PRAISE FOR
AN UNBREA[KABLE...]

"Unmissable. Ren Hutch[ings...]
Gareth L. Powell, author of the *Embers of War* series

"Deeper, darker, and more immense, full of fresh mysteries and glimpses of the familiar. Hutchings is a bright light in space opera, and her sophomore novel shouldn't be missed."
Bethany Jacobs, Philip K. Dick Award-winning author of *These Burning Stars*

"Interweaves the past and present in an exciting story about faith, revenge, and the redemptive nature of curiosity."
Taran Hunt, author of *The Immortality Thief*

"Beautiful hopepunk at its best... an amazing story about finding yourself, and about how the smallest things are the most important."
K. B. Wagers, author of *A Pale Light in the Black*

"This tale of memory, identity, and vengeance is rich with lore, deep worldbuilding, and deft character work, a Hutchings hallmark."
Khan Wong, author of *The Circus Infinite*

"An instantly engaging premise and unforgettable characters... in Hutchings' writing, there's no such thing as a person that doesn't matter or a story that can't be changed."
Rebecca Fraimow, author of *Lady Eve's Last Con*

"A compelling story of politics, religion—and longing for family, identity, and connection."
Una McCormack, author of *Star Trek: Asylum*

PRAISE FOR
UNDER FORTUNATE STARS

"A deeply human book. With a sweeping setting that encompasses galaxies and more than a century, the focus remains on the people living there."

Locus

"If the Guardians of the Galaxy crashed the Foundation... A twisty, enthralling space-time opera. Fortunate readers, and a future star."

Stephen Baxter

"A compelling look at how past and future are created not only by those who live it but by those who record it."

Library Journal (starred review)

"A perfect novel featuring my favorite time-travel paradox. This is an absolute must-read for anyone needing a little hope."

K. B. Wagers

"Despite its far-reaching plot, this time travel space opera debut is deeply character-driven. It's an entertaining, engrossing read."

Buzzfeed

"One of the best books I've read this year."

Gareth L. Powell

"Ren Hutchings has earned comparisons to Becky Chambers, Alex White, and S. K. Dunstall."

Den of Geek

"Hutchings lovingly fuses a sprawling cast of charmingly flawed characters and a plot with many moving parts into a smooth and satisfying whole."

Publishers Weekly

"Exciting, funny, truthful—and a thoughtful account of the necessity of trusting both ourselves and strangers to secure our future and live in peace."

Una McCormack

"Strong characterisation propels the narrative, from the outlaw *Jonah*'s passengers to the *Gallion*'s supposedly squeaky-clean corporate crew. An engrossing interstellar escapade."

Booklist

"Ren Hutchings has written a space opera that is close and personal in its conflicts and, at the same time, wide-reaching in its scope."

Michael Mammay

"Questions of fate, predetermination and stepping into history are cleverly wrapped in an engrossing tale."

Sci-Fi Bulletin

"A fun puzzle box of a mystery!"

Megan E. O'Keefe

"One of the most entertaining time travel space adventures that you will ever read today, tomorrow—or even yesterday."

SFBook Review

"An immensely fun space opera adventure, chock full of surprises and wonderful characters, laced through with humor and heart."

John Appel

"A time-bending, character-driven space adventure that's sure to leave you with a smile on your face. You're sure to feel very fortunate indeed."

FanFiAddict

"Smart, slick, and mind-blowingly twisty, *Under Fortunate Stars* pits a memorable ensemble cast against impossible odds: fragile timelines, fifth-dimension science, and explosive politics."

Claire Winn

"A fast-paced, easy-read story, done with style. The main characters, when not bickering or working through the action set-pieces, show frailty and vulnerability. The action is page-turning. There are fights, rescues, improbable fixes, near misses and beat-the-clock moments."

British Fantasy Society

"Boasting a heart full of hope, characters you can't help but root for, and a breathless, high-octane mystery, this is the space opera we need right now."

Karen Osborne

"The sort of book which becomes impossible to put down, and leaves you both torn up and uplifted by its conclusion. In short, it's must-read SF."

Track of Words

AN UNBREAKABLE WORLD

Also by Ren Hutchings

Under Fortunate Stars
The Legend Liminal

AN UNBREAKABLE WORLD

REN HUTCHINGS

SOLARIS

First published in 2025 by Solaris
an imprint of Rebellion Publishing Ltd,
Riverside House, Osney Mead,
Oxford, OX2 0ES, United Kingdom

www.solarisbooks.com

ISBN: 978-1-83786-579-6

Copyright © Ren Hutchings 2025

The right of the author to be identified as the author of this work has been asserted in accordance with the Copyright, Designs and Patents Act 1988.

All rights reserved. No part of this publication may be reproduced, stored in a retrieval system, or transmitted, in any form or by any means, electronic, mechanical, photocopying, recording or otherwise, without the prior permission of the copyright owners.

This is a work of fiction. All the characters and events portrayed in this book are fictional, and any resemblance to real people or incidents is purely coincidental.

10 9 8 7 6 5 4 3 2 1

A CIP catalogue record for this book is available from the British Library.

Designed & typeset by Rebellion Publishing
Cover by Dominic Forbes

Printed in Denmark

To Monica and Rebecca,
whose belief in this story was unbreakable.

THE STORYTELLER

Recording start 00:00:00

So. We're recording... right. Let's see, then. [*clears throat*] Where should I start?

I suppose we all like to think of stories as having a beginning and an ending, 'cause that's the way stories are supposed to work, isn't it? It's neat that way. All makes sense. "Once there was a little lost soul with pure intentions, *da-dee-da-da*... so on and so forth... and then, after all was said and done, they sailed happily into the stars." I sure used to think that way.

In stories, things end. Our heroes got what they wanted, or else they didn't. They won, or they lost. They lived, or they died. It's over, there's nothing more to say. All neat and tidy, the way real life never damn well is. Maybe that's why we like to hear 'em told that way. But out here in reality... well. Out here, things tend to get messy.

Now, I'll tell you this: I've never been much for second chances. Most of the time, I'm just not the fresh-start kind. See, I hold a gods-damned grudge. There's no blank scoreboard in life, you get the dice rolls you get, you did what you did. There's no starting over.

But I do like to see what gets built from the mess, afterwards. The monsters that rise from the wreckage, you know what I'm sayin'? That's what interests me. And yeah, all right... maybe there's a bit of personal experience talking there.

Real stories aren't clean, and they aren't straightforward, or fair. Who's winning and who's losing... it doesn't always make sense, no matter how you spin it.

Sometimes, we all get what we don't deserve. But there's one way to make real sure that the last bad thing that happened won't be the ending, not for you.

And that's to keep living.

PAGE FOUND
Kuuj Deep Space Outpost

If something seems too good to be real, you've got to get out of there.

That's one rule that Page usually abides by. But on a baking-hot day, crouching in the sweat-stink of the upper levels and staring at the most perfect score of the year, it's easy enough to forget her own rules. This is the very definition of easy money.

She focuses her binoculars and zooms in, studying the mark. There are only two sorts of people on Kuuj Outpost—the locals and the passers-through—and this fool is most definitely the latter. He cuts a tall, angular figure in a dark coat with diamond-shaped patches on the elbows. His polished boots have blocky heels and far too many buckles to be practical, the kind of footwear that doesn't exactly lend itself to running.

Page pans over to the stranger's hands. His pale, slender fingers are stacked with shiny rings as high as the bony knuckle will allow. Those rings alone are probably worth a fortune, but they're not what Page is after. Heart pounding, she moves her binoculars down to the stranger's belt and checks again to make sure her eyes aren't deceiving her.

Unbelievably, the thing is still there in plain view: a Q-link comms device, military-grade. The type of box you can seldom swipe off anyone who isn't a soldier. As if the mark's clothes didn't give off enough of a not-from-around-here vibe, the fact that he's clearly flashing a Q-link device, in public, is a dead giveaway. If she can nab that, she can knock as much off her debt as she'd make in a month of chasing hapless ship workers for yet another scuffed walkie.

Pickings have been worse than slim lately, and the usual hauler crews have long been wising up to the dockyard pickpockets. The workers who regularly stop over here have all been keeping their expensive devices firmly up their sleeves and securing their locker-rooms after hours. An outsider like this is Page's best chance at a score this week.

Page leans unsteadily on the pillar she crouches behind. It really is unbearably hot up here. Her skull feels too heavy for her neck to hold up, and her chin dips, a sharp ache blooming behind her eyeballs. Her vision blurs, and she grits her teeth.

Gods, how is this shit still happening? Is it getting worse? One of the air recyclers must've broken down. *Again*.

Kuuj's lower levels are sweltering, the humidity curdling in thick, musty air. Up here in the higher decks, it's somewhat cooler most of the time, but the mix still isn't right—there are too many chemicals leaching into the flow systems, the bad air making everyone light-headed and argumentative. Being hungry probably isn't helping, either. Page hasn't eaten a proper meal since sometime yesterday, and the stale energy bar she pilfered from a corner kiosk earlier hasn't done much to restore her.

She gives herself a quick mental shakedown, blinking hard to clear her vision. She's *fine*. This is perfectly normal—or whatever passes for normal on Kuuj. There's absolutely nothing wrong in her head that isn't also wrong with every single other inhabitant of this wreckhole.

Well... besides the occasional weird visions. And maybe the fact that she's lost twenty-odd years of memories... But no, no, *no*. She's not going to think about any of that today. Not with the score of the year right down there, just waiting to be robbed. She has to focus.

There'll be plenty of time to dwell on her meaningless existence later. Maybe when she's laid out for an hour or two in a temperature-controlled room with a chilled drink, spending a sliver of the profits from this fool's device. Right before she responsibly chucks the rest of her windfall against her bottomless debt.

The mark. *Eyes on the prize.* This might look straightforward, but she can't afford to get distracted now.

Page adjusts her binoculars and pans back up to the stranger's face. It's always unsettling, being able to see someone this clearly from such a distance. She can see the movement of his pupils, the way his eyes are tracking from left to right over the docks. He's probably waiting to meet someone. Someone who might be about to arrive at any minute and screw this whole thing up. Page swears under her breath. An opportunity this good won't last. If she doesn't get her ass down there and swipe that box, one of the dockyard kids is going to get it. This guy seriously looks that damn easy.

She stuffs her binoculars in her satchel and hauls herself to her feet, leaning against the pillar for support as her head swims nauseatingly. She'll be all right. Of course. *Perfectly fine.* She just needs a minute to get her bearings. Taking a steadying breath, ignoring the taste of the nasty air, she pulls down her *Leviahunter* AR game headset and snaps the slim visor into place over her eyes.

Go time. It's now or never.

Shakily, Page half-slides, half-climbs four storeys down a rickety metal utility ladder, until she drops into a narrow alleyway leading onto the main concourse. But when she gets down there, she can't see the stranger's fancy-cut coat anywhere. Her heart pounds. Is he gone? Maybe she's too late, and the Q-link box has vanished along with her hope of spending the afternoon in a cool-room.

But... no, wait! *There he is!* Unbelievably, the mark has moved into an even better position. He's wandered over into the loading space in front of one of the unoccupied docking bays, where he's now partly hidden by another wide metal pillar. To everyone out on the main concourse, that slight sunken gap will be invisible from view. The Q-link box glints, still swinging against his thigh, suspended on that tantalizingly thin strap.

Page palms her small pocketknife and saunters out into the concourse. She adjusts the gaming headset and mimes switching it on. It's not even a working one—the left lens is on the fritz and it has a busted graphics chip—but she's installed a small green light in the top corner of the visor to make it look authentic.

Leviahunter Augmented Reality Adventure is all the rage in this sector, and there are always a few people wandering around the dockyard playing the game, collecting virtual treasure and taking swipes at nonexistent monsters while they walk. There's not a lot to see on Kuuj Outpost in real life, but she's heard more than one hauler pilot mention the lucky *Leviahunter* treasure drops they've found on this concourse. The game is the perfect ruse.

Setting her jaw with determination, Page starts moving toward the mark. As she walks, she weaves unsteadily through the concourse exactly the way a *Leviahunter* gamer would, swinging her left hand in front of her to mimic a monster-sweeper with a virtual sword. She dips and swerves, dodging a couple of disgruntled-looking dock workers before she carries on.

She pauses dramatically, making a deliberate final swipe with her sword hand—*monster vanquished!* Then she takes one more long, deep breath, and runs headlong right into the mark.

"Oh! Ah, excuse me!" She feigns shock and contrition as she collides with the stranger, knocking him backwards. "Whoops! Sorry! There's an ultra-rare star chest behind you, back in there! Mind if I grab it?"

The stranger laughs. "There's a what where now?"

"An ultra-rare star chest," Page repeats with an exasperated sigh. "Don't you play *Leviahunter*? Excuse me! I need to collect that before it disintegrates!"

She pushes him roughly to one side, reaching out to scoop up the imaginary prize. As she moves past him, she slips the Q-link box from his belt, neatly snicking through the strap with her knife and looping the end around her own wrist in one fluid motion. A bit of sleight of hand, that's all this situation needs. Page has a talent for distracting people—and making them believe absolute nonsense.

He chuckles again. "*Leviahunter*, huh? Nope. Never heard of it."

"I've got it! Ultra-rare chest acquired!" Page smacks her hand against the pillar with triumph as she shifts the stolen box into her satchel. "Oooh, wow! It's a good one! Major score. Thanks." Her breath levels out as she starts backing out of the bay.

"No problem," he says, rolling his eyes.

He adjusts his strange coat, one hand rummaging idly in his pocket, but he doesn't so much as glance down at the empty space on his belt where his precious device used to be. What an unbelievable fool. Page takes another step back and pushes the *Leviahunter* visor to one side, peeling the translucent strip away from her eyes.

"It's a virtual game," she says. "You've seen people with these things on, right?" She taps the visor for emphasis. "*Leviahunter Augmented Reality Adventure.* You look around, and you collect all these different items that spawn. You have to watch out for the monsters, and pick the right weapon to defend yourself, and then you…" She glances back at the concourse. "Oh, hey, my friends are waiting for me over there! I've gotta run—"

Page's words die in her throat as the stranger suddenly lunges forward. One ringed hand closes tightly around Page's wrist. He looks pointedly at the nearly empty concourse, smirking as if her lie amuses him more than it bothers him.

And then, before she can wrench her wrist away, his voice changes into something at once strange and familiar. A curling cadence of melodious syllables raises the small hairs on the back of her neck. "*Drop the bag now, if you want to live.*"

The words are not in Union Basic, and yet their meaning blooms fully formed in her memory. Page can hardly breathe, hardly think. He's still holding her wrist tightly, but her other hand flies immediately to the strap of her satchel. Whether she means to protect it or to unclip it and hand it over to him, she can't say for sure, because just then, a rippling shock hits her nerves like ice water.

At once, it's as if her limbs are locked in place, and she's suddenly lost all ability to move. It feels like she's grabbed a live wire. She can't make a sound. What in the five hells is happening?

Fuck. He's holding a palm stunner—which he must have just pulled out of his pocket, right in front of her. This was sure a great gods-damned time to have let her guard down.

Then a second person darts out of the shadows from the empty docking bay to her left. Page has only a moment to glimpse another black jacket and a flash of blue-black hair before a fabric sack comes down over her head. She's vaguely aware of her numb arms being yanked behind her, her tingling wrists being cuffed together. There's a hand pressed into the small of her back—or is that another weapon?—pushing her forward. She stumbles in that direction, her legs like jelly.

Surely they aren't going to march her back into the middle of the concourse with a bag stuck over her head. Kuuj Outpost is heartless, but it's not entirely lawless. The patrollers might look the other way for a local dispute, especially if they've been paid off, but they wouldn't stand for outsiders pulling shit like this. No. Page must've lost her sense of direction in the scuffle—they must've turned her around.

They aren't taking her through the concourse, they're going deeper into the docks, down the side way. Through another one of those little alleys where the dockyard kids usually skulk, waiting to nick something from a passer-by's satchel. Page will get no help from them, though. If the little shits know what's good for them, they'll stay well clear of something like this and lay low. This is real bad.

She thinks about struggling, but her lungs ache with the lack of air. Her knees shake with every shambling step, and she's losing feeling in her feet. The sack that's been pulled over her head isn't airtight, but it certainly isn't hospitable, and suddenly it reeks of chemicals. Whatever she's inhaling right now, it's in the process of putting her under. She coughs weakly, still unable to make her mouth form a word.

There are stairs beneath Page's feet now, and she's being led down them, one precarious step at a time. The two strangers are half-carrying her between them. Six steps, Page counts, and they clang like corrugated metal under her dragging boots. Must be a drop-ramp in one of the smaller bays. They're taking her down into a small ship, or maybe a shuttlecraft.

"Where are you taking me?" she tries to say, her voice a garbled mumble. It comes out more like: "*Whuuu-uh-uuh-huh.*"

There's no response from her captors, only a shove between her shoulder blades as they reach the bottom of the staircase and carry on walking over a flatter surface. She hears the faint beep of an ident-chip being scanned, then a rolling door being pulled open. There's a long, rasping squeak of metal on metal.

Page tries again: "*Huu-uuh?*"

No answer.

She grits her teeth, determined not to lose consciousness—not yet. She's already been fighting a blackout since this morning, and she certainly isn't about to give in now. She needs to get her bearings and figure out where she's being taken.

Page *hates* the dark, but thankfully the fabric that covers her eyes admits some light. She notices immediately when the lighting around her changes. The fluorescent-white glow of the Kuuj concourse is gone, replaced by a cool blueish hue. Maybe a bright control panel, or a ship's bridge with a lot of lit computer screens? She's marched through the bright room, and onwards into another, dimmer space.

Her kidnappers haven't searched her, and they haven't actually touched any of her things. Despite the demand to drop her bag, they have done nothing with it; she can feel the familiar weight of the satchel still hanging there over her shoulder, with the Q-link box inside. No one has made any move to relieve her of it. If what they want is to retrieve the stolen Q-link, why would they kidnap her instead of just snatching her satchel and roughing her up a bit? Doesn't make any damn sense.

Maybe they think that Page is someone else, someone worth kidnapping. Some twisted part of her laughs internally at the thought of these people demanding a ransom for her. She pictures the kidnappers barging into Tully's office, announcing that they've seized the irreplaceable, indomitable petty thief Page Found, and she imagines the look on her boss's face. That asshole Tully wouldn't pay two chits for her. And it isn't like Page knows anybody wealthy.

Her heart jerks with sudden, soaring hope. *Unless*—

Before she can finish the thought, the two strangers hoist her under her arms and lug her upwards, settling her into what feels like a flight chair. They click a harness over her shoulders and buckle her in, talking to one another in low, hurried voices. They're speaking Union Basic again now, and she catches snippets of something that sounds terrifyingly like 'prepare to take off.'

Take off? Page trembles, sweat pooling at the base of her neck. She can no longer feel any of her limbs, just that heavy numbness that crawls over her skin, spreading to her brain. Are they really taking her off Kuuj Outpost? Where in the hells to?

She strains to listen to their conversation through the fog in her mind, but she's rapidly losing the ability to process the words. Syllables blur into indistinct sounds, then fade again into a low, distant warble that drones in her ears as her senses leave her.

Page tilts her head back against the flight seat, no longer able to hold her heavy skull upright. Bursts of light flicker at the edges of her vision.

And then everything goes completely black.

※ ※ ※

WHEN PAGE COMES to again, her mind still feels fuzzy and off-kilter. Each thought feels *strained*, as if it's taking some enormous effort just to make sense of words or sensations. She still can't move her hands and feet, but she can tell there's an engine hum reverberating in the floor, rattling under the worn soles of her shoes.

The whirr of a small vehicle in flight. These assholes seriously have taken her off Kuuj.

Amidst all the other thoughts clawing for attention in Page's confused mind, she struggles to identify the emotion that *leaving Kuuj* evokes in her. For all the times she has contemplated the idea in the abstract, she cannot quite wrap her head around the thought that she's no longer on the outpost. Much less that these people may never return her there.

Or return her *anywhere*.

As the direst of possibilities sink in, Page thinks about the apartment she left behind—if such a word can even be applied to that shoddy, poorly ventilated container hab that scarcely resembled a proper dwelling. Was there anything she would've wanted to grab from among her possessions and take with her, if she'd been given a chance to pack? If she had *planned* this departure?

Probably not, besides the personal digipad she has in her satchel—the one that contains her diaries and notes from the past eight years. Nothing else Page has ever owned on Kuuj has felt much like it belongs to her anyway. After all, how could anything truly be 'hers' when she has no idea who she is?

Page doesn't own a single sentimental thing. She has no old cartridges of photos, no mementos of trips or lovers or achievements. She doesn't know what job she used to do or what skills she used to have. She doesn't know what her favourite books were, or her favourite foods, or her favourite music. And she has spent so much time in pursuit of her missing old life, that she has actively resisted making any new memories.

Every time she discovers something new that interests her on the network, she can't help but *wonder*. Did she like this thing in her old life? Has she ever danced a dance that looked like this, or listened to this kind of poetry before? Has she ever read this book?

When she guessed the end of a particularly twisty mystery novel, she studied the pixelated cover page for an hour, trying to force herself to recall if she'd ever seen that title or that author's name before. But no matter what kinds of memory tricks she has tried, her past has remained stubbornly blank.

Well... not *entirely* blank. Memories sometimes pop into her head without any context at all, images of places she can't identify. And of course, there are simple things she knows that she must have learned somewhere—like how to tie up laced boots, or how to type on a standard 3D keyboard. But who taught her these things? Whenever she can access Kuuj's glitchy network connections, she flips through countless imagined lives she might have led. But none of them quite feel like they fit.

Occasionally, she's uncovered a thrilling new piece to the puzzle of her identity. But most of the time, each clue raises more questions than it answers. Once, a group of out-system traders sat down in the restobar on Kuuj, discussing their illicit plans for the evening... and Page discovered to her shock that she knows another language.

It took a good few minutes of listening before she even processed what was happening. This unmistakably foreign tongue, sounding nothing like Union Basic, was completely comprehensible to her. The oddly familiar words flowed easily into her mind, complete with their nuances and meanings. She wasn't *translating*, she was just... understanding.

It was the same feeling she'd experienced in some of her blackout visions, and for a moment as she sat there listening to those traders, Page wondered if maybe she'd actually passed out.

During her blackouts, she'd often heard words and phrases

that she was sure were in some other language. But she could never hold on to the recollection for long enough after waking to write any of it down. Mostly, she'd convinced herself that this *dream-language* was just something her scrambled brain had made up.

But that day in the restobar, it became real. She sat there with her breath half-held, pretending to be engrossed in reading something on her 'pad while she listened intently. The traders were discussing a shipment they planned to transfer through the Kuuj dockyard without proper permits. That info ended up yielding Page a nice bonus when she sold the details to the dockyard guards—who in turn surely charged the traders a hefty fee to keep it quiet instead of calling down the patrollers.

Page's heart starts pounding again at the memory, and a chill runs through her. *Those out-system traders.* Shit. Back in the bay, her kidnapper spoke in the same language. Almost as if he were *testing* Page to check if she understood—seeing if she'd reach for her bag when he demanded she drop it.

Could this whole mess all be something to do with those traders somehow? They couldn't possibly have marked Page as the source of that information... could they? How? She was just another unremarkable patron sitting in that grotty bar, and she didn't even look at them, nor give any outward sign that she could understand them! How could they possibly have—

At once, Page hears the slide of a door opening. And the next moment, the sack covering her eyes is suddenly gone. Someone holds a bright blue cup to her lips, nudging it forward to get her to drink what's inside.

The liquid in the cup is piping hot, and the steam rising from it further clouds Page's still-blurred vision. Her captor hasn't entirely removed the sack over her head, only rolled it up as far as her forehead. Page's hands and feet are very much still bound, and the broken *Leviahunter* headset is still hanging around her neck. She can't feel the strap of her satchel on her shoulder anymore, though. They've taken away her bag.

"*Whaahhhyou?*" Page manages, choking a little on the water. That's what it seems to be, *water*, not tea or alga, just very hot water with a strong metallic tang. *Who are you?*

"Shush. Be quiet, just drink," an unfamiliar voice whispers in Union Basic. "Zhak will be back soon."

Zhak. That must be her mark, the stranger in the funny coat. Damn him. She shouldn't have let her guard down like that. What was she *thinking?*

A hand wipes away the water that has dribbled onto Page's chin. The touch is not gentle, but nor is it very rough.

"Sorry about the disgusting water, by the way," the voice says. "The filtration system's a bit off, so I always dispense it boiling, just in case."

Tastes better than most of the water on Kuuj, Page wants to say, but instead she wraps her numb lips around the edge of the cup and lets her mysterious warden—Water Girl, she privately names her—tip more hot water into her mouth. It burns and soothes her throat in equal measure, and she drinks it down gratefully.

Then the cup is suddenly pulled away, and the rough fabric is tugged back down over Page's face.

"Shhh, shhh! He's coming," Water Girl whispers. "Quiet now."

Page hears the *whoosh* of the metal door sliding open again, and the sound of heavy boot-heels approaching, echoing over an uneven floor—those blocky, fancy-buckled boots the stranger wore, she remembers with a silent curse.

"Well? She waking up yet?" Page recognizes the voice of her careless mark, the man in the funny coat. *Zhak*. Officially the biggest mistake she's ever made—that she can remember.

"Not properly. Not in any state to interrogate yet, anyway," says Water Girl. "Probably needs another hour or so."

"I want her talking before we get back, understand?" He sounds anxious.

"Yeah? Well, maybe you should've thought about that before you stunned her hard enough to drop a battle squad *and* used the chem-sedative. Told you it was overkill."

There's a weighty silence, and a little shuffle of movement. "Watch yourself," Zhak says warningly, his voice lowering with threat. "Look... you just get her talking, all right? Call me when she's up."

The booted footsteps recede, the door opens and closes again, and—

Page's awareness is fading again, her mind fogging even as she struggles to hold on to consciousness. She thinks she feels a small, comforting squeeze on her wrist, before she realizes that Water Girl is simply checking on her bindings.

And then, the black takes her again.

This time, it's punctuated by the bright, searing rush of what Page has come to think of as a *blackout dream*, a fractured vision pouring into her head. The experience is no longer terrifying to her, but no less unpleasant than the first time.

It always starts with a sharp headache, then a feeling like *falling too slowly*—that stomach-turning lurch, like when Kuuj's artificial gravity has momentarily failed and restarted. And then, the sensation of bile rising in her throat, though she has nothing to throw up but a few mouthfuls of water.

And then, at last, the images start to pour in. They usually flash by too quickly to be easily distinguished: blurred scenes and sounds all layered over each other, like a dozen holo-vids being played at the same time. Voices, sometimes indistinct, sometimes speaking in that language she shouldn't understand—

A floor that looks like it's made of smooth wood, polished to a glossy sheen.

The clink of crockery and the hum of conversation, like a distant dinner party.

A soft, fleecy blanket being wrapped around her shoulders, softer than anything she's ever felt on Kuuj. A pair of arms wrapped around her—she's so small that she's being carried over someone's shoulder.

A sprawling house perched at the top of a green hill, tall and white-bricked, with long rows of wide windows and a balcony with a shiny rail.

A round-faced doll with two gold ribbons tied into its hair. Such beautiful shiny ribbons, so sleek and smooth against her fingers.

That's new, the doll. Page has never seen it before. She'll need to add a description of it to her journal while she still remembers it—

She bobs slowly back to wakefulness, shaking herself awake, surfacing enough to question her surroundings. How long has she been out? Where is she, and why can't she move her hands?

She needs to add the doll to her log. Where is her 'pad?

But no, wait. Perhaps she needs to stay in the dream. There might be more to see, yet. In her mind, she sinks claws into the image, pulling herself back into that disjointed, fragmentary world. The *doll*.

Ribbons, gold ribbons, two soft gold ribbons.

Bells, ringing so loudly that she can feel the sound in her chest as though her ribs are being physically struck with each peal, a glorious harmony of sound—

When Page wakes again, her head snaps up with a jolt, her body lurching painfully against her bindings. The stun is wearing off, and whatever drug was in the sack on her head is definitely leaving her system. The sensation is returning to her hands and feet, and she can now feel the cables biting into her wrists.

The memories of how she got here come flooding back into her consciousness once more. The well-dressed stranger in the coat (*Zhak*, damn him); that Q-link device she so foolishly stole; the kidnapping; and that language—

Page feels a surge of hope as she realizes the engine rumble beneath her feet has stopped. Of course they haven't really left Kuuj, that would be ridiculous. She was just being paranoid before, addled by whatever they dosed her with. Why in the worlds would anyone want to take her off the outpost?

No. This is some kind of trick. They obviously just shoved off and took her on a little spin to shake her up. Probably some new intimidation tactic of Tully's. Messing with her head. It's *got* to be Tully's doing.

She's certain it's his furious, red-cheeked face she's going to see in a moment, and she prepares her steely, irreverent defiance.

"Hey! Hey, you out there!" Page shouts, before she can think the better of it. She's almost surprised by the sound of her own voice, strong and restored. "If you think this is fucking scaring me, Tully, you can try again. C'mon, stop this, lemme out. Look... I'm good for the money... You know damn well I'm good for it! Just been a bad month. You don't have to pull shit like this—"

A moment later, the sack is yanked away from her head again, and she's blinking blearily in the sudden light. It's not Tully in front of her, but the one called Zhak. He's staring at her with something between disgust and disdain, calculating and predatory. For all his earlier demands that she talk, he doesn't ask her anything, just circles her slowly, as if sizing her up.

Page is probably meant to be real scared right now. And maybe she is. Maybe she's just repressing the inevitable panic that will soon spill forth with mortifying predictability. But she just lets loose a bitter laugh, and summons that surly, unbothered scowl that she usually reserves for uncomfortable confrontations in Tully's office.

Zhak stops in his tracks, glaring at her. For a second, Page thinks he might be about to slap her, and she forces herself not to flinch as his richly ringed hand jerks up toward her cheek. But all he does is move her head, taking hold of her chin and turning it roughly to one side. He leans over to peer at the back of her neck.

He mutters approvingly to himself, and Page shivers as she feels him running a fingernail along the scars at the top of her spine, where the three neat indentations from her stasis port form a perfect triangle. They're unusual stasis scars, she knows—small and surgically precise, compared to the round, gnarled port scars usually borne by former stasis prisoners. She's never been in prison, to her knowledge. *Clinical trial,* she was told. A stasis experiment. Why is this stranger so interested in her scars?

While Zhak is occupied with examining her, Page takes the opportunity to cast a furtive glance around. There's not much to see; they seem to be inside some kind of an empty storage locker, like a segment of a ship's cargo bay. There's thick, elastic netting held to the walls by carabiners, the kind of stuff that's used to restrain cargo in zero-grav, but there are no crates. Just a small rectangular table bracketed to the floor, and this *seat,* which is probably equally immovable. Almost like this place has been set up as an interrogation room. Page holds back a shudder.

At least she can't see any torture implements on the table; there are no flaying knives or weird tools for digging out fingernails or anything like that. *Ugh.* She deeply regrets downloading so many old horror dramas from the local troves. She's got to stop letting her imagination run away with her.

Nothing is going to happen to her here, she tells herself. For all of Tully's big talk and bluster, he'd never actually hurt her. He'd never get some grunt to break her fingers when he wants those fingers picking pockets for him. And the last thing Page intends to do is break down. Fuck Tully if he thinks she's going to piss herself scared. He'll have to try harder than this.

"Look, I'm getting fed up here, I don't have all day," Page snaps. "Who in the hells are you? Where have you taken me? And where's my bag?"

Zhak's lip curls in annoyance, and she wonders again if he's going to strike her. But he just snaps his fingers over his shoulder, and his dark-haired accomplice brings forward Page's beat-up old satchel. He takes hold of it gingerly, as if it's contaminated, and makes a revolted noise.

From this angle, Page can see Water Girl quite clearly. She's probably about the same height as Page, but broad-shouldered and stout where Page is thin and wiry. Her wavy blue-black hair falls well past her shoulders; most of it is caught up in a ponytail, but a few escaped strands cling to her neck. She has a sandy complexion and a pretty, heart-shaped face, her earlobes studded with several metallic piercings.

One of the rings in her ear has some sort of iridescent geometric shape hanging from it. Page squints at it with fascination—but she's quickly distracted by the contents of the satchel as Zhak upends her bag over the table and everything inside comes crashing out.

There's not much to Page's belongings. It's almost embarrassing to see her stuff laid out like this. A couple of low-end comm units she lifted yesterday, one half-decent battery brick, some charging cables... her binoculars, a nearly empty water flask, an elastic hair tie, a loose carabiner... and her scratched-up digipad. Conspicuously absent is the Q-link device she stole from Zhak; he must have taken that back already while she was out cold.

"Garbage, garbage... Oh, look—More garbage," Zhak says as he picks through it. He sweeps it all dismissively to one side with his hand, and gestures to Water Girl. "Throw this shit in the disposal, would you?"

"Hey! Stop it, that's a day's work!" Her composure cracking, Page thrashes uselessly against her restraints. The cables hold frustratingly firm, immovably attached to her wrists. "Those things are *mine;* I need them! Give them back!"

Zhak's thin lips are quirking up now with something like wry amusement. "Oh, I'm sorry—How awfully rude of me. Taking something that isn't mine." He grins, and it's more of a threatening flash of teeth than a smile. "You find me so terribly distasteful and uncourteous, don't you, little thief? I see how it is. But then again... given what I've seen of your previous employer... I suspect you may in fact come to find me positively charming."

Page's nausea is back with a vengeance. *Tully.* Of course it's him, this is all him, she knows it. "Right. Can we just cut to the chase here? Tully knows damn well I'm gonna pay up, I always do. I already told him I'll catch up on my quota by month-end! And I'm definitely going to—"

Zhak throws his head back with a long, full-throated laugh. "Good gracious goddess! You seriously think this whole thing is about your debt to that junk-hawking loser?"

"Well, I'm open to other explanations, but I've not heard any yet." The words slip between Page's clenched teeth, sharp as a blade. "This is ridiculous."

Sometimes, Page wonders where she gets this brash, unshakeable resilience. Somehow, she always manages to dredge up this ability to talk shit—a talent that has branded her as either suicidally brave or senselessly reckless. But it's not like she *tries* to do it. She just… shuts out the reality of the situation. Like she's found some alternate reality where she's got the guts to stand behind her words; where she's actually got bargaining power.

Maybe it's just eight years of working on Kuuj. You don't get far on Kuuj unless you're willing to fight for yourself. Sometimes, though, Page thinks this fortitude is much older. Perhaps it has run in her blood far longer than she's been stealing for Tully, longer than she's been a thief haunting the passageways of Kuuj. What kind of person might she have been? What kind of life could she have lived that called for this kind of bravery?

Behind Zhak, Water Girl is now busy collecting the contents of Page's satchel. She's slowly putting it all back into the bag, picking up and examining one item at a time. She hesitates over the digipad, and for the briefest moment, her eyes meet Page's.

When she looks back down again, much to Page's shock, Water Girl slips the 'pad surreptitiously under her black jacket. Then she walks over to what must be a disposal box by the wall and lets the satchel containing the rest of Page's stuff clatter down inside, dusting her hands off for emphasis. "Bye-bye. All gone."

She winks, tapping the side of her jacket where she hid the 'pad.

But before Page can think on what just happened, Zhak whisks out the military Q-link box she tried to steal from him and holds it up to her face. "Oops. Missed *this one*," he says in a mocking whisper. "Would you look at that? Hmm? Recognize this box, little thief?" he asks, stroking the shiny front panel. "Looks *gorgeous,* doesn't it? Quite the score in a place like Kuuj, I'd imagine. Don't see many out there like this one."

He slips one of his polished black fingernails into the groove on the front cover and dramatically prises it open, exposing a mess of fried, melted wires at the front of the casing... and nothing behind them. The Q-brick that should be inside—the actual communication device—is missing.

The gods-damned thing is completely hollow. Page swears under her breath.

"Pity, hmm? That lovely things are not exactly as they appear on the outside?" Zhak says with a self-satisfied tilt of his head. "But sometimes, illusions *are* the only thing that counts. I hope you are about to prove that very true, my new little friend."

Page grits her teeth at the mocking endearment.

"I hear your head is as empty as this box," he goes on. "But that's not going to matter when we're through with you." A dramatic pause. "*Page Found*, is it? Is that the only name you've got, or is it some kind of alias?"

"Tch! Shouldn't you know that already?" Page says glibly. "Wasn't that included in your kidnap brief?"

"Smartass, huh?" He jerks the cable on her left wrist, tightening it painfully with a smirk. "You see anywhere to run to around here? You'd better think carefully before you start running your mouth."

"Zhak, c'mon. Cool it," says Water Girl, turning back to Page. "We just want to talk, all right? We're not here to hurt you." She rests a fist briefly against her chest. "My name's Maelle," she says with a grim-looking smile. "I'm the less egregiously annoying half of this operation."

"You can call me Page," Page says grudgingly, feeling obligated to return the thin attempt at civility. "And yeah, that's the only name I've got... the only name I can remember, anyway. If the fact that I made it up myself makes it an alias, then... I guess it's that, too." She manages what she hopes is a defiant smirk. "I'm also known as Debt 4945 on Tully's books. You might be more familiar with that one."

For the first time, though, a hint of doubt finds its way into her voice. Maybe Tully really *didn't* send this guy. How much should she really be telling these people?

When she came to, Page did briefly consider being cagey about her identity, or what passes for one. But if these people really *have* mistaken her for someone else—probably someone to whom they intend to deliver a gnarly end—it's probably better to clear this shit up sooner rather than later. They might even somehow be persuaded to take her back to Kuuj when they figure out their mistake, instead of just airlocking her.

The irony is not lost on her, that the first time someone actually tries to give her an identity in eight years, they'd get it wrong and try to off her for something a stranger did, whatever that might be. She smiles at the sheer absurdity of it.

"What's so funny?" snaps Zhak.

"What's funny is that I don't actually remember a gods-damned thing from before I landed on that dump eight years ago," Page says. "I woke up from a stint in suspended animation with all those holes down my spine and a giant medical debt, and literally nothing else to my name. So whatever it is you think you're after... you're probably about to be real disappointed." She sighs. "If Tully *didn't* put you up to this, I don't suppose it's too much to ask that you drop me back off on Kuuj Outpost? Just take me back and we can forget this ever happened. I'm Tully's best worker. I'm sure he'd be happy to pay a small fee for my return."

The lie is bitter in her mouth. Some of Tully's other thieving crew or a couple of the dockyard pickpockets might try to knock together a few credits for Page, if they were feeling particularly charitable. More likely, though, they'd just shrug and think themselves lucky to be rid of the competition. She hasn't exactly made many friends on Kuuj.

No matter. The truth is incidental here. All she needs right now is for Zhak to turn this ship around and take her back; she'll deal with the rest of it when they get there.

How far from Kuuj could they even be? How long was she out of it?

"Well? I'm waiting," she says through clenched teeth.

Zhak looks completely unruffled by her bravado, studying her with that bemused expression on his face that only half-conceals the glint of rage in his eyes. He hoists himself up to perch on the now-empty table next to her, his booted feet swinging off the floor with elegant nonchalance.

"Listen here, Page Found. You can lie to me all you want about who's gonna be coming to your rescue if that makes you feel better. We both know no one gives a shit what happens to you. But before you tell me that you *want* me to take you back to that wreckhole, at least do me the courtesy of listening to my proposal. Can you do that? It could even be to your benefit."

Page leans over and spits on the floor. "I might be more inclined to consider *courtesy* if I wasn't currently tied to a *chair*."

When she lifts her head, Water Girl—*Maelle*—catches her eye, and Page sees the laugh she's suppressing. It's the smallest twitch of one corner of her lip, quickly stifled as she clears her throat and covers her mouth with her palm.

Zhak doesn't look the least bit amused as he hops down from the table again and resumes that slow circling. He doesn't so much walk as he *stalks*, Page thinks. He projects a blend of authority and utter indifference that's somehow more threatening than the alternative. Tully would cuff you alongside the head, or send someone to rough you up. Zhak, though… Zhak is unpredictable. He's the kind who wants you to think that he'd really make you suffer.

"Page," he intones, his voice honey-smooth. "I'm sorry. I've been impolite to you. What do you say we start over again with the proper introductions? Perhaps with a little more decorum this time?" He gives her a low, theatrical bow. And he speaks, with those curling, flowery words that sound so unlike the Union's common language. "*Greetings, esteemed guest. You can call me Zhak. And I am here to present you with a most incomparable proposal. I'm the key to changing your desolate fortunes. Do you understand?*"

"*What I understand is that I am at the mercy of an abhorrent, untrustworthy individual, hell-hound,*" she replies in the same tongue. "*And I do not care for such proposals.*"

Page's mouth forms the mellifluous words almost before her mind has conceived of them; it is as if she is listening to someone else speaking through her. And yet her voice has never felt more *her own*. Her breath catches.

Zhak smiles then, a wild and unhinged grin. He removes a small, plain folding knife from his pocket, and Page recognizes her own pocketknife, the one she used to snip off the Q-link. *Gods damn it*.

He walks over to Maelle and tosses the folded knife into her hand, looming over her as he does, his tall form made even taller by his big, block-heeled boots.

"Cut her loose," he tells Maelle in Union Basic. "We're about to dock, so we'll have to take the rest of it up later." He wrinkles his nose as he looks back at Page. "And get her some clean clothes and a shower when we board, would you? She *stinks*."

The Descent of the Fair-Feathered Goddess

And so came the Fair-Feathered Goddess to the world of Teyr,
strange and powerful and unspeakably glorious.
Above the Greenworld she spread her wide and graceful wings,
and her tail was as a bright flame, searing as fire through the sky.

In her great and infinite foresight, she gave us her love.
In her great and infinite compassion, she claimed us as her own.
She flew on blessed wings, young but strong in spirit,
and always she saw more than she had been made to see.
She descended from the darkness of realms unexplored,
and called humanity to rise with courage toward the stars.

In her great and infinite foresight, she gave us her love.
In her great and infinite compassion, she claimed us as her own.
In her great and infinite wisdom, she will call us home once more.
She will call us home once more, once more, once more.

> "The Descent of the Fair-Feathered Goddess,"
> Traditional [translated from Graya]

DALYA
OF HOUSE EDAMAUN, IN HER NINTH YEAR
First-City, Teyr

On the morning of the festivities of welcome, when the ship from the Moon-City on Meneyr had just come down, it stormed more fiercely than it had all year.

By the time the High Speaker's long transit convoy pulled into the city centre, all the fancy white and gold pavilions that had been erected for the celebration were already swaying dangerously. Almost half of the flags that had adorned the surrounding buildings had been ripped away, carried off in the whipping wind.

"An ill omen," Dalya's uncle said, tutting to himself and shaking his head as he looked out the window of the moving vehicle. The glass was streaming with raindrops, obscuring their view of the green hills beyond. "A day like this brings no auspices. Still, our duty calls us. We've no choice but to get on with it."

The voyager from Meneyr had made landfall late last night, at the main spaceport high in the mountains. Dalya, who ought to have been long abed by that time, had sneaked out onto her balcony to watch the big ship coming down.

It had shone in the dark like a falling star, streaming across the sky in a blaze of fiery glory. It reminded Dalya of a painting of the Descent of the Fair-Feathered Goddess, when the Curious One dove down to survey the green lands of Teyr in the form of a gold-plumed bird.

It was hard to believe that bright, distant flame in the night was actually a *starship*. A passenger ship, to be precise, the first of the year. And it carried more than two thousand souls. New citizens come to Teyr, all of them good believers returning from a faraway city on Meneyr, Teyr's singular moon. All of them were Teyrians who had been too long separated from their beloved land, and who had felt the divine call to return planetside—or so Uncle said.

Dalya pressed her face to the window of their ground transport, squinting harder through the pelting rain, and she wondered what a *divine call* felt like. She was pretty sure she'd never felt anything like that. Right now, all she could feel was cold, her fingertips almost numb despite her gloves and the industrious hum of the heating vent between the seats.

She had boarded the transport in the warm shelter of the underground garage, but when they disembarked at the city centre, they would have to walk under the elements. She *loathed* walking in her heavy ceremonial gown at the best of times, much less when she was cold and waterlogged. Her pale, soft-sided shoes would be no match for the muddy water streaming over the streets, and yet Uncle would surely complain if she dirtied another pair. She had ruined her last ones with ugly grass stains when she'd failed to stick to the paved path during the parade last feast day.

Their transport pulled up smoothly, slowing down close to the side of the square, and then floated through a succession of barriers that lifted to admit it to the restricted area. When the vehicle came to a complete stop, Uncle gestured for Dalya to remain in her seat—as usual, they'd have to wait for the security detail to surround them before they could get out.

At last, the door was opened from outside. Uncle stepped out first, his deep green cloak billowing around him as the wind caught it. He looked decidedly displeased as he motioned for Dalya to follow.

She clung to his offered hand as she stepped down from the

vehicle, an indulgence he seldom allowed her. Dalya was in her ninth year now, far too old to need childlike comfort. She was old enough to attend the festivities of welcome alongside Uncle. As the sole heir of House Edamaun besides, Uncle was always reminding her, she needed to conduct herself with more grown-up grace.

But Uncle did not pull his hand away from her this time; instead, he simply swung her down, lifting her easily over the muddy puddle next to the transport and setting her on the other side of the stone walkway.

Dalya's other hand clutched at the ornate circlet nestled in her hair. The careful updo that Heral had woven into it was already falling to the destructive whims of the wind. And she could feel the golden runes painted on her forehead melting most inelegantly, the thick paint running in rivulets down to her cheeks as the rain pelted down on her. She dabbed at her face with the back of one sleeve, but it was unlikely to be doing much good.

"No umbrellas?" Uncle snapped at one of the attendants, pointing to Dalya. "Get her covered, now."

He stopped short of actually raising his voice—Uncle was always careful not to allow his temper to get the best of him when there were surely news cameras rolling—but there was no mistaking the cold rebuke in his voice. His tone always set Dalya on edge when he spoke this way, even when she was not its intended target.

"Apologies, Speaker Edamaun. Too windy, the umbrellas were unusable," the steward protested weakly.

Uncle said nothing more, just lifted one edge of his cloak to shelter Dalya. A moment later, another attendant rushed to pull a transparent hood over her, a thin rain covering that shielded her head and gown while keeping her finery visible. Under the hood, the icy wind wailed in her ears as if it were trapped there, as if it raged against its constraints as much as Dalya wished she could.

Then Uncle nudged her forward, and she walked with the rest of the delegation toward the nearest pavilion. They reached it just as one of the front panels was ripped clean off its lashings, bending the supporting post like a meagre sapling. Dalya watched a flurry of shouting, panicked attendants rushing to catch the ropes before it was completely torn asunder. It was strangely satisfying to watch it break free, though she could hardly admit to such a thought.

There was nothing good about this day. Perhaps Uncle was right, and these bad storms were an ill omen, indeed.

Dalya wore the mantle of House Edamaun like a poorly fitting dress, and it weighed upon her like all those layers of itchy ceremonial garments she longed to remove. She had always known that she did not truly belong at Uncle's side, and yet here she was. In the position that was always meant to be filled by Uncle's firstborn, Nathin.

Fifteen years Dalya's elder, Nathin had already been training as a politician when he died. He'd been well-spoken and smart like his father, she imagined, and ready to follow in Luwan Edamaun's clever footsteps.

But then the accident happened, and Nathin passed from the world along with the rest of Dalya's family. All her kin had been swept away, and Uncle's kin too—the whole Edamaun line extinguished, save for the two of them. And so they were left to carry the great burden of their House together. That is what Uncle told Dalya. Theirs was a special duty, and one that was theirs to bear alone.

House Edamaun of the Highborn of Teyr had always been destined for greatness, and the responsibility the two of them now bore could hardly be overstated. She and Uncle had been left alive for a reason, because they both had an important part to play in their people's future. Surely Dalya could endure a little rain. The fact that she found this duty so insufferable simply attested to her unworthiness, to the place she had yet to earn.

Suffering presents a path to grace and learning. That's what Uncle would say. And Uncle was wise, perhaps the wisest on the entire planet. He was the High Speaker of the Gepcot, after all—the Great, Everlasting Planetary Council of Teyr. And with Nathin gone, Dalya was the only one left to uphold the Edamaun legacy.

Dalya had not yet seen her fourth year when Nathin died, but even then, she had known that her family was important to Teyr. And she had known, always, that Teyr itself was special. To be born on Teyr was to be a child of never-ending bounty. It was the most blessed of all planets, the only world that would be spared when the void claimed the rest of the galaxy. Here on Teyr, Dalya belonged to the safest known haven of humankind, a cradle of plenty which had never known war or conflict or lack.

Teyr, the Greenworld, the Everlasting, protected by the Fair-Feathered Goddess. Forever and always held to her blessed bosom, in this universe and the next.

For most of her life, the protection of the Goddess had been a fact that Dalya seldom questioned. Of course it was a wondrous thing to be Teyrian, and an enormous privilege besides to be part of one of its noble families... but for Dalya in her youth, it was a thing that simply *was*, like the sunrise or the flow of the river or the existence of gravity.

She knew there were other worlds out there, many places she would never see. But none mattered so much as this one, the Infinite and Unbreakable World. The planet on which all human life had begun. There was no reason anyone should want to be anywhere else. To be on Teyr was to be blessed.

This was the one most important truth that every tiny schoolchild knew: this was humanity's Origin world, the cradle of the Source civilization. All humans had once come from the Greenworld of Teyr. Humanity had dwelled here for many thousands of years, believing they were alone in the universe, until the Fair-Feathered Goddess had come down to the world and found them. It was the Goddess who had lifted humanity higher, who'd gifted them with the divine knowledge of the seedships and sent them scattering off into the galaxy to populate the Prime Worlds.

But as humanity ventured further into the darkness, they began to slip from the righteous path of the Goddess. And thus, the inevitable destruction of the cosmos by her dark rival, the demon queen known as the Oblivion, was set into motion. Prophecies foretold that there would come a great cataclysm, heralded by the onslaught of the Oblivion's demon-spawn, and thus the entire universe would eventually be destroyed... except for Teyr, which would endure under the Goddess's protection. And then the cycle of life would begin anew, with the good and loving children of Teyr repopulating a newborn galaxy.

It all sounded so wonderful in the tales. How could one not be grateful for such a blessing? And yet... if only being born Teyrian didn't come with quite so much responsibility. In the deep, dark corners of her heart, Dalya sometimes wished she had *not* been born a Teyrian, that she had not been 'born blessed' at all.

She knew better than to speak these thoughts aloud, knowing they'd be met with a harsh rebuke from Uncle and a threat to send her before the sages. But sometimes, Dalya secretly resented Nathin for dying. He got to be away in his next life somewhere, while she'd been the one left standing here in the rain in front of this half-collapsed pavilion, wiping more gold paint from where it had dripped into the crease of her eyelid.

Standing stoically next to Uncle, Dalya held her shoulders as straight as she could. She kept her chin raised, her face graceful and serene despite the weight of her lopsided, dripping hairdo under the plastic cape. She imagined what Nathin would have done, and for a moment she pictured him here instead of her.

Nathin, who she only knew from old pictures she wasn't meant to look at. He seemed so tall and grown-up and obedient, looking so much like Uncle with his perfect posture and his long dark hair combed into perfect order.

She could not remember much about Nathin, but she was absolutely certain that his ceremonial runes would *not* have been dripping down his face during an important appearance. He would not have been standing here questioning his destiny.

And Nathin would definitely not have complained about the rain.

INSIDE THE WIND-SWEPT pavilion, Dalya watched as her uncle was received with all the usual fanfare due to the High Speaker. He stepped up before the crowd and gave a long, inspiring speech on the stage, speaking proudly and profoundly to the gathered news cameras.

He spoke of *homecoming* and *answering one's calling,* and the ties that bound Teyr to the Goddess. He spoke of bounty and safety and warmly welcoming the newcomers, and the crowd listened with rapt attention, hanging on his every word. All across Teyr, thousands upon thousands of others would be watching this broadcast over the network, the cameras conveying Uncle's confident face and unwavering words.

The golden symbols of the Goddess that were painted on Uncle's face had somehow remained neat and crisp despite him making the same walk through the rain, Dalya noticed resentfully. It was as if Uncle's very presence bent the weather around him. Of course it did. He was a strong and respected leader, or so the newscasts always said.

High Speaker Edamaun was one of the most powerful people on the entire world. But more than that, he inspired people by example. He led through his imposing *righteousness*, that steely calm that Dalya could never hope to approximate. When he spoke, he could make one believe he channelled the words of the Goddess herself.

The people called him *charismatic* and *affable*; words Dalya had learned from stories about him. Words she imagined might have been applied to Nathin if he'd lived, but that were certainly never applied to her. She was the replacement heir, the girl whose dress collar was always askew, who never seemed to be smiling at the right time for the cameras. For all her careful pretending, she had nothing of the High Speaker's poise, and at best a fraction of his aura of confidence.

Beloved as High Speaker Edamaun was, it was little wonder that the Council had voted almost unanimously in Uncle's favour when he'd advanced the much-discussed cause of the Returning. That's what they were celebrating now—the ongoing gathering of Teyrians from the moon of Meneyr and the Outer System, bringing them back to the surface of Teyr. Bringing them back to where they would be safe from the oncoming cataclysm.

The signs that the End of Time was near had already been observed by the sages, though *when precisely* the end would happen, none could say. And as for *who* would be spared... that, too, was painfully unclear. There was disagreement even among the wisest interpreters of the sacred texts. When the Goddess said that 'Teyr alone' would survive the cataclysm, that 'only Teyr' would be preserved when the rest of the galaxy disappeared... did that include Teyr's orbiting space stations and hubs? And what of the second capital, the Moon-City on Meneyr, Teyr's settled moon?

Most good believers supposed that Meneyr, too, should be safe from the coming apocalypse. Sages and monks alike broadly reassured people that the moon would certainly be considered a part of Teyr, that their moonside families would still be saved. Surely when the Fair-Feathered Goddess had pledged to protect Teyr, she would have included its sun and its moon, the whole solar system and all its natural and artificial satellites in that protection.

But there had always been theologians who disagreed. Those who took the sacred texts more literally believed that the moon Meneyr would perish along with the sun and all the rest of the galaxy, and that these, too, would be remade anew at the moment the cataclysm passed. 'Only Teyr' meant *only Teyr*. And those voices had grown louder now that the end seemed to be growing more imminent.

Now, the aliens had appeared in deep space, and the Union had gone to war. *Aliens* was what some people called the Oblivion's demon-spawn, those strange creatures who came from somewhere beyond the galaxy. The monsters who were not humans, who intended to destroy all the works and civilizations of humanity.

There was increasing pressure on the good believer families on Meneyr to migrate back to the Teyrian surface before the end came, to ensure their safety and survival. And Dalya's uncle, the High Speaker, the trusted leader of Teyr, was the leading voice behind that call.

Dalya had been told over and over again that she was too young to fully understand what was happening, but she understood the shape of it well enough. The Teyrians—her people—had long ago cut themselves off from the Union that joined the other human worlds in the galaxy. Teyr had withdrawn from the United Worlds of Humanity in order to take control of their own affairs. The Gepcot, of which her uncle was High Speaker, governed with sole and complete authority over the Teyrian Protectorate, and they were no longer subjected to the whims or the wars of the Union. Nor were they bound to humanity's unwinnable fight against the aliens.

They would be spared when the end came, here on the Unbreakable World. Safe and secure, without the need for weapons, without the need to make war. They just needed to get everyone back to Teyr.

Dalya knew a little bit about the war, which is to say, much more than she was meant to. She was altogether too good at listening in on conversations she shouldn't hear, particularly when high-ranking members of the Gepcot were so often visitors in her household. Some of them were surprisingly loose-lipped—or else they were so thoroughly determined to ignore a small, quiet child that they forgot to censor themselves in her presence.

There was absolutely no mention of the alien war in Uncle's speech at the festivities of welcome. He did not speak of the cataclysm, nor of the Oblivion, nor of any of the dire predictions that had brought these new citizens to the planet. That was mostly the realm of the sages. And perhaps there was no need to mention it to *these* people; why would there be? They had already made the right choice.

The messages of doom and destruction, Dalya thought, would be better sent to the people who still remained stubbornly on Meneyr. The ones whose fate and safety were still uncertain. Uncle wanted them all to return to Teyr, even the ones who didn't wish to come. He cared for them, despite how they refused to listen. It would be *them* who needed the warnings of what might befall them. But this gathered group in front of her—the ones who had already earned their place—were being told of the *rewards*.

Dalya felt a little self-satisfied at that deduction, at having understood the purpose of Uncle's speech. She liked it when she felt a bit clever, like she'd *worked something out...* though it happened disappointingly rarely. She wondered what the newcomers made of Uncle's speech, or what they made of seeing the High Speaker in person. It must be spectacular to them, seeing Luwan Edamaun in the flesh in front of them—whole and real, instead of just a familiar face on their vid-screens.

There were quite a few of the newly arrived moonfolk here, huddled under the lopsided pavilion. One hundred and twenty of the people who'd arrived last night from Meneyr had been randomly selected, invited to the formal ceremony and to meet the High Speaker. They'd all been inside that ship Dalya had seen burning bright in its descent.

This rainstorm must be so very strange to them, Dalya thought. There was no rain or wind on the moon Meneyr; this she had learned in her studies about Teyr's off-world settlements. There was only an artificial atmosphere up there, and a big, cold city huddling under a dome. The inhabitants of the Moon-City didn't even get to feel the real sun on their faces, and that seemed like the saddest thing of all.

It was good, Dalya thought, that these people had come here. Even if they probably thought the rainstorm was very annoying. There would be sunshine tomorrow.

AFTER THE CEREMONY in the pavilion ended, the procession moved on to the First-City's grand temple for a prayer-raising dedicated to the Great Goddess. Thankfully, it wasn't very far to walk, and the pelting rain and wind had abated enough now for an attendant to hold a wide umbrella over them as they went.

And there, in the temple of the Goddess, Dalya first saw some of the newcomers from Meneyr up close.

The moonfolk looked exactly the same as ordinary Teyrians, but there was something about their manner that immediately marked them as different. For one thing, they all made eye contact a little too long to be polite, and they seemed to speak a bit too loudly when they repeated the prayers. Their gestures during the prayer cycles, too, were subtly different—Dalya had noticed it in the pavilion when the opening prayer was being read, and she saw it again now in the rows where they sat in the temple.

"You need not concern yourself with their strange ways," Heral had told her that morning, as she helped Dalya to dress in her ceremonial gown. "If they seem an oddity, do not stare at them, nor look on them with contempt. We must welcome them as they are, as Teyrians like ourselves. We bring them into our fold and we accept them, and that is that. The rest, we'll leave up to the impeccable judgement of the Goddess."

Dalya had nodded solemnly, wondering what kinds of *oddities* she might see in them. Now, she remembered Heral's admonition not to stare at them, and turned quickly back to her own prayers. She held her prayer beads tightly, flicking out the traditional gestures with her fingers as she repeated the words she knew by heart.

But she couldn't help looking over at the newcomers again, watching the way they flicked their hands in the opposite direction on some of the prayers. The way they made different shapes with their hands as the beads flowed through them. When Uncle wasn't looking, she tried holding hers that way, just once.

And much to her embarrassment, one of the newcomers saw her do it. A girl with orange flowers in her hair caught Dalya's eye from the opposite row. She smiled from the corner of her mouth, and for an instant her cool gaze danced with amusement. It wasn't judgement in her eyes, but something almost like conspiratorial glee.

Dalya quickly looked away again, her cheeks burning, and resumed the correct prayer forms. Her heart raced as she glanced toward Uncle to make sure he hadn't seen it. Thankfully, there were no news cameras in the temple, nothing to capture her foolish action, save maybe for the watchful gaze of the Goddess herself. What had she been thinking, foolish girl?

Perhaps Uncle was right, all the times he told Dalya that she did not think hard enough about how to conduct herself. Perhaps she just didn't understand yet why things had to be done a certain way—*you are so young, Dalya, so very young*, Heral always said.

But she had *felt* something then, some small spark of curious joy when she turned her string of prayer beads over and started from the other side.

Later, she would look back on that small moment and wonder if that was when everything had started to change.

PAGE FOUND
A big ship, she thinks — wherever the hells this is

ZHAK'S SMALL SPEEDSHIP has flown directly into a much larger ship and clamped down inside the bay. As Maelle ushers Page out into the cavernous space, Page sees that a network of flimsy metal scaffoldings has been pushed up against the smaller vessel, forming a sort of bridge to the catwalk around the bay's walls.

The whole place is strangely silent. There's no engine rumble—this larger ship is evidently drifting—and there isn't a single other crew member in sight. Zhak, too, is conspicuously absent. It occurs to Page that there was probably someone else piloting the speedship, but there's no sign of them in the bay, either.

"No shenanigans, all right?" Maelle says, holding up a warning finger as she leads Page out. "Just do what Zhak says and you'll be good. He's an asshole, but trust me when I say you're better off not antagonizing him. Things'll go much smoother for all of us if you don't fuck around."

"Got it," Page says, sarcasm thick in her voice. "What're you, then, Zhak's enforcer? Is he your shitty boss?"

Maelle makes a disgusted face. "Tch, no, I'm an independent contractor. I deal in information. Zhak's more of a... colleague. We work together on occasion." She gives Page a cutting look. "But I do know my way around a weapons cabinet, so I wouldn't suggest fucking around with me either." She dips one hand into her jacket and pulls out Page's scratched-up digipad. "Tell you what. Be on your best behaviour... and I might even be persuaded to give *this* back to you."

"Whatever." Page shrugs. "Why should I care about that? It's just some stolen piece of junk."

"Yeeeah. I don't think so, pal. I saw the look on your face when I picked this up. This is *yours*." Maelle smirks. "From one liar to another, be aware that you'll find it very hard to fool me. Understood?"

"Understood."

"Go this way," Maelle commands, pointing to a door at the far end of the catwalk. "We'll go in through the service entrance and get you to the showers." She laughs, not entirely unkindly. "Apparently, you 'stink.'"

Page nods wordlessly. She supposes she can cooperate for a little while, just until she gets her bearings. She can *be on her best behaviour* until she gets her eyes on an escape route. Then it's game over.

She walks where she's directed, keeping her eyes mostly lowered, pretending not to look around. But she's spent years perfecting the art of casually glancing at her surroundings without letting on that she's looking. She tips her head forward, allowing her too-long fringe to fall over her eyes, providing an additional layer of obfuscation.

There's only the one speedship docked in the bay right now, and what looks like a half-dozen small, fast cruising vessels parked along the far wall. An operation like this can surely move huge amounts of cargo. Page bites her tongue, holding back the innumerable questions that flood her as they walk, and continues to observe silently.

The large metal door at the end of the catwalk is not locked, and they proceed through it into a half-darkened hallway that smells faintly of cleaner fluid and bolt grease.

"Fuck's sake. I keep telling Zhak we need to replace the bulbs in here," Maelle says as she clicks a light switch back and forth to no avail. Even in the dark, Page can hear the eyeroll in her voice. There's a sort of casual camaraderie in her words, something that reminds Page of small talk on Kuuj—the customary complaints about maintenance.

"Guess he hasn't taken that suggestion to heart," Page says.

"You might have guessed that Zhak doesn't take too well to suggestions in general," Maelle says.

Maelle bashes her closed fist against one of the flat, flickering panels as they pass. The bulb on the other side of it returns to full brightness for a few seconds before fading again, and Page can't suppress a bitter laugh. There's something poetic in that show of absolute futility. But she can't quite put words to it.

The service passage Maelle takes her through is narrow enough that they have to walk single file, and Maelle drops behind her. Page should probably be more concerned about whether there's a weapon levelled at her back, but—whether or not camaraderie was Maelle's intent—Page feels far more at ease with Maelle right now than she likely ought to be with an armed pirate. *Independent contractor.* Whatever she is.

They walk on in silence until the passage opens up again into a little chamber a few paces wide. To the left, there are hooks, shelves and cubbies attached to the wall that might once have held equipment or space-suits. They're all empty, save for a single disused helmet sitting on the top shelf.

To their right is a metal blast door which seems to be Maelle's destination. Whatever sign was once affixed to it has been removed, leaving a square of peeling adhesive. Below that, it has been hand-lettered with a roughly drawn lavatory symbol, outlined in luminous paint.

Maelle punches a code into the access panel next to the door, then leads the way into a big, echoey room that's tiled on every side. She points across the room. "We're going through there. To the showers."

The door she's pointing at is emblazoned with another symbol that Page immediately recognizes: *Biohazard*.

"Uh... the sign doesn't really inspire much confidence," Page quips nervously.

"Hah! Well, you've got a point there. Technically, they're decontamination showers." Maelle's voice echoes through the wide chamber. "Place has got great water pressure, though, so I always come down here to wash up. Creepy signs aside, it's totally fine. I promise, it hasn't been used for its intended purpose in years. The worst biohazard in there today will be whatever's currently crawling on *you*."

Before Page has even finished taking in her surroundings, Maelle lifts the big emergency latch over the door, the one labelled ALARMED EXIT, DO NOT OPEN. No alarms sound. Instead, an overhead light comes on, illuminating a long chamber a few paces wide.

"Go on, then," Maelle says. "Walk on through. You can just dump your old clothes in the disposal in there. I presume you're not attached to them?" She pokes her booted toe toward a bright yellow disposal hatch embedded in the floor. "There are clean towels over on the other side. I'll hand you one on your way out. And I'll grab you some clean clothes, yeah? You can just borrow something of mine for now."

Page is suddenly self-conscious, realizing there's no privacy barrier. Not that she's *shy* or anything; she's been using the communal shower rooms on Kuuj for years, and she has no qualms with her naked body. It's not like everybody doesn't have ass cheeks. But there's something altogether too vulnerable about this, about relinquishing even the slim shield of her clothing and leaving herself utterly bare.

"I, ah—I..." she mumbles, feeling her face flush.

"Don't worry, darlin'. I'm not gonna stand here staring at you," Maelle says with an exasperated look. "I'll go around and meet you on the other side. There's nowhere you can run to anyway. Here, take this." She digs around in a box on one of the shelves just outside, then hands Page a small, clear packet filled with bright green granules.

Page stares down at the item in puzzlement, her mind supplying any number of explanations for the substance inside. *Poison? Hallucinogens? Some kind of sugar candy?*

"It's just soap," Maelle says, seeing the confusion on Page's face as she sniffs the packet. "Y'know... soap? As in, suds? Bubbles? Washing up? The scent of a luxurious garden in your hair?"

Page clutches the packet with a sheepish nod. "Uh. Right, soap. Thanks." She summons a laugh to cover the sting of her embarrassment. "Believe it or not, we *have* heard of soap on Kuuj. Old legends and all that. The tale has been told."

Maelle's dark eyes dance with amusement. "Hey, I'm saying nothing. See you on the other side."

Page steps cautiously over the threshold into the shower room. Then Maelle pushes a button. The clear wall between them slides shut, and Page is sealed in.

"*STAND CLEAR! D-D-DE-DECONTAMINATION CHAMBER IN USE!*" a glitching, tinny voice announces. "*W-WA-WARNING. D-D-DE-DECONTAMINATION CHAMBER IN USE!*"

Page holds the soap packet between her teeth while she quickly strips off her clothing, bunching her sweaty clothes up in her hands before she throws them away. She can hardly imagine that it was only a few hours ago she was getting dressed back in her hab-cube on Kuuj, preparing herself for a perfectly ordinary day on the concourse.

Maelle is right. She's not exactly attached to any of what she's wearing. And yet, the thought of *throwing her clothes away* still evokes a strange sense of loss. She's never thrown *any* of her clothes away on Kuuj. Nothing is ever wasted on a deep space outpost; nothing is destroyed that still has the slightest utility to it.

As Page drops each piece through the yellow trapdoor,

releasing the very last of her worldly possessions, it feels strangely as if she's peeling away the layers of her years on Kuuj. Layers of the only years of her life that she actually remembers.

First goes the nondescript beige shirt that she's owned practically the entire time she lived on the outpost, stained under the arms and stretched in the elbows.

Then goes the synthetic temperature-regulating vest she acquired the first time Kuuj had a long-term thermoregulator systems failure, when she got too uncomfortable to sleep and resentfully had to spend almost a whole week's earnings on it.

Her work shoes, the only ones she's ever had that were actually the right size, their corrugated soles thinned with years of wear.

Her baggy black trousers, considerably too long but rolled up and cuffed to fit her, found in a backpack she pinched from the Kuuj dockyard half a year ago.

Her threadbare underthings and socks, all plain grey and utilitarian. (Nothing one could buy on Kuuj had been designed with much thought to aesthetics.)

Finally, she pulls off the broken *Leviahunter* headset that still hangs looped around her neck. This, she holds on to the longest, running her hand over the lenses, stroking the faded elastic strap. Clicking on the little light she installed to make it look legit and functional. *Her own work*. The closest she's really come to something feeling like *hers*.

But even this isn't truly hers to keep, is it? Everything she's ever made, everything she's done, all her long hours... she's thrown it all into the bottomless pit of her debt to Tully. She bites the inside of her lip as she smashes the *Leviahunter* headset against the wall, destroying the lenses and synthetic frame before she hurls the device into the disposal chute.

And just like that... the last of her life on Kuuj is gone. All that remains is the digipad that Maelle is holding on to for her, but she tries not to think of that. Best not to get her hopes up. She can't trust these people.

Now completely denuded, Page is conscious that she can never remember having been more alone than she is right now. She steps forward, her bare feet following the decals on the floor as the decontamination sequence begins. There's a humming rumble and clank of pipes… and then a spray of warm, sharp-smelling water comes on overhead. She clenches her eyes shut as it hits her.

The spray strikes her upturned face with such force that Page yelps and jumps back in surprise, nearly slipping on the tiled floor. The communal showers on Kuuj barely mustered a thin, pissing trickle of water. An overpriced two minutes of shower time barely allowed her to scrub herself down and rinse off properly—and after Tully's latest *resource restructuring*, you had to buy three minutes of time to get the same measly water allocation.

Page rolls her sore shoulders under the cascade of warm water, stretching out her arms, checking herself over for injuries. She rubs resentfully at the red marks on her wrists and ankles, where the cables held her to that chair in Zhak's makeshift interrogation chamber. But aside from the still-fading bruises on her elbows from the last time she blacked out on a ladder on Kuuj, she seems unharmed.

After a minute, she tears open one corner of the soap packet, pouring the bright green granules into her hand. True to Maelle's word, a wonderfully fragrant scent hits her nostrils as water makes contact with the granules. It overpowers the chemical stench of the water, and a cloud of billowing suds starts to form on her palm. Page rubs the soap all over herself, scrubbing it through her hair and all over her skin, closing her eyes and focusing on the unfamiliar sensation. None of the little pink soap bars you could buy on Kuuj produced *bubbles*.

As she focuses on the feel of it, she *wonders*, as she always does when she feels something new. Has she ever felt this much water running over her skin at once before? Has she ever smelled a soap so fragrant while steam rose around her? But nothing specific comes to her, only a familiar disappointment.

The truth has never been further from her grasp. Whatever hope she once had of discovering her identity, it's gone, left behind on Kuuj. That chance is spiralling away down the drain, along with whatever remained of the outpost on her skin. She doesn't even know why she's here. And now her semblance of a home, her semblance of a life, her only true memories, will be gone like everything else.

Washed away.

MAELLE KRESS
Zhaklam Evelor's Ship

THE OUTPOST GIRL will be your responsibility, Zhak had said. *You're going to look after her and get her ready. That's your part in this. I don't want to deal with her any more than I have to.*

And Maelle had nodded dutifully, grumbling and talking back just the right amount to make Zhak growl some threat under his breath, yet not quite enough to make him think she'd consider crossing him. It's a delicate balance, playing Zhak, but Maelle has had years of practice.

Practice that's about to pay off, if Maelle keeps her head. *If* this gamble with the junk thief pans out.

It was a big risk to take on the basis of one anonymous tip. To go after this nobody with an alleged memory wipe, no Union ident, and apparently no ambitions of her own beyond thieving for some wreckhole low-life. But Zhak needed a decent stand-in for a Teyrian-highborn-turned-monk, and Page clearly needed an out from a dead-end life. It's like a fairytale in the making, Maelle thinks wryly to herself.

And here in front of her is the unlikely candidate herself. A petty thief with no past, no prospects, and a mess of tangled hair that's currently dripping all over the shoulders of her borrowed clothes. She looks kind of stunned and awkward, and it doesn't help that Maelle's jumpsuit doesn't fit her in the slightest.

Maelle and Page might be close to the same height, but that's where their similarity ends. Page is thin as a rail, her shoulders narrow, her lanky limbs completely lost in a black synthetic suit that would neatly hug Maelle's ample curves. The waist, at least, has a drawstring; Page pulls it tight, bunching the ill-fitting thing awkwardly around her middle.

"It's, uh… hmm. Yeah. I guess I can make this work," Page says as she ties a double knot in the string.

"We'll find you something more your size later," Maelle says. "We've got tons of stuff to choose from, but I didn't have time to go through the crates. At least this is clean, right? And hopefully *slightly* less stinky."

Maelle allows herself the hint of a laugh as she pats Page's shoulder. It won't hurt to build up a little camaraderie, to establish herself as the more *relatable* one here. She's the ally Page needs, a haven from Zhak's 'aloof, soulless asshole' routine.

Not that he has to try very hard to play at that. Zhak's a natural asshole if ever there was one.

"It's not a problem, really. This is fine," Page says with a shrug. "I mean… it's not like I had high standards back on Kuuj." She's still threading her fingers through her newly washed hair, wincing as she catches a nest of tangles above her ear.

"I should find you a hairbrush," Maelle says. "You do know what a hairbrush is, right?"

The junk thief glares, but she can't keep a smile from her face. "Yeah, sure," she says with a sarcastic grimace. "Learned about it in the same legend as the soap. I've heard of toothpaste, too, believe it or not. You got any of that?"

"Absolutely," Maelle grins. "Although, be warned that Zhak'll threaten to charge you if you use too much of it. *We're not running a hotel here.*" She drops into an imitation of Zhak's enunciation, which makes Page laugh again.

It always winds Zhak up when Maelle mocks his highbrow accent. He tries so damn hard to disguise it, adopting something closer to a Latter-Worlds drawl, but to a keen observer, his speech patterns still scream 'aristo with a Prime World education.' Which happens to be exactly what Zhak is, among other things. Maelle wonders if Page has picked up on it.

Page's own accent is unusual to Maelle's ears. She talks like someone who's travelled, like maybe she speaks a mix of dialects. It's hard to pin down. Maelle knows very little of the language variations from this part of the sector, and isolated deep space outposts like Kuuj tend to develop their own pocket dialects over time. The dockyard slang in some places is almost unrecognizable as Union Basic.

The more remarkable thing, of course, is that Page apparently speaks *Graya*. One of the ancient human tongues. It's still spoken in a few places—Teyr among them—but it's not exactly common anymore outside of scholarly pursuits. Which makes her all the more mysterious. And all the more perfect for their purposes.

Graya is an exceptionally complex language, layered with metaphor and poetic turns of phrase and ornate modifiers. It sounds the way an over-rich cake tastes. It takes years to master the spoken form of the ancient tongue with anything even close to native fluency. And yet Maelle's source claimed that Page comprehended it perfectly. So far, so good: Page obviously understood that command Zhak threw at her on Kuuj. And whatever she said to Zhak back on the speedship must have impressed him. The junk thief is a fascinating enigma.

Maelle watches Page from the corner of her eye as they leave the decontamination area, and she's well aware that Page is watching her too. Page seems to think she's being discreet about it, sneaking glances from under the mess of her tangled fringe.

It's impossible to guess what's going through the girl's head right now, but on the whole she really seems to have taken this kidnapping remarkably well. She's not asking as many questions as Maelle would've expected—or any questions at all, really.

Which either means she's afraid of something... or, more likely, that she doesn't see the point in asking, because she wouldn't trust Maelle's answers anyway. Which is exactly why Maelle needs to work the camaraderie angle a little harder.

The corridor widens enough for them to walk side by side, though they have to stick close enough that their shoulders are nearly touching. Page is frowning slightly, still glancing around like she's trying to get her bearings or searching for hidden exits. But that vague, blank look remains in her eyes.

They come to the end of the corridor, where they'll have to climb into a claustrophobically narrow lift to proceed. Maelle stops and waits for Page's reaction, but after all those years sneaking around on Kuuj Outpost, she's surely no stranger to small spaces. She didn't flinch much at having that bag over her head earlier, and she's equally unfazed here, climbing into the tiny, brightly lit lift without hesitation. Maelle presses the button, and the mechanism around them squeals to life, climbing slowly to the main deck.

With little else to look at, Maelle takes the opportunity to study the junk thief up close. Page is around thirty-odd standard, according to her medical records on Kuuj, but her stint in stasis and those ill-fed years on the outpost have aged her. Her skin has a greyish tint to it, and there are deep shadows in the hollows below her eyes. Still, there's an ethereal sort of charm about her, a confidence and grace in the way she holds herself when she's not slouching to avoid attention. There's something almost *noble* about her bearing.

The dossier Maelle bought on the junk thief included everything Kuuj knew about her past, and it wasn't much. Apparently, Page had signed up for some kind of clinical trial involving stasis. An experiment that could just as likely have become a death sentence. These shady sci-tech companies use all kinds of bribes to exploit people now: putting up lots of money for volunteers, or else offering transport to a more protected part of the galaxy, getting people to sign themselves away for science... because demand has never been higher for the development of new, allegedly *safer* forms of stasis tech.

But stasis has never been safe. It's a quiet form of torture, one that probably shouldn't have *any* legal use. How many people have died in unsuccessful revivals, or else woken with parts of their minds missing or bodies forever altered?

Stasis research was once the niche realm of scientists planning for wider-ranging venture-ships: theoretical ships full of long-term sleepers that might blaze their way far out of Union territory, or even outside the galaxy itself. A safe form of suspended animation, if the kinks could ever be worked out, would open up the prospect of crossing long stretches of deep space while scanning for new potential subspace jump points that could shorten the journey.

But then, the war started. Not just *a* war, but *The* War. An alien conflict, far beyond the petty territorial squabbles between human factions that had peppered the Union Quadrant's history. Calamity struck, a disastrous first contact with a species far more technologically advanced than humanity. A threat greater than anything else humanity has ever faced.

The Felen. Aliens with unimaginable firepower and endless endurance, with whom it was impossible to negotiate or communicate. Aliens far too advanced to stand for any human provocation. It was a mistake, all of it. A mistake for which humanity has been paying for two generations already, with no end in sight.

Religious types, of course, immediately jumped to the darkest prophecies in the sacred texts. They spouted predictions of the demise of the universe, equating the violent first contact with the Felen with the prophesied attack of the Oblivion's demon-spawn. Pragmatic survivalists started burying doomsday bunkers in far-flung asteroid belts and building deep-space hideouts. Less optimistic catastrophizers started investing in explorations outside the Union Quadrant, hoping to find new places to run.

And, as it turns out... *some* of them also sent ships full of suspended monks into space—reviving an old tradition in the name of some sort of purification ritual. Monks exactly like the one they need Page Found to impersonate.

A lot of these monks never wake up from their self-imposed stasis. But with a little luck and a little subterfuge—and one cooperative junk thief—they might just convince the right people that they've found one who did.

A Boy Found a Bird

One day a boy found a bird,
Found a little fallen bird.
On the ground, she was stone-still,
Perhaps she was dead.
The boy placed a flower by the bird,
By the little fallen bird.
Then cried a bitter tear for her,
Mourned her sad fate.
The bloom smelled so sweet to the bird,
To the little fallen bird.
She opened up her shining eyes,
And she took in a breath.
Then the boy sang a song for the bird,
For the little fallen bird.
He sang loud and clear, of joy and love,
And her heart began to beat in time.
Then she rose and spread her wings,
Did the little fallen bird.
She found her bell-bright voice
And she sang back the song.
A song so sweet, from the bird,
From the little fallen bird.
All who heard it were changed,
And blessed with everlasting life.

"A Boy Found a Bird,"
Traditional [translated from Graya]

DALYA
OF HOUSE EDAMAUN, IN HER NINTH YEAR
First-City, Teyr

ALL THROUGH THE temple prayers, Dalya watched the moon-born girl.

The girl kept glancing over at her from across the aisle, long after Dalya had corrected her prayer sequence, and for a long while she wondered what she could possibly be looking at. But then again, wasn't *she* staring too? The newcomers must be just as curious about the Teyrians as Dalya was about them.

What did the girl think, she wondered, of the Greenworld of legend and renown? What stories had she heard about the bountiful lands of Teyr? What did she make of the festivities of welcome?

They were locked in a loop as elegant as a dance: the moon girl would glance over at Dalya, and whenever Dalya looked up in turn, she'd avert her eyes for a while and stare straight ahead. Then she'd look over at the man standing next to her before she looked back at Dalya again.

The man—the girl's father, probably—rested his hand protectively on her shoulder, looking down at her with a reassuring nod. He was pale-skinned and wiry, taller even than Uncle, and his hair was pulled back in a long white braid. Dalya had seen the two of them back at the welcoming ceremony, and they didn't seem to have any other family with them. Perhaps, like Dalya and her uncle, they were a family of two.

As the delegation had walked to the temple, Uncle had told Dalya to be courteous, to keep her head up, to smile. He reminded her several times again to be *welcoming*. It was part of her duty, after all. And so, at the gathering after the prayers had concluded—when the moon girl suddenly darted over and pulled on Dalya's arm—Dalya hid her shock and instead dipped her head in a respectful greeting.

"Greetings, god-sibling," she said to the girl. The honorific indicated the collective of *Teyrian humanity*—all those whose ancestors had never left the Teyrian system, the group in which the inhabitants of Meneyr had been so tenuously included. "We pray that you will flourish among us, that you will find healthy new roots in our blessed soil."

The girl blinked slowly. Stared at her for a moment. And then, much to Dalya's surprise, she stifled a *giggle*. She brought one skinny hand up to her face as if she had to physically stop herself from laughing, and when she pulled her hand away, she had put on a serious expression that looked just a little too stiff.

"Greetings... *god-sibling*," she choked out, clearly still trying not to laugh. She spoke the Perfect Cadence with remarkable clarity, though with an accent that sounded slightly too harsh for the words. "It is... It is very good to meet you."

"What do you find funny? What are you laughing at?" Dalya demanded, immediately forgetting her good graces as her face grew hot. Had she offended the girl somehow? Had she done something wrong?

"Oh! I... no, I... I really didn't mean to laugh, I was... it's just..." The girl looked like she was clenching her teeth now, scrambling for an answer. Her expression went as rigid as a waxen mannequin. She looked at the floor, lowered her head down and bowed deeply. "I'm so sorry. It's just that... everyone is so very formal here! I'm not used to it. Forgive me for disturbing you. I only wanted to say hello."

Dalya's shoulders relaxed. She hadn't made a mistake after all. "It's all right," she said. "I... I can be less formal. I am only trying to carry out my duty." She glanced over her shoulder; Uncle was busy talking to one of the other council members, not looking at her. "It is my calling, you see. It is my solemn responsibility to welcome you to—Oh, goodness, I'm doing it again, aren't I? I'm sorry. I'll stop."

Then the girl's awkward grimace finally broke into a wide, gap-toothed smile. She glanced behind her as if she thought someone might be coming to admonish her, but seeing no one there, she turned back to Dalya again.

"Is it all right that I'm talking to you?" she asked Dalya. "One of the guards over there told me I wasn't to bother you unless it was on *official business*. But I'm not quite sure what that means."

"I... I think it's all right if we talk," said Dalya. She, too, looked nervously at the row of handlers all eyeing her vigilantly. But they remained unmoving and impassive, watching over her like so many stern-faced statues. "Talking is what this gathering is meant to be for, isn't it? We are meant to welcome you! But I must behave myself, I must *be serious*. We should not laugh in the temple. We should discuss an important matter," Dalya said.

The tall man who might be the moon girl's father was also watching them, his keen eyes fixed on his little ward, like he was worried that she might misstep. Dalya wondered if even the grown moonfolk weren't quite sure how they were meant to act here.

"All right. Listen," the girl whispered to Dalya. "If anyone comes round and asks what we're talking about... we'll simply say that we're discussing our favourite lines from the sacred texts. That's an important matter, isn't it? That seems perfectly all right for the temple. What do you think?"

Dalya bobbed her head in agreement. "Yes," she said. "All right. Yes. We can do that."

They stood facing each other in silence for a few seconds, Dalya twisting her prayer beads in her hand, trying to think of anything else to say.

"So... what's yours, then?" The girl's gappy smile widened even more. Her other teeth were straight and dazzlingly white. "Tell it to me, please!"

"What is... my what?" Dalya looked at her in confusion. Had the girl asked her name?

"Your favourite line, of course. From the sacred texts! Like we just said."

"Oh." Dalya blinked. "I... hmm. All right, let me think. You go first."

"Mine is: *And so it was that the curiosity of the Goddess led her to the Greenworld, and thus she brought humankind to their divine destiny,*" the girl recited. "I like it because it gives us permission to be curious. And that's why it's never rude to ask a well-intentioned question!"

Dalya shifted her feet awkwardly, realizing at once that she still didn't know which line to choose. She had spent so long memorizing lines and verses and tenets from the sacred texts, but it had never occurred to her to pick out a *favourite* line.

She stared at the girl, at the strange cut of the dark blue dress she wore, with the orange blooms of the Goddess-blossom printed on it. There were lots of orange flowers clipped into her hair, too—synthetic blooms stuck to little gold barrettes that didn't look at all like real flowers, even less so now that they were droopy and damp from the downpour.

Flowers, Dalya thought, racking her brain for a snippet of the sacred texts. She liked flowers, there were lots of lines about those—

"I suppose I... I do like all the lines about flowers. And about courage," she said at last. "*Courage is not always a bright flower in full bloom; sometimes it is a bud awaiting the moment to open.*"

"Ah! Yes!" The girl looked delighted. "That's a good one. It tells us... Even if you aren't one of the people everyone else sees as courageous, you have inner qualities that count, too! Yes. I like it very much."

The girl rocked back and forth on her heels, like this was genuinely exciting to her. But then she caught herself and stopped, glancing back at her watchful guardian again. Like he might come and pull her away from Dalya before she'd finished her conversation.

Dalya's row of handlers seemed to have relaxed now. Most of their attention was back on the High Speaker as he made his way down the procession of newcomers, pausing along the way to pose for the news cameras. He wasn't far from the girls. It was nearly time to leave; any moment now, Uncle would signal to Dalya to rejoin the delegation, and she'd have to step back to his side for their exit.

But before Dalya could say anything else, the moon girl suddenly reached up into her hair and plucked out one of the orange flowers—the largest of the blooms, with a wider gold clip than the others, which she'd had pinned over one ear. Perhaps she'd seen Dalya's eyes on it, and thought she was admiring it.

"Here," she said. She clipped the big gold barrette with the flower stuck to it onto the edge of Dalya's rain-cape. "Take this. In friendship. Thank you so much for welcoming us here."

Then, with one more quick bow, the girl ducked away and ran back over to the tall man.

Dalya touched the flower with something like wonder, watching the girl's retreating back. "Thank you," she mumbled.

Not long after that, Uncle signalled Dalya to his side. The delegation swept past and collected her, and the security escort shepherded them away toward their waiting transport. And thus, her duty at the festivities of welcome was done.

"You did well today, Dalya," Uncle said as she climbed into the transport. Dalya beamed with pride at his rare approval.

"Was I welcoming to the newcomers? Bright as a beacon, like you said?" she asked. "Did you see me, Uncle?"

"I did." He reached over and plucked the synthetic Goddess-blossom from the edge of Dalya's rain cape, and to her great surprise, he pinned the gold bauble to his own collar as he settled back into his seat. "I saw you, Dalya. And I am very proud of you."

Their transport eased through the barriers and pulled away.

MAELLE KRESS
Zhaklam Evelor's Ship

MAELLE CAREFULLY DIRECTS Page down a side hallway that Zhak has declared off-limits to the rest of the ship's crew, keeping her out of sight. They've got the smallest possible skeleton crew on this mission, and they've all been strictly ordered to stay out of the way. It's mostly new contractors, grunts who've had absolutely no prior dealings with Zhak. And a raider crew, of course, who also don't know where they're going. They've got no reason to suspect that this mission is anything out of the ordinary.

Zhak has many different business ventures, but on this occasion he's playing the out-system debt collector. Most of this crew think he's tracking down a couple of elderly debt-dodgers who've fled from somewhere in the Monaxan system.

Maelle wonders if it's ever occurred to anyone to question any of it. Like how an old couple from Monaxas would even have ended up in the ass-end of a deep-space sector in a place like Kuuj, when there's a thousand different travel bans in effect. Or how setting a debt collector on them would serve any purpose whatsoever, when the debt laws on their planet would've allowed their assets to be seized the minute they were confirmed out-of-system. Or why Zhak needs an *entire raider crew* to capture them.

It figures that Zhak would just… make some random shit up, with no thought to how much sense it made. This is exactly the kind of sloppy work he does. Maelle could have come up with something better in her sleep. But then again, she supposes that most of this crew aren't the type to think about stuff too hard. They're just here to do the job; they're happy to know nothing at all about what's actually going on as long as they're getting paid on time.

"Come on," Maelle says to Page, leading her toward the open doorway at the end of the corridor. "It's this way. Time to get your questions answered, whether you want to or not."

Zhak is waiting for the two of them in what he calls his 'boardroom.' Inside is what probably used to be some kind of records room when this ship was operating as a hauler. All that's left is a few rows of empty shelves pushed to the sides of the room, replaced by an octagonal table with seven chairs around it. On the side without a chair, a portable computer sits on top of a couple of storage boxes.

Zhak's still wearing the same clothes he had on when he came to interrogate Page in the speedship, but in typical theatrical fashion, he's now added an ornate, cream-coloured ruffled jacket to the ensemble. There are little pointed jewels dangling around the collar and sleeves, and the chains jangle as he moves.

The jewelled chains are painfully obvious, cheap replicas. A mockery of ostentation, a disguise upon a disguise like just about everything else Zhak does. Because what golden-assed aristocrat would wear *fake jewels*? He comes across as some kind of social climber who doesn't know anything about actual aesthetics. Exactly what he wants people to think—that he's a Latter-Worlder trying to put on a fake posh air, not the other way around.

"Well! It's about time, isn't it?" Zhak stands up expectantly when Page and Maelle come in. "Have fun at the baths?" He sniffs at the air. "Hmm. I don't smell stale sweat and outpost fumes the minute you walk in anymore… so I guess that's an improvement."

Would it really kill him to be polite? At moments like these, it's hard to believe that he's had any sort of respectable upbringing—which is undoubtedly exactly why he acts this way.

Maelle glances nervously at Page, but she doesn't rise to the bait. She just gives him an icy, even stare.

He motions Page toward the chairs. "Sit."

The junk thief seems to hesitate for a moment before cautiously obeying. She folds herself into a hard-backed orange seat with evident apprehension, as if she's not quite sure that it doesn't hold some kind of trap. Maelle gives her what she hopes is a reassuring look, and slides into the chair beside her.

"So. You must be wondering why I've brought you here," Zhak says with an irreverent laugh. "Why I ripped you from your life of luxury in the palatial halls of Kuuj Outpost?"

Page stares straight ahead, saying nothing.

"Oh, I see. We're being *serious*," he says, waving a dismissive hand. "Fine. Forget about that. Kuuj, whatever you were doing there, that's all in the past. It's time to meet your *new* destiny. Behold!"

The display on Zhak's computer lights up, showing a close still image of what looks like a half-dozen monks in long white robes. They stand shoulder to shoulder around some grandiose altar, with a round object resting on it. They all wear winglike capes, and feather-covered, avian-looking masks.

Some of the details in the capture are remarkably sharp, but the image as a whole is indistinct—as though it's been cut from a piece of security footage, or taken from very far away and then enhanced. Still, Maelle has seen this image so many times, now, that she could probably sketch the angles of all their beaked heads and the designs on their robes from memory.

"Monks of the Sanctum of the Golden-Feather, the Awakened from the Blessed Sleep," Zhak says. He enunciates the lengthy name with dramatic flair as he brings up the projection. "You ever seen these little birdies before?"

Maelle watches Page squinting at the image. She leans forward in her chair, her eyes scanning it as if she's taking in every detail. Deeply considering the question, as if her life depends on it.

"Nope," Page finally says with a shrug. "Don't think so. Never seen 'em in my life."

"Hmmm." Zhak's ringed fingers drum along the edge of the table. "Not surprising. They're downright impossible to track down... as I've learned firsthand," he says enigmatically. "Underneath these cute little bird costumes, they're utterly deranged. Most of them are highborn heirs from the Teyrian Protectorate. They put themselves into stasis *voluntarily*, to experience some kind of transcendence. To *commune with the Goddess*, see? As you do, I suppose, when you come from some noble Teyrian house and you've run out of things to do with your limitless wealth." He chuckles to himself. "Prime aristos, huh? Am I right? Bunch of weirdos."

"Look, I... uh... I dunno," says Page. Her gaze darts to Maelle, as if she's not quite sure what's expected and hopes to find the answer in Maelle's eyes. Then she squares her shoulders, recovering some of her earlier sass. "Shocking as it might be, we don't see many Prime aristos on Kuuj."

"Ha! Well, no matter," Zhak says. "We can teach you all you need to know. You see... I happen to need one of these monks in my employ for a little business venture, Page. One which stands to benefit *you* a great deal, should you choose to cooperate. And I strongly suggest that you do."

Page just glowers at him and slouches down in the chair.

He turns back to the picture of the gathered monks. "Long story short, these monks like to launch their ships into space on multi-year circuits, with routes that are kept a closely guarded secret. At any given time, most of the monks are in suspension, or else dead in their pods—except for a small living contingent to crew the ship." He pauses dramatically and grins. "But as it happens, these monk-ships don't just haul stasis corpses around. *Some* of them are also rumoured to carry significant caches of rare old-world artifacts. Pieces that would be of great interest to a... certain *client* of mine. And so... I would very much like to secure access to such a ship."

"Right," Page says flatly. "And why are you telling me all of this?"

"Well." Zhak chuckles again. "As special as they believe themselves to be, these monks are just ordinary people, exactly like everybody else. Except for a couple of crucial little difficult-to-replicate details." He raises a finger and taps the base of his neck, then points back to the image of the Golden-Feather monks.

Page doesn't react when he repeats the gesture twice, staring at him without comprehension.

"Ugh! I'm talking about *stasis!*" Zhak finally huffs. "You're exactly what I need, Page. You'd have been about the right age to have made one of those flights already... and you're a wakeling with uniquely *delicate* stasis scarring... It's a gods-damned miracle I found you, because I'm on a pretty tight deadline right now."

"What? You don't mean—" Page looks incredulously from Zhak to Maelle, then back at Zhak again. "You want to pass me off as one of *them*? I don't know a damn thing about being a monk *or* an aristocrat. I mean... I'm a swindler, sure, but I'm not a damn *actor*."

Zhak hums with amusement. "Oh, really? Not an actor? *'Excuse me, oh, sorry—I just need to grab that super-rare chest over there, see, it's a little game called Leviahunter...'*" He winks. "Could've fooled me. And as I understand it... you don't remember anything at *all* about your past, or so you claim. Post-suspension syndrome. So... what's to say you're *not* a monk of the Golden-Feather?"

There's something more than anger or annoyance in Page's expression. For a moment, Maelle sees something soft and fragile in her gaze. Fleeting, like there's a momentary glitch in her shields. If Maelle didn't know better, she might think it was hope.

"Well... presumably an identity scan, for one thing?" Page

says sarcastically. That soft flicker of vulnerability in her face has vanished; her shields are back up and immovable. "Whatever it is you want your fake aristo-monk to do... if they have access to anything even remotely important, I assume there'd be basic biometric protocols in place. I'm no expert, but I've seen enough holo-dramas to know that Prime aristos aren't exactly easy to impersonate."

"Nuh-uh," says Zhak smugly. "This is the Teyrian Protectorate we're talking about. Whole system's notoriously reclusive. They reject most Union protocols, biometric idents among them. And as for any *other* identity coming to light if anyone happens to check you for Union records... well..."

Zhak smiles slowly as he takes a flat grey data card out of his jacket pocket and taps it against the table. "I have your medical file right here, courtesy of your dear old boss Tully. Full genetic sweep included. We ran it against every official Union database that's still up and running, and a few unofficial ones too. And guess what we learned, *Page Found*?"

The junk thief's face contorts into something that might be joy and might be horror, a chaos of sudden emotion. She lurches forward in the chair like the weight of his words has thrown her right over, and Maelle almost feels bad for her.

"You... you found out who I *really* am?" she half-whispers.

Zhak almost chokes with laughter. "Oh, no no no! Heaven's stars, no! Exactly the opposite, Page! You're a total phantom! You're no child who's been officially registered for citizenship on a Prime or Latter world in the past sixty years. You've never been arrested, never been to prison, never served in the United Worlds Defence Forces. And that is why you're *perfect*. You could be anybody at all."

Maelle leans back in her chair and crosses her arms, watching Zhak, saying nothing. By the look on the junk thief's face, she's not having any of this.

"I still don't get it," Page says. "Why me? I can't be the only thirty-something around with a few stasis port scars and no

Union ident. Why go through all the trouble of setting a trap for me on Kuuj?"

"Ahhh. *This is all the answer you need, little bird*," Zhak says in Graya. It's one of the few Graya sentences Maelle recognizes—a stock saying that Zhak is fond of repeating.

But when he says it, it's as if something in the junk thief's gaze fractures in real-time, breaking apart before Maelle's eyes. For a moment Page sits there blinking, and then some kind of *understanding* dawns on her all at once. She crumbles like a building collapsing, like a planet being blown apart. A soft gasp emits from her throat.

Page says something to him in reply, speaking in the same ancient tongue, effortlessly forming the mellifluous syllables. The Perfect Cadence. She looks stunned—almost incredulous—as she speaks, as if the sound of her own voice surprises her.

"Brilliant! Yes!" Zhak smiles slowly, the triumph plain on his face as he switches back into Union Basic. "And *this* is why you're special. There's no shortage of stasis survivors if you know where to look for 'em. But you tell me how many of them speak fluent Graya! Not many. Aristos don't get into that kind of trouble unless it's on purpose." He grins toothily as he switches off the projection, his sleeves jangling. "You, my dear, are a most unique commodity. The rarest of jewels."

Page is still sitting there with her mouth slightly open, working her jaw like she's struggling to speak again.

"Well? What do you say?" Zhak prompts her. "Would you like to learn more about the... job requirements?"

Page finds her voice at last. "What if I say no?" she asks. "Supposing I just don't give a damn about your *job*? Supposing I don't even care if you airlock me? What then?"

"Oh, I think you do care, Page." The derision in Zhak's voice crawls over Maelle's skin. "You didn't scrape and claw and beg for eight years on that wreckhole, barely surviving, only to give up a chance at freedom now." He smirks darkly. "Besides... there will be ample compensation. It will all be very fair."

It occurs to Maelle that Page hasn't even asked about payment. Damn. That could be a real problem. If money won't tempt her, then this operation could be in trouble.

Page straightens her shoulders and sits up, as if she's armouring herself with that foolhardy bravado again. She slams her fists down on the table so hard that the stack of crates shifts, and the portable computer nearly tips over.

"I didn't ask for any of this! I didn't ask to be taken off Kuuj!" she shouts. She jumps furiously out of her chair, nearly tripping over herself on still-unsteady feet.

And then, she turns around and she bolts out the door.

Zhak stands there for a moment with two fingers pinched over the bridge of his nose, his eyes closed, fury radiating off him. Finally, he snaps his head up and whirls around, moving to follow Page.

"Leave it. Stop, Zhak, no. Let her go." Maelle grabs hold of his arm, pulling back roughly as he passes. Those silly little fake jewels jangle on their chains at his wrists, and she fights the impulse to rip them off.

"Let her *go*? She can't just go wandering wherever the hells she likes—"

"Where exactly is she gonna run to, Zhak? Just give her a minute."

"She needs to listen! I can't fuck around here, Maelle, this is my big chance—"

"And that's exactly why you need to leave her be. Let *me* handle her. You can't threaten her into this. You haven't offered her *anything* yet, much less anything she actually *wants*."

"A generous fee was implied from the start, surely," he huffs. "Two hundred thousand credits, on success. She could have asked. I haven't even briefed her about the job! She has no idea what—"

"Zhak… look. Sit back and let me take over, before you burn down whatever goodwill we have with her," Maelle says. She soothes the sharpness in her tone, casting him a look that's more pleading than combative, and she releases her hold on his fancy sleeve. "I can get her to trust me. I know it. You just need to let me work on her, *my* way. I know what I'm doing, Zhak."

She's pressing her luck defying him like this—he's petulant when he doesn't get his way—but this situation is precarious. Maelle has waited too long for an opportunity like this. She can't let him screw it up because he can't keep his gods-damned mouth shut.

And Maelle understands some of what was written in the junk thief's broken gaze, because she's seen the same in *herself*. Page is as stubborn as a rusted bolt, and her anger runs deeper than her common sense. She's exactly the type who'd refuse a hefty payday out of spite. It's not money or the prospect of comfort that drives her, Maelle is certain. If that was the case, she'd surely have bailed from Kuuj long ago.

"Find her and calm her down," Zhak says, jabbing a finger at Maelle. "And from now on, you don't let her out of your sight, Maelle. If I see her alone, I'm cuffing her again. Do I make myself clear?"

"Perfectly," says Maelle with a crisp smile. She tosses her hair over her shoulder and walks unhurriedly out the door after Page.

For all of Zhak's assumptions about Page's naivety, the junk thief's more than clever enough to have slipped the net on that asshole Tully if she'd wanted to. She's more than clever enough to have escaped Kuuj; surely she could have bartered herself onto a ship out of there somehow in *eight gods-damned years*.

Something else must have been holding her there, on Kuuj. Something that burns in her blood and drives her onward, whatever it is that has kept her going.

And Maelle intends to find out exactly what that is.

THE STORYTELLER

Recording start 02:19:03

There's this old saying from the Primes that goes something like: 'There's been war from the minute we figured out the first thing to disagree about.'

And most of the time, I think that's probably not too far off the mark. [*chuckles*] I mean... looking at recorded history, going back all the way to the Imperial Ages... most of that's just centuries on centuries of conflict. Planetside, on orbitals, on outposts, on ships, in space. We fight and we fight, for whatever reason we can come up with.

But *this* war, well... this war with the aliens... it's different. Because this might be the first time we've fought a war where nobody's got any idea what we're even fighting about! All we know is that we want to survive... and the Felen don't seem to want us to.

I can see how folks might think that makes it a lost cause. Bunch of aliens show up, they're way more advanced, they're way stronger than us... and hey. Maybe our time's up. Humanity's age of intrepid exploration and great civilizations is just... over.

And if that's true... maybe it's pointless to lay your life down for a cause when you don't even know what it's all for. Maybe those aliens know better than us, maybe they know something we don't.

Can't deny that the galaxy will move on without us. The stars'll burn long after we're gone, one way or another.

Is fighting the Felen really any less pointless than dying in some squabble over one terraformed rock, like in the olden days? Was it better to get the knife out over some shit about who gets to send mining ships to that fuckin' asteroid belt? Humanity even found a way to argue about the *gods*, of all things! Ready to tear each other apart over whether this story or that story was the *right way* to tell the divine journeys. Tch!

But anyway... [*clears throat*] Where was I? Ahhh. The war, right. This incomprehensible war's been goin' on for a long, long time. First contact – well, the first one they admit to publicly – that happened when I hadn't even cut my baby teeth. Safe to say I've never known a single day without those aliens out there in the background. And I'm no young'un, that's for sure.

So, what do you do with a situation like that, assuming you're not gonna fight? You live, that's what you do. Life goes on. People eat and drink, sing and dance, fuck and fall in love. And sure, aliens are slowly picking us off... but that's *way out there* in deep space! If you're sitting on one of the Primes with a hundred and twenty squadrons guarding your orbit, you're probably feeling pretty good about things.

Or else you're in a real shit situation out in the deeps or the far reaches... in which case you've got bigger things to worry about, like whether or not your water's drinkable. Even now, some of those backwater Union settlements still deny the Felen are out there at all. They think the Union's just making excuses for why they abandoned the terraforming projects.

The fact is... most people haven't seen an alien with their own eyes. Not a live one, not a dead one, not even a ship or a piece of their tech, 'cept in holos. Most people never will. So, tell me... does it matter all that much if they're real or not?

If it's money or power you're looking for, then what's real and what's not real has always made very little difference. Because the people's *fear* is real. And where you find a lot of fear... you'll always find a lot of profit.

See, for certain kinds of entrepreneurs, interstellar war is an opportunity. All these new travel restrictions, they're absolutely smothering the trade and cargo transport businesses. Shit's hard out there. But if you deal in illegal cargo, and your shipments aren't on the record to begin with... [*chuckles*] Well, let's just say rule changes don't matter if you're not following the rules to begin with. And what with the authorities so busy chasin' aliens around, there's been less and less eyes on what the rest of us upstanding citizens are doing.

This war's brought in lots of new ways to make a living. There's almost limitless money to be made on selling *safety*. And if you market it right... the *idea* of safety can be worth more than safety itself, you get me?

Like, take all those ditch ships they're building out at Baedenoch. Now that's an outrageous racket – 'Course, they're total sham shows, claiming they can replicate the old seedships that founded the Primes. Telling people that they're sending these great venture-ships outside the Union Quadrant to find new worlds. There's a pretty pile of chits to be made selling one-way tickets for that, and it's not like those poor suckers will be coming back looking for refunds.

Oh, and of course the venturers all want weapons, too. They want to buy illegal, unstable planetary defence systems, to protect all those new planets they're never actually gonna find. But as long as there's someone who wants to buy, there'll always be work for the folks who have it to sell. And that's where we come in.

Now, you can say what you want about the morality of it all, but this war's certainly brought out the innovators. If there's one thing I appreciate, it's a bit of ingenuity. And if we're all going to die anyway... I suppose we might as well take it for all it's worth before everything burns to ash.

PAGE FOUND
Kuuj Deep Space Outpost, Before

FOR MONTHS AFTER her revival from suspended animation, the exhaustion had clung to Page like a weight. She had struggled to complete the most basic tasks—not because she couldn't *remember* how to do them, but because she was simply too tired to continue.

She would leave food uneaten because of the sheer effort involved in getting it from the bowl into her mouth. She kept her hair twisted up in a greasy knot, rarely expending the time or the extra water cost to wash it. She would lie on the cot in her hab-cube, staring at the wall as if it were too much effort just to *think*.

Those were the worst days, at the beginning. Her improvement, in fact, went relatively swiftly—at least, so the half-trained medics on Kuuj told her. She may have been unlucky with the severity of her memory loss, but her physical recovery was labelled 'encouraging.'

Half a year after the revival, Page had regained most of her strength and some of her appetite, and—she surmised—she had some of her *old self* back, if not her memories. She kept a journal in her 'pad, meticulously noting mundane details, as if to convince herself she wouldn't lose them.

[File: Daily_musings]
"Old self" is such an odd term. What does it even mean?
An old self can only exist in relation to a new self, and I only
have this one. Page Found. Because everything else is lost.

She tried to remember what came before. Where had she been, before she was on Kuuj? There must be *something* she could dredge from her fractured mind, some snippet of truth she could extract and cling to. Something to build on. But it remained frustratingly elusive.

She wasn't born on Kuuj Outpost, that much she knew. For all its disorganization, Kuuj did keep a record of every newborn child who had been registered there, including a genetic profile. And for all that she was a thief by trade and lacked an official Union ident, Page *was* a registered resident of the outpost. A Kuuj registration was necessary to access the basic infrastructure of the outpost, to purchase water, to visit the local marketplace areas that outsiders couldn't.

Kuuj's scant legal system tied blood relatives together, but her outpost file had always listed hers as a *family of one*. And, so, she knew she was no genetic relative of anyone who had ever been registered on Kuuj. She was alone. And she would have to make her own way if she intended to find out the secrets of her missing past.

[File: Hunt_log]
Couple dock workers I talked to today reckoned I should ask
around the underground marketplace for answers, if I want to
figure out how I got to Kuuj. Not holding out a ton of hope,
but it seems as good a place as any to keep looking, even if
I'm not keen to hang around down there too long.
 Telling them Tully sent me might work for basic snooping,
long as I don't ask anything too weird and as long as he
doesn't find out. But I reckon if there's anybody here who
brokers shady medical debt transfers, it's a good bet they're
operating from the under-market. I guess I'll try anything once.

Kuuj's under-market was small, poorly stocked and unlikely to satisfy even the most cursory of unscrupulous customers. There was a shop that purported to forge transit permits, but they were terrible facsimiles, the kind of obvious fakes that would fool none but the most willingly uninterested of backwater authorities. There were also a few folks down there who dealt in weapons, but the selection was truly dire.

Page had never had any occasion to trade with any of those merchants, but she'd certainly heard talk of how useless the under-market was in the restobar. If you didn't bring your own good-quality weapon to Kuuj, you were unlikely to leave with one. It seemed, Page had overheard, you'd be better off using the synthetic breadknives from one of the grubby cafs than whatever the vendors down below had to offer.

Still, she thought, there was a chance that someone down there would turn up some lost piece of information, some crucial clue that would lead her to the truth of her origins. There must be somebody who knew what vessel she'd been taken from, or what company might have sold her medical debt to Tully. Alas, it seemed that no one could remember *anything*.

[File: Hunt_log]
Covered the whole lower mall, no one remembers anything in particular. Or they just aren't interested in talking.

•

Thirteen hours walking the lower decks. Don't know why I bother going down there.

•

Back downstairs to investigate again. Nothing. Wonder if it's getting too long ago now for anyone to remember.

•

Almost got robbed downstairs again. Knew I shouldn't have taken my pack and gone straight after work. Knocked one of the fool's teeth out, though – figure I probably shouldn't go down there for a while. But I didn't lose any of my take.

•

Lower mall again. How many times? Is this pointless?
SOMEONE HAS TO KNOW SOMETHING.

Two years had passed, then three, then four. The truth faded even further into the outpost's shoddily documented history, and Page had begun to despair.

There were probably more expensive ways to search for her heritage outside the outpost—genealogy services and Union archives and whatnot—but the worlds-wide identity net had already started fragmenting when the war broke out. By now, it was almost non-existent. Information from mainspace barely flowed into Kuuj. There was very little chance of anyone's record being available outside the sector where they'd been born.

All those years, Page didn't know if she'd been a Union-registered birth at all. Or if either of her parents, or *their* parents, had ever held a Union ident. She couldn't afford any of those lines of investigation anyway—not while she still owed her entire life to Tully. Kuuj itself, and whatever secrets might still be found somewhere within it, was all she had.

Sometimes, she looked into the mirror and tried to imagine what a relative of hers might look like. In most aspects, Page's appearance was unmemorable.

She was slightly taller than average, but not by much. Like most people on Kuuj, she was thinner than she should be from years of poor nutrition and unhealthy air.

Her hair was a very common shade of dark brown, though her natural complexion was more difficult to discern, as she'd never recovered a healthy colour in her face after her revival. It was not an uncommon symptom for stasis wakelings, the medics said. One of the many faces of post-suspension syndrome. Her original skin tone was probably on the paler side, but it was now tinged a sickly grey. Aside from that, Page had no real distinguishing features besides the triangle of scars on her neck that marked the entry point of her stasis port, and a row of similar markings down her back where the suspension tubes had been inserted. That, she supposed, was the most interesting thing about her.

Page had never directly spoken to another person who'd been woken from suspension, although she'd seen a few folks with prison scars in the dockyard over the years. She'd read as much as she could find about the procedure under all its names, researching *suspended animation technology* and *SAT-sleep* and *stasis* as thoroughly as she could on Kuuj's spotty network connection.

Wakelings seldom recovered very well. There were almost always physical and neurological effects, even from short suspensions. Page perused the long lists of potential health problems that revival could cause. Tremors, seizures, numbness in extremities. Dizziness, headaches, vision irregularities, difficulty breathing. Permanent organ damage. Memory loss—rarer, but sometimes severe. Some survivors lost their senses or their coordination, their balance, their ability to distinguish distance, their ability to speak or walk.

Approximately two in fifteen people never woke up at all, regardless of the length of the suspension. Not something anyone would've voluntarily entered into without serious forethought. Or desperation.

> [File: Hunt_log]
> Got on the net today for a bit. Cost a fortune and I didn't find a single useful thing. Turns out there's not much on the public channels about 'clinical trials for faster stasis revival.' Mostly just a bunch of paywalled articles in medical journals. Real useful.
> [Linked file: List_of_potential_company_names]
>
> - Methods to improve revival outcomes and the speed of suspension reversal are being trialled by several different research companies

- "Race for commercial success" due to "exacerbating factors including the future building of new venture-ships to leave Union space."
- The goal is "improved outcomes in restoration of life" HAHAHAHA. Memories may or may not be included, huh? What a bunch of rubbish.

Tully didn't seem to know much about Page's origin. Her scant medical record concluded she had been put under for a 'median' period—likely no more than five years—and then she'd been revived.

And then… somehow, she'd been brought to Kuuj. She'd already been pulled out of deep stasis when she arrived on the outpost, but she was still in a comatose state with an incomplete revival and no funds to complete it. Marked for an inevitable death.

A transport ship would have brought her to Kuuj from deep space, that's all she knew for sure. Tully had bought the debt from some middle-broker, and that was that. He looked for people in desperate situations and he profited, and her case was no exception. She had seen the ledger, those stark numbers detailing the cost of every individual medical procedure that saved her life. Basic revival completion, price. Name of a medicine she could not pronounce, price. Name of some scan or piece of equipment, price. Lump sum debt from whoever was the previous holder of her account, price. A gross tally of the worth of her continued existence.

Page remembered only tiny fragments from her awakening, bits and pieces from the first days when she woke up on Kuuj. She recalled a hazy view of the people examining her, checking her vital signs, drawing her blood. She remembered wires and tubes surrounding her. She remembered trying to speak to someone, to ask them where she was, and a medic asking her very, very slowly if she could speak any Union Basic—

All things considered, though Kuuj's medical facilities were far from sophisticated, the care that was provided to her had fulfilled its intended purpose. It had saved her from death, and mended *most* of what was wrong with her as well as could be expected, fractured past aside.

In the matter of her ongoing blackouts, the medics said, she would need to consult a specialist if she wanted any further treatment or diagnostics. Page scoffed at the idea—there was no such specialist on Kuuj. Not that that she'd ever be able to afford their opinion anyway. And so that was the end of it. She stopped attending the medical facility for any kind of consultation if she could help it—the last thing she needed was to incur more debt. Page was never going to be able to pay it off anyway.

Of course, the labour she did for Tully should already have more than repaid the original amount a few years into her service. But there was still the matter of rent, and Tully's exorbitant interest fees, and the charges he insisted on leveraging for every little mishap. *Maintenance fees. Utility fees. Administration fees.* Page's debt had barely moved in the last few years, what with all the rent hikes he'd imposed.

Late rents for the hab-cubes were collected by a decrepit old drone that made its way up from door to door, buzzing relentlessly at the panels until someone emerged to shove some chits at it. The infuriating thing was covered in dents and dings, doubtless from having doors slammed on it or boots taken to it. But there was no escaping it. Every fortnight it would be back, tapping at the flimsy panels again, shrieking its pre-recorded message about penalties for lateness.

Page hated that drone, and she'd been tempted to take a swipe at it more than once. But damaging Tully's property would only incur further fines, the likes of which she didn't feel like facing. She always paid on time when she could, adding on whatever surcharges it demanded, while she worked to further offset her debt by stealing comm-tech for Tully to sell in his shop.

Day after day, week after week, year after year, that was her life.

She had always known what this *really* was, what Tully had really done by saving her. She had a life debt. She was in a stasis of another kind, one she could only escape if she fled the outpost.

> [File: Daily_musings]
> Owning a person is illegal. But paying to save their life, and then making them work for you for the rest of their days to pay it off? Apparently that's a 'grey area.' And that's how I know I'm never, ever getting out of here.
>
> Oh well. I can't leave Kuuj anyway. Because someone, somewhere here HAS to know something! I'm going to find something, I know it.

Leaving Kuuj had never been a viable option. Not when it would mean leaving behind whatever clues still lay hidden between those creaking metal walls.

And so she stayed, and she worked, and she waited.

Always, always she *waited*.

Until the stranger with the weird coat and buckled boots, with his too-pretty Water Girl, smashed through all of her stagnant plans like an asteroid on a collision course.

PAGE FOUND
Zhaklam Evelor's Ship

Something wild and furious takes hold of Page when she flees from Zhak's makeshift boardroom. She runs down the corridor, flinging herself headlong toward the nearest unmarked door, her feet pounding with all the speed that should have carried her off that concourse when she saw the too-good-to-be-true mark.

Damn it, damn it, damn it.

With every step and slip of the ill-fitting, slippery-soled boots Maelle gave her, Page regrets having tossed her comfortable old shoes down that disposal chute. She regrets it all, especially the tiny spark of unreasonable, foolish *hope* that kindles in the back of her mind.

That idealistic, daydreaming part of her that has fantasized about something exactly like this. A highborn Teyrian? *Long-lost heir to a wealthy family* was once on her list of imagined identities, wasn't it? This feels like a slap in the face, like a deliberate mockery of everything she's held on to for comfort.

The picture of the bird-masked monks is burned into her mind, and the more she thinks about them, the more she could almost convince herself that there's something *familiar* about them. The sight of them evoked an odd feeling in her stomach—not dread or fear, exactly, but a wariness she can't quite place. But when Zhak asked if she had seen them before, she somehow doubted he was asking about the vague blurry feelings of a girl with no memories. It could just as easily be something she saw in a holo.

Try as she might to shake some sense into herself, Zhak's words won't leave her head. *What's to say you're not a monk of the Golden-Feather?*

No. *Stop it*, she tells herself. There's no sense getting sentimental about this, or allowing whatever game these scammers are playing to get under her skin. But for an instant, when he spoke to her in *that language*... it felt as if all the air had rushed out of Page's lungs. Like that time she fell out of a maintenance chute and blacked out in an alleyway. It felt like the whole world was dropping away, about to be replaced with something new and wild and wonderful, like her mind was stretching toward something just out of reach.

Like the start of one of her blackout dreams.

It's almost as if the very thought of blacking out brings on the attack. Page doesn't get halfway to the metal door she's aiming for before she loses her balance and collapses, her still-wobbly knees buckling.

Her heart beats a panicked drum as her body crumples unceremoniously to the ground, her limbs suddenly refusing to obey her. For a moment, she wonders if she's just suffering with the remnant of whatever it was they drugged her with, or the after-effects of the stun. She hasn't been steady on her feet since Maelle snapped her bindings off back on the speedship.

But then she feels that familiar pressure at the base of her skull, the pinpricks of light creeping in at the edges of her vision, signalling an oncoming blackout. *Gods damn it*. This *always* happens at the worst possible moment. But she can't ever recall having two of them this close together.

Page reaches her hand out to grab the door handle in front of her and misses, her fingertips bending painfully backwards as she falls. Her forehead strikes the cold metal panelling, making her head ring.

And she sinks down, down... down into the dark.

* * *

A STRINGED INSTRUMENT playing, its music high and clear and sweet, rising in a crescendo that lifts her heart with joy.

A hand pressed onto her shoulder, reassuring. Someone gently fixing her hair.

That house again—always that white-bricked house, grand and imposing with its many windows and the large garden stretching away from it.

A shining balcony, the rail cool and smooth against her palms as she tilts her head up. A sky so full of stars.

And bright orange flowers, scattered over a flat plane of marbled stone.

A BRIEF HISTORY OF TEYR

Encyclopedia of Humanity
Union school text, 6th revision, 39th edition

> A BRIEF HISTORY OF THE UNITED WORLDS
>> PRIME WORLDS
>>> FIRST PRIMES (see: SOURCE SETTLEMENTS)
>>>> **TEYR**

TEYR is one of twenty-eight worlds collectively known as the Prime Worlds, and one of the six planets known as First Primes. The First Primes are the worlds in the settled galaxy that made up the Source Settlements, believed to be among the first worlds of humanity.

> The First Primes are all characterized by two factors: advanced planetary civilizations that date back multiple thousands of years, and evidence of seedship cities – the oldest settlements that sprang up around the landing sites of the arrival ships. All of the First Prime worlds have between two and seven seedship cities, in varying degrees of archaeological preservation, all of which are considered important heritage sites.

Teyr was once a member of the United Worlds of Humanity, and it was one of the founding planets of the Union. However, its leadership ultimately chose to break Teyr away from the Union, isolating the planet along with its settled moon Meneyr. (See also: Isolationism on Teyr)

The Teyrian Protectorate was governed by the Great, Everlasting Planetary Council of Teyr, informally known as the Gepcot. The ruling powers of the Gepcot rejected many of the tenets of the Union and wanted more self-governance. Further, while they generally drew from the same pantheon of deities as the rest of the Union planets, Teyr came to embrace a divisive spiritual movement known as the

Teyrian Primacy – one which placed Teyr's divine significance above that of all other First Prime worlds.

This movement stems from the legend of a mythological planet known as the Unbreakable World, which was believed to be the cosmological epicentre of the expansion and subsequent collapse of the known universe. The universe, the legend says, is created and destroyed in a repeating cycle, but the Unbreakable World endures, and the things which are preserved there will remake the next universe. From this Unbreakable World, all life as we know it today has sprung, and at the end of everything, it is the one world that will survive to seed the next iteration of creation. The Unbreakable World is protected by the promise of the Fair-Feathered Goddess, one of the aspects of the Great Goddess of the Source Pantheon.

> [*The above section has been flagged as conjecture; it is suggested to move this into the article Teyrian Primacy in a future edition.*]

At first, the Gepcot's claim was that the seedship cities on Teyr were older than all others, thereby claiming Teyr as the eldest and first of the Source Settlements (see also: Teyrian Origin Theory). However, over time this evolved into a much more dramatic claim: that the planet Teyr had never been settled by seedships at all, because Teyr was in fact the true Origin world of humanity, the cradle of all life in the universe – the Unbreakable World itself.

This claim is widely rejected by the scientific community. It is completely unsubstantiated, and in fact disproven by the material existence of three seedship cities on the Teyrian surface. The Gepcot, in turn, claims that the Teyrian seedship rings are actually a natural formation.

At the time of Teyr's break from the Union, the Gepcot declared that the teaching of the Teyrian Primacy was to be instituted in all schools and universities, replacing the scientifically verifiable history of Teyr as a First Prime settlement.

DALYA
OF HOUSE EDAMAUN, IN HER NINTH YEAR
First-City, Teyr

A WEEK AFTER the festivities of welcome, Dalya saw the newcomer girl again at the temple. She hadn't ever expected to see her again—most of the newcomers to Teyr, Heral had told her, would be settling in the mountain cities, and not here in the capital. Few moonfolk ever remained in the First-City.

But the girl and her guardian, it seemed, had stayed—at least for now.

After the prayers, Dalya waited carefully until Uncle was occupied with one of the council members and checked that her handlers had spread out before she approached the girl. It wasn't that she thought she was doing anything *wrong,* exactly. But something about the girl had evoked a curiosity in her, and she longed to ask her some questions that Uncle probably wouldn't approve of. There was something secretive about it, something that she wanted to keep all to herself.

"Hello," Dalya said, and the girl wheeled around as if startled, eyes wide. "I am not sure if you remember who I am," Dalya blurted, "but we met here last week, and you gave me—"

The girl's slightly nervous giggle interrupted her. "Of *course* I remember you," she said. "I know who you are. You're the Honoured Daughter Dalya of House Edamaun! The child of High Speaker Luwan Edamaun of the Gepcot! I gave you a flower." She had a strange, awed look on her face.

Dalya should probably have felt proud, faced with such unabashed admiration. But in the moment, all she felt was resentment. She did not want her new friend to talk about Uncle and his position, nor to ask her about the responsibilities she had as the heir of House Edamaun. She didn't want to feel that weight on her shoulders. She only wanted to talk to the girl, to ask her things about living on Meneyr. She wanted to hear more about the moon, or perhaps to learn more about her favourite stories from the sacred texts. She just wanted to talk to her some more.

"I... ah... well, I'm High Speaker Edamaun's *brother's* child, actually," Dalya corrected her. Technically, Dalya *was* Uncle's child now, in the sense that she was his only heir. But he rarely addressed her as such, and she didn't wish to start this new friendship with any kind of dishonesty. "My uncle holds my guardianship," she explained.

"Oh! Really!" The moon girl's eyes widened. "Me, too! That's *my* uncle, right over there." She tipped her head toward her guardian—that tall man with the white braid, who was standing and talking to a small group of other adults near the doors. "I came to Teyr with him. We, ah... we used to live moonside, before this," she added.

It was an odd addition, Dalya thought—as if this fact weren't already obvious, given their place in the newcomers' procession last week. Did she really think Dalya so very foolish? Had Dalya done something that made the girl think her unintelligent?

Perhaps it was her failure to quickly name a favourite passage from the sacred texts last week that had put the girl off. Resentment curled bitterly in Dalya's chest; she should have done better, she chided herself.

It only occurred to Dalya much later that the girl was probably just as anxious as she was, that her hesitation and her stating the obvious was better ascribed to nerves than to judgement.

Dalya bit back her reaction, instead reaching for some of the sentiments she'd heard repeated in Uncle's welcomes. "I hope you are settling in well, and that you have found the expected contentment in your new lodgings," she said stiffly. "The embrace of the Goddess is strong here. You should soon feel at home." And then, remembering the girl's dislike for formalities, she concluded: "I hope something has entertained you."

To her surprise, the moon girl gave a long, mournful sigh, and her shoulders slumped. "Not really," she huffed. "This has all been terribly boring, if I'm honest with you. My uncle hasn't taken very well to the atmospheric changes, so he's been resting most of the time. I've not been out anywhere all week, and I don't start my lessons until next month. I've not even had the chance to meet anyone properly yet!"

She made no apology when she'd finished complaining, and Dalya's heart rose. Someone *else* thought this was boring—and said so without reservation. The very boldness of it made Dalya's heart race a little.

She'd been right, it would certainly not do to have Uncle overhear any of this. But perhaps she could impress Uncle yet, if she showed special care to the girl. She remembered his constant reminders to be courteous and welcoming. To be *a conduit of divine love*.

"I... am sorry that you haven't been adequately entertained," Dalya said. "And that you've not had a chance to enjoy Teyr's bountiful hospitality. I would like for us to rectify that." She took a deep breath. "Would you and your uncle like to dine at our table tonight? We would be honoured to welcome you to our house."

"To your *house?*" The girl looked shocked for a moment, then lifted her hand to her mouth. "Wait... what? Really? You are inviting us to dine with... with *the High Speaker of the Gepcot?*"

"Why not?" Dalya said with a small shrug. "It is our duty to invite others to share our bounty, as our forebears shared with the Goddess. Our bread is yours."

"Are you certain that we are welcome?" the girl asked. She cast a furtive glance back toward her own uncle. "You can ask us over? Just like that?"

In truth, Dalya had never invited *anyone* to dine at the High Speaker's table before, though many a diplomat and council member's family had shared meals with them over the years. She'd had a friend or two over for dinner with their families, on occasion—mostly children she'd met through her music conservatory—but it was always Heral who organized it all with formal invitations. A few days ahead of the dinner, Heral would send out a crisp handwritten note with the date and time of the invitation. This would then be folded into a thick beige envelope, sealed with the Edamaun family crest, and she'd send it off by messenger to be delivered to the head of the family they were inviting.

But perhaps this moon-born girl's own unworried boldness made Dalya uncharacteristically forward, and so she followed through on her offer with earnest confidence. "Of course I'm certain," she declared. "I can do whatever I like, I am allowed to invite whomever I choose. It will be no trouble at all. Come along to our house for a meal this evening, just before sunset. We will be glad of your company!"

The girl stared at her for another long beat. "Well, all right, then," she finally said. "I will ask my uncle if we can. But... ah, where do you live?"

Dalya blinked, stunned at the question. Of course, the girl had not been here very long, not in First-City, nor even on Teyr itself. But Dalya had never met anyone who needed telling where the High Speaker dwelled.

"I live in the same place as the High Speaker, naturally," she said. "The residence of House Edamaun. Any driver will know where to bring you. You do have a driver, don't you?"

"O-of course," the girl stammered, her face telling an entirely different story. "I mean... I'm sure we can find one. We'll be there. Just before sunset, I promise!"

She started to turn on her heels, whirling to see where her uncle had gone, but Dalya reached out to grab her arm. "Wait, wait! Stop!"

The girl froze in her tracks. "What is it?"

"Ah... sorry." Dalya shifted her feet. "I probably need to know your names. For the place cards on the table, you see. We usually have those, to show where everyone should sit. What are you called?"

"I'm called Anda," the girl breathed out, her voice barely more than a whisper. "My name is Anda Agote. And... my uncle is Derin Agote."

"Right," Dalya nodded. "I've got it, thank you."

Anda, she repeated to herself, and the name danced in her head like music. *Anda Anda Anda Anda*. It was the most beautiful name she had ever heard.

"I shall look forward to seeing you tonight," Anda said with a hasty bow, and when she straightened back up, she had recovered her cheeky, gap-toothed grin. "I have every hope that the house of the High Speaker will prove most entertaining. Thank you, Dalya."

"No, thank *you*," Dalya said, clasping her hands excitedly to her chin. "See you soon!"

AFTER THEY LEFT the temple, Dalya walked back to the transport next to Uncle, and her heart swelled with pride. This, she was certain, was exactly what Nathin would have done in her place. This was exactly what the Goddess's beloved ones were meant to do, embracing the newcomers as if they were their own kin. Because they *were*. The children of Meneyr were also the children of the Goddess's love, after all—born so near her blessed lands so that she might reach out and gather them up into her embrace.

Uncle would be so pleased with this.

But when they slid into their seats inside the transport, and Dalya excitedly leaned over to tell Uncle what she had done, he was not pleased at all. His mouth went thin, his lips pale and pressed close together, the way he always looked when he was trying not to lose his temper.

"Dalya," he whispered sharply. "What were you thinking? Why in the name of the Everlasting Lady would you do such a thing?"

"Did you not say we should be welcoming to our new neighbours?" Dalya protested. "You said that we should treat them as we treat our own friends! That we ought to show them the bounty and the blessings of Teyr! And we have those at our table in ample supply—"

"Yes, of course," Uncle said. "But that does not mean that you should *invite people unannounced to our home*." He let out his breath with a weary sound, rubbing the bridge of his nose. "Goddess in the stars, I don't know what got into you, Dalya."

The Great Goddess herself came unannounced when the golden bird fell from the Cosmic Void, Dalya thought to herself. Hadn't one of the sages just told that story in the temple? She didn't understand why Uncle was so angry, and his cold disappointment swiftly extinguished her happiness.

Out loud, she said: "I'm sorry, Uncle. I will not do it again." She lowered her eyes. "I... I should have asked your permission. But I am not sure how I should retract the invitation—"

"No, no," he said. "You must not retract it, above all do not do that. That would do more harm than good." He sighed again, and the expression on his face was the same as the one he always had when he'd just taken a difficult call in his study. "It won't do to draw more attention to this. What's done is done, I suppose they must come to dinner now. We will get through this."

"Uncle, I—truly, I didn't know—"

"No more excuses. Let this be an exercise in discipline for you," he said firmly, raising a finger to silence her. "You will have to take care of all the arrangements—this is *your* dinner, not mine, do you understand? I knew nothing about this, I do not know these people. I am busy all afternoon. So, you will have to inform Heral that we will have two unexpected guests, and get her to help you make preparations. You will select the menu, secure the entertainment, and recite the opening prayer for the meal." He shook his raised finger. "And you are not to do anything like this again, Dalya. Is that clear?"

"Yes, Uncle." She nodded, keeping her eyes fixed on her feet. "I will see to everything, Uncle."

"And," he added, "you will apologize to Heral for the late notice. She was due to have the evening off tonight, now she will have to help you. Explain to her that you will not repeat this mistake."

"I will make many apologies, Uncle."

"Good." Uncle settled back in his seat.

He stared out the window for a long time after that, his stiff back turned to Dalya, before he finally looked over at her again. His expression had softened a bit, the furrow between his brows less pronounced, his eyes no longer as cold. There was something different in his face now, something more like exhausted resignation.

"Sometimes fate pulls us in a direction we do not understand. And at times, the Goddess guides us toward some greater purpose that is yet unseen to us," Uncle said. "Let us pray that this is one of those times."

It would be many years before Dalya understood what he meant.

PAGE FOUND
Zhaklam Evelor's Ship

WHEN PAGE OPENS her eyes, she's lying in a small, narrow cot with a thick blanket laid over her. Her mouth is parched, and there's a throbbing pain in her head.

Where *is* she? How many times is she going to wake up disoriented and confused this week?

For a moment, she thinks she sees the familiar patched-metal ceiling of Kuuj's medibay, where she's woken up one too many times after a blackout with a fresh bill added to her endless debt. She expects to see Tully there at her bedside, chewing her out and reminding her to be more careful.

Part of her still wonders if she did actually pass out in the dockyard back on Kuuj. Maybe she collapsed while she was scoping that Q-link score back on the concourse. Maybe all of this is just some long, weird dream, and none of the rest of it happened at all, and she's still lying unconscious at the bottom of that rickety ladder.

It's plain as can be that her mind's not right, that it hasn't been right in a damn long time. She's been lying to herself, telling herself she was fine to keep working... and maybe it's finally caught up with her.

But it's not Tully's pitiless scowl that greets her when she turns her head. Tully certainly wouldn't be pressing a cup of warm, metallic-tasting water against her lips with this kind of gentleness.

No, it's Water Girl crouching there beside her cot.

Maelle.

"Hey, pal," Maelle says, her voice soft and soothing. "Relax. You're good, all right? I've got you. You're safe here."

"Get *away* from me," Page growls. She raises her shaky hand and tries to shove the cup of water away, but only manages to spill some of it down her neck. "Augh!"

She summons the implacable glower she always throws at Tully's muscleheads, on the rare occasions when Tully bothers to send an enforcer to collect instead of just that infuriating drone. (Usually, that means someone has kicked the drone down the stairwell again and knocked it out, and they're going door to door to find out who's to blame.)

"Listen... I'm not your enemy here, Page. I *want* to be on your side," Maelle says quietly. "I've lost things, too."

There's a deep sadness in her dark eyes, a veneer of sincerity that Page absolutely doesn't trust. Finding an ally here would definitely be too good to be real. Like the Q-link score. Like those traders—

At once, she remembers them again. Those two out-system traders sitting in the corner booth at the restobar that night, quietly discussing their illegal shipment as they sat right behind her. Speaking that language she'd somehow *recognized*. And her stomach turns as she realizes what an absolute setup that must have been. They had gone into the details of their drop in astonishing detail, right down to the shipment codes and the container measurements—

Damn it all.

"The traders. Back on Kuuj, in the restobar..." Page chokes out. "Did you set that up?"

"What?" Maelle looks confused.

"A while back, I overheard these two guys talking about a cargo drop they didn't have permits for. They were talking in another language, and I... I realized I understood them. I sold their information to the dockyard guards, snitched 'em out! But... that was never real, was it? That was all to trap *me*."

Of course it was. How much of a fool could she have been?

Maelle nods thoughtfully. "It's possible. The dossier we got on you claimed it had been independently verified that you could understand Graya to a high level of fluency. It came in as an anonymous tip on one of my contact lines."

Page's cheeks burn with fury. Those traders, whoever they really were, were just checking whether she could understand what they were saying. And then, when the shipment they described actually got nailed by the guards—when they picked out the right containers and went straight for the bait—then they would have known for sure.

"We got off to a bad start, I know. But I'd like to change that, Page. If you'll let me," Maelle says. "I know better than anyone that Zhak isn't easy to work with. And I'm not going to ask you to trust me after what you've just been through. But I'll give it my best shot to prove it to you, all right? You want to know what's going on here, I'll tell you. Ask me anything."

Page clenches her fists, weighing up the idea of asking for more information and abandoning her stony refusal to engage. Curiosity and stubbornness war briefly in her mind, but her curiosity wins out in the end. She lets her head drop back on the pillow with a tired sigh. It's not like she really has any other options, lying here hardly able to lift her head up. She might as well hear it.

"Okay, what's the big deal about this language?" Page asks. "*Graya*... that's what you called it? What's so damn special about knowing it?"

Until those traders came, she was almost sure the odd *dream language* was a product of her broken mind, unable as she was to recall anything but the smallest fragments of it while she was awake. But there was something she saw in that patchy medical record she got access to back on Kuuj. The note that said, 'the patient spoke unintelligibly for several days when she first regained consciousness.' And Page remembers that medic's voice... *Shhh, stay calm. Do you speak any Union Basic at all? Can you understand me?*

Now, she realizes what happened with a shiver. When she first woke, she must have been speaking Graya.

"Graya is an ancient tongue. It's one of the oldest known human languages," Maelle says. "On Teyr, they call it the *Perfect Cadence*. Of course, it's not entirely unheard of to find Graya still spoken on some of the Prime Worlds, especially in high society. It's still taught on most of the Primes, if you go to an expensive university." This last, she says with unmistakable disdain. "As far as we know, the Teyrian Protectorate mostly reverted to Graya after they split from the Union, and they stopped teaching Union Basic altogether." She pauses. "Those Golden-Feather monks would definitely speak Graya amongst themselves. But it's a notoriously difficult language—very hard to learn with anything like native fluency."

"Wow. All right, then." Page sighs, tucking that information away under *Weird Information to Deal With Later*. Right now, though, she's almost annoyed that Maelle is being so straightforward with her. Some part of her would rather these scammers lied more blatantly, or refused to answer anything, so she could hold on to her rage. She's always known how to pull her solitude around herself like a shield, how to count on herself alone. Pull herself out of trouble. She shouldn't even *think* about trusting anything she's told by these people. Hasn't she fallen for enough scams this week already?

Page struggles to sit up again, propping herself up on her elbows. She's still wearing that ridiculous-looking jumpsuit, bunched up around her waist. The fabric does feel great, though, surprisingly soft compared to the rough, starched feel of her old clothes. Her clothes *did* stink, she has to admit. The strong-smelling chemicals from the dry-clean laundrette never quite wear off; ironically, most of her clothes on Kuuj smelled better after a few days of wear.

She turns her head to look around, searching for something to anchor her next question to. The room around her is absolutely spartan. There is not a scrap of decoration anywhere, no sign of habitation, no clothing hanging on the hooks next to the door. There are no pictures in frames or any personal items on display. It's as utilitarian and sparse as Page's cube on Kuuj. Even the sheets on the bunks look crisp and fresh. There's an unmistakable engine hum, now—the ship is on the move.

"Where are we right now?" she asks.

"A grand palace on Teyr," Maelle says with a teasing smile. "Nahhh, I'm just kidding. You're still on our ship," she says. "I think we're just about crossing the sector border. We're at the edge of mainspace."

"It's so… quiet on this ship. Are you and Zhak the only ones here?"

"There's a crew, but they're all newbies. Hired hands. Zhak's ordered everyone to keep out of the way, 'cause you're top secret, pal. So, for now, you've got to stick with me."

"You mean I've got to stay locked in this room?" Page bristles.

"Only for a little while. But if Zhak finds you alone, he said he's gonna cuff you. So it's probably better if you don't leave."

"What? That's ridiculous! Besides, what am I gonna do? It's not like I'm gonna steal your speedship and fly away back to Kuuj."

For one irrational, unthinking moment, she wonders if maybe she *could*. The fact that she's never piloted a speedship before—as far as she knows—feels like a minor issue when she considers the thought of staying *here*.

"Yeah, that's what I told Zhak!" Maelle laughs. "Wouldn't put it past you, though, to find a way. You're a sneaky one. Clever."

And Page, despite herself, feels a momentary sliver of pride before the anger rushes back in again.

"Oh, yeah, I'm *real* clever," Page sighs, rolling her eyes. "Falling for that Q-link scam? That's got to be one of the least clever things I ever did."

"Look... if it's any consolation, Zhak would've found a way to take you from Kuuj Outpost anyway," Maelle says. "His original plan was to buy your debt from Tully, and then blackmail you into working for us. We already had a contract ready and everything. It was me who suggested the alternative."

"What?" Page feels her eyes go wide. "Wait... Tully was going to *sell me out?*"

"Your boss was a piece of work, wasn't he? He wanted two hundred thousand for the transfer of your debt, and Zhak would've paid it. But I didn't want that asshole to get a damn chit more than we already gave him for the information on you. So look on the bright side. You got a bag over your head, but at least your shitty boss didn't make any more money off this."

"Ugh." Page's stomach turns. "Two hundred thousand! My debt wasn't worth that. But I guess I was a lost cause, as far as Tully was concerned. I wasn't making him money anymore, especially with how bad business has been. He probably reckoned it was way more profitable to get rid of me, if he had a buyer willing to pay that much."

Rage tightens in her throat. Tully would've known damn well that whatever they wanted with her wasn't anything good. Nobody would ever buy a dead-end debt like that, unless they were trying to entrap someone. Tully had no idea what they were going to do to her or where she'd be taken... and apparently, he didn't care, as long as he lined his pockets.

Page has always known, as well as Tully did, that his 'business' on Kuuj is dying slowly. The outpost's prospects have been crumbling along with the steadily closing commerce routes. Now, some months, fewer than a half-dozen big cargo stopovers go past Kuuj. And the orange zones, where deep-space alien skirmishes are heating up, have been creeping ever closer. More and more transit companies are shutting down operations completely because of the Union's travel restrictions. There are fewer and fewer people to steal from, and fewer people to buy the shop's wares.

But while Tully's income has been faltering for years, he's always reacted to his decreasing profits by raising rents on the hab-cubes, raising quotas for his crew, and hiking the interest on his outstanding loans. He's always going to find a way, and if that means selling his underlings out, he'd have no qualms about it.

"So... I *was* right, wasn't I?" Maelle says. "I was right to tell Zhak we should go the kidnap route? This way, all we paid Tully was a fee for more information about you."

Page sits up, suddenly wondering if Tully had disclosed anything to them that he'd kept from her. Maybe, just maybe—

"Did Tully say anything else about me?" she blurts. "Did he show you anything else he kept from... from before? Documents other than my medical record?"

Maelle shakes her head. "No. Your docs on Kuuj were pretty sparse. He told us your birth date was just guesswork from whoever did your initial stasis revival, and that you'd submitted your own registration name with no supporting ident. But listen, Page, this is a *good* thing for you! Tully's hardly going to chase you down, or put a sector hold on your debt—how could he? You've got no legal identity! You have no Union ident, and he has no idea where we took you!"

As far as Tully's concerned, Page has always remained Debt 4945, regardless of what she calls herself. She remembers him telling her to put down whatever name she wanted when he submitted her Kuuj residence registration, but she had no idea what to choose. When she clicked through to *View Identity Documents* on her intake form, she saw for the first time the message that would haunt her for years: PAGE NOT FOUND.

And so, on the registration form, she entered *Page Found*. She didn't know much about herself, but apparently she had a sense of humour.

"What I'm saying is... you've made a clean getaway," Maelle says gently. "Page Found doesn't even *exist*, outside of Kuuj. Nothing Tully can do will get to you. You're free, if you want to be."

"You mean free to work with you? To impersonate some feathery monk for you? Whatever." Page scowls. Right now it feels an awful lot like she's just landed herself another life debt. She can't exactly get out of here.

She *was* briefly tempted by Zhak's suggestion that she'd be well-paid for her cooperation. It has occurred to her that a windfall could help with her search, or that she might be able to secure herself a proper identity—but she cuts those thoughts off in a hurry.

Whatever good-gal game Maelle thinks she's playing here, it's not going to work on her. Maelle is *not* her friend, and these people are not to be trusted. They're certainly not doing Page any favours out of the goodness of their hearts, any more than the rest of Tully's crew have ever been her allies. To them, you're either competition or you're a mark. Page would prefer to be neither.

Wordlessly, she takes the cup of water Maelle is still holding and gulps the remainder of it down—this much, at least, she's too thirsty not to accept. She swishes the last mouthful around in her cheeks as she examines the cup in her hands.

It's made of cheap blue metal, and there are a couple of stickers on it—the one on the bottom is a manufacturer's label that has almost worn off, the text illegible, but the one on the side is a decorative cartoon drawing of a planet and a star. She runs her finger over the bubbled surface of the sticker, smoothing it down.

"You're curious about the weirdest little things, huh?" Maelle says, an amused look on her face. "I see the way you're always sizing everything up. Always examining every damned little thing, like you're some kind of detective. I've got to ask, what's so interesting about that cup?"

Page feels her cheeks flush. "I... I don't know. Nothing, really... I'm just..." Five different quips fight their way to her tongue, ranging from sarcastic to downright vicious. But for some godsforsaken reason, she decides to answer sincerely. "I guess I'm just always wondering if something might trigger a memory. Like the picture might be something I recognize, or maybe I might've seen a cup like this somewhere…" She squints at it for a moment more before she drops it onto the blanket next to her. "Don't think so, though."

"Oh." Maelle looks sheepish. "Sorry. Right, the memory loss. That must be rough."

Page shrugs. "It is what it is."

"Look… I know this is weird and all, but… I want you to know you *can* talk to me if you need to," Maelle says.

"I'm *fine,* thanks," Page says, more coldly than she means to. "I got by on my own on Kuuj for eight damn years. I don't need a protector, okay? I don't need your pity."

"That's not what I'm—"

"And I don't need you pretending to be my friend, either, to make yourself look good and Zhak look like the bad guy while you gain my trust!" Page snaps. "I know that tactic. I've seen more than enough holo-dramas. I know exactly what you're up to. We all gotta do what we gotta do, okay? I get it. But at least respect me enough not to sell me yet another damned scam."

Maelle opens her mouth like she's going to speak, then closes it, and there's that flash of sadness in her eyes again.

"You're right not to trust Zhak," she finally says, her voice soft. "And you're right not to trust me either. You've got no reason to believe me. But what I said still stands." She picks up the empty cup and tucks the blanket back up around Page. "So if you change your mind and decide you *do* want an ally… well… you've got one."

She places Page's scratched, beat-up digipad on the blanket beside her.

And then she turns and walks away.

UNCHANGING AND UNBREAKABLE

Excerpted from "Fringe Movements in Teyrian Spiritual Practice"
[Author Redacted]

While Teyr has prided itself on the 'unchanging and unbreakable' nature of its traditions over the centuries, the Teyrian spiritual practice of veneration for the Great Goddess has in fact undergone many changes in recorded history.

Teyr's path to independence from the United Worlds of Humanity gave rise to a wide variety of fringe practices and beliefs. Many of these movements proliferated just before the planet's split from the Union and quite likely blossomed in its subsequent isolation, when various Temple powers were vying for prominence and seeking alliances with the newly empowered Gepcot.

The Sanctum of the Golden-Feather and the Purification Flight
See: Monks of the Golden-Feather

While many spiritual orders throughout the Primes are notoriously secretive, and those of Teyr even more so, the rites of the Sanctum of the Golden-Feather remain some of the only Teyrian practices that extend their activities beyond the Teyrian Protectorate. Monks of the order are initiated by a so-called 'purification flight': a long, low-speed space circuit in suspended animation, spending months or years in transit through space before returning to the Protectorate and being reawakened.

This 'ritual of awakening' is meant to emulate the Descent of the Goddess through the cosmic void, as well as her reawakening from a temporary death after falling to the Greenworld in bird form. The journey culminates in a symbolic return to Teyr, invoking the eventual return of the Goddess to protect the Greenworld from destruction at the End of Time.

Such ritual practices are illegal in the United Worlds due to the high risks inherent in long-term stasis. Under Union Law [*citation*], suspension of an individual is not permitted for 'spiritual or recreational purposes,' and to place a person into such a suspension is a criminal act. The rituals involving stasis were rarely practised while Teyr was a part of the United Worlds. However, after Teyr's departure from the Union, the rite experienced a resurgence in the Teyrian Protectorate, and such 'monk-ships' of Teyrian provenance are occasionally apprehended traversing Union space during their space circuits.

Most sects that practise suspension rituals believe that divine oversight will spare the monks from any of the dangerous ramifications of stasis, and in transit they are thought to be protected under the traveller-god Yhannis' guiding hands. But other practitioners consider the damage inflicted by the suspension to be a desirable part of the process – a penance of sorts, or a purification, in imitation of the difficult journey of the goddess they seek to emulate.

A death in the 'void-sleep' is considered a 'blessed calling.' Monks who perish during stasis or who do not survive revival are believed to be reincarnated directly to the beginning and the end of everything – called to watch the first sunrise of the next iteration of the universe from the hills of the Everlasting Greenworld.

PAGE FOUND
Zhaklam Evelor's Ship

A MONK OF *Teyr*.

Of all the places Page has read about as she's clicked through the fragmented network on Kuuj, she has never given Teyr a second thought. She knows next to nothing about it, save that it was a First Prime that used to be a part of the Union before it chose to isolate itself and its territories from the rest of humanity. Very few Teyrians have ever left the Protectorate since then, so it would have seemed a highly unlikely place to consider.

Now, Page finds that Maelle has added dozens of dense and lengthy academic articles about Teyr to her 'pad, covering everything from history to politics to language to 'fringe spiritual practices.' Something about the information compels Page, pulling at those loose strings in her head the same way the picture of the bird-masked monks did.

What does she really remember of *anything* that came before? There are her blackout dreams, or visions, or whatever... but those have always been too fragmentary to make sense of. For all her careful journal-keeping, she can barely distinguish what's actually a damaged memory and what's a half-remembered documentary she saw once, or a lyric from a song, or a scene from a book—

Could there really be something that connects *her* to Teyr? To these Golden-Feather monks? Of course she'd love nothing better than some dramatic, exciting tale about how a lost aristocrat-turned-monk ended up on Kuuj. Finding out that she's *somebody*? That she might actually have a *family*, and one of some importance at that? It's the fairytale ending she dreamed of through many a long night crouched in the dockyard waiting to snatch a couple of cheap comm boxes.

But surely, her logical mind insists, an imaginary aristocratic background is exactly that: a fantasy. Whatever she was, she doubts she was any kind of *monk*. It's far more likely that she was just a foolish girl who signed her life away in a clinical trial for money—probably because of some even older debt she can't remember.

And yet, somehow, she speaks Graya, this rare and ancient language. The so-called Perfect Cadence. It has to mean *something*.

As soon as Maelle leaves the room, Page picks up the 'pad and devours each article, re-reading it twice, scanning every line of the text like it might contain some hidden key or cipher.

Maelle comes back to check on Page several times, bringing food and drink, and taking her over to use the lav. Page throws her device down quickly every time she hears the door opening, and feigns sleep. But once, she fails to switch it off before tossing it back onto the blanket, and Maelle smiles smugly at the telltale glow. She says nothing, just lets her eyes rest knowingly on it for a moment before she turns and walks out again.

Page refuses to ask any more questions, and she's not entirely sure why. She supposes that it's a point of stubbornness now, a show of intent to suss out the truth on her own without begging for information. Perhaps she can discover something of what Zhak's scheme is by going through these articles again. Artifacts from a monk-ship, that's what his client is after. What kind of artifacts? Does he expect Page to steal something?

Regardless of what this *job* turns out to be, one certainty is slowly sinking into Page's bones—she's never going to be able to go back to Kuuj Outpost, so she'd better start making some plans.

She wonders if Tully has noticed yet that she's gone. Realistically, he'll probably just wash his hands of her as soon as he figures out that she's not on the outpost anymore. He'll repossess her hab-cube, split it in two and rent it back out again. Her time on Kuuj is over.

This is a good thing, Maelle said. A fresh start, in a way.

Page tries to convince herself of it. Eight years is surely enough to exhaust whatever chance there was of finding a clue there, anyway. There's a kind of relief in letting go. She should be glad not to be shackled to that wreckhole anymore, even if she's exchanged the prison she chose for a new one she didn't.

Page sets down the 'pad again, stares at the ceiling and thinks of her Kuuj hab-cube. She pictures the too-thin walls, the shared toilet that constantly backed up, the air recyclers that hummed and rattled relentlessly, which at least meant they were working.

Will she *miss* anything about the only home she can remember? Anything at all? Maybe she'll miss that one holo series she left unfinished, she thinks—an obscure bootleg of an adventure-fantasy disc, snagged from one of the dockyard workers in exchange for a charger cable he needed. She doubts she'll be able to find it again. But it hardly matters that much.

She picks up her 'pad and opens up her blackout journal. The file is still there, created a little less than eight years ago, last edited a week ago.

[File: Blackout_dream_log]

The doll, she remembers suddenly. The doll with the two soft gold ribbons, she meant to add that to her vision log.

Holding a doll. Gold ribbons, long hair.

She types only the briefest summary of the new image, but her heart isn't in it; she doesn't even bother to describe the way the light hit the gold fabric, nor its sumptuous texture under her hands.

But there was something else, more recently, wasn't there? Something in that second blackout, when she fell in the corridor. *Flowers.*

She's seen those orange flowers in her visions many times before—sometimes growing on bushes, sometimes enclosed in pretty vases, sometimes clasped in her hands. *Goddess-blossom*, that's what the species is called—she looked it up long ago. An extremely common flower that grows on dozens of green worlds, hardly a useful lead. This time, the bright blooms were laid out on that pretty flat stone surface, marbled and smooth.

Loose flowers (Goddess-blossom) on some kind of... altar?

She sighs. What good has all this been, collecting fragments and scraps, hoarding bits of half-remembered visions as though she could ever make anything useful of it? She feels an awful lot like deleting it all, and she would, if she wasn't so sure she'd regret it.

Of course, there were some few-and-far-between triumphs in her early investigations on Kuuj, moments when she made a little bit of progress that lifted her heart.

The ships, for example—those seemed so promising, back then. She'd been determined to find the name of the ship that conveyed her unconscious body to the outpost, and to figure out the exact date of its arrival. There were eight candidates, at first, which she slowly eliminated through careful research. And after a while, there were only two possible ship names left on her shortlist.

The first was a privately owned cargo hauler called the *Beauty Ninefold*, which had docked about a week before Page regained consciousness in Kuuj's medibay. That ship had stayed in dock for four days, and the purpose of its stay was unmarked.

The second candidate was a ship called *Starhelm 23-2*, which had landed two days before her awakening and remained for only half a day before moving onward. It was of unspecified provenance—like her—with no description of its purpose of visit and its captain's signature left blank.

It took two years before Page finally found more information about the *Beauty Ninefold*, in the form of a purchase order at a hardware stall down in the lower levels. She'd paid dearly for the privilege of digging through their charges and receipts from all those years ago, mostly to no avail. The majority of Kuuj's shopkeepers, she'd discovered, were absolutely terrible at keeping reliable records. Or perhaps they just found it safer not to know who exactly it was that bought their wares.

But at that hardware stall, she'd struck lucky: a record of a single mechanical part being sold, the receipt made out to the captain of the *Beauty Ninefold*. The ship had needed a replacement for a systems component that had broken down, but it would take a few days for the print-shop to produce and install it. There was a long note included about the complexities of the repair. The *Beauty Ninefold* had clearly never planned to stop at all; only the need for a new part had made them pull up. It was highly unlikely that they'd spontaneously decided to drop off a half-revived stasis wakeling.

Silently, Page raised a prayer, thanking whatever backroom clerk had bothered to take down this very detailed message. And, with some trepidation, she crossed off the *Beauty Ninefold* from her list. That left only *one* ship, the one she never managed to learn any more about, no matter how hard she looked.

Until her final candidate, *Starhelm 23-2*, finally came back to Kuuj.

One of the annoying little dockyard kids spotted it coming in and remembered the five-chit reward that Page had set on that information. It was mid-morning, and Page was cleaning a keyboard in Tully's shop when the kid ran in, shrieking and breathless, shouting her name.

"Page! Page! *Page Found!*"

She'd bolted to her feet, morbidly certain that some disaster must be happening. Had the life support systems finally given out, was this decrepit wreckhole about to vent them all into space?

But no, the kid was grinning. "Page! The *Starhelm 23-2* is docking!" he shouted. "Bay Four! I spotted it, I spotted it! How's about those five chits?"

Page had dropped the keyboard she was working on and dashed for the door.

"Hey!" the kid shouted behind her. "My reward! Page, come on! Where's my five chits?"

"Later, kid! I've got to see if your intel checks out first!"

She already knew that it would. Her feet pounded down to the docks, her heart threatening to hammer out of her chest as she ran. Was this *it*? The answer she was looking for? The ship that had brought her here?

But when she turned the corner and ran out into the dockyard ring, her heart sank. The ship in Bay Four was a tiny single-engine sector-hopper with barely any room up front to seat two. It didn't even have a cargo bay, much less enough space to house a stasis casket or a medical setup of any kind. The owner was a grouchy-looking man who seemed very taken aback by this panicked, sweating stranger accosting him, asking him if his ship had ever passed this way before.

Yes, he reckoned, he'd been here a few years back, on the way to a meeting in mainspace. He had hoped never to see Kuuj again. What a disgusting place, he added, full of disgusting people. He couldn't believe he'd stopped here again, and *my gods, this place has not improved*. Was there anything else she wanted?

When the asshole went to check in at the dockyard office, Page had lifted his rucksack. He had a decent comms device and a nice supply of expensive snacks that she kept hidden in her wall for weeks afterwards, supplying bribes to the kids for various watch duties and tip-offs. And of course, she paid out the promised five-chit reward to her little informant, with a bag of salted cakes on top, muttering to herself the entire time.

All her imagined stories about the *Starhelm 23-2* were dead, along with any hope of further leads. Whatever ship had brought her here, there was no trace of it. Of course there wasn't. Everything she'd read about liquidation of medical debts suggested it probably wouldn't be on the record, but she hadn't wanted to believe it.

And now... well, *now*, being forced to leave Kuuj has suddenly laid bare the futility of it all. This is who she is now: *Page Found*. She wears an identity she constructed out of thin air in the first place. So what difference would it make if she *did* let them turn her into some long-gone monk?

She could reinvent herself as a monk of the Golden-Feather and concoct any back story she likes. Part of the purpose of the purification rite is *pledging to leave the weight of your past behind*, so she's practically done it already by definition. She almost laughs to herself.

Who's to say you're not a monk of the Golden-Feather?

Agreeing to play their bird-costumed monk seems like a way off this bucket, at least. Maybe there's a piece of good fortune to be scraped from this mess. If they intend to take her to some kind of floating monastery, surely Page Found can turn that into an escape route. She's a sneaky one, after all, she reminds herself. She's *clever*.

She picks up her 'pad and dives back into the list of documents.

THE BIRD'S HEART

See also: BIRD'S ORB
Excerpted from *Lost Artifacts of the Old Worlds: The Facts Behind the Legends*

The *Bird's Heart* or *Bird's Orb* is a legendary relic that is briefly mentioned in several Source texts. It is variously described as a repository of knowledge that can be accessed by touch, a divinely created orb with strong healing properties, or simply a small globe of the Origin world.

The Heart's existence as a physical object has long been debated, with some scholars believing these stories to be entirely metaphorical[1], while others purport that the object described did in fact exist historically, and that it may have been carried from the Origin world on one of the seedships[2]. Others have proposed that there could even have been several such Hearts, based on similar descriptions of the object found in pre-unification Prime sources[3].

Various hypotheses have been set forward as to the object's practical purpose, and the topic has long intrigued academics and treasure-hunters alike. Some of the more widely discussed theories include:

- An archive or digital storage system from the Source civilization
- A lost star chart or navigation instrument that shows the location of the Origin world
- A map to a cache of advanced weapons of Source provenance

A reclusive order of Teyrian monks, known as the Sanctum of the Golden-Feather, has sometimes been tied to the supposed guardianship of the Bird's Orb. This, however, is a fringe theory, connected to the belief in Teyrian Primacy – the false claim that Teyr is the Origin world[4].

Many works of fiction have touched on the subject of a hunt for the Heart or the consequences of its discovery. However, to date, no material evidence has ever been found of this object's existence.

DALYA
OF HOUSE EDAMAUN, IN HER NINTH YEAR
First-City, Teyr

WHEN ANDA AND her uncle arrived at the front gates of the Edamaun residence, Dalya's heart was hammering in her throat. She had chosen an elegant blue dress and jacket for the evening, with matching shoes and high socks embroidered with the crest of House Edamaun. Her hair was pulled back into a quick, simple braided updo—it was all Heral had time for, much plainer than at ceremonies.

But secretly, Dalya was glad of the simplicity of their preparations. Perhaps it was better if she looked more like the newcomers, if things were not as formal. It might make them feel more at ease here.

Ushering them inside, showing them to the carefully laid table with its gilded place cards, she had never felt more grown-up. It almost seemed worth the price of Uncle's earlier disapproval—her *own* dinner party, hosted and arranged by her. It was like a little glimpse of the future, she thought: the day when she'd more fully take on her responsibilities as Uncle's heir.

Perhaps this would help him see, in the end. Perhaps he'd notice how good she could be, how responsible, how *organized*. Even Nathin couldn't have done better on such short notice.

Uncle joined them at the dining table just as Dalya started to lead the evening prayer, and he took his seat across from Anda's uncle, Derin Agote. As dinner began, the two men exchanged stiff pleasantries, barely speaking to one another at first—and Dalya found this awfully strange, given how talkative Uncle usually was in company. But eventually they seemed to settle on a lively discussion on the finer points of a piece of classical music, and Dalya was quietly relieved.

She turned her focus to Anda—bright, inquisitive, wide-eyed Anda, perhaps the most interesting acquaintance she had ever made. They spoke of all manner of things while they ate: ball games and dresses, the names of trees, Teyrian food and how it differed from moonside cuisine. And of course, the sacred texts and the many stories they contained. Anda *loved* the sacred texts, and she spoke of them with an excitement that made Dalya sit up and take interest.

Dalya smiled then, and said that perhaps when Anda grew older she might officiate in the Goddess's temple. She would be ever so good at telling the divine stories—so much better than the mumbling sage who'd spoken at last week's gathering. But Anda demurred at this, and she grew oddly shy at the suggestion she might speak in the temple.

"I don't think so," she whispered. "I... I do not imagine that I would be allowed to."

What did she mean? Dalya wondered. Perhaps moonfolk were not permitted to officiate at the temple, Dalya thought. Could that be true? She would have to ask Heral about it; Heral knew such things.

But Dalya's heart grew heavy at the thought—after all, had they not been told to accept the moonfolk as their own? Was it not said that they were no different from planet-born Teyrians? Why *couldn't* it be Anda who spoke from the great glimmering arch, with the light of the brazier on her face and the divine light in her eyes? It was glorious to imagine it.

Still, Dalya spoke no more of it that evening, for it seemed to have upset her new friend.

After dinner, the two uncles retired to the drawing-room,

speaking to one another in low, serious voices. It was clear to Dalya that the girls were not meant to follow, so she took the opportunity to slip away with Anda into the back gardens, where she could show the moon girl all the dazzling fronds and flowers that Uncle's gardeners had cultivated.

All around us is the beauty and the bounty of the Goddess. Nothing anywhere in the galaxy grew the way it did on Teyr, for the soil here had been blessed by the Goddess's very footsteps. And bright Anda appreciated it all. She even kicked off her shoes and spun around barefoot over the sweet-smelling grasses. Dalya gasped at the brazenness of it, and after a moment she followed her suit. The grass tickled against her feet.

But it was there in the gardens, while they twirled barefoot together and the sunset played over the golden honey-blossoms, that Dalya made a terrible mistake.

Afterwards, she asked herself how she could possibly have said such a thing, how she could have slipped and become quite so familiar with the girl who was still a stranger. Something about Anda must have put her at such ease that any filter of common sense had apparently left her. She spoke her mind as freely as flowing water.

"Did your parents die, too?" Dalya asked her, the foolish words tumbling too quickly from her mouth. "Is that why your uncle has your guardianship?"

Anda recoiled, her whole body drawing back as if she'd been slapped. And Dalya instantly regretted the blunt nature of her question. What a daft thing that had been to ask her! She had only wondered if Anda had come into her uncle's guardianship the same way that Dalya had come to her own uncle's—thinking to find one more strand of shining kinship connecting them.

But Anda seemed to freeze. She stopped twirling and stood there blinking with her head tipped down, looking at the grass. Her eyes went glassy.

"Anda…"

"Yes. Yes, they died," she said quietly. "There was... there was a fire. About a year ago. And then... Well, then my uncle brought me to Teyr with him." Fat tears were rolling down her cheeks—it seemed that the half-hidden sadness inside her had found purchase and clawed its way to the surface. "I never... never thought we'd leave Meneyr! My parents wouldn't have wanted me to leave. But he... he said we had to... and I was scared..." She bit down hard on her lower lip, leaving bright pink indentations with her gappy teeth. "Honestly, I... I'm still scared. I don't know anybody here. And... I really miss my parents."

"I know what you mean," Dalya said softly. "I miss mine, too."

It was not a lie, not exactly. Dalya did miss the *idea* of having parents... but can you really miss someone you never really knew? Still, it seemed like the right thing to say, to sympathize with the girl, even though in truth Dalya's own departed parents were no more than a blur in her recollection. She was so very young when they died, she didn't remember much of anything about them. If she'd been wounded by their departure from this world, that wound had long ago healed. By contrast, Anda's grief was a fresh cut, and Dalya's insensitive words had torn it wide open.

"It's all right, Anda," she said confidently, patting the girl's arm. "You'll see your parents again, at the beginning and at the end of everything! At the end of it all, we'll return to the beginning! It will be exactly like the sacred texts say. You'll find your family in the Renewal, and you'll all be reunited. Here, on the Greenworld of Teyr!"

The girl shook her head, and the tears fell fast as raindrops from beneath her dark lashes. "No..." she whispered. "No, I don't think that's going to happen. Not for me. Never for me."

"It will," Dalya insisted stubbornly. How could this girl be so familiar with the divine teachings, and yet lack such an important bit of knowledge? "You must know this, Anda. The sacred texts tell us that at the end of it all, we'll be together on the Greenworld. All the good believers will find one another again, on that blessed day when the universe begins anew—"

"Yes... but... not my parents." Anda wiped at her reddening eyes with the back of her arm. "They weren't good believers, Dalya. They... they would not have come to Teyr with us, even if they were still alive. They had both refused the call. And so... they won't be with us at the beginning and the end of everything." She takes a hiccupping breath. "They wanted us all to stay on Meneyr."

"Is that what *you* wanted? To stay?" Dalya asked. Again with the bold questions. But a line had been crossed now, and Dalya didn't hesitate. Of course Anda must have wanted to come to Teyr, even if she was a little scared. Didn't she? "What did you want to do?"

"It doesn't matter what I wanted. I'm a *child*, why would that matter?" Anda said, almost angrily. She looked at Dalya as if she were being quite unreasonable. "My parents are dead, and I'm here now. This is where I am meant to be. *Doing my duty*."

And in that moment, awkward as it was, Dalya felt like she'd suddenly found all the kinship in the world. Not just a god-sibling, but a true friend. At last, perhaps, here was someone who might understand her.

A friend who understood exactly what it was to wear a mantle that didn't fit, and to serve a destiny she didn't want.

"I understand," Dalya said, and she reached for Anda's hand. "Truly. I really, really do."

Anda was silent for a little while, idly flicking the end of her dark braid between two fingernails of her other hand. Her eyes still had that distant, bottomless sadness, but something in her air of skittish apprehension had lifted, and she didn't pull away from Dalya's grip. Then she finally took Dalya's hand properly, meshing their palms together with a determined squeeze.

"Thank you," she said. "Thank you for listening, Honoured Daughter Dalya."

"I'd really like to be your friend. That is... if you'd like that, too," Dalya said. "You should just call me Dalya, if we're to be friends."

"Hello, Dalya," said Anda, and her face lit up with a tearful smile, as if they were meeting again for the first time. "I would like that very much. And, well, uh... I guess you can still call me Anda, so there's no change there." She giggled and sniffled at the same time. "Hello, *friend*."

THE STORYTELLER

Recording start 03:22:09

What else... Oh, of course, there's the scamships. A niche business, that one, and something I don't deal in myself, though we've... [clears throat] crossed paths on occasion.

It's a bold kind of deception, but a damn lucrative one. See, there's always folks who go trawling around looking for Felen wrecks in the orange zones. Alien salvage is hard to come by, of course, 'cause mostly the military grabs the wreckage if they ever manage to take out any enemy craft. But every so often, these trawlers do hit a payday, and they find stuff that's nearly intact.

Then these scamship mechanics, they buy up the stripped-out Felen hulls. They mount 'em right on top of a regular human-made ship chassis. They put a totally normal human ship underneath. And then they sell them on to deep-space pirate raiders.

Of course, some of these fakes are better than others – frankly, I'd say most scamships aren't exactly convincing on a closer look. They don't move anything like real alien craft, they've got nowhere near the acceleration and of course, none of the weapons. But it's human nature to let panic overtake logic, isn't it? [chuckles] The most important thing is that these fakes can fool a cargo ship's scanners at a distance. And so these pirate raiders can whip up a little bit of 'alien contact' whenever it might be useful.

See, there's only one thing a cargo crew wants to see less than the authorities, and that's alien traffic. Absolutely nobody wants to come face to face with the Felen, or find out what happens if you get boarded by 'em. If most people so much as glimpse the shape of those hulls on their scans, they'll go straight into lockdown mode. Cut their engines, run for their panic rooms, eject themselves in emergency pods, whatever.

They know they can't outrun the Felen, so they don't even try it. Makes it a hell of a lot easier for pirates to board the ship and unload all the cargo without a whiff of confrontation. Hells, you might even argue it's more ethical that way – less casualties if people just get out of the damn way. [*laughs*]

Well, anyway. It's like I was saying before. The further you get into this shit, the more you realize just how little it matters what's real and what's not.

It only matters what you can *convince people of*.

MAELLE KRESS
Zhaklam Evelor's Ship

THE JUNK THIEF stays in bed for almost a whole day more, sleeping most of the time—little wonder, after everything she's been through. Miraculously, Zhak doesn't insist on dragging her out again, and accepts Maelle's promise that she'll brief the girl on the next steps of the plan. Something else currently has Zhak preoccupied, and Maelle is too relieved to question it.

She reminds herself to smile every time she comes in to check on Page. Affable, friendly, approachable. *Trustworthy*. She needs to be the one who's helpful, the one who's answering questions and giving Page information without reservation. The one who's not *hiding things*.

Maelle would tell Page everything, the whole plan, if only Page were willing to listen. Like how Zhak has accomplished the rarest of feats: he's somehow picked up a piece of priceless intel on the planned route of a monk-ship. And not just any monk-ship, but the longest-flying flagship of the Sanctum of the Golden-Feather.

That thing will be full of corpses, of course, in addition to its live crew—there's no way anyone survives stasis for anywhere near as long as it's meant to have been out there. But more importantly, that monk-ship is alleged to be carrying some long-sought Source artifact. Something one of Zhak's clients will pay dearly for, to the tune of *millions*.

Monk-ships fly entirely dark, but now Zhak knows exactly where its route will dip along the edge of mainspace, as it makes a rare stop to resupply for its living contingent. He's perfectly placed to intercept it. Unfortunately, the window to rendezvous with it has been steadily narrowing, and they were still missing a feathery accomplice. Maelle had all but lost hope that she'd find a way to get in on this.

And then... Page's file appeared. Maelle couldn't believe her luck when such a perfect dossier came through. A short, unsigned scrawltext woke her in the middle of ship's night:

Candidate of interest, it said simply. *Outer Sectors. About 30 years old. Scars from a clinical stasis trial. Fluent in Graya, verified*. This last was underlined three times. *Let me know if you want particulars/location.*

Maelle replied instantly. And Zhak, thank the gods, was willing to take a chance on it. He was all in, despite the exorbitant figure that came through when Maelle asked about the cost for more information. Just like he was ready to pay Tully for that damned debt contract.

A contract which, Maelle thinks smugly to herself, *she* found a way to evade. It eases her conscience a little, the fact that they didn't pay Tully for Page's debt note, that they actually managed to *help* the junk thief in the process.

Zhak has spent far too long interviewing potential false monks, and so far all of them have proven to be terrible flops. The last candidate was a grifter who didn't even have real stasis scars; a cursory glance was enough to tell that the 'ports' on her neck and spine were only skin-deep. Her spoken Graya was almost non-existent when Zhak tested her. And she still somehow thought she'd pull one over on them.

It doesn't much matter if you lie at a job interview for *being a con artist*, Maelle thinks wryly—it's more or less expected. But you've damn well got to be able to lie *effectively*. That's the whole point of the job.

This girl, Page, though? Page is different. She's a decent liar, that much is clear. Her bit with that aug-reality game might even have worked on most people. She'll suit Zhak's plan just fine. And a petty thief with no prospects is a better match for Maelle's own plan than she ever dared to hope for.

If Page ever comes around to wanting to hear about the plan, much less participate in it. If Zhak acting like the biggest asshole in the Union Quadrant doesn't scare her off completely.

Negative thoughts have no home here, Maelle thinks to herself. *Let it go, let it go.*

She reaches into her pocket for the little talisman she always carries, feeling its reassuring smoothness against her palm. It's an inexpensive trinket, mass-produced and probably not even properly blessed, for whatever that's worth. But it was Rodin's, once. It was among his things when he departed this mortal plane... and now it's hers.

It had surprised Maelle a little to learn that Rodin kept something like this—she never knew him to be particularly observant. Perhaps he simply saw the Traveller's talisman as a good luck charm, or something to speak the night's prayer to, the way many spacefarers did. But this is something Rodin touched, something he held. And most of the time, that's more than blessing enough for Maelle.

She takes the talisman out of her pocket and rests it on the flat of her hand, looking it over like she has a thousand times. A glossy, greyish-white synthstone with an image of Yhannis, the travelling god, carved in the middle. The inscription around the edge was once traced with gold paint, which has long worn off except for a few flecks still clinging to the grooves like stars. There's something poetic in it, Maelle thinks—those tiny flecks of gold still holding on, the same way she holds Rodin's memory.

There's a deep valley running over the back of the talisman where Rodin's thumb might have worried back and forth over it. Sometimes, when she's feeling particularly melancholy, Maelle imagines that it still feels a little warm when she reaches into her pocket to seek it, as though Rodin has just placed it into her hand.

I've got this, Rodin, she tells him silently. *I've got you, the way you always had me. Not long now. Not long to go.*

Maelle shoves the little stone back into her pocket and marches down the hall to Zhak's boardroom door. One of the ship's hired crew is just coming out of the room as she passes, but the man lowers his head and wordlessly ducks away, pretending he hasn't seen her. They're all getting discretion pay on this job, and none of them want to risk it with unnecessary eye contact.

Maelle shoulders the door release and stomps into the boardroom with all of Rodin's old swagger.

There's a navigation chart open on Zhak's computer screen, but he shoves the device aside as she walks in, that familiar pique flashing across his face when he sees that she's alone.

"Don't tell me," he sighs. "She *still* sleeping?"

"She passed out, Zhak, you saw it. Right out cold in the hallway. We're damn lucky she didn't crack her head open when she hit that door," Maelle says.

"Who knows, maybe it would've knocked some of those lost memories back into her head," says Zhak with a sarcastic grimace. "But I think we've done her enough favours already, don't you?"

He leans back in his chair and takes out that tacky jewelled knife he likes to play with—some kind of antique tool meant for opening paper letters. He rotates it slowly, making a great show of examining its sharpened edge, running it under each of his varnished nails before he sets it back down next to his computer.

"Look, Zhak, just give her a damn break, all right?" Maelle says. "She needs a minute to deal with all this. And while we're on the subject, how about you thank me for getting us out of Kuuj without paying anything to that piss-merchant Tully, huh? I told you my plan was way easier."

Zhak spins the knife on the table, a blur of glittering shine. "More importantly," he says, "do you reckon she'll be convincing as a monk?"

"She's the best we were ever gonna find," says Maelle confidently. "Your time's run out anyway. It's her or nobody. But we need to get her on board, which means *you* need to let *me* play nice." She leans on the back of one of the chairs, bracing herself to hide how she's shaking.

"I got the update today from our contact, confirming the rendezvous point," Zhak says. "The monk-ship itself never docks, but they send out a shuttle for resupply runs. I know exactly where their party's going to be and when, for a day or so. That's how long we'll have to get our own little birdie onto that shuttle."

"Right. Where's that, exactly?"

"Nice try," Zhak says with a toothy grin. "Wouldn't you like to know? Let's just say we still have time to run an intercept course, but we need to get a move on."

Maelle holds back a biting reply and nods, schooling her face into something approximating compliance, or as close to it as she's ever likely to get.

"Now... the girl needs to understand that her payment will only come when the job's successfully completed, and when my client has acquired the merchandise... right?" Zhak arches a dark eyebrow. "Make that *very* clear to her."

Maelle grits her teeth. Sometimes, she wonders about the consequences of challenging Zhak, and about what will happen if her own plan should fail. Even if Page cooperates, Maelle's plan is beyond risky. If it doesn't go off without a hitch, Zhak is most definitely going to kill her.

Zhak may have pissed off some of the sector underworld, but he's still well-connected in ways she can only dream of, ways that could easily thwart any attempt to overturn him. He's got enough puppets dancing on his strings to make her life very difficult. And of course, Zhak has one particularly influential associate... his *client:* the Nightblade, one of the biggest crime bosses in the reaches. And that alone makes Zhak almost invulnerable.

Zhak's been working for the Nightblade ever since the beginning—a smuggler and arms dealer who's by every account just as reprehensible as Zhak, but a dozen times as powerful. A man who seized his criminal enterprise with a betrayal that Zhaklam Evelor helped him carry out. It's little wonder they're allies.

But Zhak has absolutely no idea that Maelle is baiting a trap of her own.

"So... if there's nothing new to report about the little birdie... is there a reason you've come back here?" Zhak asks, drawling each syllable in that way that somehow makes his underlying aristo accent stand out all the clearer. He bares enough of his teeth to expose the jewel on his incisor. "Your company, unfortunately, is not exactly compelling these days."

Maelle tries not to flinch. She holds her tongue and affixes a tight-lipped smile to her face. She's rehearsed this conversation so many times. *Scamships. This raid has to be done with scamships.*

"I was thinking. This crew you've got..." She glances toward the door with a grimace. "They're totally untested in a raid, Zhak. Now, I get it, you don't want anybody to know what we're doing out there, or scuppering this job—but if that's the case, wouldn't it be easier if the three of us—you, me and Page—just did this raid on our own? No boarding party, just us? There's less mess, less chance any artifacts get damaged—"

Zhak stops her with a raised palm. "Look, Maelle. I know these monks are pacifists and all, but this ship's carrying a *legendary artifact.* There'll be guards in there or something, even if there aren't very many. This ship's bound to be protected. We might have our birdie on the inside... but a raid like this without backup? That could be suicide."

"Hear me out." Maelle takes a long, steadying breath. "The Teyrians believe that the Felen are the demon-spawn of the Oblivion, right?" she says. "*You* told me that once. And what do you suppose Teyrians are meant to do when the Oblivion's creatures look upon them?" She fixes Zhak with a long, triumphant look. "Their sacred texts cover this very clearly. Only the gods can fight the Oblivion or her shadows. Humans are supposed to turn their backs, to avoid the cursing gaze. If those monks think they're being boarded by *aliens*... then they'll go to ground just as quick as any Union cargo crew."

Zhak studies her, slowly licking his lips. "Hmmm."

There's a spark of interest in his eyes, but something suspicious too—or wary—that Maelle can't quite read. His lip curls, and for one nauseating second, she wonders if he's pieced something together.

"So I have an idea—" she begins.

Zhak holds his hand up again, dismissing her. "I'll think on it," he says. "Now get out. Go check on the girl, see if she's up. We'll talk about this later."

PAGE FOUND
Zhaklam Evelor's Ship

"LISTEN, THERE'S ONE thing I really don't understand about all of this Teyr stuff," Page says. She's sitting up in bed, holding her scratched 'pad against her knees and squinting at the glitchy screen. Her curiosity has got the better of her, and she's given up on hiding the fact that she's *looking* from Maelle.

"Look at this. It says: *Their traditions have long taught that Teyr is the Origin world. The wellspring of human civilization, the Greenworld from whence we all took to the stars. The sacred crèche to which the Union owes all its ages of prosperity*," she reads out, making a face.

"What about it?" Maelle sits down on the edge of the bed.

Page might have spent the only eight years she remembers living in an isolated deep-space piss-can, but she's not completely ignorant. Maybe this is meant to be some kind of test.

"Well... I'm no scholar, that's for sure, but I thought *nobody* knew where humanity's Origin world was. So how can they just... tell people a lie like that?" she asks. "The First Primes are the oldest known settlements, right? And even those were all settled by the old seedships, centuries back—"

"Well, yeah, of course. If you employ empirical evidence, that's all real obvious," Maelle says with a smile. "It's like it says in there—Teyr was a Prime World. It's not like their history wasn't already known. Teyr was a founding member of the Union. It has seedship landing sites and everything. The same as all the other First Primes."

She cranes her neck to see the 'pad, looking over Page's shoulder at the article.

"But I think one reason the Teyrians ignore the evidence is that most of them probably can't access it," she explains. "See, their government cut off the public Q-link connections when they left the Union. So almost nobody in the quadrant knows what they're up to on Teyr right now. And the common people on Teyr don't know what anyone else is doing out *here*, either. Hard to believe, right? They're just… floating out there, all on their own."

Page shrugs. "I guess it's not really that hard to imagine," she says, thinking it over. "It's probably not that much different from living on a deep space outpost. Kuuj only ever has spotty network access, and it costs so much to get on a link that a lot of people don't even bother. They just pick up whatever news is available on the local troves. So I reckon it's probably a lot like that."

Maelle looks surprised, like maybe she's never really looked at it that way before. If you've never lived somewhere like Kuuj, Page supposes there'd be no real reason to even contemplate the idea. It strikes her, not for the first time, how little she really knows of the galaxy outside that one outpost.

"The only reason I paid for a connection sometimes was 'cause of my research," Page tells her. "I read the news and books and stuff because I wanted to see if I could jog my memory about anything. But for most people? Why the fuck would anyone on Kuuj care what's going on with the Primes, or who's losing some war out in the reaches? We were more worried about whether the water recycler was going to break down again, or how shitty the air quality was. A bad vent was way more likely to kill us than any aliens."

"Yeah," Maelle says, still sounding a little stunned. "That makes total sense."

Page looks back down to the 'pad, scrolling through an article about how Teyrians believed themselves to be the centre of the known universe. "I can tell you this, though. If I'd looked it up and some article told me *Kuuj Outpost* was the most important place in the universe? That one might've pushed me over the edge."

Maelle laughs, then, a soft, genuine laugh that almost startles Page. She looks completely different when her smile reaches her eyes for a moment—her whole face lights up, her chin tips upward, and it's as if something in her entire being *softens*. Like she's relinquishing something of the invisible armour she keeps around herself.

But it's gone as quickly as it came, and the next second her guard is back up and her smile looks tight and pasted-on again. She clears her throat against the back of her hand, wipes the softness from her face as if she's caught herself doing something involuntary.

"Right. I'm here to brief you when you feel ready," she says after a long pause. "If you're ready to hear more now, about the… job we have for you. The *offer*," she clarifies.

Sure, *offer* sounds better than *job*.

"The offer." Page tosses the 'pad down on the bed. She folds her arms over her chest. "How about you start by explaining to me how working for you will be any different from working under Tully? This is worse. Because now I'm stuck here on your ship, *and* I'm basically a prisoner. You might not have bought my debt, but I can't exactly leave. So…?" She looks at Maelle expectantly.

"This isn't at all like your contract with Tully," Maelle protests. She looks disgusted at the thought. "For one thing, Tully wasn't offering you anything like a fair wage. And we're willing to offer you two hundred thousand credits for approximately two weeks of work."

Don't react, Page tells herself, even as her heartbeat accelerates a little, and she wipes sweat from her palms against the blanket.

She has long ago taught herself that the last thing you want to do is show someone who you don't trust your true reaction. She holds it in, holds it back, and says nothing.

Maelle pauses before she goes on, as if weighing up her next words carefully. "Look, I'll level with you. Zhak's angling to steal this artifact for his client. Some old Source relic that they say is protected by the Golden-Feather monks," she says. "He's got good intel that a real important monk-ship will be passing not far from here, and that it'll be sending a shuttle out to resupply. I reckon it'll be on one of the ancillaries, though he won't tell me where. I'm sure he paid a fortune for this information."

Page swallows, and tilts her head to one side. "So what is it that you need me to do, exactly, that's worth two hundred thousand credits?" While she talks, she studies the ceiling, where the flickering bulbs are barely clinging to life. Playing it cool, as if this is something she does every day. Like she's a calm, collected character in a holo-drama.

"Your job will be to get that shuttle to pick you up," Maelle says. "You'll need to talk to these monks on the ancillary, do one of your little acts, and convince them *you're* a Teyrian monk of the Golden-Feather for long enough to finagle your way on board the shuttle. We'll give you a special Q-link device that we can use to track your location at a short distance. Once you get onto the monk-ship, you'll find out where exactly the artifact is located inside it, and you'll send us the info. Then we'll ambush the ship as it crosses back into deep space, we'll board it, and Zhak will get his target. Simple. That's all there is to it!"

"Right. Sounds real simple." Page rolls her eyes.

"When we're on board, we'll also extract you from the ship. We'll pick you up—safe and sound. Once Zhak's client has authenticated the artifact, then you'll get your payment." She rests her hand briefly on Page's wrist, as if in reassurance. "And then we part ways, all right? You'll be free *and* you'll have the money to go wherever you want."

Page scowls. There are a thousand questions she wants to ask about the logistics of this endeavour, but that would imply she's even considering accepting. So she sticks to the obvious. "And why should I believe you'll come good on your side of the deal?"

"Look. I'm not going to tell you that you'll have to take our word for it," Maelle says. She holds up a hand and smiles, and there's something mysterious in it, like there's a secret hiding just behind her lips. Something she won't say. Or can't say *yet*. "You'd be a gods-damned fool to work with Zhak. But Page... I'm hoping to show you that you can work with *me*," she whispers. "Together? You and me on the same side? We might actually pull this thing off."

LATER, WHEN PAGE is feeling more rested, Maelle takes her to the other side of Zhak's sprawling ship, to something she calls the *Dressing Room*. What it actually amounts to is a row of cleaned-out storage lockers, full of what look like various costumes and disguises. Every locker is crammed full of small, identical crates, their warped lids bearing peeling labels handwritten in blue marking-pen:

STARPORT CREW (BASIC UNION)
STARPORT CREW (S. PRIME)
SECURITY GUARD
MAINTENANCE WORKER
PERMIT OFFICIAL (MID RANK)

"What in the hells *is* all this stuff?" Page asks, kicking at the nearest crate. She studies the labels with narrowed eyes. "Costumes? What other scams is Zhak running with these?"

"A bunch. Some of which you can probably guess and others it's best not to think about," Maelle says as she moves between the crates, dragging her hand over them like she's looking for something. "Hmm... let's see, where did he put it... Look, here. I think this one's yours."

She drags a crate down from high up on one of the stacks, letting it drop the rest of the way to the floor with a metallic clang.

TEYRIAN TRADITIONAL, says the label.

"Go on, have a look," she says, prising off the lid. "Some impeccable Teyrian fashion. Just for you."

Page steps closer and peers into the box, and her heart skips. On the very top is an elaborately shaped bird mask and feathered cloak. The pieces are wrapped in clear packaging, indistinguishable from the ones in that blurry security camera capture. But when Maelle lifts them out and sets them gently to one side, there's much more to see below: layers upon layers of soft finery, silky suits and flowing shirts in pale pastel colours. Soft neckties and ornate hairpieces, filmy scarves and lace veils.

Page stares into the box for a long time before she turns back to Maelle.

"I've seen stuff like this," she says in a near-whisper. She blinks slowly, pursing her chapped lips when she finishes the sentence. The words feel delicate in her mouth, and she's not sure she should be saying them. "It was... in a holo, I think?" she adds weakly. "I'm not sure."

"Huh," says Maelle. "Did you know very much about Teyr, before all this?"

"Nope." There's that *pull* at the back of Page's mind again, like she's trying to remember something she can't quite get to take its full shape. "I don't think so. Well... maybe? I guess anything's possible when your memory's a black hole."

Maelle doesn't press her further. She situates Page in front of a long, cracked mirror in the corner of the Dressing Room, and unpacks several items of clothing for her to try on. Most of the tailored pieces that are long enough for Page are at least slightly too large for her gaunt frame. But one pale green jacket with bright gold buttons fits her almost perfectly, except for some extra room in the shoulders.

"We could pad this out," Maelle says, tugging at the extra fabric, "but that would ruin the shape. It would look better if I just take this in for you. How about that?"

Take this in is a strange phrase, one Page doesn't think she's heard. At least, not in Union Basic. She's uncertain what it means, or what exactly Maelle plans to do. But she nods her agreement.

Maelle seats her on top of two piled-up crates, turned toward the mirror. She rummages around in one of the other crates, and brings back a small, rectangular box containing various widths of thread, bobbins of ribbon, pins and buttons. Page tries not to stare too obviously, but she's fascinated by the delicate materials.

Of course she knows that clothes, and even fabrics, *can* be handmade. She's certainly seen enough mending, patching and amalgamation of threadbare pieces. But she's never had a piece of clothing on Kuuj that wasn't initially mass-produced. The two clothing shops in the concourse have only ever stocked cheap synthetics that never quite hang together properly, and she hasn't found anything much better in any of the luggage she's stolen. These are fine quality clothes—clothes that could really have belonged to a Teyrian aristo.

"Hmm... I guess this stuff would probably be long out of fashion by now," Page muses. "If Teyr's been out of contact with the Union for so long..."

It's not like the idea of 'fashion' could really be applied on Kuuj Outpost, but Page has been on the network enough and seen enough holos to know how swiftly trends in mainspace and planetside clothing change. They vary from city to city, planet to planet.

"*Change* like that doesn't really happen on Teyr," Maelle says matter-of-factly. "They like tradition, their stuff always stays the same. That's kind of their whole deal." She's putting pins in her mouth, mumbling around them as she continues: "Even before the Isolation, Teyrian dress hadn't really changed in hundreds of years. Remember, their whole story is about how they're the one and only unchanging and everlasting world, the planet that's been the same for all time, how it'll remain the same at the beginning and end of everything. They're all about *how things have always been.*"

Maelle makes a new fold in Page's sleeve, then secures it with one of the pins. She squints at the opposing shoulder, then carefully places another pin before she steps back to look at Page again, readjusting her stance.

"Where'd you learn to do this?" Page asks. "How to... *sew* clothes?"

"Tutorial vids, mostly," Maelle says. "It's a big deal on some of the Worlds, has been for ages. Making stuff by hand, making your own clothes. It's about... fighting against the reckless capitalism of factory-made things and all of that." She shrugs. "I do it because I find it soothing. I guess I just like making nice things sometimes, I dunno. I like seeing something I made myself."

Maelle holds out several bobbins of thread against the jacket's collar, comparing them to the colour of the fabric before she makes the best-matching selection. She slips the thread through the eye of a large needle and begins to stitch the garment while Page is still wearing it, fitting the sleeve to the curve of her arm as she moves toward the collar. The needle dances in her hand, dipping in and out of the fabric with careful precision, and Page doesn't even flinch.

She stares into the mirror, examining how the soft, wide sleeves of the jacket drape over her slender arm. She isn't quite as thin now as when she first awoke on Kuuj, but her cheeks are still hollowed from too many skipped meals. Her eyes look bright and feverish. Has her face always looked this... intense?

She almost doesn't recognize herself. Maybe it's the strangeness of being dressed in clothes that clearly don't belong to her, when she should be back in a dockyard alley on Kuuj with her bag of stolen junk, trying to scrape together the rent for her flimsy hab-cube. She wonders idly if that damned drone is banging on her apartment door yet.

"Stop tensing up," Maelle says, rearranging the bell of Page's sleeve. "Here. Bring your arms up a little, and keep your shoulders straight." She looks down at Page's balled fists with something like amusement, taking the last of the pins out from between her teeth. "You look like you're about to punch me. Warn me beforehand, will you? I've got sharp things in my mouth." She laughs. "Just try to relax."

It's been a long time since Page has been *relaxed* this close to another person. But when Maelle moves her arm again to reposition her, there's a strange tenderness in it. A touch that's calm and undemanding and… *gentle*. There is something in it that she's almost forgotten she's been lacking. She closes her eyes and thinks of being carried in that soft blanket, of being laid down gently somewhere safe and warm.

Maelle snips the thread and turns Page to one side again, examining her handiwork on the left sleeve. "So… I've been wondering. Why *did* you stay on Kuuj so long?" she asks. "You must've figured out that there was no way Tully could track you down if you left. So why keep working for him, when he was never going to let you pay off your debt? Why not run?"

Page shrugs. "What else was I gonna do? With no money to my name, no Union ident, no proof of any qualifications? Sticking with Tully was about the only option I had."

And there it is. The lie, the weakness in her story that she senses Maelle has already seen through. She suddenly feels exposed, a raw nerve laid out before Maelle's scrutiny.

Maelle straightens up, fixing Page with a sceptical look. "You know… somehow, I don't buy that," she says. "You're pretty damn resourceful. You've got guts, and like I said, you're *sneaky*. And lots of people out in the reaches have skills but no formal qualifications. It's not like you were gonna be applying to a corporate job on a Prime World or something." She narrows her eyes, studying Page for a reaction. "You don't need a Union ident to stow away on some dungheap outpost-hopper. You probably could've just robbed that asshole's shop on the way out and taken off. So why *didn't* you?"

Page bristles, her hands tightening into fists again, looking away from Maelle. It's a painful question, one she's asked herself too many times.

"Because I didn't know where to go," she finally whispers. "And I wanted to figure out *who I was*. So long as I stayed there, there was still a chance that I might find some clue what I was *doing* before I went under." She lets out a long breath. "But now... Well, I guess now I'll never know."

Maelle is quiet for a long moment.

"I'm sorry," she says, her voice soft. "Really. If there was anything I could do—"

"Look, don't worry about it. I'm pretty sure I already found out everything I was likely to—basically that I came out of some kind of clinical trial of faster stasis revival methods, and nobody knew more'n that." Page tilts her head and lifts up her hair, exposing the port scars at the back of her neck. "See how weird my stasis scars are?"

"Yeah, I saw them." Maelle nods, leaning in without getting too close. "They're unusual, that's for sure. They're so... neat, and small. Like, super precise. They don't usually look like that."

"I know. I've seen the regular kind." Page shrugs. "Nice scars, head empty, huh?"

"Ugh," says Maelle. "They're always claiming that they're doing something new or better with stasis, but it ends up just being the same old shit. I think humans are just not meant to hibernate." She shakes her head. "No one's done anything to *actually* improve stasis in like... sixty years. It's not safe long-term. Maybe it never will be. Nobody who goes down for more than a year or two ever walks away unscathed."

"They figured I was probably down for less than five years, based on the condition of my organs," Page says. "Guess that was enough to scramble my brains. Memory loss isn't a super common side effect, but it's not rare either. Scrambled brains is just one of the risks you take." She looks at her reflection again, staring into her own eyes like they might hold some elusive answer. "I reckon I must've really needed money for some reason if I signed on to something like that. These clinical trials are supposed to pay well. Sometimes I think... maybe I did it for someone else, like... to get money for my family or something." She blinks away tears. "Whatever it was, hope it was worth it."

"You never found a copy of your suspension contract, then, huh? I guess that would've had your real name and details on it. There wasn't anything like that in what we got from Tully."

"Nope, never found that." Page wipes at her eyes, careful to use the arm on the side Maelle isn't currently working on. "For years, I convinced myself that Tully must have a copy somewhere, that it was definitely somewhere in his records, if I could only get my hands on it. But then I realized—of *course* he wouldn't keep any of that around, even if he got it when he bought my debt. It was better for him not to." She sighs.

"Did he ever tell you *anything* more? Anything to go on?"

"Not much. Just that the research company went under and couldn't afford to properly finish my care after the revival. That's what usually happens with this kind of stuff, if the trial outcome fails. And that's how I ended up working for Tully, 'cause he paid off the cost of completing my revival and my rehabilitation."

"Fuck. That's one hell of a business," Maelle says, making a face. She takes one more look at her finished alterations on the jacket, then folds away the sewing kit. She motions for Page to spin all the way around and look in the mirror at the finished product. "Not bad, huh? I knew it would look nice."

Something flickers in the back of Page's mind when she looks at her reflection, at the way the shadows fall in that multi-layered soft fabric. Something almost like *recollection*.

Her cheeks heat at the compliment. "Thank you," she says. And it's a beat before she realizes that what came out was in Graya. *I give you thanks.*

Maelle's eyebrows go up. "I wish I knew how you learned to speak Graya. I'm guessing you must be from a Prime World. Or you went to some posh university, at least, like Zhak did." She smiles.

Page's face burns again. She can't possibly let on how badly she wishes that were true. "I have no idea where I learned Graya. I didn't even know what it *was* until I met you," she says. "And I've certainly never heard anyone else speaking it on Kuuj, except for that one time when those traders came through, and I realized I understood them."

Maelle looks at her thoughtfully. "I was wondering..." she says. "When you realized you understood them, why didn't you just extort the traders yourself? Or try to talk to them, if you were curious about the language?"

"No way. I'd never get my hands dirty with something like that," Page says. "Tully would've killed me if I attracted the wrong kind of attention. That's exactly the sort of thing that could bring real trouble down on us. See, Tully runs everything on the outpost, but Kuuj is small shit, in the scheme of things. We had a sort of... *non-interference policy* with the bigger guns in the sector. So we'd run our little shady business, and let them run theirs, and we'd just politely nod and look the other way if other operations did business in our space."

"You're talking about the Nightblade's crews, aren't you?" Maelle says, almost a growl.

The Nightblade. Page startles in recognition. She'd often heard that name whispered around the docks on Kuuj, and for a long time she thought it was the name of a shipping company. But she later learned that it's the alias of a crime boss who runs some kind of big-time smuggling operation, and possibly deals arms on the side. Page grimaces.

"By the look on your face, I gather you know him?" Maelle says. "Well, the Nightblade is Zhak's client. He's the one who wants to buy that Source artifact."

"I don't, like, know him *personally*." Page laughs. "Mainly we just saw his symbol on the shipping crates from time to time, back on Kuuj. A black dagger stamp. It meant you shouldn't mess with those." Page drops her shoulders dramatically. "Sure sucked when our only big drop in a fortnight was a Nightblade shipment. No chance for a take at all."

"It always comes back to him somehow," Maelle sighs. "Wouldn't be surprised if it was one of his people who got that intel on you. If you hadn't got yourself involved with those traders and their shipment, they wouldn't have had the proof you speak Graya."

"But I was cautious!" Page protests. "I was sure those traders never even noticed me there!" She winces at the memory. "All I did was tell the guards what I overheard, so that they could show up and demand a price for looking the other way on the missing permit. As they do." She sighs again. "See, the dockyard guards used to pay us for information about permit-dodging. And with the take so low these last few months, I couldn't afford not to chance it. Guess the joke's on me, huh? I'm the one that got played."

She makes a show of laughing as she says it, but in truth, she's way too embarrassed to find any amusement in this. Either she's losing her edge, or she never really had one. Maybe being a smooth operator on Kuuj isn't exactly the accomplishment she thought it was.

"Look... I really am sorry about how the kidnapping went down. And for how incredibly shitty Zhak's been to you." Maelle looks away. "Seriously, though, Page. This is the break we've *all* been waiting for. Finding you when we did was a gods-damned gift. Zhak says your Graya is remarkable."

"I... I have these dreams sometimes," Page blurts out before she can think.

"Dreams?"

"When I black out. I think they're bits of memories, maybe. Or visions, or something. I've never really been sure what they are. But when I'm unconscious... it's like... I'm always in this green place. And *that's* where I've heard Graya before."

"Hmm." A pensive look drifts over Maelle's face. "A green world?"

"I want to see more pictures of Teyr. Do you think maybe you could get me some new ones from the network?"

"Sure," Maelle says. "Well, I mean... not *new* ones. They're all going to be old—"

"It's all right." Page smiles. "Nothing on Teyr ever changes."

THAT NIGHT SHE sleeps, and she dreams of the green place.

The sound of a child laughing, a sound that's somehow gentler and more irreverent than any mirth she has heard from the dockyard urchins.

Bells tolling—four, five, six times—then a pause, then six chimes again.

The feeling of grass, warm grass beneath her bare feet, the strangest feeling. Can she ever remember feeling grass under her toes before?

She stands in a garden surrounded by flowers, her head tilted up to a wide sky above. A sky so big and unbroken and endless that it somehow seems bigger than the expanse of space. So impossibly blue but for a few pale clouds.

"Come, little darling," someone says. "It's time to come inside."

And those words are in Graya.

HUMANITY'S GIFT

Excerpt from Weekly Reflection Essay submitted by
[Student ID 1116]
First year Mythological and Spiritual Studies, University of Monaxas
Course Title: 'On Folk Traditions in the Primes and Beyond'
Essay Title: 'Music: Humanity's Gift to the Gods'

Of special note in this week's readings was the significance of music in many Prime traditions. Music has been called 'the lifeblood of art and civilization'[1] and 'the most human of the artistic pursuits.'[2] Some of the very oldest human texts we have – including some so old they may date back to the Source – have arrangements and rhythms that suggest they may once have been sung.[3] [Expand > References]

Many tales of the gods have been put to music in later ages, some in their original forms and others with alterations to their text as they migrated into other planetary cultures. This essay will examine three such musical pieces – which are presented in full in the appendices – and will compare two different versions of each piece. [Expand > List of titles and citations]

I will break down and analyse a translation of the earliest Prime (or Source) material – in each case, a text more than six hundred years old – and compare it to a modern rendition dated to within the past sixty years. I will focus here on the story element that is shared between the three: the idea of humanity bringing music to the gods.

The use of music in spiritual and religious contexts, in traditions across the Prime and Latter Worlds, has been connected to the myth of the Descent of the Great Goddess. In traditional tellings, it is said that while many other artistic and philosophical gifts were granted to humanity by their benevolent gods, music was an exception. Humans already had music before they had gods.

More than that: music was the gift that humanity gave to the gods in return.

DALYA
OF HOUSE EDAMAUN, IN HER TENTH YEAR
First-City, Teyr

ANDA AGOTE WAS as compelling as she was confusing, Dalya thought. She looked at the world in a way Dalya could not quite understand, but found endlessly fascinating.

Anda usually did not mind what kind of questions Dalya asked her, and she herself asked questions constantly. Not only did she *ask* them, she actually expected them to be *answered*, reacting with shock whenever Dalya confessed that she had never pressed Uncle for an explanation for something or other.

It is important to surround yourself with friends who will lead you in the right direction, Uncle always said. It was the reason why the Gepcot held counsel to advise the High Speaker. Why, even the Great Goddess did not rule the celestial realm alone, but instead consulted the gods of the Pantheon in all things. She heard their opinions, both fierce and gentle, and the Pantheon governed all things together. Even the gods were not infallible—*the goal is not perfect harmony, but perfect self-knowledge.*

Anda certainly did lead Dalya in new and unexpected directions. Whether or not that amounted to the *right* direction, or the direction of self-knowledge, Dalya was never quite sure. The moon girl had come into Dalya's life like the storm that had blown away that pavilion the day after the voyager landed.

Anda was an unstoppable gale, a force of nature that would come to sweep her along more swiftly and more easily than Dalya would have thought possible.

In Anda's company, Dalya always felt off-kilter, uncertain. But it was not an unpleasant feeling—she felt excited, too. For the first time since her parents died, since Uncle had declared her the heir of House Edamaun—perhaps for the first time since she could actually remember—Dalya felt *alive*. And she wanted to spend all the time she could with the girl from the moon.

Anda's uncle, Derin Agote, never came to the Edamaun house again after that first impromptu dinner. In the weeks and months that followed, Anda's driver would always drop her off alone, and Dalya would run across the grounds to the side gate to meet her. But Anda often brought gifts to Uncle from Ker Agote, which she dutifully delivered to his study: a plate of spicy baked goods, a bottle of plum wine, a box of fruit. Once, she brought a packet of seeds for the garden, some unique and exquisite variety of white lunar flower that had been developed on Meneyr.

To Dalya's surprise, not only did Uncle receive Ker Agote's gifts with great interest, he, too, seemed to be almost charmed by Anda. At the very least, he was interested in acknowledging her presence, which was more than he'd done for any of Dalya's music conservatory friends. Uncle had never been bothered to interact with any of them, few as they'd been. But Uncle always asked after Anda, and mentioned her absence if she hadn't been to visit for a week or two.

"Where is Derin Agote's scamp?" he would ask. "I haven't seen her here lately. I hope they are both well." Occasionally, Uncle sent a small gift back to Ker Agote in Anda's care: once a soft green necktie in a fancy box, once a tiny glass vase, once a brick of luxury butter.

But Derin Agote himself never did return to the house, despite Dalya's frequent exhortations that Anda bring him along. He had seemed an interesting fellow, and Dalya wondered sometimes if he got lonely when Anda wasn't at home, especially when she came to stay with the Edamauns for several days running. She always found it odd how Ker Agote stayed away, but in her youthful enthusiasm over Anda's visits, she never gave it much thought.

"He is just terribly busy right now," Anda would say. And another time, "He is travelling up north, to see the new voyager ships. Perhaps he will come to dinner next month."

Sometimes, Anda said, she had to stay with a neighbour for a while when her uncle was travelling to the launchyards. The neighbour was very kind, but Anda missed her uncle. And she was awfully bored there.

"Why not come stay with us, then?" Dalya asked her. And of course, Anda did.

As little as they heard from Ker Agote, Anda's visits became increasingly frequent, sometimes lasting for a whole week or more. The girls shared everything, and with Anda, Dalya was the furthest thing from timid. With Anda, she did not question herself constantly anymore, nor wonder if she was saying the right thing or playing the part of the Edamaun heir with sufficient gravitas.

No, with Anda she was just *Dalya*, in a way she had never known she could be.

They spoke often of the Moon-City, and of Anda's life there, and of how it was different from living on Teyr. Anda was fascinated with the planetside weather, with the sun and the rain and the wind and the variations in temperature on her skin. Under the dome on Meneyr, she said, nothing ever changed.

Something about that struck Dalya as odd—that Meneyr should change less than Teyr, when it was Teyr, after all, that was the everlasting and *unchanging* world. She wondered what the sages made of it, or if they'd discussed it when they debated whether Meneyr would be saved in the cataclysm.

Anda always wanted to hear music, and Dalya often played

for her on her gold-stringed lyren. Dalya had never thought herself the most gifted musician—Nathin surely would have far outmatched her, she always thought—but after many years of lessons at the conservatory, she could coax many beautiful melodies from the instrument. She played and played—songs of beauty and bounty, of love and legend, all the songs she could remember—and Anda sat entranced through every verse.

"What sort of music did you have on Meneyr?" Dalya asked one day. "Was it like ours?"

"Some was the same as here," Anda said. "But we had... more. More kinds, I suppose." She looked down at Dalya's instrument. "I used to play a lyren back home, too. It wasn't so pretty as this one, and it sounded a little bit different, but—"

"Oh! You must teach me one of your songs!" Dalya demanded excitedly, holding out the gold-stringed lyren. "Please. Sing me something from Meneyr. Can you play me something I haven't heard before?"

Anda laughed and took the lyren. "Yes, of course! I can try." She plucked at the instrument and tuned its strings to a slightly different pitch, manipulating it with such familiarity that she seemed to do it almost by instinct. "Do you want to hear a happy song, or a sad one?"

"Happy, please," Dalya said. "I'd like something to cheer me up today."

"I know exactly which one you need, then. Listen. This one is *really* funny."

Anda hoisted the instrument up onto her hip, holding it at an angle, her fingers finding their places on the strings. And then she began to sing, in a voice deeper and more resonant than her speaking voice.

It was a bawdy ballad, in which Dalya recognized several words she'd been told never to say, and a good few others whose meaning she could only guess at through context. The song told of a goddess who'd once claimed a human lover, with some... *intimate* details of the act that Dalya had never heard spoken out loud.

"Everlasting Lady have mercy... where did you learn *that?*" Dalya asked breathlessly when Anda had finished. Her cheeks were hot, her pulse pounding in her wrists, and she hoped by all that was good that Heral was not nearby to hear any of those words. Heral did have an inconvenient habit of hovering at doorways.

Anda grinned. "I didn't learn it at the temple," she said slyly. "I thought you might fancy something a bit less *serious*. Everything here is always so... solemn."

That's because our souls and our safety are at stake, and we must take our godly duties seriously, Dalya thought, hearing the words in Uncle's stern voice. But she didn't correct Anda. Instead, she took the instrument and held it as Anda had, twisting her fingers into the unfamiliar forms.

"Show me," she said. "How do you play a chord that goes all... wobbly like that?" Anda had made the instrument *trill,* a sound Dalya hadn't even known it could make, by dragging her fingernail backward over the string, then tapping it with the flat of her hand. "I'm pretty sure that isn't how you're meant to play it."

"There is no one right way to play it, there are a lot of different ways," Anda said, no malice in her voice. "It's all music. And it doesn't belong to Teyr alone." She pursed her lips. "Did you know music doesn't even belong to the gods? We taught it to *them!* There's a song about that, too—it says that hearing the music from a celebration on the Greenworld was what drew the Little Bird down to investigate."

"Really?" Dalya leaned forward, her mouth open. She had taken to collecting these stories of Anda's about the Goddess, telling them back to herself when she found it hard to sleep. Even now, she was still discovering new ones all the time—Anda seemed to know an endless parade of them. "People always say that music is godly. I suppose I just... assumed that the gods must've invented it," she muses.

"Well, maybe it's godly *now*. But no, it was all ours at the beginning. That's why music is our most human creation! The gods taught us many things, but there are some things we have always done better than they do."

"I am certain that some of the elders would not like to hear you say that." Dalya laughed.

Anda fixed her clear gaze on Dalya. "Well… the elders aren't right about *everything*. Neither are the sages or the monks. And neither is your uncle."

Neither is your uncle. Dalya felt the words settle in the pit of her stomach, along with all the things she held back and shared with no one but Anda.

She had scarcely realized it yet, but the more time she spent with Anda, the more she began to wonder what other not-quite-right things she might believe.

MAELLE KRESS
Zhaklam Evelor's Ship

"So. This idea of yours... Scamships, huh? I'm listening." Zhak sits back in his chair and looks at her expectantly. "Where is it you think I'm gonna get a hold of a scamship crew on such short notice? We haven't got a lot of time here."

"I have a lead." Maelle forces herself to look him directly in the eye, steadying her nerve. "What if we contacted Reece Bereda? No one makes 'em better."

"What?" Zhak's eyebrows jump at the mention of Bereda, as if he's surprised Maelle even knows that name. "No. Nuh-uh. Absolutely not." He laughs darkly. "Reece Bereda's not too fond of me, to put it mildly. I haven't seen her since the Void Snake went down. And I wouldn't have a fucking clue how to get in touch with her, anyway, *if* she's even in business anymore. I heard she retired."

"Yeah, well, I heard otherwise." Maelle looks down at Zhak's knife on the table instead of looking at him. "What if I said I can get a direct line to Bereda? There's no need to mention your name. She won't even know you're involved in this."

She can feel Zhak's unyielding stare on her. He seems torn between derisive disbelief and burning curiosity. "*You* have a line to Reece Bereda? The little scamship matriarch herself?"

"I have a contact on the inside," Maelle says obliquely. "I

can get right to her. But I'd need to go to the Laithe system, in person. Bereda doesn't deal over comms."

"Laithe? Fuck *me*." Zhak curses, shaking his head. "C'mon, Maelle. You know I can't risk goin' anywhere near the Laithe system. That's where some of the Void Snake's old buddies are holed up. I'm sure there's more than a couple of 'em who are still hot enough about what happened to put a plasma shot through me—not to mention Bereda herself."

"Fine. Then let me go there alone," says Maelle. "You don't even have to enter the system. Drop me off at Felwae Outpost with Page, and we'll take a hopper over to the Laithe orbital."

"Even Felwae's a bit of a risk," Zhak says with a wince. "It's gonna take too much time to get out there. Our timeline's tight already."

"Yeah? Well, I saw that nav chart you had up the last time," Maelle says, folding her arms. "I don't know where exactly we're going, but Felwae's not *that* far out of the way."

An irritated fury flashes in his eyes. "Be that as it may, Maelle, I am not letting you *take our monk* off this ship—"

"*I* would keep the girl until we meet back up again," Maelle says matter-of-factly. "That's not negotiable."

Zhak makes a show of examining his knife. "Who says I'm negotiating with you?"

"If you want me to get you Bereda's scamships, then Page stays with me." She raises her chin. "Call it insurance."

"Call it whatever you want, but I'm still in charge of this operation, in case there's been some misunderstanding." He smiles cruelly, his fingers tightening on the jewelled hilt of the ornamental blade.

"You're in charge of exactly nothing if Page doesn't cooperate," Maelle says. "If she refuses to do it, or she gets on that monk-ship and decides to tell them she's been put up to it, this'll be over in a hot second. I need to sell her on this thing!" She folds her arms. "Listen, if I take Page with me to Laithe, I can keep working on her in the meantime. I'll get her to trust me. We need to treat her like a *friend*. Right now she has no reason to believe us. But I can see damn well that she's desperate for something to believe *in*. We can exploit that, Zhak! We can pull this off."

It puts a bad taste in Maelle's mouth, talking about Page like this. She feels oddly like she's betraying the junk thief's confidence. But Zhak is nodding in slow, thoughtful approval.

"Zhak, I can do this. I know I can get to Bereda. Do you want the scamships or not?"

"Hmmm," he says, like he wants her to think he's still debating it. And yet, the little quirk of his lip tells Maelle he's already made up his mind. "You'd have to be real quick about it. Get in and get out, Maelle. Make damn sure you leave my name out of it. And don't tell Bereda's people what we're lifting, or that the client is the Nightblade—"

"Look, I'll keep it discreet. They generally don't ask too many questions."

Zhak gives the knife on the table a long spin. Maelle watches it circle round and round and round, her eyes fixed on it like a portent. When it comes to rest, the blade is pointing toward him.

"You'll have less than three days to get into the Laithe system, find Bereda, make the deal, and get back," Zhak says. "So you'd better be damn sure your contact will be good for setting up a meeting that fast."

"I can get the meeting." Maelle pulls in another steadying breath. "I grew up around there. And… I know Reece Bereda's daughter."

WHEN MAELLE POPS her head into the junk thief's room, Page is sitting on her cot in silence. She's staring into the middle distance, her 'pad open on her folded knees.

"Hey. Uh… Hey, Page. You doing all right?" Maelle says. The words sound hollow, insufficient. "You look a little freaked out."

"I'll be fine," says Page. "Just... been having some more weird dreams, that's all."

"What, you mean the blackout dreams?"

"Sort of," Page says. "It's like that, only... it's kind of... merging now. I think it's blending in with all the stuff I've been reading about Teyr. It's kind of creepy, to be honest." She takes a deep breath. "Last night I heard this bell chiming, and—I mean, I've heard that same bell in my head for years. But this time I specifically noticed that it rang *six times*." She holds up the 'pad. "*The six-chime of the bells.* That's a Teyrian thing."

"Wow. Maybe you really *are* a lost monk from the Teyrian Protectorate! Wouldn't that be something?"

Maelle laughs, but the junk thief doesn't crack a smile. Instead, she draws back and pulls her arms tight around her knees, dropping the 'pad onto the blanket next to her. She says nothing. There's an inscrutable look on her grey-tinged face, like she might be about to cry, or maybe she's thinking about punching Maelle. It could really go either way.

"Look... maybe when this is all through, you could try again to find out who you are," Maelle says, pivoting quickly to sincerity. "With two hundred thousand to your name, you could widen the search, right? You could even go back to Kuuj, if you decided—"

"Yeah. Sure, maybe," Page mumbles.

"Page..." Maelle reaches out and rests a tentative hand on Page's arm. "I'm sorry. I wish there was something I could do to help you *right now*, but there isn't."

"Oh, yeah?" The junk thief scowls. "Well, if you're so serious about helping, how about you get me those pictures of Teyr, like I asked for?" Her gaze hardens, like something of her resolve has suddenly recovered. "If I'm supposed to convince these people I've ever been on Teyr, I'm gonna need a little more to go on."

Maelle lets her breath out in relief. "On it," she says. "I pulled another archive for you already, with a bit more recent stuff in it." She smiles tentatively. "There's really not a lot on the public network, though, so it takes some digging. There hasn't been a newsfeed out of Teyr for ages, and even before the split they were pretty reclusive."

"How'd they do it?" Page asks curiously. "Cut themselves off, I mean. They just... deactivated all their Q-link devices? Destroyed their satellites?"

"Something like that," Maelle says. "The official story goes that they shut off their interplanetary comm links when they broke with the Union, and the Union cut off their side of the feeds, too. So in theory, there should be total signal silence between us and them." She draws a finger across her lips, then pauses. "But of course, that's not *entirely* true. They definitely *do* have operational Q-links left. There's groups inside the Protectorate who've been in contact with the outside world this whole time. As with everything, you just need to pay the right people."

"Yeah." Page looks thoughtful. "You know, I was also wondering how I'm—"

Maelle holds up a hand and smiles slowly. "Shhh, shhh. Listen, pal. Hold those questions, all right? I'm going to tell you some things soon, but not here." She tries to keep her tone nonchalant. "How'd you fancy a little trip planetside with me?"

"Planetside!" Page's eyes go saucer-wide, and despite her immediate attempt to hide her interest, she can't quite keep the startled wonder from her voice. "Where?"

"I'm heading down to Laithe for a couple days to look after some business," Maelle says. "And I managed to convince Zhak to let you come. How's that sound? It'll be just you and me."

Page bites at her lip, looking somewhere between concerned and outright alarmed. "You're serious? You... you could take me planetside with you?"

"Absolutely. And to a green world, no less! I think you're going to love Laithe. It's where I grew up." Maelle cringes inwardly at the overly bright excitement in her voice. She misses home, in a manner of speaking, but she's not exactly relishing the thought of landing on Laithe.

Page shoots her a dubious look, like she's trying to figure out what kind of game Maelle is running. But she does sit up straighter, adjusting the collar of her shirt. She's wearing one of the billowing, lacy Teyrian blouses in a pastel green today, and she's paired it with some baggy navy-and-yellow trousers that look like they came out of one of the security guard getups. Quite the combination.

"Well? What do you say?" Maelle prompts her again. "You want to see a planet?"

There's a long, drawn-out silence while Page stares down at the 'pad on the bed beside her. Maelle holds her breath without meaning to.

And then, at last, Page looks up and says, "All right. Let's go to Laithe."

"Yes!" Maelle grins with unabashed triumph before she lowers her voice to a conspiratorial whisper. "Down there, we'll be on our own, pal," she says. "And then... I can tell you everything."

THE STORYTELLER

Recording start 04:28:15

You want more stories? Oh, I got stories. Too many, maybe. More than one person should really have rolling around in their head, even one as old as me. [*chuckles*] More than I have the time to tell. Some I've forgotten, and some I wish I could.

Thing is, every time I start to tell one... gods damn it. I realize it's got *him* in it somewhere. It's inevitable, in the end. Where I went, he went. It was that way for years, his fingerprints all over my life, long before his knife was in my back.

Look... I wasn't going to talk about him in this thing at all. That's what I told myself, when I started recordin' this. A man like him, he doesn't deserve any kind of memorial. But I suppose some parts of my stories – and some parts of *me* – wouldn't quite make sense without him.

I won't give him his proper name, in any case, or any of the other aliases he gave himself later. Fuck that. We'll just call him Vonnie, 'cause that's how he introduced himself to me when I first met him.

We ran into each other at a bar when I was – what? Nineteen, maybe twenty standard? Damn. A long, long time ago. Vonnie was about the same age, and he was a charmer in this irreverent, nihilistic sort of way. The type who wore 'not giving a shit' like a fancy jacket, you know what I mean? But truth be told, my first impression was that he was naive as a babe. And he was. He was a rich kid who'd watched too many action holos and decided he wanted to be some kind of a big-time gangster.

See, Vonnie was always this way. He thought he was complicated, and that's the most charitable thing I can say about him. Came from an old family, born on Saymu Prime with stars in his eyes and a taste for fine things. He had a real rebellious streak, and a nose for drama. But I thought I was safe from all of that, see, because I knew all about resilience when I met him. I thought Vonnie was soft and foolish, and I was clever and hard. I thought we complemented each other that way. But I never really knew what surviving meant until he tried to take it all from me.

Anyway... Well, let's leave all that aside. This story isn't about Vonnie and me. But it's important that you know these things about him, when I tell you about how he got us mixed up in all this business with the Teyrian Protectorate. Because Vonnie was born with all the opportunities anybody could possibly have, and yet he always wanted to be doing something different. Wanted to 'make his own way,' that's what he always said. He did whatever the hells he wanted, even if he did do it with inherited money. What Vonnie wanted, Vonnie took.

It wasn't long after we met that we went into business together, and he started us out with a pile of that family money he'd siphoned off from some relative. One-point-nine million, that's what we had. To me, at the time, that seemed like an incomprehensible fortune. It was enough to buy us a decent cargo ship and some expensive plasma guns he didn't know how to use. I had to teach him how to shoot, and he never did get any good at it. [*laughs*]

Vonnie always thought he was the mastermind between us. But he never had the faintest clue how to run a business, because they don't show you *that* in the holos. Between his money and my brains, though... There was a point when I thought maybe we'd manage all right. I thought that maybe we'd – that we could –

[*There is a long pause. Static. Possibly a splice in the recording, before the Storyteller carries on.*]

Well, never mind that. Like I said, this story isn't about him, it's about the business. Yes. That's what I'm talking about here. How we got into our dealings with the Teyrian Protectorate, before Vonnie burned down my life.

I can't exactly recall how it was that we ended up running that first transport job to the Teyrian system. It was definitely Vonnie who brought it in originally, but I remember it was supposed to be a one-off. Just some basic smuggling run, some completely pointless shit that paid a heap – bringing crates of Prime-made booze or something like that out to Meneyr.

See, there was always this bunch of rich fucks out there on that Teyrian moon who got off on the fact that they could buy the banned interplanetary stuff. They wanted anything they could get a hold of from the Union. Things you couldn't get on Teyr itself. They'd pay any price for it, whether it was booze or literature or art... or just plain old Q-link comms so they could tap into some of the Union networks. There was always a market. And that's where we started out, believe it or not. Running offworld booze to the dark side of Meneyr, hooked up by some Saymu buddy of Vonnie's.

Now, I had some experience in the biz, in the practical sense – I mean, I'd been a small-time smuggler since I was old enough to work a cargo clamp – but I didn't know a damn thing about something like *this*. It felt like such a big deal to me. Trading with a system that had left the Union?

At first, I was learnin' all kinds of new things. Like how the money transfer was even gonna work, 'cause of course, the Teyrian Protectorate didn't officially have any Union currency anymore. And [*laughs*] well, it's also fucking illegal to trade with them at all. Whatever Union chits anyone might've hoarded in the Protectorate, those would've been deactivated years ago. So I didn't understand how we'd even get paid for this job.

But did any of that ever stop 'em from finding a way? No, of course not! I'll say this: one thing you learn as soon as you get your hands on a little bit of money is how often 'that's impossible' just means 'you haven't put up enough of a bribe yet.'

So how did Meneyr's rich fucks pay for their Union goods? Well, they'd just run all the payments through Saymu Prime! Those ties go waaay back, we're talking pre-Union, and gods know that the weird dealings between Teyr and the old SP imperial territories are still a whole thing. Anyway, so these bigshot Teyrian moonfolk, they all had secret Union bank accounts on Saymu Prime, and they accessed them with their illegal Q-links. They'd just casually transfer us thousands and thousands of credits through Union channels. Just like that. I tell you, my mouth dropped open like a gawping fish.

Gods, that was a time. I was young and wide-eyed, seeing those kinds of sums for the first time... and fuck, I was *fascinated*. That was probably my first real glimpse of 'how the worlds work' or whatnot. And I knew, even then, that this was exactly how I was going to build my business. This was what I wanted to do with my life, finding the gaps between what people wanted and what they were allowed to have.

On the surface, Vonnie had the connections and the money to get it all started. And me, I had the *other* kind of connections. I knew how and where you could travel with unregistered ships. I knew what outposts were good for fake permits. I knew the ways to move so you didn't get hassled by the patrols. That's the kind of shit that a Prime education doesn't teach you. [*laughs*]

So anyway. Off we went to the Teyrian Protectorate, just us and a crew of three, and all these crates of booze in the hold... and that was only the beginning. One job led to another, and before too long, we'd dropped most of our other business to focus on that Meneyr run. Absolutely nothing else was paying as high as that route. All we were doing was running holds full of random Union-made shit for them, hauling all this Saymu stuff to Meneyr. I didn't know what half of it was.

Now, even back then it was getting more dangerous out in the deeps, with the Felen moving in closer. There were dozens of orange zones all along the routes we took... but the war heating up also meant the Union had no time to chase illegal trading like what we were doing. The logistics of travel got a bit trickier, but the authorities... well, the Union authorities definitely got laxer. Especially when we were heading out of Union space. They didn't really seem to give much of a fuck about us or what we were doing out there.

Those were the days when we had it all. We were good. We were fast, we were reliable, trustworthy and untraceable. We moved things for years like that – it was seven, maybe eight years that we were doing this constant back and forth. It would take about three months for a ship to get out to the Protectorate, and then we'd turn straight back around to the Saymu system and do it again. After a while we had a fleet of about a dozen ships flying our routes on a constant loop, and Vonnie and I stopped running ships ourselves – we were just takin' care of admin. Occasionally, we went out to Meneyr, but mostly we coordinated things from the safety of Union space.

We had a base in the Saymu outer system, and Vonnie took care of all the negotiations with the Graya speakers. I learned a few little bits and pieces of Graya over the years, but Meneyr still teaches Union Basic, so I could get by in Basic with most of our contacts. Thing is, most of those moonfolk still preferred to do all their business in Graya. And so there was a lot I didn't know about what Vonnie was doing. Things that went over my head, even when I heard the commcalls. Things I probably should've kept an eye on. But, you see, I trusted him. I had these wild ideas about loyalty. And back then, well, maybe none of us really knew any better.

After it all went down... The way it ended, well, for a long time I wished I hadn't met Vonnie at all. I wished I'd walked the other way that night at the bar. I wished that I'd left earlier, or that a different song had come on the speakers – that's the very first thing Vonnie ever said to me, you know? He asked me about the song. He turned to me, yelling over this loud music, and he leaned in and said to me: 'Hey, do you know this song? What song is this?' [*laughs*]

Gods damn it. I guess that probably should've been my first clue, if you believe in such things. Sometimes, the universe speaks. 'Cause that fucking song... it was 'You'll Know It When It's Over.'

PAGE FOUND
Felwae Deep Space Outpost

FELWAE OUTPOST IS a run-down deep-space stopover that reminds Page all too much of Kuuj. It's perhaps a little newer and less patched-together, and the air is significantly more breathable, but parts of it look startlingly like they fell out of the same dingy mould. Page can't help but wonder if this place has its own Tully, and its own dockyard kids fist-fighting for territory. If she squints a little, she could almost pretend she's back on Kuuj again—except there are *so* many more people jostling for space here. *Overwhelming* is the word that comes to mind.

Maelle winds her way confidently through the crowded concourse, ducking expertly through the throng, turning corners without checking the signs. Page struggles to keep up, walking unsteadily in those slippery-soled blue boots. She's constantly finding herself in someone's way, her sleeve catching on someone's bag, her foot snagging the edge of a vent. It's so much noisier than the Kuuj concourse, even on its busiest days. She's not sure if she's *ever* seen this many people packed into such a small area.

Page is more than relieved when they finally find a place to sit down. Maelle buys them a couple of cold drinks, and they slide into a booth in the grimy bar on the upper level while they wait for their hopper to the Laithe system. This place is equally reminiscent of Page's old haunts, and she hunches down in the peeling seat, trying to make herself as small as possible.

Page knows there's nothing particularly memorable about her, especially with the plain sweater currently covering most of her gold-trimmed Teyrian blouse. Still, it feels like everyone in the room is eyeing her suspiciously, like she doesn't belong here. She probably should have worn something less conspicuous, but she's grown so attached to these delicate Teyrian fashions—there's something oddly comforting about them. She quickly shoves the gilded collar of her blouse back under the sweater.

Beside her, Maelle closes her eyes and sniffs at the bar air. "You smell that? Mmm. Cheap liquor and coolant!" A wistful smile crosses her face. "This always reminds me of almost being back home."

Almost back home. The phrase elicits a pang of something Page can't quite name, like an echo deep in her chest. If she were capable of anything like homesickness for Kuuj, she supposes she might feel it now. But for the people who live here on Felwae, these walls probably feel just as much a prison as a protection. Page sinks down even further in the seat, resting the side of her head against the faded panel wall.

Directly in her line of sight, she idly watches a figure leaning on the end of the bar: a young man with a half-finished drink in front of him, constantly checking his comm like he's waiting for a message. There's a pair of pink-tinted glasses sitting on the top of his head, nestled in his shoulder-length curly hair. He wears what looks like a shipping guild jacket, dark green with round patches from an unfamiliar guild on the arms. Kuuj didn't get many guild types, but Page has seen them from time to time.

She regards the man with curiosity, leaning over to whisper to Maelle. "That guy over there... over at the bar? He's got a guild jacket. Do you get a lot of guildsfolk round here?"

Maelle looks up with little interest as the man turns back to his comm again. "A few. Sometimes."

"Think he's going to Laithe?"

"Doubt it. He's probably headed in the other direction, out to the deeps," Maelle says. "Could be a supply-aider." Seeing the lack of comprehension on Page's face, she clarifies: "Humanitarian aid delivery."

"Oh." Page pauses, searches her memory and comes up blank. "What's that mean?"

"Well, there's all these outposts and space stations waaay out in deep space, like your Kuuj... but a lot of 'em have been totally cut off by the orange zones. And the gods know the Union's been doing a piss-poor job resupplying them. People are starving out there, and with all the travel bans and comms blackouts, it's tough for anyone to get to them. So some of the shipping guilds stepped in. They've put together these quasi-legal supply chains to bring food and medicines out to the deeps."

"Wow. Right." Page hadn't ever seen anything like that on Kuuj. In that respect, she supposes, Kuuj has been very lucky. Traffic through their hub may have been dropping, but they had never been cut off from regular supply chains. Tully's merchants in the marketplace seldom seemed to have trouble getting in the cheap, mass-produced merchandise and crappy food they overcharged for.

Page has never really thought about what would have happened if Kuuj *couldn't* be resupplied; how little food was actually produced in their meagre hydroponic decks, how there was virtually no manufacturing besides a couple of industrial printers that mostly did ship parts for repairs. She had not considered how quickly they would all starve, just like the outposts Maelle's talking about.

In truth, though, it's like she told Maelle: Kuuj's inhabitants were generally way more worried about the life support systems blowing than anything else. A fatal failure in some critical, creaking system has always felt much more likely than a slow death from an external disaster. Still, the thought is chilling. Deep space is terribly lonely. Would anyone even notice if one outpost was cut off, the people left behind? Kuuj's fate never seemed to matter that much to anyone. Maybe even the supply-aiders would forget about it.

Page studies the stranger standing by the bar again. Guild Jacket is talking to another man now, someone new who just arrived. The well-dressed newcomer hands him a small, flat package.

"What do you think about that guy in the fancy suit, then?" Page asks Maelle. "What'd you reckon is up with that?"

"Private courier from a rich investor, maybe?" Maelle shrugs. "Who do you think pays for all those supplies, pouring that money into the guilds? It's not the guilds themselves, that's for sure."

"Rich people?" Page widens her eyes. "Rich people who... actually want to help?"

Maelle gives a cynical little cough in the back of her throat. "Well. Help *themselves*, mostly. Or their consciences, if you wanna be nice about it." She follows Page's gaze to the two figures, watching them along with her. "The supply-aid chain is bankrolled by Prime World billionaires. Guess at least a few of those assholes feel guilty about sitting safe in their mansions and asteroid-belt strongholds while the rest of the galaxy's being rinsed by the Felen." Her voice drips with sarcasm.

"'Course, even for the soulless ones who have more greed than empathy running in their veins, there's advantages to be had," she goes on. "They make a deal *now* to keep one of the guilds afloat, banking on the fact that when trade *does* start up again, they'll get a better contract. These big Prime families, they think long-term. It's not one human lifetime they're thinking of. Some of their corporations are hundreds of years old. Old money will outlast the war, and they're still making connections to protect that power."

"Huh," Page says.

"I guess it's as good a gamble as any," Maelle laughs. "Assuming humanity's even around in another couple hundred years."

The Graya word for *everlasting* flashes up in Page's mind, too briefly for her to wrap a thought around it. She sips slowly from her drink and continues to stare in front of her.

And then, there's a ping on Maelle's device—a local ping, one that sounds on every single device in the bar. All around them, people are fishing out their devices, looking around curiously, checking their screens.

Maelle scrambles to grab her comm. But when she flicks it open and angles it over for Page to see, it's a generic alert. One sent to all local devices from Felwae's outpost network.

BULLETIN – FELWAE OUTPOST – Hopper terminating at LAITHE SYSTEM, PLANETARY ORBITAL is delayed due to a temporary power outage. Apologies for any inconvenience.

"Gods damn it," Maelle mutters.

"A power outage again? These hoppers are a gods-damned joke," says the guy in the guild jacket. He's moved closer to them now, Page notices with a start—he's no longer over at the bar. Now he's sitting alone in the booth directly across from them. He gives Maelle an exasperated, commiserating look as he turns his handheld toward them, showing the same brightly coloured dispatch on his screen.

"Yep. Outrageous," Maelle sighs. She shoots Page an eyeroll that says she's not really in the mood for outpost small-talk. But there's no avoiding it when people are stuck in a transit hub and there's any kind of delay.

Guild Jacket slides his comm back into his pocket. "I guess you two must be heading toward the Laithe system, then?"

"Maybe," Maelle says, looking at him askance. "What's it to you?"

The guild trader gives a good-natured shrug, raising his hands in mock defence. "Hey, just making conversation. I'm heading for the deeps shortly, myself. Just waiting on a colleague." He's smiling in that way that *might* be flirtatious, but could equally just be the slightly vacuous words of a bored stranger making conversation. "Name's Dex, by the way."

"You doing guild work in the deeps?" Page asks, before she can think the better of it. "Or something else?" She doesn't offer her name in return.

Dex just laughs, adjusting the pink glasses perched on his head. "Definitely *something else,*" he says. "I do a little bit of everything these days."

Page studies him. Most people would consider Dex plenty handsome, she thinks. His bronze skin has that ruddy tone that usually only comes from spending time on actual worlds, or access to expensive sunlamps, and he has the kind of plump cheeks that one never sees on Kuuj.

On the whole, he looks very much like how Page imagined the characters in some of the adventure novels that she used to download. He's charming, but there's something clever and calculating in his gaze. Like he's looking out for something.

"Are you a supply-aider? Like... for the orange zone outposts?" Page ventures. She probably shouldn't be asking so many questions, but she's curious about the humanitarian deliveries.

He shrugs. "Yeah, sure! Much as anyone. I do a bit of aid work where I can, run a little medicine out to the deeps. Gotta do my civic duty, right? Especially if I'm already heading out there," he says. "To be honest, most of what I do's off the books already. So I might as well throw in a little help."

Maelle is still eyeing him suspiciously, and Page gets the sense she's just about to tell him to shove off.

But before either of them can say anything more, Dex gets a comm ping. It's not the device he was using before. Instead, he pulls a different device from an inner pocket of his guild jacket, and Page can't help but case it out as he checks the screen and taps out a reply. It's an expensive-looking box, non-military, but probably Q-capable. That would have fetched a pretty price, she thinks wryly.

"Oop!" he says when he's done. "That was my colleague. I've gotta go—real nice chatting to you."

He drains the last of his drink, glancing over his shoulder to check the local time displayed on the wall next to the bar. Then he shoves his device back into his jacket, picks up his carryall, and strides off in the direction of the concourse.

Page watches him go until he's out of sight around the corner. "Whoa. That was a sweet-looking device." She laughs. "Good thing I'm out of the comms resale business, huh?"

"Yeeeah. That guy was definitely doing something shady as all hells," Maelle says with an eyeroll. "You meet all sorts on these outposts."

The delayed hopper to Laithe still hasn't come in, and after a while Maelle pulls some snacks out of her bag. She passes Page a packet of sour candy, and Page eats it slowly, grimacing at the odd tang on her tongue. It's an unfamiliar flavour that she rolls around in her mouth. She tries to recall anything she could compare it to. Certainly, there was nothing exactly like it on Kuuj. But it doesn't stir anything in the depths of her before-memory, either. No, she decides, this flavour must be entirely new to her.

If she tastes it again, she'll undoubtedly associate it with *this* place: with these warped metal stairs leading back down to the concourse; with the way one of the neon lights is catching a strand of Maelle's blue-black hair.

"What're you thinking, there?" Maelle asks her. "You're giving me a weird look."

"I was just thinking that... I'm..." Page pauses, trying to find the right words to articulate it. "Right now, here in this moment, I'm making new memories." She holds up the little bag of candy. "I don't think I've had this stuff before. It's not attached to anything in my memory. But if I ever taste it again, I know I'm probably gonna think of *this*. This moment, you and me right here, waiting for the hopper. Me, about to go planetside for the first time I can remember. And... feeling impatient."

"I always used to *hate* waiting," Maelle says quietly. There's a halting hesitation in the words, as if she's not quite sure she should be telling Page this. "But now... Well, now, whenever I find myself feeling impatient, I always think back to the day I found out my friend Rodin was killed on a job."

"*Oh.*" Page is so startled by the unexpected words that something like a small gasp escapes her. The admission feels achingly personal, as if Maelle has allowed her to see into a small, private sanctuary, and she's not quite sure how to react. "I'm... sorry. I mean, about your friend."

Page knows grief, she thinks. She, too, has grieved for much. But she doesn't know the pain of remembering what it is she lost.

Maelle blinks slowly. "I was so impatient for him to come back. I kept messaging him, asking why in the hells they were all so late. I was so damn annoyed. Why couldn't he answer faster, why couldn't they be back already, why didn't he send me a *message*..." She tilts her head back, and Page sees the glimmer of a tear slipping down her cheek, taking an inky trail of black kohl from her eye with it.

"Eventually, the rest of them turned up, and we found out what happened. Rodin didn't make it out of that job alive. He was never coming back at all." She wipes her cheek with the edge of her sleeve. "And after that... I only *wished* I was still waiting for him. So now I try to think of it like this: waiting is *possibility*. As long as you're waiting, it means there's still a future to wait for."

"I... yeah. I think... I understand what you mean," Page says. "That's like me waiting on Kuuj. As long as I didn't stop working at it, as long as I was always scoping out one more record or buying one more old logfile, I didn't have to admit it was over, that my past was gone." She toys with the edge of the crumpled, empty candy bag. "Sorry. I—I guess it's not the same as someone dying."

"Nah, Page. You're right," Maelle says. "You're grieving

someone you can't get back, too. Whoever it was that you used to be."

She reaches for Page's hand. For the briefest moment, her warm palm presses over Page's fingers where they rest on the table, and Page's heartbeat stutters. But then Maelle suddenly jerks her hand away, startled by the high *ping* of a local notification coming into her comm.

"There it is! It's time to go," Maelle says as she snatches up the device and checks the screen.

Their hopper to the Laithe orbital is here.

ON HOW CURIOSITY SAVED ALL THE WORLD

Adapted from the Sacred Texts; this version translated from 'Folktales of the Eternal: A Volume of Traditional Stories.' Original author unknown.

So begins the tale of the Fair-Feathered Goddess, who we call She Who Was Raised on High and She of the Gorgeous Gifts. But she was not always so. When first she came into being, she was counted among the Small Spirits, of the kind that guard doorways and bless gardens. Important tasks, of course, but very small tasks nonetheless. Like all great things, the Goddess was once not very great at all.

Indeed, even amid the Small Spirits, she was ranked among the lesser of her kind. Her work was small, and her calling was small, and her courage was small. But it was she, the tiniest of divinities, who first found the green world of Teyr, who first walked its sweet-smelling fields and cool rivers, and spoke divine words to its children. It was she who raised humanity to their rightful inheritance, who named them as successors of the gods, even as she herself was raised to her greatest triumph.

It began like this: the Small Spirit was rebellious and unruly in her youth, and to the eyes of the other gods, she seemed quite awkward and strange. While the Higher Gods were content to remain in their Celestial Kingdom, studying the mysteries of the universe from afar, the Small Spirit could not contain her curiosity about what lay behind the kingdom's starry walls. And she wanted to see it all for herself, all the beauty and majesty in the galaxy. She wanted to taste starlight, and step through the cosmic prism to explore the worlds beyond.

And thus it was that she descended to the Greenworld, and encountered Humanity in their earliest dawn. She watched the humans at first from afar, not daring to interfere with them, but she found in them a great warmth and delight and kinship. She did not reveal her presence to them, but she returned many times over to observe them, to watch them as they learned and grew. And the more she saw of them, the more love she felt for them.

The Small Spirit wished very much to walk among the humans; to know them and to have them know her in turn, to share with them all she had learned in the Celestial Kingdom. But still she did not speak to them, for she was timid in those days and had not yet come into her great Divine Voice. And as the Higher Gods had not permitted her to leave her home, she did not know how she could ever tell the other gods about what she'd found beyond the starry walls.

One day, the Small Spirit had climbed again from a window of the grand palace in the Celestial Kingdom. And as she slipped through the darkness of the cosmic void on her way to visit the Greenworld, quite by chance she came upon a secret gathering of divine beings. A gathering that was being held in the depths of the shadows. A meeting that had been kept from the eyes of the Higher Gods.

Here spoke the Oblivion, the oldest enemy of the gods, seeking new allies among the host of the Celestial Kingdom. The Small Spirit hid herself, and she listened to what transpired. The Oblivion, Queen of Demons, spoke with honeyed words. She offered promises of great reward to those who would follow her. She called upon the gathered spirits to betray the gods, to join her in a war to overthrow the Divine Pantheon. Many of the spirits were swayed by her words, ensnared by her lies. But the Small Spirit saw the Oblivion for what she truly was – the Bringer of Darkness, the Destroyer of All Things. And the Small Spirit was terrified.

At once she raced back toward the realm of the gods to tell them of all that she'd seen, to warn the Divine Pantheon of the treachery that slithered among them. She flew as fast as she could, but being so distressed and frightened, or perhaps confused by the Oblivion's shadowy spells, she lost her way in the cosmic void, and she could not find her way back home.

For many days and nights the Small Spirit wandered, until she stumbled once again upon a little green planet in the dark, and she recognized the beautiful hills and vales of the Greenworld. She sighed with weariness and great relief to see it.

She hastened to descend to the Greenworld. And there, she came to a small village, and at last she revealed herself and beseeched the humans for help. She knew her way back to the Celestial Kingdom from here, but her strength had faded too much, and she feared she could not go on.

The humans did not recognize her for what she was. They had no knowledge yet of the gods, nor of anything beyond their own world. They could not understand her pleas, nor could they hear her speak. They saw only a small, wounded bird before them, for that was the shape she took.

But, being good and kind of heart, the people in the village restored the little bird's strength. They lifted her from the ground where she fell, and soothed her with gifts of cool, clear water and sweet-smelling flowers. And the joy and spark of life within them kindled in the Small Spirit enough strength to fly home once again, in time to warn the Divine Pantheon of the Oblivion's impending attack.

In the gods' immense gratitude, the Small Spirit was elevated to full divinity. And in time, she would win the leadership of the entire Pantheon, and she would become the greatest among them – the Great Goddess we all know.

The humans did not seek any reward for their selfless act. But in time, the Fair-Feathered Goddess would do many things to reward the hearts of humanity, to thank them for their help in her most dreadful hour.

Her story is as long as the comet's tail, and infinite is her cosmic ballad. But we must remember that she began – like all things do – as something small.

And so it was that the curiosity of a Small Spirit saved all the world, and everything that exists in the universe.

PAGE FOUND
Laithe Planetary System

JUST AS MAELLE predicted, no one checks them for Union idents when they board the hopper. In fact, no one so much as looks at them for the duration of the nine-hour journey to the Laithe orbital, nor the two further hours they spend waiting for the shuttle pod Maelle has booked.

Maelle speaks little to her, and Page mostly buries herself in the lengthy tome of legends that Maelle downloaded to her 'pad, along with the new cache of Teyr images: *Folktales of the Eternal: A Volume of Traditional Stories.*

There's an odd familiarity to these stories, Page thinks—something soft and vaguely comforting. Like the Teyrian clothes, or that memory of the blanket being wrapped around her shoulders.

Page reads the whole book three times, lingering a long while over certain passages, willing herself to recall where she first heard these tales. But that memory remains as elusive as a dream slipping away upon waking.

And before she knows it, they're already in view of the green globe of Laithe.

* * *

[File: Planetside_trip]
Laithe is a relatively small planet, an offshoot settlement of one of the Latter Worlds, settled during the Fourth Expansion. It's classified as 'Highly Habitable' on the Union's habitability scale. The climate is temperate, the soil is fruitful, and it's mostly self-sufficient when it comes to resources. It's particularly known for its dense forests, and prior to the war, its exports were chiefly natural wood and wood products.

ALL OF THIS, Page learns from the vid presentation before their descent, a grainy holo hosted by a pair of smiling children that plays in the waiting area on the orbital. Page tucks the information away in her mind like everything else she learns, preserving facts in her memory like delicate keepsakes.

And then, she copies the facts down into her 'pad for good measure. Even if she doesn't need them later, they're nice to look at. It feels good to remember something.

The experience of riding in the shuttle pod is entirely strange. The cylindrical chamber they're in has about twenty seats inside, but Maelle and Page are its only passengers. There doesn't seem to be a pilot, a fact which captures Page's curiosity until she looks out the round windows and realizes that the pod is held by a wide metal claw, and secured to the side of a larger craft that's towing it down to the surface. The craft makes its way all around the ring of the orbital, collecting a few more pods before it descends toward the planet.

The descent itself is bumpy and erratic. Page rests her head against the window and listens to the hum of movement, the intensifying vibration rattling her teeth as they breach the atmosphere. She doesn't realize how hard she's clutching Maelle's arm until Maelle gives a loud yelp and pulls herself free.

"You don't have to hang on to me for dear life, you know," Maelle says. But there's no harshness in it; she regards Page with a startlingly affectionate smile. "There's a handle for that, right there." She gestures to the smooth blue handhold curving between their seats, clearly built for the purpose, and Page gives an embarrassed laugh.

"Sorry," she mumbles. "It's, uh… well, I *think* it's my first time going planetside. That I can recall. I guess I'm kind of nervous."

Page examines the statement for the feeling of *truth*. She has been turning over the sights and sensations of the descent in her mind, focusing on each of her senses in turn: the vibration of the descending craft, the smell of the vessel's interior (old sweat, cleaning chemicals, something vaguely like burning wires), the view of the orbital above, the green and brown curve of the planet welcoming them below, outlined against the black expanse of space.

"You're trying to remember again, aren't you?" Maelle says gently. "You're thinking about whether you've ever done this before?"

Page nods wordlessly. She keeps staring out the window, studying the approaching landscape below. A brief moment of vertigo unsettles her insides as the craft tips and realigns itself for its final descent. She wonders what Teyr would look like from above. Then she closes her eyes and clutches that blue handhold, gripping it tightly until their pod is on the ground, and she feels almost safe again.

The pod is set down at a small spaceport, and the towing shuttle has barely retracted its clamps before it takes straight back off again, rising away into the sky. The spaceport is nothing but an open outdoor lot, with one squat brick building at the far end housing a couple of tiny shopfronts, both boarded up. On the other side, the landing area is framed by high fences.

When Maelle swings open the exterior door and they disembark from the pod, Page is quite sure that she's not meant to be impressed by any of this. She's seen holos, after all, of things far more awe-inspiring than this on the Union's worlds. Stunning natural formations, lakes and mountains and oceans, views that would surely take her breath away if they were stretched before her.

But a holo doesn't compare to the strange experience of actually standing on a planet. Breathing air that's *in motion* somehow, feeling the wind brushing against her face, cold and organic-smelling in a way she can't compare to anything else.

There's no one checking for idents or scanning for tickets where they disembark. There seems to be no one else here at all. The metal barrier at the side of the landing pad opens up for them, and... they just walk right on out.

Is this normal? Page wonders. She's suddenly aware of how empty the surrounding area is, after the bustling commotion on Felwae. This might be the biggest open space she's ever seen. Has she ever been this far away from other people?

"Come on," Maelle says, hoisting her small pack high up onto her back. "Let's go. This way! It's only about an hour's walk to the Compound from here."

"Wait, we're gonna walk?" Page doesn't hide her surprise. She doesn't know exactly what she expected, but she'd certainly imagined there would be some sort of ground transport collecting them. The idea of *walking in a straight line* for an hour and not having reached her destination yet is mind-boggling. It only takes about fifteen minutes to walk from one end of Kuuj to the other, ten at a clip.

"I like to go on foot," says Maelle. "Gets me re-acclimated after a long time in space. Balance, gravity and that. And you can enjoy all this fresh air!"

Page peers further into the distance, up into the hills beyond the small brick building. There's what looks like a woodland up there—is this one of the dense forests the intro vid talked about? But there's something strange about it. The treetops are blotches of yellow and orange and brown, peppering the hill like some kind of sickly mushrooms, the kind Kuuj grows for food.

Page looks down and sees that the ground all around the spaceport is barren, except where it's pocked with a few stray grasses and small green shrubs. The green bits look stark and incongruous against the desolate landscape, so much less verdant than it appeared from above.

She kneels on the ground and examines a furled leaf that has caught on a stone beside the footpath. It, too, is crumpled and yellow. What has done this? Some kind of chemical weapon? Is it even safe to be outside? Why isn't Maelle reacting? Page's heart is pounding under her ribcage.

"What's happened here?" she whispers, holding up the crumpled leaf. "Look at this! Look at those trees up there! The leaves are falling off. Everything is all dried out, like it's *dying!*"

To her surprise, Maelle only laughs. "Yeah, that happens. It's autumn."

Page stares at her blankly. "It's... what?"

"Oh, my gods, Page. You never heard of seasons?"

"I have, yeah, sure... I mean I've read about them, but..." Page gazes around. "I didn't think it would be like *this*. It looks like some kind of apocalypse happened! And that smell in the air... It smells like... decay. Like *death*."

"Well, it is death... of a sort, I suppose," Maelle says. "Dropping the old and growing new leaves. Kind of poetic, isn't it? I think it has a certain romance about it."

Page makes a face. "Dead things? You have some strange ideas of romance."

"Renewal," Maelle corrects.

"*Renewal*... right," Page repeats, and she uses the Graya word. The word that means *the beginning and the end of everything*, the apocalypse that destroys and regenerates. "*For there can be no renewal without death. Not without letting things go.*"

The saying surfaces in Page's mind fully formed, dredged from somewhere in the depths of her memory. Her voice always sounds strange to her when she speaks Graya, as though the words come from somebody else. Someone who memorizes quotes.

Maelle laughs. "I'm not a Prime scholar here. Translation, please?"

"It's like... I think it's trying to say that you have to let things go in exchange for new things."

"Yeah," Maelle says with a faraway look. "I guess you do."

Page collects herself and gets back to her feet. She gingerly drops the dead leaf back onto the edge of the footpath where she found it, and the wind immediately sweeps it away to join its dry-husked brethren. She watches it racing and tumbling up the hill until she loses sight of it.

Autumn or not, there's something funerary about this. Even the wind sounds a little creepy. It's not how she imagined it would sound—it is no light, comforting thing, no gentle kiss of the Goddess like the Teyrians describe in their poems. This wind is cold, and the sound of it is eerie and wailing.

"I... I'm not sure if I like being planetside," Page says with a grimace. "This really isn't what I thought it would be like."

"Right. Well, how about you give it more than a couple of minutes?" Maelle says with another laugh. "At least get a good meal in you before you make up your mind. Wait till you taste some home-cooked food and a glass of shine. Then we'll revisit your opinion on it, yeah?"

"Sure," Page mumbles. But this doesn't seem *right*. It's not like the verdant world in her memories, or visions or... whatever they are. She is sure she has never seen anything like this. The green of the Greenworld is *everlasting*.

"You know, maybe Teyr's climate would be more to your taste, li'l monk," Maelle says teasingly as they walk. She turns to Page and grins. "It's green all year there. All over the planet. No seasons."

But there are still storms on Teyr, sometimes. Page is not entirely sure where that thought came from, but she is certain that it's true.

* * *

They follow a half-paved road not far from the back of the spaceport, moving along it for what feels like ages. They must walk slower than Maelle would have travelled if she were alone, because it takes them well over an hour—nearly two, in fact—to get close to what Maelle calls 'the Compound.' Damn these impractical boots. Page might have only owned one pair of shoes on Kuuj, but they had a grippy sole and a firm ankle support that never let her down.

Page really should ask Maelle now to cough up more information about this robbing-a-monk-ship plan. She should ask what it was that Maelle wanted to tell her back on Zhak's ship. She should ask what they're even *doing* on this planet.

But somehow, the words don't find their way to her lips. Here, walking side by side with Maelle under a real sky, breathing real air, all Page wants is to ignore the obvious. To talk about something else for a while.

"So, uh. This is Laithe. And… you said this is near where you grew up?" She looks over at Maelle, and wonders not for the first time what a *homecoming* feels like.

"Yep. Lotta childhood memories here. I grew up on the Compound, right here, actually! You'll see it when we get there—not far now."

And not for the first time, Page wishes she could remember something of her own childhood. She wonders who was carrying her in that soft blanket.

"Must be… nice for you," Page says awkwardly. "Being back home, I mean."

"Yeah. Parts of it are nice. Unfortunately, family stuff can also be kind of messy." There's that uncharacteristic hesitation in Maelle's voice again, like when she'd talked about her friend Rodin back at the bar.

Page thinks of the holo-dramas she's seen, of feuds between siblings, of backstabbing parents and murderous schemes. She drags her feet, certain that the ill-fitting blue boots are wearing blisters into her heels. "Messy how?"

"You mean my family in particular? Well... Let's just say that some of them aren't happy with my life choices," Maelle says.

"You mean because your line of work is a bit illegal?"

Maelle laughs loudly at that. "No, no... definitely not that," she says, shaking her head. "Believe me, my family's business is as illegal as they come. It's more my choice of business partner that has their backs up." Her brow furrows. "They think I should stop working with Zhak."

"To be fair, so do I, and I've barely known you a minute," Page says flippantly. "Zhak's a total piss-merchant."

Not that Page believes that Maelle would care about her opinion on her career path, or Zhak, or anything really. Not when Maelle's just said that her own family failed to sway her.

"You're not wrong," Maelle says. "I told you, you're absolutely right not to trust him. Working for Zhak is a dangerous business, always has been." She winces. "But my family... We hold a grudge against him. And it's real *personal*."

Maelle turns away and kicks at a stone on the road, digging it free from the dirt with her toe and sending it skittering violently toward the tree line.

"I, uh... I guess that's why you said you don't work *for* him. I remember. You said you're an independent contractor."

"Yeah, exactly." Maelle lets out a wry laugh. She looks at Page intently. "You ever heard of Reece Bereda and her crew?"

Page shakes her head. "No, I don't think so. What do they do?"

"Depends on who you ask, I guess," Maelle says. "On the record? They run Bereda's Fine Wood Furnishings. Long-time exporters of handmade furniture, carved from genuine Laithe wood." She watches Page's eyebrows go up before she laughs again. "In practice? They make scamships. You know, like... fake alien ships."

"Wait, what?" Page squints, not entirely sure she's understanding correctly. "*Fake* alien ships? What for?"

"Piracy, mainly," says Maelle with a shrug. "Turns out, when impenetrable alien materials pop up on the proximity scanners, and it looks like Felen skirmishers are approaching, cargo crews don't put up a resistance. So raiders can board a target without a shootout. One or two scamships can do the job of a whole raider fleet."

Page thinks on this for a moment, then opens her mouth to ask something else. But the words die on her lips, immediately forgotten. Because at once, she notices the barbed, black metal gate that's straight ahead of them, covered with brightly coloured warning signs.

ALARMED ENTRY.
DANGER—LETHAL CHARGE IN FENCE.
TRESPASSERS BEWARE.
YOU ARE ON SURVEILLANCE CAM, WELL IN RANGE OF OUR SNIPERS.

Maelle carries on walking, entirely unbothered by all of this. She flips open a little control pad on the gate, presses her thumb to the round lens inside, and taps in a security code. A moment later, the black gate rumbles slowly open.

Although the moving part of the gate looks more than wide enough to accommodate a large land vehicle, it slides smoothly aside just enough to admit one person through the gap. Page can't help but notice the serrated metal teeth lining the inside of the gate, as if it might just chew down on you if it changed its mind. She eyes it suspiciously, not moving from where she stands until Maelle goes through first.

Maelle shimmies her pack off her back, then swiftly eases her larger frame through the gap sideways. She holds out her hand to Page. There's clearly more than enough space for Page to pass, and she stares at Page expectantly. "Come on, what're you waiting for?"

Wordlessly, Page places her hand into Maelle's, and lets Maelle pull her through the gate.

When they're both on the other side, Maelle pushes a button and the gate slams shut behind them with a clanging snap of those metal teeth. Page tries not to shudder. They carry on slightly uphill, following the curve of the road to where several buildings crouch around a little courtyard.

Buildings? Yes, they are definitely *buildings*, to be sure, but there is not a hint of architecture to them. They'd perhaps better be described as grey cubes stacked atop each other, as functional and devoid of aesthetic intent as Page's hab-cube on Kuuj was. Here, though, nestled in the middle of this tiled courtyard and surrounded by the whispering dry trees, even their brutal simplicity feels like some kind of highbrow art piece.

Across the side of the largest building, tall letters in worn blue paint proclaim:

BEREDA FINE WOOD FURNISHINGS

Page tries not to stare too much, keeping her gaze impassive and steady, as though she's just calmly assessing her new surroundings. But it doesn't take a moment for her to lose her cool, her head whipping around as she starts. Because there's something *moving* under the nearby building. Something *alive* is over there, she's sure of it—an ominous rustle is coming from the pile of dead leaves that the wind has collected against the foot of the entrance stairway.

Suddenly, Page rues having skipped the vid segment about Laithe's local wildlife. She stumbles backwards, clutching at Maelle's arm.

"What? What's wrong, Page?" Maelle whispers.

"I think there's... there might be an... *animal!* There! Look... it's right over there. See it moving?"

Page squints, nervously looking back to where the movement had been. And sees to her dismay that there are *two* moving things there. Two creatures. A pair of indistinct, furred shapes, jostling against each other just under the space where the building meets the decking around it.

The leaves rustle and move one more time. And then, two small, round, short-legged beasts suddenly come hurtling out from under the decking, bounding toward them faster than they have a right to, on those tiny legs. The creatures are absolutely covered in leaves and dry grass, the debris entangled in grey and brown fur that's so long and shaggy that their eyes are scarcely visible. As Page looks on in horror, they both run directly toward Maelle.

They launch themselves upward, their clawed front feet hooking into Maelle's thighs, and Page screams. To her shame, she does nothing at all to help Maelle against their attack. She just stands there, frozen in shock and fear.

But Maelle is still laughing, and now she's *picking up* one of the little beasts with her hands, lifting it up into her arms. It wriggles around as she clutches it to her chest and rakes one hand over it, combing a shower of dead leaves out from its fur with her fingers.

The creature's long pink tongue lolls out, flicking out of an invisible mouth buried under its coat of fluff, and it starts licking at her face. The other creature is still trying and failing to climb up her leg. It's yelping loudly as it tries to claw its way up, struggling to gain purchase on the canvas of Maelle's trousers.

"Wh—what in the five hells are *those?*" Page gasps when she can breathe again. She clutches her pack with both hands, holding it to her chest like a shield.

"They're only jibbles, silly!" Maelle says, like that's the most obvious thing in the world. "They won't hurt you. They're pets!"

The creature still on the ground continues jumping and snuffling at Maelle's knee, making that high barking sound, evidently jealous of its companion. Maelle nudges it gently toward Page with the side of her foot as Page shrinks back.

"Go on. Pet him. I swear, he won't bite you."

Hesitantly, Page stoops to a crouch, sets down her pack, and extends her hand. The creature turns in a circle, then sniffs at her curiously, pressing its small warm face into her palm before she feels the lick of its spindly tongue. It feels strange and rough against her fingers. Page lightly pats the top of the beast's head with her other hand.

And then a high whistle sounds from the direction of the nearest outbuilding, and an absolutely enormous man comes out through the doors. He's easily head and shoulders taller than Page, with a broad, muscular build and a thick braid of reddish hair. As he approaches, he waves at Maelle, wiping his sweaty forehead with one sleeve.

"Oi!" he's shouting. "Maelle! So, that's how it is, hmm? The gods-damned jibbles get a hello before I do, huh?"

Maelle grins back, setting the wriggling animal in her arms back down on the ground. The one near Page takes off as well, and both of the jibbles dart straight to the broad man's feet, where they start running in frantic circles and yapping excitedly.

"All right, there. Calm down, you little shits!" the man says, laughter in his voice. "They always lose their tiny minds when we have visitors."

"They do make the best welcoming squad," Maelle says, smiling back at him warmly.

Page has never seen Maelle smile quite like *this* before, so very openly. So... familiarly. With Zhak, on the ship, her smiles are stiff and guarded. Aside from those occasional slips of softness that Page can almost convince herself she's imagined, Maelle's emotions remain hidden behind an impenetrable wall.

But here, she seems instantly different. She doesn't hold her shoulders so straight, or keep her laughter contained. Here, Maelle seems at home.

The big man steps carefully over the jumping jibbles, pulls Maelle close and embraces her in a hug, patting her on the back. "Ahhh, that's right! Hey, now. There's my girl!" He looks in the direction of the gate they came from. "Got a ping that a pod was coming down and I just *knew* it would be you. Then I saw you on the gate cam."

"Page, this is Garin. Closest thing I've got to a father," Maelle says. "And Garin, this is... this is my friend, Page."

My friend. Page's cheeks warm unexpectedly at the endearment. Is that what they are, then? *Friends?* Or is Maelle just being polite for the sake of introductions? Perhaps 'this is the petty thief we kidnapped to impersonate a monk' would be considered uncouth. She wonders how much Garin knows of it, if he knows anything at all.

"Well! Page, how about that. Nice to meet ya!" Garin turns back to look at Page with the same affable smile. "Any friend of Maelle's is a friend of ours."

Garin has the kind of face that seems set into a perpetual half-scowl, but clearly balanced by an incredibly jovial disposition. There's a pair of safety goggles hanging from the collar of his coveralls, and the shape of the goggles is still outlined on his ruddy face, the indentation running over his nose and across his forehead as though he's just taken them off. He has spark lines over his left cheek and reaching up toward his eye, where some kind of comms implant might once have been fused.

There's a world-weariness about him that Page has seen in some of the oldest members of the Kuuj dockyard crew. The look of someone who has been 'in the business' longer than they care to admit. Garin looks like someone who's *seen things*... but there's a kindness in his eyes that immediately puts her at ease.

Garin takes Maelle's pack from her, slinging it over his own shoulder. It looks as small as a child's bag against his thick arm. But when he holds his hand out for Page's bag, she decides to hang on to it. Kindly stranger or not, Page Found doesn't let anyone handle her stuff if she can help it.

"Right. C'mon inside," Garin says, lowering his hand and brushing off Page's refusal without any comment. "Let's get you two into the upstairs canteen, and I'll pop some tea on!" He glances pointedly at Maelle. "And then you can tell me what kind of trouble you've got yourself into this time."

They follow him into the building next door to the one the jibbles had been hiding under, leading them up a narrow metal ramp with flimsy railings that Page wouldn't trust to hold any weight. But those rails must be a lot sturdier than they look, because Garin stomps onto the structure with no apparent concern. The big man leads them up the ramp, the overexcited jibbles still jumping around his heels, and they climb two more levels up the side of the building before they reach a thick, black-painted door.

Here, Garin stoops to pick up the jibbles, collecting them both under one arm. They yap and squirm as he opens the door, then he turns around and deposits them behind him, shooing them back to the outer side. It seems the creatures aren't allowed through to this secure stairwell.

At the top of the next flight of stairs, Garin stops and looks back at Maelle again with something like fatherly reprimand on his face. "You didn't tell her you were coming, did you?"

"I thought about it." Maelle rolls her eyes. "But I reckoned maybe a surprise would go down better."

"Well, it probably saved me an earful, I'll give you that." Garin shakes his head and lets out a long, weary sigh. "Gods. You couldn't have called ahead for once?"

"Oh, come on, Garin. I don't need you giving me shit, too." Maelle raises both hands defensively. "Can I not just come home for a surprise visit if I feel like it?"

Garin huffs like he's blowing hair out of his eyes. "You know you're welcome here any time, far as I'm concerned. I just wish you two could get past this," he says. "I wish you'd settle things properly. But I also know damn well you're not just here for a vis—"

Just then, a panelled lift door at the end of the corridor slams open. Another person swiftly steps out of the lift and storms toward them, carrying an overflowing crate of loose electronics.

At first, Page mistakes her for a child. She's slender-limbed and slight of build, with a round, wide-eyed face. At her full height, even in thick-soled work boots, she barely comes to Page's shoulder. But from closer up, she's clearly a woman much older than she first appears. Her light brown skin is creased at the corners of her eyes, and the temples of her wavy dark hair are greying.

She looks... exactly like an older, more compact version of Maelle.

"Well, well, well," the woman says with a long, disapproving sigh. "Hello, *Maelle*."

"Page... this is Reece Bereda," Maelle says through gritted teeth. "My mother."

DALYA
OF HOUSE EDAMAUN, IN HER TWELFTH YEAR
First-City, Teyr

ONE DAY, WHEN rain was sleeting down the windows for the second week in a row and Dalya had grown weary of being stuck indoors, Anda declared that they should go have a look inside Luwan Edamaun's library.

Dalya had never been particularly interested in the library, but from the moment she'd become aware of its existence, Anda was insistent that she wanted to see it one day. There would never be a better opportunity than today, when the library wing had seemingly been left unlocked despite Uncle's absence.

"I can't believe there are old *books* in there!" Anda whispered. "Books! Oh! I've never held a really old one! These will be *hundreds* of years old!"

She was so excited that she rocked on her heels with glee, and Dalya wondered how anyone could possibly be that interested in looking at some dry old books, of all things. But Anda was like that: she could find wonder in absolutely anything. She seized her life with both hands and shook it until it gave her what she desired. And today, she wanted to see the inside of the library.

Dalya sighed, knowing before Anda had finished speaking that she would give in. She took Anda by the hand, and after checking to ensure that none of the household staff were in sight of them, they sneaked away together to the library wing. Dalya ducked into the stairwell as silently as a ghost and led Anda carefully down the winding staircase to the basement library.

Dalya didn't know where to find the light switch, so they descended in the dark. They felt their way down along the wooden banister, until Dalya located one of the reading nooks in the library foyer and clicked on a small lamp. The air down here was a few degrees colder than upstairs, and the strangely ancient scents of stone and paper filled the air. Anda looked around with her eyes wide and sparkling. She leaned close to the bookshelves in the low light, scanning the labels along the bottom of each shelf.

"Wow! Just *look* at all this!" she said, pulling down a thick volume titled *On the Oldest of Philosophies* and flipping it open to a random page. "I'll bet we could find loads of interesting things in here."

Dalya felt slightly sick to her stomach. "We can't stay here for too long," she whispered. "Take a quick look around, and then we'll leave. Uncle won't like it if we poke about too much. Make sure you put that back *exactly* where you found it."

"Come on, Dalya. We're just being *curious!*" Anda laughed and pulled another book out from the shelf. "That's a good thing! Don't you remember the story of how the curiosity of the Great Goddess saved the whole wide world?"

It was not the first time Anda had mentioned that story. One of her favourites, she'd told Dalya, way back when they'd first spoken. Dalya had always been too embarrassed to admit it was unfamiliar to her. But now, she gave in to her own curiosity. "No," she said. "Actually, I… I don't think I do know it. Is it in the sacred texts?"

"Of *course* it is!" Anda said. "I've read it for myself, right from the original Source text! It's from one of the early volumes, when the Fair-Feathered Goddess was still only a lowly spirit."

"Ah. Well… our sages mostly read from the later parts of the story," said Dalya. "You must have noticed that we usually start from when the beautiful golden bird fell down to the Greenworld."

"Yes. And I've always thought that was strange. Because how do you suppose the little bird got there, then?" Anda said, her eyes sparkling with mirth.

"I... well, I really don't know." Dalya's cheeks burned. "The sages don't usually talk much about that. I'm not sure why."

"My parents loved the early tales best of all," Anda said. "They sang me so many songs about the journeys of the Curious One, and all the adventures she had when she was still small."

Dalya paused, processing what Anda had said, and a question that had tugged at her mind for years now suddenly spilled from her mouth. "I don't understand, Anda. You always say that your parents weren't good believers. But somehow... you know the stories in the sacred texts *way* better than I do." Her skin heated again with the admission of her own insufficiency—surely Nathin would have known all of these stories, even the ones the sages didn't read from very often. "How is that possible, Anda? Your parents must have been good."

Anda slid the book she was holding slowly back into its place on the bookshelf, and she stood there for a long time with her back turned to Dalya before she replied. It was as if a great weight balanced on her shoulders—something she was considering putting down, but feared to move.

"It wasn't because they didn't know the divine stories that my parents shunned their godly duties," she said at last, and her voice came out unusually timid. She still didn't turn around to meet Dalya's eyes. "They got into trouble because they held some scientific opinions that were... heretical. They wrote some things about the Origin world. Published some papers that were..." She paused as if searching her memory for an unfamiliar word. "*Controversial*. Do you know what that word means?"

From the way it was inflected, Dalya recognized the common tongue of the United Worlds. Not the Perfect Cadence, but the imperfect, corrupted language that some of the moonfolk uttered amongst themselves. Union Basic.

"I'm... not sure," Dalya said. She didn't like the sound of the word, and she was certain that it must mean something bad.

"It means divisive. Something that makes people argue, or that makes them upset to talk about," Anda said. "And my parents' papers did upset people, a lot." She bit her lip, and something like terror flashed up in her eyes. "Listen, Dalya... you absolutely cannot tell *anyone* about this. Ever, do you understand? If we talk about what my parents did, my uncle said there could be big trouble for us here on Teyr. We could get hurt, or he could be taken away. He said I mustn't speak of them to anyone."

"Of course. I won't tell anybody. I can keep it secret, I promise." Dalya pressed an earnest, reassuring hand onto her friend's shoulder. "But... what do you think your parents could have said that was so bad?" She leaned closer, lowering her voice. "Do you know what they wrote about? The things that were... *controversial?*"

"I can't tell you. I—I don't know, I c-cannot speak of it, I'm s-sorry," Anda stammered, pinching her lips shut. "It's too dangerous, Dalya! I shouldn't have mentioned it at all. Please... just let it drop."

Dalya swallowed hard, once again certain that she had pushed too hard, asked too many questions. But hadn't Anda said that curiosity saved the whole wide world? She needed to *know*. Shouldn't the heir of the High Speaker know all that went on in the Protectorate, even the bad things? Even the *controversial* things?

"Why don't you tell me your story from the sacred texts, then," Dalya said, to break the awkward silence. "Tell me about how the Great Goddess saved the world with curiosity. We should speak of the divine stories instead."

Anda's worried eyes brightened again, her relief plain on her face.

"All right," she said. And she did.

Anda told the story like this:

"Way back in the days of old, before she descended to the Greenworld, the Great Goddess was still a lowly spirit. She was... sort of a house-servant to the other gods. But she wasn't very good at it. She was always getting into mischief and doing lots of things she oughtn't do. She was more like a troublesome little child, back then... always late to ceremonies, and she never had her clothes properly tucked in—"

"What? A *little child*?" Dalya frowned. She did not remember ever hearing anything like this story, and it made her feel a little uneasy. Saying that the Great Goddess used to be a clumsy house-servant felt strangely disrespectful. The gods' tales shouldn't be *funny*.

Was *this* what Anda's parents had written about, she wondered? Goddess-stories that upset people?

But no, Anda had said this one was in the sacred texts. And what harm could possibly be done in speaking of the sacred texts? She wanted Anda to continue—she loved listening to her talk.

"It's true, all of it. You can look it up for yourself!" Anda said, crossing her arms with triumph. "Our Great Goddess was once a mischievous little brat! And whenever the affairs of the gods got too boring for her, she'd run off and go frolic around all over the cosmos. She went off exploring all around the planets, to see what else she could find. And *that's* how she ran into the humans. She thought they were rather lovely and interesting, and so she kept coming back to visit them. But she always had to hurry back to the Celestial Realm, because otherwise the Higher Gods would catch her, and they'd scold her for looking around where she shouldn't—"

At once, the big overhead lights in the library stairwell came on in a bright blaze, and Dalya stifled a shocked scream. Someone was *coming*.

She seized Anda's sleeve, her grip tight with panic as the girls tried to crouch down and hide themselves behind the wooden bookshelf.

But it was already too late.

"Dalya!" It was Heral there on the stairs, looking straight at the two of them with something between worry and fury etched on her face. "What in the Everlasting Lady's name are you doing here? You know the library's off limits!"

"I'm sorry," Dalya began weakly. "We—we were only—"

"It is my fault, Ker Heral," Anda interrupted, scrambling up to her feet. "Please, don't be cross with us. We were only playing hide-and-seek. I ran down here to hide, and... and I didn't know we weren't allowed! Dalya came to find me."

She smiled stiffly, her wide-eyed, contrite expression betraying no hint of the lie. Dalya's heart raced.

Heral looked sceptical, staring past them at the shelf behind Anda's head. Dalya hoped to all the gods that Anda had returned any books she'd touched into the correct places. But nothing was obviously amiss, and Heral's gaze shifted back to Dalya.

"Get upstairs, both of you," Heral hissed. "Hurry up, now. Swiftly, Dalya! Your uncle has a meeting down here, and he's already on his way."

Uncle? A meeting in the *library*, in the middle of the day? She supposed this must be why the wing was unlocked. Oh, how foolish she'd been—

Dalya wanted to ask why Uncle was *here* when the Gepcot was still meant to be in session, but she immediately thought the better of it when she saw the storm in Heral's eyes. Anda was already running up the steps, following Heral's pointing finger, and Dalya followed her.

As Dalya passed, Heral grabbed her arm hard, and Dalya startled with the pain as her fingernails dug in sharply. In all the years she'd known her, Heral had never laid a hand on her before.

"Be *careful*," Heral hissed. "Rules are in place for a reason, Dalya. You'd do well to follow them. Understand?"

"What?" Dalya whispered, taken aback. But Heral said no more, she just all but dragged Dalya the rest of the way up the stairs, elbowing her out the door. Dalya could hear Uncle's voice drifting toward them—snippets of the conversation he was having as he approached from around the corner—but she could hear no other voice replying to him. He must be taking a call on his commpiece.

"—to speak with Agote—no, absolutely not!—as a matter of utmost urgency—the timeline—this is not negotiable—we need Meneyr cut off—"

Further up the hall, Anda was motioning for Dalya to hurry onward. "Quick, Dalya," she hissed, her hand flailing urgently. "Come on! Let's go!"

And they scrambled away down the corridor, running to turn the corner before Uncle could see them.

MAELLE KRESS
Bereda Compound, Laithe

MAELLE WATCHES IN shock as the junk thief bends her knees and half-crouches into a strange little bow of greeting in front of Reece.

"Hello, Ker Bereda. It's so lovely to meet you," Page says. Then she straightens up again and stands demurely with her hands folded in front of her like some kind of stiff-shouldered aristo. One edge of her gilded Teyrian collar is sticking out askew over the plain grey fabric of her sweater.

It suddenly occurs to Maelle that this is probably Page's first time interacting with anyone new outside of her backwater outpost. It's her first time being a *guest* anywhere. And she's just walked into the most awkward possible family reunion.

"Oh, please. None of that *Ker Bereda* stuff, now. Just *Reece* will do." Reece looks at Page askance and gives her a brisk nod before she turns right back to Maelle. "This is quite the surprise, I must say. What's the occasion?"

"Blessings to you, too, Reece," Maelle bites out, forcing her mouth into a grimacing smile. "Mother."

Her eyes go to Reece's hands, gripping the sides of the crate. Familiar hands, small but strong, showing signs of a lifetime of hard work—her fingernails are cut short, the knuckle of one finger bruised and blue as if she's caught it in some hinge or tool. Both of her wrists are scarred with half-healed burns.

Reece glances from Maelle to Page and back again, this time with thinly veiled suspicion. "She's trusted, I take it, if you brought her here?" She jerks her chin in the junk thief's direction. "You haven't lost your senses completely?"

Those are two different questions, Maelle thinks, but does not say.

"Yeah. Yeah, Page is good. She's—one of us." Maelle hesitates, so briefly that no one else could possibly have perceived it. But it's true. She's not entirely sure why, but she *does* trust Page. She takes a deep breath through her nose. "Page and I are here to bring a business proposition, actually. I need to borrow a couple of scamships—"

"What! Borrow? For who?" Reece spits through her teeth. She drops the crate in her hands, or throws it, more like. It hurtles to the ground with an angry crash. "Get real, Maelle! What, you think I just have *a couple of scamships* lying around for your joy rides? There is a six-month waitlist right now." She narrows her eyes. "And if you think you're going to come here and call in *family favours*—"

"Hey, now. Hey. Don't think of it as a family favour," Maelle says, forcing the calm that she very much doesn't feel into her voice. She curses herself silently for rushing into this argument. She really should have waited before bringing this up. But then again, Reece never would have bought the *surprise visit just to see you* line. Maybe it's better to get this over with. "Look, just take it as a mutually beneficial business proposition to the greatest pilot in the business—"

"What's that got to do with it?" Reece cuts in. "*Retired* pilot."

"In your grand old age," Garin says, obviously trying to ease the tension with a soft, sarcastic laugh. "Reece here used to be an absolute ace pilot," he says to Page in a whispered aside. "She really was one of the best ever."

"Cht! You stay out of this!" Reece says sharply. "That was a long time ago."

"Ohhh. Must be nice to just bury your head and never think about the past, huh?" Maelle's tone is equally harsh, and she doesn't try to soften it. "Must be great to forget it all, to pretend it never happened—"

"Me?" Reece's eyes flash fury. "Me? Oh, you've got some nerve saying that to me, Maelle. I'm not the one working with *Zhaklam Evelor*. Your own kin's murderer! Believe me, I've forgotten *nothing*."

"Come on, now, come on," Garin says softly. "Please. Let's not start with this, all right? We've got a guest here."

Reece shrugs, looking pointedly at Page. "I thought Maelle said she was *one of us*. You choose to walk into family business, you're gonna see family business."

Page is just standing there wide-eyed, looking baffled.

Garin tentatively rests a hand on Page's shoulder. "Hey, listen... Page, why don't I take you outside to see our orchard?" he says. "Let's give them some space."

At once, Maelle recalls a flash of a childhood memory: Reece arguing loudly with Rodin in the kitchen, the two of them getting into it with heated voices about something or other. And Garin in the doorway, his hand on Maelle's shoulder, gently leading her away. *Let's give them some space, shall we?* How old had she been, then? Twelve or thirteen standard, maybe—which would've made Rodin about seventeen. She almost smiles at the recollection despite her anger. Garin has always been the peacemaker in this household.

"Page?" Garin prompts again. "Shall we?"

The junk thief looks sceptical. But she doesn't look worried about going with Garin. No—confusingly, she looks like she's worried about *leaving Maelle here*.

Maelle motions Page toward Garin. "Go on, go with him. It's fine, pal." She can feel a muscle in her jaw twitching, and her cheeks are practically aching from her faked smile. "Fresh fruit from the orchard! I'm jealous."

Garin echoes her grin with obvious relief. "Ever had fruit

right off a tree, Page?"

"I... don't know," Page says. "Maybe? But I... I guess I'd like to try it."

Reece stands impatiently with her arms folded in front of her, her eyes still cold and glaring. Maelle had known this would be no joyous homecoming, but she'd expected it to go a little better than *this*.

Garin quickly shepherds Page away, back toward the stairwell that leads to the exterior door, and Page doesn't look back.

Then Reece kneels down and starts picking up all the bits and bobs that have scattered out of her fallen crate, throwing them back into the container with unnecessary violence.

"Reece," Maelle says. "Come on... please. Stop acting like this. I know you're not happy with me, okay? I get that, I totally get it. But I'm almost there! I have a real good plan this time. I wish you'd just *listen* to me—"

Reece continues to collect wires and bolt-heads and converters, not looking up. "Something stopping you from talking? Didn't think so."

Maelle sighs as she slouches against the wall. She doesn't look at Reece any more than Reece looks at her. "I know you can't see it... but I'm doing this for Rodin," she says. "I'm never fucking going to be over it, Reece. But you have your own way of dealing with things, and I have mine."

"Doing it for Rodin?" Reece stops and straightens up, slamming the metal crate furiously against the floor. "Maelle, you are delusional. You think you're avenging Rodin's life, but all you're doing is wasting your own!"

"Why can't you understand that this is about the *family?*"

"Tch!" Reece makes a disdainful choking sound in the back of her throat. "Family? Forgive me if I can't understand where your loyalties actually lie. The only time you ever show up here is when you're in trouble or when you want something. Garin has a soft heart, you know he'll never speak his mind to you. But if he hadn't begged me, I'd have revoked your codes, changed the keys... I'd never allow you to come and go as you please—"

"*Allow* me? To come into *my own damn house?*" Maelle's voice rises. "You could at least hear me out before you question my loyalties!" She smacks the flat of her palm against the wall. "I'm about to take Zhak for *millions* of credits, Reece!"

There's a long silence, and then Reece steps forward. She puts her hand over Maelle's, squeezing her wrist the way she used to do to soothe her when she was a child, her thumb stroking over the top of her hand. Her jaw is still set with anger, but there are unmistakable tears welling in those iron-hard eyes.

"What use is millions of credits if I have two dead children instead of one?" she whispers. "I may as well carve your name onto that memorial stone right now, Maelle, because it's only a matter of time. Haven't we lost enough?"

"It wasn't supposed to *be* this way." Maelle blinks back furious tears of her own. "None of it. It's not fair! Rodin should still be here."

"Nothing in this damn universe is the way it's supposed to be. If any gods were watching, I think they gave up on us long ago," says Reece. "We can't afford to give up on each other, too."

Maelle nods, swallowing past the tightness in her throat.

"Come on, then, let's have it." Reece sighs. "Let's hear this plan of yours so your mother can talk you out of it."

PAGE FOUND
Bereda Compound, Laithe

GARIN LEADS PAGE outside, around the other side of the courtyard. The jibbles are at their feet in an instant, running and yipping and jumping excitedly through piles of scattered dead leaves. They're so small they disappear almost completely from sight before their little heads pop back out again. Page suddenly feels quite foolish for having been so afraid of them before.

The orchard that Garin spoke of is just beyond the far edge of the Compound. There's not much to it—only about twenty trees growing in neat rows behind one of the buildings—but Page is captivated nonetheless. The leaves on these trees are still green despite the season, and the branches are heavy with round, purplish fruits.

"Our autumn harvest," Garin proclaims proudly, plucking a fruit from the nearest tree and polishing it against his shirtsleeve. He bites into it and holds it out to show Page; the light green flesh beneath the rind looks soft and moist, peppered with pale, thin seeds. "Try one," he says, motioning up at the low-hanging branch. "That one right there looks ripe. Pull it off."

Page pulls on the fruit like he did, giving it a gentle tug until its stem separates from the branch, and she wipes it against her own sleeve to polish it to a shine before she bites in. It tastes incredible, sharp and sweet and sour at the same time. Has she ever tasted its like?

Garin must notice her enraptured expression as she chews it, because he laughs good-naturedly and says: "Something special, isn't it? This variety only grows on Laithe."

"I'm not sure I've ever had anything like this," Page says. "Fruit from a tree. Or, you know. Fruit at all, except for the dried kind."

"Hmm. You spaceborn, then?"

"Might be." Page shrugs, realizing as she says it that this probably sounds either rude or intentionally evasive. But Garin is unfazed, and he doesn't press her. She supposes that in his line of work, he's used to vague answers about people's identities. "I, uh… well, I spent the last eight years on a deep-space wreckhole called Kuuj Outpost," she adds after a while. "Doubt you've ever heard of it."

"Doesn't ring a bell. But trust me, kid, I've been on my share of deep-space wreckholes. Still a lot better than living on a mining rig. I spent most of *my* youth working on rock crackers." He shakes his head, swiping fruit juice off his chin with the back of his hand. "Gods damn, though, I wouldn't want to live anywhere in deep space right now. I'm so glad we have *this* place. We're real lucky to be down here with the earth under our feet."

Page is listening, but her mind is whirling with dozens of questions. She's suddenly flooded with the sheer enormity of it all, the idea of how much there is to see out here, how little she knows of anything at all beyond the walls of Kuuj.

Garin walks a short way into the orchard, running his hands through the branches like he's looking for something. He reaches up to one of the trees and carefully selects one large green leaf, examining its fine points and turning it over in his hands before he tucks it carefully into a pocket of his coveralls. Then he circles back to Page.

"You all right, there, kid?" he asks, sounding genuinely concerned. It's funny, Page thinks, how he calls her *kid*, considering she's somewhere close to thirty standard.

"Yeah." She answers honestly. "I... I think I'm good."

"You look a little overwhelmed."

"It's just... I've seen a lot today," she says. "It's been a long while since I've been off Kuuj Outpost. Can't even remember the last time. There's so much to see here."

"And you haven't even seen our famous workshop yet," Garin grins. "You ever seen alien ships before? Felen craft?"

Page shudders. "No. Well, not outside a holo, anyway."

She feels deeply certain that it's true—she hasn't seen the aliens. No stirrings of memories from her former life have ever echoed back to her when she looked at images of Felen ships on the network. She'd felt nothing about the fathomless ink-black shine of their hulls, only an unsettling emptiness. Whatever horror or awe the sight of the alien ships evoked in her, it was new to her.

"You want to see some?" Garin asks. "Up close? We can pop over to the workshop right now, if you like. I'll show you."

"I—for real? They're just...right *here*? Alien tech?" Page shifts her feet anxiously, looking back at the cubic grey buildings.

"Well... it's just the hulls," Garin clarifies. "That's all we deal with here, as far as alien tech goes. Underneath, it's just a normal human ship. We build the hybrids here."

"Huh. Kinda weird building ships *on a planet*, isn't it? Wouldn't it be easier to have your shipyard in orbit?" Page asks.

"Easier, sure. But we like it here." Garin takes another bite of fruit. "And besides, with this kind of work, the last thing you want to do is attract attention. We usually take the finished ships up in big transport crates four or five times a year, and tow them to our deep-space warehouse out on Ancillary Nineteen. That's where we sell from. Meantime, nobody's looking for a shipyard down here." He tips his head toward the signage on the building. "Officially, we export *handmade wooden furniture*. Bereda Fine Wood Furnishings. That business has been here longer than I've been alive."

"Huh. So... I guess the government officials or whatever don't come down here to see what you're really doing?"

Another laugh. "You kidding? Haven't come across a Union patrol this side of the system in years. We're in the lawless zone here, kid. Anything goes." He raises a finger with a wink. "Our furniture shop pays generously in sector taxes... so what's to look into?"

"I noticed there weren't any checkpoints anywhere when we landed here... or back on Felwae, either," Page says. "Good thing, too, 'cause I've got no Union ident." She's not entirely sure why she's telling a complete stranger this, but as he's just shared the logistics of his family's trade in fake alien craft, it seems unlikely that Garin will judge.

"That spaceport down the road there is all ours," Garin tells her. "Makes hauling our stuff up to orbit a lot simpler. It did used to be a small Union port, but they decommissioned it years ago. With the war effort, seems they can't be bothered with us at all. Which suits us *just fine*."

Page has gnawed her fruit down to the stem now, and she chews thoughtfully on the end of the bitter little stick. She's pretty sure you aren't meant to eat it.

"C'mon." Garin flicks the stem of his own fruit away into the grass, then motions toward the largest of the outbuildings. "Let's go see some ships. Workshop's over this way."

Page follows Garin into the largest of the buildings, waiting while he wrangles the jibbles. He feeds them a handful of treats in a little side room, and slides a wire grate across the door to enclose them there before he takes Page into the workshop.

Page remains two paces behind him, dragging her blistered feet until he turns his head to see where she's gone. There's a nervous apprehension buzzing in her chest at the thought of what she's about to see, but it's excitement, too. A deep and burning curiosity. The need to *look*, no matter what it is she might behold. She holds her breath.

The floor here has turned to a corrugated metal, and their

boots echo hollowly as they step into a wide hangar. And there, right ahead, are the scamships—the *hybrids*, as Garin called them. Three glossy black alien hulls are suspended in workbays around the place, each one lit by several bright spotlights from above. Page thought she'd prepared herself to hide her reaction, but a gasp still catches in her throat.

A tall man with sandy hair and a scruffy beard is walking toward them, flashing them a wide, genial smile. "Oi! What's this, Garin?" he shouts. "I didn't know we had guests!"

"Look, here's one of our main artisans!" Garin says. "Page, meet Edlin. Our chief mechanic." He turns to the bearded man. "This is Page. She's a friend of Maelle's."

"Hey, Page," the mechanic says, raising a grease-stained palm to introduce himself. He's a lot younger than Garin—he doesn't look much more than twenty-five standard—but he carries himself with the same easy assurance. "No way! Maelle's home?"

"Yep," Garin says. "She's next door, talking to Reece."

"Ah." The look on Edlin's face says that's all he needs to know.

"I'm just taking Page here around the workshop," Garin tells him. "You want to show us what you're working on right now?"

"Hells, yeah!" Edlin enthuses. "Come on, over here. I'll show you one of our little alien beauties up close."

"All right," Page whispers, her words barely an exhale.

The Felen ships are sharp and angular, something like great black thorns. They're so close that Page imagines reaching out and touching one of them. And when Edlin leads her right underneath the belly of the nearest craft, she really could, if she dared.

But what's hanging there above her head looks like ordinary metal, with none of that strange black iridescence. The underbelly of the ship looks as normal as can be. This is the human ship that sits beneath the Felen hull material.

Edlin reaches over his head to pat the metal with the palm of his hand. "Haven't put the bottom on this one yet. As you can see, under here this is a standard Union-made fighter chassis, military-grade. Basically the same as what the UWDF flies." He walks a little further, running his hand over the edge of the join as he talks. "The alien hulls we work with are already stripped pretty clean when we get 'em. Electronics, interiors and the like, that's not our department. We pick these pieces up from salvagers in the orange zones."

He leads Page onward into the middle of the workshop space, beaming proudly as he spins around with his arms spread. "Amazing, isn't it? Here, look, those two over there are still being prepped for integration." He points out the larger of the two hulls on the left side. "That big one is real interesting, we haven't worked with that kind before, but it came in almost intact."

"Wow," Page says. She pictures those black shapes slicing through space like deadly sharp thorns. They do look terrifying.

"Most of what we get from the salvagers is in pieces, so we need to pick and choose, to assemble them into complete hulls. It takes a long time to finish one," says Edlin. "See over there? There's a piece we just got last week. Sal's been working on shaping that one." He indicates a workstation over in the far corner, where a jagged piece of the black material is clamped to a huge table, surrounded by power tools.

"We look for pieces that match well enough to fit together… and then we have to make the final product spaceworthy. You see that weird shiny coating they have on the surface? That black stuff? Nobody has any idea what that is exactly, or how to make it—even the molecular analysis is weird," he says. "That's what makes the Felen hulls resistant to all our ship scans. We actually had to develop a totally new form of plasma welding to work with it—we call it the Bereda method." He grins again.

Page studies the gleaming ship, letting her eyes linger over the finer details of the elegantly curved alien hull. She's seen so many images of Felen craft in newscasts, and renderings of the aliens, too, and yet the whole idea has always seemed so... abstract. This was something *other* people experienced, something utterly removed from her own reality. She stands there in silence for a moment, still staring at that smooth, iridescent surface.

"Wow," she repeats. It seems the only reasonable response. "They're... incredible."

"Those Felen sure are somethin'. Their tech's more advanced than anything we've made since the Source, that's for sure," Garin says, coming back over to them. "We haven't figured out what half of it even does. Course, when I say 'we' I mean the smart-brains at the research centres. The ones studying the Felen."

"What happens to the, uh..." Page stumbles over the right words. "The... pilots that were inside the ships, before?"

"What, you mean the aliens?" Edlin makes a face. "No clue. We don't mess with any of that. Trust me, we've got no interest in running across those things."

There's a strange look on Garin's face, and he gives a halting chuckle, as if to cover his revulsion.

"I've wondered about them, sometimes," Page says. "The Felen, the aliens, the... whatever you call them. We didn't get a ton of recent news out on Kuuj, where I'm from, but people still talked about them. Some people think they're robots. But... they're *alive*, aren't they? They're... organic?"

"Oh, yeah. Definitely," Garin says. "They're made of flesh and blood, just like the lot of us. Under all those shields they generate, they bleed, and they die. They feel pain." He winces almost imperceptibly.

"Do you think the salvage hunters have seen them alive?" Page asks.

Edlin shrugs. "I reckon most of them haven't ever seen a live one. The wrecks they find have been drifting out there for months, if not years, before they get picked up. There's hardly ever anything left living. But... yeah, sometimes it happens." He glances toward Garin with a look that Page can't quite parse. "You've seen 'em, haven't you, old man? You wanna tell her your story?"

"Oh, yeah. I sure did. Long time ago."

"Tell her," Edlin says, nudging Garin's shoulder. "C'mon! Tell how you saw the Felen, when you were working on the mining rig!"

Garin clears his throat, and pulls a flask out of the wide pocket on his belt. He takes a long swig of whatever's inside it before he elaborates. "Well, all right, then. So... Back when I had my very first job, I used to work as a mechanic's assistant on a rock cracker. My team got posted waaay out in the far reaches, doing some mining work deep in this asteroid belt. And then, about a year after I went out there, this weird ship crashed down on one of the big rocks just outside our perimeter. We didn't know what it was, exactly, but a bunch of us got sent to check it out. This was a company job, see, and they didn't want competitors snooping around. But this... *thing* that came down out there... Well, it wasn't anything human. Wasn't robots in there, either."

He takes another drink from his flask and swishes it around in his mouth before he continues. "There were three aliens that got dragged out from that wreckage, and I saw it happen. Reckon it must have been some kind of Felen scout ship. But we had no clue what we were lookin' at."

"The Felen... They were still alive?" Page whispers.

"I swear at least one of 'em was still moving. Two of our guys pulled it out, an' it was sort of... y'know... twitchin' around a bit," Garin says, flailing one arm up and down. "All these years later, that whole scene's still burned into my head, clear as can be. 'Course, that was back in the day when *most* people thought any talk of 'alien contact' was a total hoax. But after that ship crashed, a whole bunch of reporters came out there to talk to us, even some from the Primes. Yep, they came all the way out there to the reaches, and they were wanting to interview everyone who saw it. Started askin' us questions, trying to catch us out on the small details, like it was some kind of publicity stunt. But this was no fuckin' hoax. What I saw was *real*. We saw a crashed alien ship."

He gulps from the flask again. "And if you think the reporters came fast... well... the military ships got there even faster. The deffies were already there. First thing the UWDF did was secure the site. They shut down our whole mining op, got everything under wraps, and then they cleared all those reporters out right quick. We workers all got paid half a year's salary and sent straight home. And after that... Well, then the networks put out a new story. Said the crash was some kind of misguided monitoring drone from a rival mining company. They were just scoping out the belt, that was it. Just the usual corporate shenanigans, nothin' to do with aliens." He rolls his eyes. "That was... hmm, what year was that? Gotta be going on fifty years ago now. But... it wasn't the last we saw of the Felen."

Page waits patiently for him to carry on speaking, vaguely aware that her mouth is hanging open.

"A few years later... I guess they came back again to scout the same sector," Garin finally continues. "This time, it was a whole damn attack. The one on the Kloswë mining settlement, the one everybody knows about. The *Declaration*. At first the Union authorities played it like *that* was our first contact with 'em, but way too many people knew the truth. The Union was forced to admit they'd known about this shit for years." He shakes his head. "Well, anyway. From then on, it was a public mobilization. We'd officially declared war. But at that point, the UWDF had already been fighting the war out in deep space for years, all in secret. We common folk just didn't know what we were dealing with. And you know what... I reckon we still don't know the half of it."

He stays silent for a moment, as if in quiet reflection, before he goes on again. "After the Kloswë attack... There was no denying this shit was big after that. The public wanted explanations. More than that, they wanted to know how we planned to retaliate."

He pops the cap back onto his flask with a decisive *clink*. Page stares at the dusty toes of her uncomfortable blue boots, wriggling her blistered feet. She doesn't quite know what to say.

"And so it all started," Garin says, almost to himself. "A war that's probably gonna end us all. But I suppose we were always going to retaliate. That's human nature, isn't it? Even if it kills us."

DALYA
OF HOUSE EDAMAUN, IN HER FIFTEENTH YEAR
First-City, Teyr

"When you think about being beloved of the Great Divine... do you ever get frightened?" Dalya asked Anda one evening while they sat together on Dalya's balcony.

It was a clear and starlit night, and they were waiting to see if they could spy the bright tail of a new voyager coming down. There was another Returning flight due to arrive soon from the Moon-City, and Anda's uncle, Derin Agote, should be on it. Ker Agote went back up to the Moon-City sometimes now, helping to gather the moonfolk for the next Returning flights.

It was a noble duty he did, Dalya thought, to leave Teyr again when he'd already reached the blessed Greenworld. But Anda was always so melancholy while he was away, and tonight, Dalya's own mood was not much better.

"What do you mean? Why would I be frightened?" Anda reached for the plate of sweet biscuits between them, taking one and biting into it as she spoke. She chewed thoughtfully, looking up at the sky. "It is a comfort, I think, that someone is looking out for us... that the Goddess watches over us. Isn't it? It feels like always having a friend, even when you're alone."

"Sometimes... I'm just not sure I'm really *good enough* for her favour," Dalya said. "What makes *me* worthy of being at the

Renewal? Of being there to meet the Goddess at the beginning and end of it all?"

"Well, you're Teyrian," Anda said with a shrug. "You were born here, you never left. You're guaranteed to be at the Renewal. If it happens like the sacred texts say it will, then I suppose you don't really need to worry about it."

"That's what I'm afraid of, though," Dalya whispered. "That I'll be there at the Renewal, but... the Goddess and all of my family will still be disappointed in me. Because I've never really proven I'm any *good* at being one of the chosen."

"What?" Anda said incredulously. "Why would you think something like that? Of course you're good enough. You work so hard. The Goddess will know all of that."

"I'm just... I'm still not sure it was ever meant to be *me* doing this work," Dalya said, her voice shaking. "You know that I've always wondered if Uncle wished it was me that died, instead of Nathin. I'm only a replacement."

"Come on, now." Anda put her arm around Dalya. "Where is this coming from? You are good enough, Dalya, of course you are," she whispered. "You're a good believer!"

Dalya just nodded in tearful silence, resting her head against Anda's soft shoulder.

"What's got into you tonight?" Anda leaned back with a searching look. She always saw right through Dalya, right to the heart of her. "What's happened to upset you like this?"

"Uncle sent me to be read by the sages," Dalya blurted out. "And when they looked at my trajectory... they said... they said that... that the Goddess had doubts about me."

It was a secret she hadn't spoken aloud to anyone, not even to Uncle. But who could she tell about it, if she couldn't tell Anda?

"What?" Anda breathed, her eyes going wide. "Why?"

"I don't know. They said they saw an ill omen around me. And..." Dalya lowered her head, her eyes stinging with tears. "They said that the gaze of the *Oblivion* had been upon me for half a moment! The Demon Queen herself!"

To Dalya's horror, Anda laughed at that. She *laughed*, as if Dalya had told her some ridiculous joke, instead of her most shameful secret.

"That's complete nonsense," Anda said with a dismissive wave of her hand. "The sages can't possibly tell where the Oblivion is looking. How would anybody know that?"

Dalya shrugged angrily. "I don't know."

"No, listen. Think about it, Dalya! Even the entire Divine Pantheon couldn't tell what the Oblivion was up to when she was plotting to destroy the entire universe! So how would a sage know what she looked at for *half a moment?*" Anda insisted.

That startled Dalya into silence. It didn't exactly make sense, did it? Another one of those things that sat slightly askew in her mind, and made her feel uneasy to look at too closely.

Anda stood up and walked to the rail of the balcony, staring up at the stars. "My uncle told me that's just an untruth that people make up sometimes, when they want to give you a fright," she said. "They tell you they sensed the Oblivion's gaze on you to make you more obedient. But they're lying. No one can really sense that."

Dalya's skin prickled. It was one thing for Anda to doubt the visions of the sages, but the idea that the sages could just *make something up* struck a cold dread into her heart. Surely Anda had just misunderstood; Ker Agote couldn't have said something like that.

"The sages interpret the things that we don't understand, Anda. They tell us what the divine words mean, and they sense the strands of the universe, but they certainly do not *make things up—*"

"No, I'm pretty sure they *do* make things up," Anda said. "They do it all the time. Just like all the lies they tell about Teyr."

"*What?*"

"They lie about loads of things, Dalya." She fell into a low, conspiratorial whisper. "The Unbreakable World *isn't even really Teyr*. My parents knew the truth, and they tried to tell people. That's how they got into trouble with—"

Dalya flew to her feet, faster than she'd thought she could move, and clapped a hand over Anda's mouth, pressing her palm down hard while her heart pounded triple time. "Shhh, shhh, stop!" she begged. "Please, Anda! Don't. You're acting like a heretic!"

"Don't touch me!" Anda braced herself against the balcony rail and shoved Dalya's hand away. "How dare you say that to me!" She pushed Dalya back with so much force that Dalya fell against the wall of the house.

Dalya shrieked as her head made contact with the brick. She dropped to her knees, biting the inside of her mouth against the pain, tears welling hotly in her eyes.

And now Anda was crying too, tears streaming unabashedly down her face. "I thought I could trust you," she hissed. "You always wanted me to tell you about my parents. You've asked me about it since we met, and this is how you repay me when I finally tell you? By calling me a heretic? Just like what people said about *them*? They *died*, Dalya!"

"Well, maybe they died because they lied," Dalya gasped out. "Your parents were wrong. They were liars!"

"Take it back. Take it back, now!" Anda grabbed hold of Dalya's braid and pulled, hard, whipping her head around and making her cry out again in pain. "My parents did not *lie*. The Gepcot did! The Gepcot is lying to everyone—"

"The Prime Worlds, first to be settled, all have rings seared down to their deep crust," Dalya recited breathlessly, the images from her school texts flashing into her mind. "The First Primes have rings from the landings of the seedships! But Teyr has no landing rings! We have no rings, that's how we know for sure—"

"Teyr *does* have rings." Anda's tear-rimmed eyes were fixed on Dalya's face, and she sounded deathly calm now, her voice measured and even. "The Circle Hills in the north. That's the landing site. Three rings. You can see them from space. Why do you think the voyagers come down at night? To keep anyone from seeing them!"

"No. It isn't true! The Circle Hills are just hills, they're *natural formations*," Dalya said. "Anything else you read is Union fabrication, this is why we don't treat with the Union—"

"Dalya. Stop it, stop!" Anda's hand was tight on her shoulder now, holding her in a viselike grip. "They're landing rings. Teyr has landing rings. That's what my parents' *controversial* papers were about, all right? That's what you wanted to know, and now you know. When Teyr split away from the Union, the Gepcot cut us off from the other worlds, so we can't learn about the truth anymore. Teyr is one of the First Primes, but it's *not* the Origin world. It's exactly the same as all the other Primes! And the Unbreakable World, wherever it is… it's somewhere else. The real Origin planet might not even be in this galaxy!"

Dalya was still staring at her, stunned speechless. She felt like she was going to be sick.

"Look, there's no point explaining it to you, Dalya, if you won't listen. You'd rather listen to *them*. I should never have told you any of it." Anda wiped at her eyes as she turned to leave.

"I'm sorry," Dalya sobbed. "Wait. Please! I shouldn't have said that about your parents. Anda, don't go, please, don't—"

"Are you going to believe me, then?" Anda sniffled, and her voice was small. "Say it. Say you believe me."

"I—I'm not—I can't—"

"Yes or no, Dalya?" she demanded. "I'm your best friend. Do you believe me or not? My parents didn't lie."

"I'll keep it secret for you. I won't tell a soul what you said." Dalya swallowed down her terror as she looked back toward the balcony exit, suddenly dreading to see Heral there lurking in the doorway. But the doorway stood empty. They were still alone.

"Dalya—"

"I'll protect you, Anda. You're my best friend, too. You know that," she whispered, squeezing Anda's hand. "But you can't say these things anymore. Please… promise me you won't ever say it again. I don't want you to get hurt."

THE STORYTELLER

Recording start 05:01:29

Ahhh... the big job, the Teyrian job. Yes. That's what we called it, *the Teyrian Job*, like something out of a holo. The big break we'd been waiting for.

Now at that time, Saymu Prime had just started manufacturing the death-hoops again. These so-called Planetary Defence Systems... 'Course, that's banned tech in the Union, because of everything that went down back in the Imperial Ages. But now these things were being manufactured again in the Saymu outer system, mostly to supply the ditch ships. And these Saymu mercs, some of the same ones we were running with... They were the ones brokering it all.

Vonnie and I had been working the Meneyr run for years already when that job came along. It was the kind of unbelievably lucrative job we could only have dreamed about. The biggest smuggling job we'd ever done. This time, it wasn't just booze or dirty art. No, this was big-time contraband. And it was the first time I'd ever dealt in weapons transport.

On the surface, it looked like wild amounts of money for an easy bunch of runs. Same thing we'd been doing for years, just different cargo. Now, what's interesting to know is this: These death-hoops were illegal to manufacture, possess or transport within the Union, that much is a given. But the Teyrian Protectorate, because of the split, was *outside* of Union jurisdiction. So once a ship had exited Union space, the whole thing became a bit of what you'd call a 'legal grey area.'

At some point, we'd cross some invisible border, and that's the point where the precise nature of what laws we were breaking changed from 'transporting illegal technology in Union space' to 'unauthorized trade with a non-Union entity.'

I guess you'll have to ask the legal system which one of those crimes was worse. But ultimately, it didn't matter, 'cause I got slapped with both of them.

[*A long, pained sigh*]

Right. I digress. I suppose you're wondering what anybody inside the Teyrian Protectorate wanted with a dodgy P-def system in the first place. Cause if there's one thing you probably know about Teyrians, it's that they're so-called pacifists. They hate the idea of weapons. They like to call themselves the only planet that's never seen a war. Well... I suppose that last part might be true. But as to the rest... I'll leave you to make your own mind up, when we reach the end of this story.

Because the buyer wasn't just some rich moon-dweller this time. It was the gods-damned Gepcot. Teyr's planetary council.

We were dealing this shit to the highest level of the Protectorate's government.

MAELLE KRESS
Bereda Compound, Laithe

REECE WILL COME around, Maelle tells herself.

She has to come around. Maelle needs to believe it. She didn't get this close just to fail at the finish line. No, as always, her mother just needs a little time to cool off.

Maelle lets herself out the side door, walks slowly down the exterior steps and goes to the other side of the courtyard. She can see the orchard from here, but Garin and Page aren't there—he must've taken her somewhere else on the grounds. Knowing him, he's giving her the grand tour.

She crosses through the orchard to the small meadow on the other side. The grass here is long and pale at this time of year, dried leaves catching everywhere in its bent strands. But the pink marbled standing stone in the middle is bright and clean—undoubtedly Garin still washes and polishes it every week. The lettering on the front is catching the light as Maelle approaches, her feet crunching over the gravel laid at the stone's base.

The memorial monument stands taller than Maelle, and the text etched into its surface has been engraved by hand. She presses her fingers to her lips and runs her hand over the curves and angles of his name. *RODIN BEREDA*.

There is no machine precision in the blocky lettering, and it strikes her suddenly to wonder who it was that carved Rodin's name here. Did Reece carve it herself? Did Garin? Maelle had never looked at this stone when it was first erected, and she had refused to look at it for years. An entire life, reduced to a few scratches on a stone and a memory held only by a few. How many people think of Rodin, still, anywhere outside these gated walls?

Maelle doesn't allow herself to cry. She just sits down cross-legged in the gravel like she always does, fishes Rodin's synthstone talisman out of her pocket and closes her fingers around it. She holds it there against her knee as she looks up at Rodin's name on the stone.

I've got you, Rodin. I've got your back. And I'm going to take care of the family.

She doesn't know how long she's been sitting there—or how long *Page* has been there. But she jumps in surprise when she notices the junk thief standing right behind her, looking curiously up at the memorial stone.

Maelle scrambles to her feet, and quickly shoves the little talisman into her pocket.

"Gods! Don't sneak up like that!" she gasps. "Not when we're not paying you to sneak, anyway."

But Page is still staring straight ahead, looking at the memorial with an inscrutable look on her face. "Rodin was your friend that you were telling me about. Your friend who died. Isn't he?" she says softly. "Rodin *Bereda*. You were related to him, then?"

Maelle blinks. Part of her resents Page for prying. And yet another part of her just wants so desperately to *talk about this*, in a way she can't with the rest of them.

"Not by blood," Maelle says. "But he was family."

"Ah," says Page. "You mean he was... *one of yours*." She speaks the phrase in Graya, but it's a loanword Maelle has heard before. A phrase from the old tongue that indicates chosen family.

"Yes, exactly," Maelle says. "The Bereda name is a gift he was given. Reece and Garin took him in when he was about thirteen standard, so we grew up together like siblings. He was only a few years older than me."

Page doesn't say anything, but she reaches out and touches the edge of the stone.

"I'm older than he ever got, now. How strange is that?" Maelle forces a smile, still blinking away stubborn tears. She's determined not to let Page see her cry *again*. "He should still be here, cussin' me out like a joker, telling me what to do about this whole mess."

And then Page lays a tentative hand on Maelle's shoulder and squeezes. "How did Rodin die?" she asks.

Maelle's fists clench at her sides. No words come, only something like a choked half-sob. But Page doesn't back off.

"Your mother said Zhak killed one of your kin," Page whispers. "Zhak killed *Rodin*, didn't he? That's what you haven't told me. That's why your family has a grudge against him."

"They were... working a job together, for the Nightblade. Something to do with stealing antiquities that were being transported. And it all went wrong," Maelle bites out, and the words stick painfully in her throat. "Reece never told me the details. Only that Zhak gave the order to shoot down his own hired scamship pilots, so he could save himself." She wipes at her eye with the back of her hand. "Reece was *there*. She saw it happen... and that's the last time she ever flew a scamship."

Page is frowning, like she's trying to put together a puzzle that doesn't quite make sense to her. "But that's—I'm not sure I understand—"

"Zhak has no idea that Rodin and I ever knew each other," Maelle says bitterly. "He doesn't know I'm a Bereda. He's never seen my Union ident, and I've always gone by an alias—I use Garin's old surname, *Kress*. Zhak doesn't have a fucking clue who I am, or that I've been in front of him this whole time."

Page's mouth forms a small, surprised 'oh.'

"Yeah. Now you see why my family's a little tense with me, huh?" Maelle rolls her eyes. "But I *had* no choice but to work with him, Page. Not if I wanted any chance to get near him. Zhak lets almost nobody get close to him, you've seen how damn paranoid he is. I needed to... to get to him somehow. *Really* get to him. Get him to trust me." She rolls her foot back and forth over the gravel. "It took me years to build up enough of a reputation for information-hawking that we were finally introduced. But here we are. And I'm going to destroy him."

"You mean... you're looking for a way to kill Zhak? Is that it?" Page asks warily.

Maelle laughs. "You think I haven't had several opportunities to kill him already?"

It's not as if Maelle hasn't thought of it. Zhak trusts her enough now that she's had him on the other side of an airlock at least twice, with the override to vent it into space under her hand. And he's left his plasma pistol right within her reach. Many times.

It's not like she hasn't got the guts to do it, it's just that—

"If I killed him, it would all be for nothing, Page. No, I'm going to get the money that he owed Rodin, and more than that. *I'm* going to get that Source artifact Zhak is after on the monk-ship. The Bird's Heart. If it's the real deal, it's supposed to be worth millions. Maybe even *hundreds* of millions. I'll find a way to sell it to the Nightblade myself! Or, hells, I can find another buyer! This thing is *legendary*."

She takes a deep breath, and she knows, at once, that Page *needs* to understand this.

"You can get so much more than those two hundred thousand credits we promised you," Maelle says. "I'm going to rip this job right out from under him, and I'm going to set up my family for *life*. Help me do this, Page... and you could probably go back and *buy* Kuuj Outpost."

PAGE FOUND
Bereda Compound, Laithe

AT DINNER THAT night, Reece and Maelle seem to have temporarily put aside their animosity, or else they've come to some uneasy truce. They're still noticeably frosty with one another, and they sit at opposite ends of the table, but they no longer seem to be in active conflict.

Page sits between Edlin and a thin, pale, red-haired older woman called Carleen, another one of the Bereda shop mechanics. Garin sits next to Edlin, and on Carleen's other side is another younger man—stocky and dark-haired with a tawny complexion—who Edlin introduces as Sal.

All of these people seem to live here, along with at least a half-dozen others who come through to fill their plates and gather around the communal table. The Compound, and the family within it, seems to extend far beyond Maelle and her immediate kin. Page tucks their names away one by one, intending to ask Maelle later how they're all related. Few of them look very much alike—maybe some of them received the Bereda name as a gift, like Rodin did.

"So, how'd you like the workshop tour?" Carleen asks, passing Page a bowl of bright green vegetables.

Page can't remember ever seeing food so *fresh* before. She scoops green sprouts onto her plate with the wooden serving spoon, wondering how many of these things you're supposed to take. She glances to Maelle's plate and follows her lead.

"The workshop was... It was really interesting," she says.

"That's one word for it," Edlin laughs. "By that you mean it was amazing, right? Or freaky as all hells. It's always a trip when folks see it for the first time. Alien hulls! What a life." He takes the bowl from Page and helps himself to a generous heap of the green sprouts. "Sometimes I forget just how *weird* our job is."

Page is suddenly conscious that all the eyes at the table have turned to her—the guest, by definition the most interesting person here. "I guess it *is* weird to think of it," she says. "But for me, it's weirder to imagine that there's been this alien war going on out there for all these years. The military fighting them, all these strange ships flying around... and meanwhile I was sitting on Kuuj Outpost wondering if the vents would give out this week or not." She spears a sprout and bites down on it, warm oil spilling into her mouth. "The aliens just didn't seem like that big of a deal, in the scheme of things, you know? It was so far from anything that was affecting us. Nothin' we could really do about it."

"Well, I suppose it's all the better for *our* business if most people don't know shit about these aliens," Carleen says. "Never mind that no ship we've ever built goes anywhere near as fast as the real thing, or that they can't possibly get the flying patterns right. We build the best hybrids on the market, but let's face it, all these fakes are half-baked if you have the first clue what you're looking for. Does it matter? Nope! All you gotta do is show a cargo crew that thorn shape on their scanners and that impenetrable hull material and they're all running for cover."

"We laugh, but I reckon *I'd* run, too, if I ever came across a *working* alien ship," says Edlin. "Wouldn't you?"

"Personally, I just wanna know where those things *came* from," Sal says. "Can you believe nobody knows, all these years into it? We don't know where their homeworld is, or what their civilization's like, or if there's more than one group of them... or anything about them, really. Damn." He pauses to cut himself another slice of the dark, thick-crusted bread loaf in the centre of the table. "Apparently there's some group that's tryin' to do genetic sequencing on 'em or something, to learn more about what they are. Like... I guess they must be harvesting cells from recovered bodies that they got from the wrecks or something? Ewww." He grimaces. "Alien dissections, am I right? That's proper horror stuff."

"Sal." Carleen swats at the back of Sal's head. "Not a topic for the table, come on. Manners. We've got a guest."

"Don't much matter what they *are*, the bigger problem is what they're *doing* to us," Edlin says grimly. "The govvies try to keep it out of the mainstream news... but apparently the Felen are absolutely demolishing the UWDF out in the deeps. They're losing this war, and badly. I reckon we're gonna start running into a shortage of components for the *human* part of our builds soon."

"Unbelievable," Sal says around a mouthful of bread. "Damn."

"Apparently the military's running real low on ships *and* pilots," Edlin goes on. "I read that the deffies have been landing out in the dust settlements now, looking for recruits. You seen that? Taking trainee pilots from the age of sixteen standard, practically still kids!" He drops his knife down on his plate for emphasis. "Fuck."

"That wouldn't surprise me one bit," Carleen says derisively. "What has the Union ever done but raid the settlements to protect the Primes? If it's not one thing, it's another. I swear the only reason they don't come knocking out here is that we've got too many resources of our own. We're not starving like the dust worlds. They know the Fourth Expansion's not desperate enough to give 'em our kids."

Garin heaves a long, weary sigh. "Got to admit the whole thing looks dire," he says.

"All feels a bit futile, doesn't it?" says Edlin. "I mean, we've got a tiny fraction of the Felen's firing power. We can't breach their body shielding, we have no idea how the fuck they communicate. We can't decipher any of their signals or intercept their data at all. They *don't even have a spoken language*. What do you do with that?"

Reece had slipped away from the table to take a call, but she walks back in from the direction of the galley just then, snapping shut her comms device and slipping it back into the clip on her belt.

"I'll tell you exactly what you do with that," she says. "You fucking stay far away from it, that's what, and you hope you'll make it to old age before these things actually wipe us all out."

"Are you saying you don't think the war is winnable?" Page ventures.

Reece shrugs. "Doubt it. Not in the long run. Making war on those things is only delaying the inevitable. Humanity finally met a natural predator."

"Oho, except there's nothin' natural about it. What's natural about a technological extinction?" Sal says.

Garin turns to Page. "Did you know that some people think this is a sign that the End of Time is coming? The onslaught of the Oblivion's spawn?" Garin's been drinking since before dinner started, and he's heading to the other side of sober now. His speech is a little slurred, his eyes drooping at the corners where his wrinkles gather. "Some people say these things are the Creatures of Torment, broken out of the dark prisons of our collective corrupted soul…"

"Oh, come on. Now *that's* rubbish," Carleen snorts. "*Creatures of Torment*, tch! That kind of crackpot shit's one step off claiming that Teyr is the Origin world." She gives Page an exaggerated look, and laughs. "What else has he been telling you?"

Edlin glances playfully toward Garin. "Old man was telling us his alien sighting stories, before."

"Yeah, an' who asked me to tell 'em, you little shit?" Garin grumbles, rolling his eyes.

"Garin, I swear," says Carleen. "If we haven't all heard those stories enough times—"

"Hey, Page hasn't heard them yet!"

"Don't you go scaring the poor girl," Carleen says, but there's a grudging smile on her lips, as if this is some kind of family joke.

"Scaring her? Nah... no way. She's got guts, she does. Don't ya, Page?" Garin reaches across Edlin to nudge Page's elbow, but he hits the edge of her plate instead, nearly knocking it off the table. "If you really wanna know what fearless is, though... Lemme tell you something. That used to be Reece's old nickname. They called her Little Fearless. Ace pilot of the age, right over here." Garin points across the table. "Have I told you how good she used to be?"

"Garin." Reece looks tense again. "That's enough, all right? Stop."

"Oh, don't let her play modest, now." Garin seems utterly unfazed by Reece's ire. "They used to say Reece Bereda would fly right into the open maw of the hells just to show 'em what's what."

"Huh. Did you ever fight in the war, then?" Page asks Reece before she can think the better of it. An ace pilot with no fear... that's who the UWDF should want to recruit, isn't it?

Out of the corner of her eye, she sees Maelle flinch, as if Page has said entirely the wrong thing.

"Hells, no. You'd never catch me in that uniform." Reece shakes her head vigorously. "And it's nothin' to do with fear. I'm not putting my life on the line for a lost cause. Protecting humankind?" Reece rolls her eyes. "Pff. Most of them aren't worth the trouble, are they?"

"Damn, that's cold," Edlin laughs.

"Be real, Eddy. You really think this shitscape of a civilization is worth dying to save?" She pushes her plate away. "It's bad enough to die for money. Was *that* even worth it? Was it worth it for Rodin? No. What did he die for?" She swears under her breath. "Nothing!"

Page glances over at Maelle, who's been all but silent the entire meal. She currently seems to be concentrating very intently on dragging a crust of bread through the remnants of the vegetable oil on her plate.

The table falls completely silent but for the clink of glasses and cutlery, as if no one dares to follow that up.

"So… what do you think, kid?" Garin asks Page after a long while, making successful contact with Page's elbow this time. "You reckon humanity's worth saving?"

"Uh… maybe. Sure," Page says with a shrug. "Probably?"

"Ringing endorsement over here," says Edlin.

"Well… I mean, humanity earned the inheritance of the gods, right?" says Page. "And even the gods didn't always get along with each other. The end goal isn't meant to be perfect harmony for us, but perfect self-knowledge. So… yeah, I'd say there's hope."

She startles a little at her own words. Where did *that* come from? There's a chorus of laughter around the table, the awkward silence finally broken. And then Garin claps her hard on the shoulder.

"That… is… profound!" Garin intones. "Not sure I quite get what you said, Page, but it damn well sounds like the truth, don't it? I think we should drink to that."

Carleen is already lining up a row of tall, narrow glasses, pouring measures of sour wine that she passes out to everyone.

"To Page, our idealist!" Garin bellows when he lifts up his glass. It looks minuscule in his large hand.

"To the idealist," the others chime in together.

Maelle raises her glass too, if a little more slowly than the others. But when she holds it aloft, her eyes meet Page's, and there's something more than sincerity in them. Maybe a tiny glimmer of hope.

* * *

PAGE WATCHES AS Garin downs a second glass of the sour wine, then moves on to the dregs of his flask before he shuffles off somewhere down the hall to retrieve more liquor. When he comes back again, he slumps down into his chair, head bowed like he might be about to fall asleep.

But then his head snaps up again, and he turns once more to Page. "Hey. Kid," he says to Page in a loud whisper. "There was one other time I saw a live Felen. Wanna hear about that one?"

"Garin," says Carleen warningly. "Come on—"

"I'm talkin' to our guest," Garin says, not unkindly. "You want to hear this one, right, kid? It wasn't but a little while ago... only happened maybe three years gone."

Page nods, unable to resist her curiosity. "Yes. Please."

"Wait, what? *Three* years ago?" Edlin leans forward, his eyes wide. "What the fuck, Garin?"

Even Reece looks rattled. "What? Where?"

"Ah, now you all wanna hear about it, huh?" Garin chortles to himself. "I didn't tell you at the time, 'cause, well. Y'know." He sniffs, gesturing around the table as if the rest of his sentence should be self-explanatory, his *told-you-so* gaze lingering the longest on Carleen. "Well, I guess I *don't* rightly know why I kept it to myself all this time. But when it happened, I just didn't wanna talk about it. Easier not to think of it. This is the first time I'm gonna tell it. So listen up."

The table has gone dead silent again, everyone staring at him expectantly.

"I was on the way to bid on some new salvage," Garin begins. His voice has gone low, almost reverent. "We'd had a call from one of our salvage dealers... and they told us about a nice solid piece of hull material being towed back from the orange zone." He looks over at Page. "New finds usually get towed out to one of the ancillaries for potential buyers to view, and they thought we might be interested in this one," he explains. "And of course, we *were* interested, so I told Reece I'd check it out." He pauses and takes a long swig from his recently refilled flask.

"They told me the seller was towing it to Anc-23. That's almost a day's haul outside our usual territory, but it sounded like a hot find. And I was already up on Anc-19 at our warehouse, so I packed my shit to go out there to see. I got the money together in a bag, the usual—with these kinds of exchanges, they tend to like the money up front, and in chits. So anyway... I head over there with our little hauler, clamps at the ready, thinking I'm gonna inspect this hull, haggle with 'em about the price if it's decent, and then crate it and haul that shit back here to Laithe."

He shakes a thick finger. "But nuh-uh. That's not what happened. I get all the way out there to Anc-23. I dock up exactly where they instruct me to. I wait there for ages... and then, finally, this old salvager comes out to the airlock to meet me. He says, hmm, the hull's not quite ready to inspect just yet. Obviously he's stalling me, right? He's talking around it, giving me a bit of a runaround. At this point I'm already suspecting something's going on, like maybe another bidder's on the way. But I'm ready to up the stakes, 'cause I always bring a bit extra for the bargaining. And then the guy leans closer... an' he says to me, real quiet-like: 'There's a specimen.'"

Page swallows hard. "He meant an *alien*, didn't he?"

"Oh, he sure did. But me, in the moment? I'm not quite getting it. I'm just staring at him like, 'There's a specimen? What in the hells are you talkin' about?' And then... well, then the guy takes me over there, takes me across the way. And he shows me this real beat-up Felen ship. They've got it suspended on clamps in the bay right there, basically still whole. Hull hasn't even been detached yet. And I can see there's ten or twelve people all standing around it lookin' real nervous, all armed to the teeth. And there's some other folks a bit closer to the ship, and they're draggin' something out. I'm looking at this thing, thinking *what in the hells*... and then it suddenly hits me. *That's* a fuckin' alien! Right there, right in front of me, closer than I've ever seen one. Closer than I was in the asteroid belt." He pauses. "And it's definitely *alive*."

"Shit," Edlin whispers. "What do they do?"

"Right? So at this point I'm thinking... there's a live alien, this is definitely not a job for salvagers, right? It's dangerous! Surely they're going to have to call the authorities to deal with this, or some kind of biohazard unit, or the military or... something? I've been in this business for a long while but I never really... I guess I never really *got* that we were just... takin' care of this kind of stuff all on our own." He looks at the flask in his hand. "Or maybe I just didn't want to know about it. Just wanted to believe we were finding these abandoned hulls floating around and pickin' them up for a little recycling. But of *course* they couldn't call the authorities, that was a fool thought to have. That salvager was knee-deep in illegal business, just trawling the orange zone in the first place! No. Of course he wasn't about to call the military."

"So what happened then?" Carleen, this time, breathless and awed, leaning forward in her chair.

"I... I don't know. They got it out, an' it was struggling around a bit, but I guess its bodysuit was damaged or whatever, 'cause they managed to overpower it. They sealed it into one of those big hazard containers that you put leaking engine cores in."

Garin wipes at his face, a faraway look in his eyes. "Then the guy in charge there took me over into the canteen, so I couldn't see much more. The folks that touched the alien all went off to the showers, and when they came back out again they brought out food and drink, a good spread, actin' like nothing ever happened. I could hardly eat anything, I was so damn shaken by the whole thing." He blinks slowly, recalling. "I never saw what they did with the alien. And I never did buy that hull. It was way more damaged than they'd said. Barely any of it would've been usable for us. I was relieved, to be honest. Passed on the deal, said thanks and goodbye, and off I went back home."

Carleen reaches for Garin's flask, prises it from his hand

and takes a long drink herself. "All right. I think that really *is* enough, now. I'll hang on to this." She looks toward the window and stares outside like she's deep in thought, and there's a long silence before anyone speaks again.

And then, Reece says: "Y'know the most surprising thing about all of this? It's that humanity has even stuck around long enough for someone else to wipe us out." She shakes her head. "It's a wonder we're still here."

"And that's why we can't give up on each other," says Maelle quietly.

AFTER DINNER, PAGE follows Maelle out to the courtyard. Maelle is still not speaking much, her hands shoved deep into the pockets of her black trousers, her gaze clouded with some impenetrable melancholy.

Laithe's huge sun is slowly setting in the sky, and Page tries not to stare too obviously at it, no matter how majestic it seems. It sinks toward the orange-and-yellow treetops in the hills, like—well, like a *regular sun*, she imagines, like any number of other suns on any number of other planets. It's not like Page hasn't seen a sunset in vids before. This one probably isn't even particularly notable. She ignores it and scuffs her ill-fitting blue boots along the edge of the courtyard.

"So, uh… what's with all the little shrines and altars around here?" Page points toward the small wooden display she's just noticed, right at the join where two of the courtyard's buildings meet. "I keep seeing those things around."

Maelle smiles that soft, fond smile that she seems to reserve for her father figure. "Ah. Those would be Garin's doing," she says. "He'll tell you that he doesn't *believe*, definitely not. Claims he's an atheist. But he still pulls leaves. And he always makes donations at the shrines when he travels."

Page moves toward the display, reaching out tentatively to touch the wooden figures. The Great Goddess stands in the centre, surrounded by smaller representations of other members of the Divine Pantheon. Her faceless head is gilded with a brush of gold paint, and at her feet is a small collection of dried-out leaves and twigs. A couple of the leaves look fresher than the others, as though they've just recently been placed there—one is still completely green.

Peering closer at the offerings, Page recognizes the pristine, many-pointed leaf that Garin snapped off the fruit tree just a few hours earlier. *Pulling leaves*. Of course. Page is familiar enough with the ritual—you're meant to collect green leaves or grass, and lay them at the feet of the goddess to thank her for the blessing of life on the Worlds. It's a rite that has survived transplantation into deep space; some outposts keep small gardens on their concourses specifically for the purpose. Even Kuuj had a meagre patch of anaemic lamp-grown shrubbery, where passing traders could grab a leaf for a two-chit donation. And surprisingly, quite a few people availed themselves of the ritual—Page knows, she's stolen the donation box enough times.

She examines Garin's altar, marvelling at the evident care with which it's been made. There's a pattern of small leaves carved all around the edge of the shrine, and a flowering vine adorns the edge of the goddess's cloud-wreathed robe.

When did Page first hear about pulling leaves?

She attempts to conjure the memory with more clarity, then tries to remember the first time she ever saw someone pull a leaf on Kuuj. She knows she wrote in her diary about it, how peculiar it had seemed, and how certain she was that it must have *meant* something to her. She had wondered what was happening and known the answer at the exact same time, that buried knowledge rushing to the front of her mind like it had always been there.

It was the first time Page ever saw anybody do it. And yet it can't have been the first. She must have seen it before, in her former life. Though that hardly narrows things down very much—pulling leaves is not exactly an obscure tradition. She contemplates the goddess's wooden likeness, wondering if any deity can answer the kind of questions she has.

"Do the Teyrians pull leaves?" she asks Maelle. "Would they hold to this tradition?"

Maelle looks thoughtful. "Hmm... I don't know. I mean... the whole thing's to do with collecting leaves from the planets the Goddess helped humanity get to, right? A ritual to thank her for spreading the gift of life to other worlds. And with Teyr... Well, their whole deal is that they're supposed to *be* the Origin world. They think they had a green world before the Goddess even got there! So why would they need to pull leaves?"

"I guess. Yeah, you're right. Probably not, then."

From everything Page has read, Teyr always held strongly to their own traditions and unique beliefs. They were very much set in their ways, even when they were still part of the United Worlds. They revered the other gods, too, and they acknowledged the whole Source Pantheon just like the Union worlds. But they held the Great Goddess in much higher regard than the rest of them. They called her the *Fair-Feathered Goddess*.

"On Teyr, I think the Goddess would've been sculpted in her bird form, not a humanoid-looking one like this," Page says. "They almost always show her as a bird."

Maelle gives her a little smile. She says nothing, but there's unmistakable delight in her eyes at the suggestion that Page has been studying the materials. Page hasn't agreed, yet, that she'll play along with Maelle's scheme. But the signs must be looking good.

Page picks up Garin's green leaf from the shrine and toys with it, twirling it around by the stem, studying the paler green veins that run along its underside. "Must be nice for those Teyrian monks, to know exactly what they believe," she muses. "Me, I've got no idea. How are you meant to know if you're a... good believer?"

Maelle shrugs. "I'm not sure. I'd say that's between you and whatever gods you hold to." She scrutinizes Page for a moment more before she reaches her hand out slowly, laying a hand on Page's shoulder with something almost like tenderness. "Look," she says. "I know you feel lost, Page. You're worried that sometimes you don't know what you really want, or what to believe. But honestly, I think that's more normal than you think, memories or no memories. We all feel it." She smiles reassuringly. "But if a little communing-with-the-gods would make you feel better, then have at it."

Page reaches out and sets the green leaf back down, laying it gently at the wooden goddess's feet. She mumbles an invocation of thanks in Graya, and she doesn't think about where she heard this one.

"There you go," Maelle says with a smile.

"Hmm. I don't know if it makes me feel *better*, exactly," Page says hesitantly. "It feels... honestly, it feels a bit silly, like I'm playing pretend. But since I don't even know who I really am... if I *did* want to pray, or meditate, or whatever... how would I know what to do? How would I know which god to invoke, or how to start?" She sighs. "I'm pretty sure you're supposed to be taught all that stuff by someone else. Not just figure it out all by yourself."

"Oh, you *can* be taught it, sure," Maelle says. "You can read the Source texts and look at relics and study the theological and philosophical implications of life's big questions. But... I think most of this stuff *is* something you've just got to discover for yourself, Page. You get there by asking your own questions. Finding your own answers, your own meanings. Figuring out what the divine means for *you*, not for anybody else." She looks back at the little shrine. "I asked Garin once why he pulls leaves. He said it reminds him to stop and feel grateful for all the living things around us. He said it makes him feel like he's connected to something. Not a god, necessarily, but all the other people who did this before. And that means something, too."

Page stays quiet for a while before she gathers herself to speak again. "Can I ask *you* a question?"

"Sure. Shoot."

"Where do *you* think I should start, if I wanted to... to try some of this? If you were me, what god would you call to for help?"

"If I were you? Oh, it would definitely be Yhannis," says Maelle after barely a moment's pause. "That's exactly who you want. The good ol' god of travellers, wandering folks, nomads and lost things. And a champion of hopeless causes, too." She fishes around in her pocket and pulls out what looks like a flat stone amulet. "Here, look. That's Yhannis, right there."

Page delicately takes the little oval from Maelle's outstretched fingers and holds it up to the waning light, examining the object. It's rubbed almost completely smooth on one side, with a deep groove in the middle. On the other side there's an engraving of the god: a tall, thin humanoid figure in a cloak, holding a long staff in one hand.

Her heart leaps. For a moment, she feels that almost-remembering, like she's slipping between sleep and waking. She stares at the tiny, faded text that runs in two rows around the edge of the amulet, surrounding the god-figure.

It's written in Union Basic:

THE END IS NOT THE END.
THE BEGINNING IS NOT THE BEGINNING.
BE WITH ME AT EVERY MOMENT OF THE JOURNEY;
REMIND ME OF THAT WHICH IS TRUE.

"What?" Page whispers. "What does it mean?"

"It's an invocation to Yhannis," Maelle says. "I think it's supposed to be about staying focused in the present. The importance of the journey, or something like that. I recite it to myself sometimes, when I need to calm myself down." She's quiet for a beat before she adds, "This talisman used to be Rodin's."

"Oh!" Page curls her other hand protectively around it, suddenly realizing how dear this object must be to Maelle. "He was devoted to Yhannis, then?"

Maelle shrugs. "You know what? I don't really know. He never really spoke about gods. Not that I can recall. But this was among his stuff, in his room here." A tear escapes one eye, and a rivulet of black kohl runs to the curve of her cheek. "I guess it must have meant something to him."

"Yeah," Page whispers. She turns it over in her hand, her eyes fixed on that carved figure. There's something about this—something so—

"What is it?" Maelle asks.

"Nothing, I just—I really think I've seen this before. Yhannis. Or… another picture of him." The words catch in her throat. "When I hold it, I feel…" She trails off. "I can't explain it. Safe?"

"Well, maybe you should hold on to it, then." Maelle sounds a little choked, but she nods at the talisman. "Keep it for now. Just for a little while. You can have it till tomorrow."

"No way," Page says. Her heartbeat quickens, and she's not sure if it's the talisman making her feel oddly emotional or the idea that Maelle really *must* trust her. "I can't take this. It was Rodin's. It's yours. And I don't know if I ought to—"

"Yhannis is a traveller." Maelle smiles tearfully, closing her hand over Page's. "He journeys to wherever he's needed. And it sounds like right now… Well, maybe he feels like taking a little trip."

MYTHOLOGIES OF THE GREAT GODDESS

Excerpt from Final Term Paper submitted by [Student ID 1116]
First year Mythological and Spiritual Studies, University of Monaxas
Course Title: 'On the Many Mythologies of the Great Goddess'

The story is often told, by children and sages alike, of the journey of the Curious Spirit to warn the gods of an oncoming doom.

In some stories, the Curious One becomes frightened after seeing the Oblivion, the Demon Queen. She runs in the wrong direction and is lost for a long time, wandering through the cosmic void until – nearly at the point of exhaustion – she finds her way back to the Greenworld that she has been observing in secret. In dire need of rest, she drops to the planet in the shape of a bird and collapses. When they care for her and revive her, she reveals her true nature to the humans whom she has already grown to love. She is given help by the kind humans, and their aid restores her for the journey home.

In other stories, the order of events is found somewhat changed. Here, it is only after her discovery of the Oblivion's plot that the Curious One finds the humans. She learns of the plotting of the Demon Queen, then flees and loses her way, and in doing so she stumbles upon the Greenworld and sees the humans for the first time.

But my essay will not be concerned with those earlier details of the Goddess's journey. In this analysis, I will seek to examine the differences found in the tellings of the Curious Spirit's story <u>after</u> her return to the Celestial Kingdom.

The oldest Source texts generally agree that after being nursed back to strength by the humans, the Curious One returns to the kingdom of the gods, bearing the dark tidings of the plot to overthrow the Divine Pantheon. And there, she warns the gods in time so they can prepare for battle, which in turn allows them to avert the

Oblivion's plans for total destruction. And not only do they save the Celestial Kingdom, they also save the Greenworld. They ward the Unbreakable World, granting the human homeworld everlasting life, so that it may be preserved beyond the ending of the universe.

It is interesting to note that many versions of the story elide the specific events of this part of the divine timeline completely. Some retellings imply that the Curious One returned to the Celestial Kingdom, reported her findings to the Higher Gods, and was immediately elevated to full divinity as a reward for her intervention – a blessing she then passed to her beloved Greenworld. They do not really go into much more detail than that. But in the Source texts themselves, we find the bones of a much more complex tale.

Some of these early texts seem to make more of the Curious One's lack of credibility before the other gods, and here we encounter the idea that the Higher Gods did not, at first, believe her when she told them what she saw. Upon her return to the Celestial Kingdom, the gods initially did not want to admit that the Oblivion could have sown such chaos in their midst, nor to believe that there were traitors among them who would wish to harm the Celestial Kingdom.

In these versions, the Higher Gods initially claim that the Curious One is lying, or that she has let her fanciful imagination get away with her. In some versions, she is even banished for daring to tell such a tale, and she must sneak back into the Celestial Kingdom a second time to find someone who is willing to heed her warning. We find one such account in an early Monaxan translation of this myth [see citation 23]:

> The words [the Curious One] spoke fell on disbelieving ears. And so decreed the Higher Gods when she begged for their attention: 'There is no such treachery here, no, there is no treason known in our divine kingdom. Go away, foolish spirit, go back to your childish games. Do not trouble yourself with the affairs of the gods.'

Another text gives a similar description, and specifically states that the Curious One is being 'banished' from the stronghold of the Celestial Kingdom [see citation 24]:

> **Banished shall you be from these walls for such tales! No more shall you dwell here in our blessed sanctuary! You shall not sow discord where there is peace, nor doubt where there is harmony.**

In the later reinterpretations of the myth, beginning from the first annals of the Latter Worlds, we find this version of the story repeated with much more frequency, often to the exclusion of the alternatives. Wherever the myth and its associated folk tales have travelled to settlements beyond the Primes, a second deity almost always features prominently in the Curious One's journey [see citation 25]:

> **Only Yhannis the Wise, the Finder of Lost Things, did listen to the Curious Spirit's tale. It was Yhannis, thenceforth known as The Interlocutor, who brought the dire warning to the High Gods, and who spoke to them on behalf of the spirit whose voice was too small to be heard.**

The idea of Yhannis's intervention to convince the other gods to listen to the Curious One's tale has become central to many retellings. This version is the one popularized and retold in most of the Latter Worlds, where the Traveller God's part of the tale is given even more embellishment and significance.

Yhannis, while present in other stories in the Source texts, is a comparatively minor figure in the other tales of the Pantheon. However, he has gained increasing popularity among spacefarers, and in more modern folk traditions.

One can easily draw parallels between the idea of a divine 'interlocutor' who speaks for lesser voices, and the politically and socially weaker position held by the Latter Worlds, relative to the power wielded by the Primes of the Union. Within the Prime systems, the imagery of Yhannis is historically found with greater frequency on satellite settlements – for example, on settled moons or in orbital communities.

In this paper, I will examine the use of Yhannis's story and imagery in the Goddess Myths, and the influence those stories have had on political and artistic movements spanning from the Imperial Ages to the founding of the Latter Worlds.

DALYA
OF HOUSE EDAMAUN, IN HER SIXTEENTH YEAR
First-City, Teyr

The Edamaun house was vast, but whenever Uncle was in a bad mood, the entire building felt like it was coiled tight with tension. Uncle seldom got *angry*, exactly—not outwardly, at least. He would not slam doors or shout or make any big show of his emotion. That would have been an affront to the Goddess. Wrath, visible anger, uncontrolled outbursts, these things did not become a good believer.

But Dalya had learned to recognize Uncle's quiet, unspoken anger, and she felt it like a building storm. Something was clearly bothering him, and it had been happening more and more often of late. The household attendants stepped more delicately than usual, whispering to one another in the halls with low, worried voices. The door to Uncle's study was kept closed. Dalya preferred to avoid him, retreating to her rooms when she finished her lessons, emerging as little as possible until those tempestuous clouds had lifted.

Uncle had been in a dark and introspective mood for several days now, taking his meals in his study, sending her away with a 'not now, Dalya' and a wave of his hand whenever she tried to speak to him.

But that evening, something unusual happened: Uncle came to see her in her rooms.

She knew it was him when his knock came at the door, because he always knocked the same way. Three times, then three times more, like the six-chime of the bells. Knocking less than six times was unholy, some said—demons may open the door.

Uncle rarely ventured to this part of the house. Long ago, Heral had told Dalya that he'd moved out of the familial wing after Nathin died, relocating his own bedchamber to the distant wing where his study was. He said it was because his work often called him to his desk at odd hours, and it was easier for him to be closer to his office—but Dalya had never believed him.

When she was a young child, Dalya had always imagined that Uncle did not like to walk this way because Nathin had once dwelt in the room that was now hers. Perhaps it pained him too much to think of it being Dalya's space now—of this *imposter* being here, this awkward, ill-suited child who disturbed his son's gentle ghost. But as she grew older, sometimes she wondered if it was quite the opposite. If entering the familial wing made Uncle too soft somehow, flaying open the parts of him that he would rather not show to her.

Dalya put down her comb and went to answer the knock. Uncle must be here to admonish her about something. And it must be dire indeed if he could not wait to see her until breakfast, when they usually spoke together.

But when Dalya opened the door, Uncle just stood there, saying nothing. He had been at a meeting with some other members of the Gepcot earlier, and he was still in formal clothes now, layers of heavy blue and gold robes cascading to the ground.

"Dalya," he said, enunciating each syllable of her name as crisply and clearly as when he read from his prayer book. "May I come in? I must speak to you in private. It is an important matter."

Dalya blinked. Uncle *never* had the time to speak to her in private, and certainly not on a day when he had important Gepcot engagements. There was something different about him tonight. His angular face, high cheekbones and sharp chin looked the same as ever, but something had changed in his eyes. There was a fierce, furious fire in the look he gave her that terrified her a little.

"Do you know why Teyr had to be made Unbreakable, Dalya?" he asked when they were seated side by side at her study table.

Dalya wondered which specific sacred text or article from her studies he wanted her to recite, but something made her hesitate, sensing that he wanted her to seek his guidance instead of giving an answer. "Why, Uncle?"

"For our survival." Uncle's eyes were distant. "For *humanity's* survival. That's what was at stake, what has always been at stake. And survival requires sacrifices, Dalya. Sometimes, we must do things that are difficult, things which run against our own desires. I have done many such things in the service of our people. Do you understand?"

Dalya nodded. She wasn't entirely sure what he meant, but she acquiesced nonetheless, lowering her eyes.

"Good. You are in your sixteenth year now—you are ready for the next steps in your education. From now on, you will have a different kind of lesson. Your new tutors will arrive tomorrow."

"New tutors?" She looked at him in confusion. "What for?"

"For the ways of the many worlds," Uncle said enigmatically. "These are excellent teachers. They come from a Union planet called Saymu Prime. They will teach you the common tongue of the United Worlds, Dalya. And you'll be guided in some offworld customs."

Dalya's pulse raced with apprehension. Was this some kind of test, to see if she would refuse? Speaking a foreign tongue was all but forbidden in the highborn houses of Teyr.

Of course, she knew there were scholars who studied the other languages of humanity. Many moonfolk knew the common tongue, like Anda and her uncle did. There were people in the Protectorate who knew much about the United Worlds and their history, who were able to read stories from other places.

But such knowledge was the realm of the Moon-City. Dalya had never known anyone like that who was born on Teyr.

There had been no contact with the outside galaxy or with the United Worlds in so many years, and she'd thought that foreigners no longer came here from worlds beyond the Moon-City. So what need could there be to learn offworld customs, or to speak anything but the Perfect Cadence here on Teyr?

"I—I don't understand why you ask this of me, Uncle. I thought we were never to treat with outsiders. It is forbidden... is it not?"

Uncle tensed, and for a moment, Dalya wondered if her question would provoke a rare outward expression of anger. But he only sighed, as though he were terribly weary.

"There are things you do not yet understand," he said. "In time, you will learn why this must be done. But trust that I am doing what is necessary to ensure our survival, Dalya. And that the secrets you keep will protect Teyr for centuries to come. You will learn from your new teachers, and you will obey them as you obeyed your old tutors. From tomorrow, your lessons with the Saymu will begin. Do you understand?"

She nodded slowly. "Yes, Uncle."

"You must speak of this to no one except Heral, Dalya. These lessons must be our secret." He looked at her gravely. "This could not be any more serious—for us, for our family, or for our people. You have a special duty, my child. But it does mean that you will have to break some rules you've been taught, and bear an unusual burden."

Dalya's heart leapt hopefully, as it always did when he referred to her as *his child*. It was a small thing, but she had always known that she could never fill the space left in his heart by Nathin's death. The implication that she belonged in that space at all felt like a boon. Surely this meant that he would have called on Nathin to do this duty, if only he still had his son. All Dalya could do was try to prove that she could live up to the responsibility.

"I suppose that the Great Goddess disobeyed the rules once, too," she said quietly. "And it was for good, in the end. It is why we are beloved of Her Divine Grace."

"What?" Uncle arched an eyebrow. "What did you say?"

"The Goddess. When she was still a lowly spirit," Dalya said. "She disobeyed the Higher Gods who told her to stay in the palace... but instead, she sneaked away from the Celestial Kingdom. And that's when she came down from the heavens to speak to the humans. She wasn't meant to do that. It wasn't allowed. But it was a good thing she did it, in the end. So... I suppose that this disobedience with the outsiders, it's... a little bit like that?"

Uncle's face softened in a way she had seldom seen it do before, and for a moment she thought she saw tears glistening in his eyes.

"Yes," he said. "It is exactly like that, Dalya. Sometimes, disobedient footsteps do take you to the right place. And sometimes, when you feel it—when you feel a path calling you to go somewhere unexpected—that's the divine inspiration in you."

She nodded again. "I will make you proud, Uncle," she said. "I will dedicate myself to my studies, just as your child should." She looked up at Uncle curiously. "Did Nathin have to study the common tongue, too?"

Uncle's back stiffened at that, his shoulders drawing together, his jaw suddenly tightening as if something she said had wounded him. "Do not speak of Nathin," he told Dalya. "I told you long ago that you are not to mention that name."

"I only thought—"

"No." Uncle shook his head. "You are *not* Nathin. You are on your own journey, Dalya, and you always have been. Do not look for his footsteps. Find your own path."

She nodded. "Yes, Uncle."

He pressed a hand to her shoulder for a brief moment before he stood up to leave.

"Oh," he said, pausing in the doorway as if he'd only just remembered something. "There is one more thing. From now on, you will spend much less time with Anda Agote," Uncle said. "I do not think she is a good influence."

"What? What do you mean?" Dalya's voice rose with shock, and for a moment she was unsure if she'd heard him correctly. "Anda is my best friend! Are—are you and Ker Agote not friends as well? He has sent us so many gifts—"

Uncle's eyebrows went up. "Ker Agote's gifts are no longer welcome," he said. "And Anda is not to be invited here anymore. That is final. I will say no more on the matter."

"But *why*—"

"Enough, Dalya," Uncle said, in that tone that brooked no further argument. "You are my heir, and that means you must rely on me for guidance while you are still young. Trust that I will not steer you wrong. If I tell you to do something, know that I will give you good counsel, and that I am doing it to protect you." He raised a finger. "Where the Agote family goes, trouble follows. I do not want trouble for you."

"Is it... because Anda's parents weren't good believers?" Dalya asked, risking the boldness it required to speak again. "Because they published those papers about the Unbreakable World?"

"What?" At this, Uncle's posture stiffened again, and he whirled abruptly. "Dalya! Where did you hear such a thing?"

Dalya had never spoken of what Anda told her that night on the balcony, not to anyone, not in all this time. They had long ago forgiven each other after that horrible argument, and guilt flooded Dalya as she let Anda's secret slip from her mouth. But surely Uncle must know already, and that's why he was banishing the Agotes. She had to make him understand that it wasn't Anda's fault that her parents—

"I can't remember where I heard it," Dalya lied, her mouth going dry. Uncle's sharp eyes scanned her face, and she could feel her cheeks reddening under his searching gaze.

"Dalya," he said. "Do not defy me on this. From today, you are no longer to speak with the Agote family, and no more will be said of it. I am not to see Anda in these halls, nor you in her company, in town or elsewhere. And under no circumstances are you to go anywhere with Ker Agote. Have I made myself very clear?"

"Yes, Uncle," Dalya whispered, and she bowed her head obediently.

"We are at a crossroads," Uncle said, his voice strangely gentle again. "It is not always easy to see the right path. Sometimes, the right path seems monstrous. But it is the only way."

THE STORYTELLER

Recording start 05:35:02

Now, the whole Teyrian Job probably never would have existed if it wasn't for one man. Luwan Edamaun, that was his name – I'll never forget it. I never met the man myself, but we heard enough bits and pieces from the Saymu mercs. He was the one behind all of it.

See, back then, Edamaun was the High Speaker of the Gepcot on Teyr. He was pretty much the most important man on that forsaken planet – as far as Teyr was concerned, he spoke for the people, for the Temple, for the Great Goddess, all of it. Outside of Teyr, practically nobody's ever heard of this guy, but in the Protectorate, he was a living icon. And of course, that means that publicly, Edamaun was all in on Teyrian Primacy. All that stuff about the apocalypse, and Teyr being the Unbreakable World, and all of that.

But it gets so much weirder. 'Cause, see, Edamaun's leadership was the big push behind this initiative they called the Returning. And the Returning... that was all about getting the moonfolk that were settled on Meneyr to move back to Teyr's surface. Just in case the moon also blew up when the whole rest of the universe disappeared. [*laughs*] Yeah, yeah, I know. Sounds real wild. But this whole thing, all those apocalyptic predictions, the Returning... Edamaun himself never believed in any of it.

See, it's like this. Edamaun knew damn well that Teyrian Primacy is a fraud. The whole Gepcot's always been well aware that Teyr's got no special divine protection, that their planet is not the gods-damned Greenworld. But now suddenly this alien war starts heating up, and they know they're absolutely fucked for defence against the Felen. They've got no real-world protection, 'cause some smartasses a few generations back decided that Teyr should leave the Union. And so now, with the cards all down... now they're on their own.

This wasn't even the worst of the war yet, of course, but things were bad enough already that it had them worried. They were getting real scared that, hey, they're sitting there undefended, wide open to the Felen. They've totally isolated themselves. And sure, they've still got these hidden Union bank accounts and illegal comm links... but they've got no more access to UWDF military intelligence.

So, what does Edamaun do to shield himself? 'Course, he's thinking, how can he protect the planet while he also protects his own power? How in the hells does the Gepcot get out of this mess?

Publicly, of course, Edamaun couldn't possibly speak the truth. There's no way he could move on any of this out in the open. His entire authority – their whole social structure, really – is built on the concept of Teyrian Primacy. On the idea that their planet is the Unbreakable World, the one and only safe place in the universe. So what in the fuck would they need military protection for? [*laughs*] Yeeaah. A mess, I'm telling you.

And here's the other thing. The whole time he's been in power, Edamaun's other big initiative was that he'd been cracking down on all the rebellious movements popping up out of Meneyr. And there's always been this real loud group of people out there in the Moon-City that want to expose the Teyrian Primacy as nonsense.

These people don't want to leave the moon and go back to Teyr. Not now and not ever. They start calling out all that end-of-the-world stuff as fabrication. And then a lot of those same people start agitating about other things, because they want the Protectorate to petition to rejoin the Union. They want back into the United Worlds, so they can actually get UWDF military protection. Which they do, in fact, need.

And then... Well, shit. Some of the people on Teyr actually started listening to these moonfolk. People on Teyr started speaking up against the Gepcot. Those little pockets of resistance on Meneyr kept flooding the local networks with banned scientific papers, showing all these proofs that debunk Teyrian Primacy. They were disseminating all the damning evidence that the Gepcot tried to keep out of Teyr. And the Gepcot, of course, went into panic mode.

And, well, I guess that's when Luwan Edamaun started making some real bad decisions. Because that's when he got in bed with an offworld mercenary cell operating out of Saymu Prime.

Now, if you're up on your history, you can probably trace all this shit back to the legacy connections between Teyr and the old SP empire. These alliances are older than the Union, they go way back to the Imperial Ages. Always there in the background. They'll still be going on as long as humanity survives.

And here's where Vonnie and I come in – 'cause of course, Vonnie got us in with those Saymu mercs. This shit was all being backed by some old-school Prime aristos – because this always comes back to old money.

And here comes the kicker. This whole damn time, Edamaun was using the Returning flights as a cover for his offworld activities. Every time one of those voyagers went back to the moon, the Gepcot was ferrying tons of Teyrian artifacts – I'm talking centuries-old Source stuff that they've been preserving – out to Meneyr. That's how they're paying for all of this.

Every time a Returning flight came down to Teyr, the empty vessels got stocked with crates upon crates of these artifacts, which were being smuggled back up to Meneyr, to the Moon-City – and then onward into Union space. Edamaun was selling tons of this stuff, sending it all to Saymu Prime. Paying for – wait for it – the construction of that illegal P-def system that he wanted built around his planet.

For years, he'd already been paying the Saymu to give Teyr military protection in Protectorate space – a mercenary fleet, effectively, since Teyr could no longer officially be covered by Union forces. And now, Edamaun wanted the Saymu to build Teyr a death-hoop.

Well, like I said... Vonnie and I never met Luwan Edamaun face to face. We only talked to Edamaun's go-between. Agote was his name. He was the one who dealt directly with us and with those Saymu mercs, so that the Gepcot didn't have to get their hands dirty.

Agote used to go back and forth to Meneyr sometimes, kind of overseeing it all. Coordinating with us to shuffle the crated artifacts out to Saymu Prime, when we came in smuggling those P-def components they were using to build the death-hoop.

Oh, that guy, Agote... He was a real live wire. I liked him. He was pretty decent to work with, which I can't say for most of them. As I recall it, he had Saymu ancestry on his mother's side, going back to before Teyr split from the Union. That's how he was connected to all of it.

And I remember that Agote had this kid he took care of. It was his dead sister's kid, I think... his niece. He was always debating whether he should send her out to Saymu Prime, so she'd be safer, but he didn't want to be that far away from her, since he was the only family she had left. And so he'd taken her down to Teyr instead. He showed me a picture of her once when we got drunk together on Meneyr, an' he was real emotional about whether he was doing right by her. [*sighs*]

Damn, that was a long time ago. Anyway... I don't know exactly what happened to Agote, in the end... but I still think about him sometimes. He wasn't there by the end of the Teyrian Job. One day he just wasn't on the links anymore. Even his private Q-link was cut off. It was like he was never there at all.

You don't ask questions in this biz, but I can guess what probably happened. Still... I like to imagine he got out. That he took the kid with him, that they went to Saymu Prime, or somewhere else... That he raised her somewhere nice and safe.

Yeah. [*long pause*] That would be nice, wouldn't it?

OPERATION ANGEL'S EYE
Private Channel

RO THE GREAT: Approaching Angel's Eye, looks clear. Fearless, you good?
LITTLE FEARLESS: I hear you, pal – already here. We're in position.
RO THE GREAT: Wooo! Two minutes to intercept... Countdown engaged.
LITTLE FEARLESS: Right, coming in. Aiming for a sweep by the cargo bay, then circle round, mark six-eight-six, confirm?
RO THE GREAT: Confirm, on target. I see you, you're good! Scanners should have you by now... Intercept in three, two, one –

[AUTOMATED TRANSMISSION TO ALL CHANNELS – EMERGENCY EMERGENCY EMERGENCY – WE ARE UNDER ATTACK – PANIC ROOM ENGAGED – EMERGENCY EMERGENCY EMERGENCY – END AUTOMATED TRANSMISSION]

LITTLE FEARLESS: Hang on. Ro – Wait, wait – What's that? You picking that up?
RO THE GREAT: Oh, wow. Yeah. [*static*] What the fuck? Is that their emergency beacon?

[AUTOMATED TRANSMISSION TO ALL CHANNELS – EMERGENCY EMERGENCY EMERGENCY – WE ARE UNDER ATTACK – PANIC ROOM ENGAGED – EMERGENCY EMERGENCY EMERGENCY – END AUTOMATED TRANSMISSION]

LITTLE FEARLESS: Hey, Zhak? Listen, we're picking up an emergency transmission from your ship. It's some kind of automatic message. Did you not cut your whole comms array? Shut that thing off!

[*static*]

LITTLE FEARLESS: Hello? Zhak!

[*static*]

[AUTOMATED TRANSMISSION TO ALL CHANNELS – EMERGENCY EMERGENCY EMERGENCY – WE ARE UNDER ATTACK – PANIC ROOM ENGAGED – EMERGENCY EMERGENCY EMERGENCY – END AUTOMATED TRANSMISSION]

LITTLE FEARLESS: Fuck. I told him to take all the internal comms offline before he pulled the panic alarm. I think he did it in the wrong order.

[*static*]

LITTLE FEARLESS: That ship's screaming for help to anyone who can hear it. Zhak! Do you read us?

[*static*]

LITTLE FEARLESS: Damn it. That fucking [*unintelligible swearing*], what is he – ?

[*AUTOMATED TRANSMISSION TO ALL CHANNELS – EMERGENCY EMERGENCY EMERGENCY – WE ARE UNDER ATTACK – PANIC ROOM ENGAGED – EMERGENCY EMERGENCY EMERGENCY – END AUTOMATED TRANSMISSION*]

RO THE GREAT: Gods, it's still goin'! You'd think when a guy hires you to rob his own ship, he could get his shit together, huh? [*laughs*] Wow. This guy's about as smart as a –

LITTLE FEARLESS: Ro, hang on. Hold off. I've got a bad feeling here. Circle wide.

RO THE GREAT: Holding off, Fearless! [*laughs*] Circling wide. Coming back to you.

[*AUTOMATED TRANSMISSION TO ALL CHANNELS – EMERGENCY EMERGENCY EMERGENCY – WE ARE UNDER ATTACK – PANIC ROOM ENGAGED – EMERGENCY EMERGENCY EMERGENCY – END AUTOMATED TRANSMISSION*]

LITTLE FEARLESS: Oh, for – Ugh. Pull up your readout, Ro. I'm looking at eight ship signatures here, closing fast. He's brought a gods-damned Union patrol down on us.

RO THE GREAT: Fuck! For real?

LITTLE FEARLESS: We've got to bail. [*static*] Zhak! Listen, we've got to abort this, I've got Union ships coming up on us. You see that?

[*static*]

LITTLE FEARLESS: Right, that's it. We're out. Pop your hull and drop it, Ro, we have to get out of here. If we're real lucky we can come back for 'em later.

RO THE GREAT: Separating hull. [*pause*] All clear, there it goes... Oh! Whoa! [*garbled*] Oh, shit!

LITTLE FEARLESS: Ro? What's happening?

RO THE GREAT: I'm – I think I'm taking fire! What the – gods damn! [*garbled*] Target's shooting at us!

[*AUTOMATED TRANSMISSION TO ALL CHANNELS – EMERGENCY EMERGENCY EMERGENCY – WE ARE UNDER ATTACK – PANIC ROOM ENGAGED – EMERGENCY EMERGENCY EMERGENCY – END AUTOMATED TRANSMISSION*]

LITTLE FEARLESS: Zhak! What in the hells is wrong with you? Are you firing on us?
RO THE GREAT: Fall back, mama! Fall back! I'm – [*explosions, static*]
LITTLE FEARLESS: Ro? Rodin! [*screaming*] RODIN!
RO THE GREAT: [*static*]

MAELLE KRESS
Bereda Compound, Laithe

NORMALLY, MAELLE RELISHES her solitude, and protects it diligently. She's certainly got enough to think about tonight. But when she walks away from Garin's wooden altar, Page keeps on walking after her, and Maelle just... doesn't send her away.

They walk side by side in the dark, their hands nearly touching but not quite, their boots crunching through piles of dead leaves as they move away from the Compound in the opposite direction from the spaceport. Behind them, the windows cast a distant yellow glow, and soon that, too, fades away. Their view back to the Compound is hidden by the copse of trees as the path dips down into a slight valley.

Maelle pulls on her headlamp and lights it on the lowest setting. It haloes them both with its warm glow as Page follows her lead, stepping cautiously on the loose earth. She sees a glimmer of reflection in the corner of her eye, and notices that Page is pulling one of the old workshop jackets out of her bag. She stops to tug it on against the evening chill. The reflective stripe on the sleeve shimmers under Maelle's light, where silvery letters surround the semicircular saw logo: *BEREDA FINE WOOD FURNISHINGS.*

"Reece gave it to me before I went out," Page says, noticing her looking.

"Oh," says Maelle. She hadn't intended to sound quite so surprised. "That's a shock."

Page gives her a withering look, but it's more sarcastic than genuinely wounded. "What, you really think I robbed your mother for a *jacket*? She said it might be cold out."

Maelle laughs. "Nah. I just, I..." She trails off, the words strangely caught behind her lips. "Sometimes I guess I... forget that she cares."

Page doesn't say anything. She just keeps walking, her eyes on the path ahead, and she steps a little closer to Maelle to make better use of the light as they descend the grassy slope.

"Over here, this way," Maelle says when they get to the bottom of the hill. "To the roamer." She points to one of the large land-roamers parked to the side of the equipment garage down here. It's a huge, multi-wheeled machine that Garin uses sometimes for moving crated ships to the spaceport. The cabin is so high up off the ground that there's a metal ladder on the side of it to get to the door.

"Whoa! Do you know how to drive that thing? We're going somewhere in *that*?" Page's voice goes up, and her laugh drifts through the dark.

"I do know how to drive it... but nah, we're not going anywhere," Maelle says, a smile breaking onto her own face at the sound. She gestures upwards. "We're gonna climb up there. The roof. C'mon, after me."

She grabs the ladder and pulls herself up. Instead of opening the door, she climbs past it and reaches up, grabbing hold of one of the roof-rails. There's a cargo bracket up there: three metal bars to strap smaller cargo to, with spools of cable and carabiners to hold them in place. But the rack is totally empty right now.

By the time Page gets to the roof, Maelle has already sat down and stretched herself out. And as soon as Page has clambered up beside her, Maelle switches off her headlamp.

Big mistake. The minute the light clicks off, Page *shrieks*. She flails around like she's drowning, fumbling for a handhold. She grabs Maelle's hair and sleeve as she hurls herself backwards, and she probably would have toppled over the side if it weren't for the rail. She yanks Maelle right to the edge along with her.

Maelle grabs hold of her with both hands, hauling Page back toward the middle of the roof. Her heart is hammering in her chest. "Whoa, whoa! Page!" she shouts. "Gods! What're you doing?"

"It's so dark!" Page gasps. "Too dark, too dark!"

Maelle's headlamp has been knocked off; she heard it land and skid away somewhere near them on the metal roof. She pats around with one hand to look for it while she holds on to Page with the other.

"Calm down, Page, shhh," she whispers. "Just give your eyes a few seconds to adjust, all right? And then… look up."

She feels Page gradually relaxing under her hand, the tension leaving her shoulders as she takes a few long, steadying breaths.

Maelle finds the headlamp at last, but she doesn't turn it on.

And then, very slowly, Page tilts her head back and looks.

Above them, the sky is alight with countless bright stars. There's the steady blink of the orbital, suspended high above them. A small white light dances low in the sky, where a dropshuttle is descending behind the distant trees.

"Oh," Page breathes, and her soft laugh is honey-warm, ringing through the quiet of the evening. "Damn. Wow."

"See! You see?" Maelle says, lifting her hand away. "That's what we came up here for."

"I… yeah." Page slumps back. "Sudden darkness freaks me out. I think it reminds me of the power failures on Kuuj. I panicked."

"Sorry." Maelle looks away guiltily. "My bad. I should've thought about that."

"No, no. It's fine," she says. "Really. I'm fine now."

She's slid against Maelle's side in the dark, so the back of her head rests on Maelle's arm. Maelle doesn't move away, and neither does Page.

They lie in silence that way for a while, looking up into the twinkling black. The descending craft must have landed and dropped off a pod at a spaceport somewhere across the lake, and a few minutes later it's ascending again, its silent cone of light rotating as it climbs.

"That's a shuttle over there, huh?" Page whispers, breaking the silence. "Same as the one that brought us?"

"Yeah, reckon so."

"Wonder where they were going."

"Don't we all," Maelle laughs.

Another silence, stretching long into the dark.

And then: "Do you really think I'm an idealist, for thinking humanity can make it?"

"Nah." Maelle shrugs her shoulders. "I mean, whether we're *worth* saving is a separate question. But I reckon we'll pull through, somehow. The human species survives. It's what we do. Even if the Union's wiped, one of these ditch ships that's trying to escape Union space will probably make it somewhere. A few people will survive."

"There's also those apocalypse bunkers in the asteroid belts," Page says. "Have you read about those?"

"Yeah. Some of them are being supplied for forty to sixty years, they say. Gods. Imagine living in a tiny little underground box for that long?"

"Better than stasis," Page laughs. "Or, you know… at least about the same as spending the next sixty years on Kuuj Outpost."

"Fair enough. But I don't know about the chances of making it out the other side. Who's to say the war will even be over by the time you run out of food?" Maelle says with a shrug. "It's probably a scam. But facts don't matter. People will still pay for it. It only matters what they *believe* is true." She clears her throat awkwardly. "Sorry. It gets kind of hard not to be cynical when your family makes a living the way mine does."

"Assuming it was for real, and you knew for sure you'd survive till the war ended... would you ever do it?" Page asks. "Get sealed into an apocalypse bunker, I mean?"

"Nah, no way," Maelle says. She stretches back, folding her hands behind her head. "I don't like hiding. It's not the way I was raised. I was always raised to confront things, to fight things face to face."

"Huh." Page looks up curiously. "How come *you* didn't go fight in the war, then? Did you ever think of signing on with the UWDF? Going up against the Felen?"

"Rodin tried, once. To join the military, I mean," Maelle says slowly. "He applied right when he finished his mechanic's apprenticeship. Thought he might work on Union ships, and help the war effort. But back then, they didn't want anyone with a less-than-perfect record, and he'd got into a little trouble with the law when he was younger. And just because of that... they thought he wasn't good enough, I guess." She laughs wryly. "Now look at them. Recruiting anyone they can find. Taking those fuckin' *kids* from the poor settlements. They're scraping for anyone and everyone they can throw into the fray. So... nah." She kicks the rail for emphasis. "Fuck the UWDF. If Rodin wasn't good enough for 'em, they can burn, for all I care. I never bothered applying, after that."

Maelle stares up into the sky, unexpected tears welling in her eyes. The shuttle is long out of sight now, the last embers of its white light melting into the darkness. It's a remarkably calm night, the air crisp and chilly, all quiet save for the occasional faint rustle of dry leaves. She wishes she could relax and enjoy it more.

"Have you thought about where you'll go after the job's done?" she asks Page at last. "I gather it won't be an apocalypse bunker."

Page is quiet for a long time, her breathing soft and steady at Maelle's side, and Maelle hopes she's thinking about her cut of their potential millions. She *has* to have made up her mind by now.

Page shifts her arm, rummaging in her pocket and taking out Rodin's little Yhannis talisman. She holds it between her fingers, tilting it up toward the sky, and the faint starlight catches on the glints of metallic paint still left in those worn grooves.

Page studies it intently, like there's some hidden meaning in it, and she runs a fingernail over the tiny text around the figure of Yhannis.

THE END IS NOT THE END. THE BEGINNING IS NOT THE BEGINNING.

And then, Page whispers something to herself in Graya.

"What?" Maelle sits up.

"I was looking at this invocation again," Page says. "It's kind of similar to that one Teyrian saying, about the *beginning and the end of everything*. Like it's... kind of the same concept, only spun around a little. I'm... not sure what I'm saying exactly."

"No, you're totally right," Maelle says. "I think that's the way it goes with a lot of the Prime World traditions. When they got taken out to the Latter Worlds, they got a bit... *remixed*. Reinterpreted through a different lens. Like... different people reading the same story and coming away with slightly different interpretations."

"Huh." Page's thumb strokes the talisman. "Do *you* ever wonder about this kind of stuff? Gods and all that?" Page asks. "I mean... All those stories and myths, the legends. Do you think it can really help with your problems?"

Maelle shrugs again. "I dunno. It's like I told you before, this stuff is real personal. It's up to you how much it can help. But if you're asking *me*... Well. It's not like I think that a god is gonna show up to give me all the answers to my problems. But sometimes... sometimes the questions themselves are comforting. Does that make sense? I like the fact that maybe there's some stuff we just can't ever know in this lifetime."

"Oh. I *hate* that," Page says matter-of-factly. "I hate that there are things I can't know. And, of course, with some things, I wonder if I *used to know*, and now I don't anymore..." She slips the talisman back into her pocket. "I guess it's probably a good thing to keep the god of lost things with me for a bit, huh? Just *in case* it helps."

Maelle tilts her head, letting the barest hint of a smile flicker over her lips. "Reckon so. It's like Garin says—these rituals can remind you that other people are out there doing the same things, too. People in the past and present and future, all looking for the same connections." She pauses. "And that it can't hurt to have someone to rely on besides yourself."

There's a long silence again. Page goes so still that for a minute Maelle wonders if she's fallen asleep. When she speaks again, there's a hesitation in her voice. "*You* don't rely on anyone... do you? Not even your family."

Maelle sighs. "It's complicated."

Another silence.

And then, swallowing against that tightness in her throat: "I used to rely on Rodin. He always had my back. But I don't know if I can trust anyone that way again."

"Yeah," Page says sadly. "At least you can *remember* trusting someone. I'm not so sure. I certainly didn't learn much in the way of trust on Kuuj." She looks back to the sky for a while. "I think... I'd like to trust *you*, though."

Maelle's heart leaps. She should take advantage of this, she knows—*of course you can trust me, of course this is real, of course you need a friend and I'm here and I like you and I care and I just happen to need you to help me hijack Zhaklam Evelor's scheme so you'd better be about to agree*—

But what comes out is: "I'm well aware of what I deserve from you, Page, and trust isn't it. It's a dangerous thing, trusting someone."

"Oh." Page sounds sad, almost hurt. "I just thought—when you let me borrow Rodin's talisman—that..." She shifts away from Maelle. "I thought that we were real friends now."

"Page, I helped kidnap you from Kuuj. I brought you here because I wanted to use you against Zhak, and I didn't feel bad about it." She sighs. "Listen, you can trust me to see this job through, to give you your cut and to see you to safety. On my honour, I'm good for that. The Bereda family doesn't raise betrayers. But beyond that... Page, this is a business partnership. And I think we should keep it at that. We get the job done, together, and then we part ways."

"Oh," Page says again. She sniffs softly, and it sounds like she might be crying.

"Page, it's nothin' personal," Maelle says. "I think it's just better to keep a distance."

She straightens her back and tucks her feet under her, looking toward the Compound. She can't see it from here, but she imagines that most of the lights are off now, except for the kitchen. That's where Reece always sits when she can't sleep at night, or when she's got too much to think about.

"Do you know about how the Nightblade got his shipping business?" Maelle asks.

"Um... nope." Page shrugs, and in the dim light Maelle imagines she sees something like relief in her face at the change of topic.

"Well, he used to have a partner, years ago. They called her the Void Snake, and apparently she was the brains behind their whole operation. She taught the Nightblade every damn thing he ever knew about smuggling. But in the end... he stabbed her in the back."

In the distance, another shuttle pod is coming down. Page is watching it intently as she listens to Maelle, tracking its slow, arcing descent.

"The Nightblade started out pretty much exactly the same way as Zhak," Maelle goes on. "Some rich, young university student. Prime educated, but no instincts. Too soft to survive in lawless space. The kind who wants other people to do everything for him... until he decides to throw them away." Her jaw clenches. "He and Zhak are both the exact same brand of asshole. The Void Snake gave the Nightblade everything, and he ruined her gods-damned life. She got sent to stasis prison when the Nightblade sold her out, and he walked away with the whole damn business they built together."

"Oh," Page says quietly.

"People like the Nightblade, and Zhak, and Tully... they're the only ones who ever get what they want," Maelle says.

Page is silent for a long time before she finally speaks again. "If I do this job with you, Maelle... I need you to know that I don't care about the damn money," she says. "I just... I thought maybe I found something else to care about again. It's too bad that *you* don't."

"It's not about *not caring*, all right?" Maelle snaps. "I care a whole fucking lot, Page. Sometimes I feel like I'm the only one who does."

"Maelle—"

"Reece is worried about me getting hurt. I get it. She's my mother. She's worried that this'll all end badly, that it's some kind of doomed revenge quest. But that's not her decision to make. I *have* to do this. I owe it to Rodin."

Page has pulled the Interlocutor's talisman back out, and she's turning it around and around in her hand again, her thumb stroking slowly over the text on its worn surface. Then she reaches out tentatively, slowly slipping her other hand over Maelle's and resting it against her knee.

"If it were you who'd been killed instead," she says, "and Rodin was the one left behind... what would you have wanted him to do?"

The question startles Maelle, and for a moment she's lost for an answer. But no, it's clear, isn't it? It's what she wishes he'd got to do, if Zhak hadn't shot that ship down.

"I'd just want him to *live*," Maelle answers. "Maybe to see the galaxy, travel around, see some *wonder* before it all burns down? To—I don't know, I'd want him to do whatever the hells he wanted! I mean, it's not like I'd want him to forget about me or anything, but... I wouldn't want him to miss out on life just because I was gone…" She trails off with shock, her cheeks burning with the realization of what she's just said as Page's hand squeezes against hers.

"See?" Page whispers. "I don't think he'd want that for you either, Maelle. But it's not really Rodin you're doing this for, is it?"

"It is," she insists stubbornly.

"It's not." Page smiles, and there's so much wisdom in those eyes for someone who has forgotten most of what she's known. For a moment, Maelle feels like she sees something more there, some fragment of whoever Page was before. "From one liar to another," Page says, "I know damn well when I'm lying to myself about why I'm doing things. And I know when other people are doing it."

"Yeah?" She looks away from Page. "So what *am* I doing all this for, then, in your opinion?"

Page tilts back her head contemplatively. "A sense of purpose," she finally whispers. "The same thing that held me on Kuuj, even when it made no sense. You tell yourself that you need to chase Zhak and get this money because otherwise you'd have to admit you have no idea what to do with the rest of your life. In some ways… you're the same as me."

"Right." Maelle lowers her gaze. Her head is pounding, her mind suddenly swirling with too many contradictions. "Fuck."

"Surviving's the first thing. Sometimes that's all you can do, I've been doing that for years already." Page presses her hand against Maelle's again. "I'm in. You have your monk," she says. "But when this is over… I want a chance to *live*."

ON REINCARNATION AND RENEWAL

Reading From 'The Divine Cycle: On Teyrian Belief Systems and Reincarnation' [Please read pages 81-93 for next lecture]

Like several other ancient Prime World cultures, the Teyrians subscribe to a belief in reincarnation. This belief is fundamental to their spiritual practice and to their general understanding of the universe and their place in it.

Reincarnation entails the idea of the human spirit's immortality, and that spirit's perpetual re-embodiment after each corporeal death. When a human being dies, the spirit will be re-housed in a new physical body, following a voyage through the cosmos that mirrors the Great Goddess's journey through the Cosmic Void.

(Note: In the undertaking of this journey, some Prime traditions invoke the god Yhannis as a guide who helps the spirit find their next incarnation. In this aspect, Yhannis is known under the epithet *He Who Guides*, and a depiction of Yhannis is included in many funerary rites across the Prime Worlds.)

Several passages in the Sacred Texts ascribe the immortality of human souls directly to the elevation of the Curious One to full godhood. When the Small Spirit was granted her divinity, she shared a sliver of her blessing with the humans. Through her intervention, never-ending life was granted to the spirits of all the people on her beloved Greenworld, 'made eternal through the impenetrable shield of her love, so that none may ever perish.' [*Divine Tenets*, 7E-87] Thus, every immortal spirit in existence is that of an individual who was born on the First World.

Philosophically, this idea does lead to some logistical problems – for instance, it is an indisputable fact that there are many more humans in existence today, scattered across many worlds and exosettlements, than could possibly have lived on humanity's Origin planet. Various religious and spiritual traditions have dealt with this contradiction in different ways – for example, by proposing that those original immortal human souls have since 'split' (so that fragments of the Source's souls now reside in more than one person, existing in several disparate pieces).

But a more divisive interpretation of the Sacred Texts – the interpretation widely held by the Teyrian tradition – teaches that **humans who are born outside the Origin world are not guaranteed an immortal soul**. And, as the general belief of the Teyrians is that *Teyr itself* is the Origin world, the result of this is a conviction that **non-Teyrians are not reincarnated**.

In this interpretation, humans without an immortal soul do not benefit from the blessing of the Goddess, and therefore will live only one single lifetime before proceeding to some indeterminate fate. Meanwhile, the Blessed Children of Teyr will return again and again to this universe or the next one, perpetually called back to the Goddess's favour.

(Note: 'Non-Teyrian' is a theoretical category rather than a literal one, since people who *were* Teyrian in a past life have souls that will not perish. Those who have *been* Teyrian have already benefited from the blessing and been made immortal, regardless of which world they were born on in their current lifetime. A Teyrian may be reborn on many other worlds in intervening lives, before finally being reincarnated again on Teyr 'at the end of all things.' Several divination techniques are purported to determine if a person possesses a Teyrian soul. It goes without saying that there is no scientific basis for any of these claims, nor any empirical method to ascertain the nature of a human soul in the first instance.)

PAGE FOUND
Somewhere outside a country town, Laithe

IN THE MORNING, Edlin takes Page and Maelle over to the local market.

It takes about twenty minutes to get there in Edlin's small three-wheeled roamer, and Page is absolutely entranced. It's an open-air marketplace, full of life and music, its colourful awnings spreading out like flowers in the bright sunshine. Out here, it almost feels possible to forget about everything that looms ahead of them. Like everything will be fine, somehow.

Page wanders between the stalls, trying to keep the awe from showing on her face as they pass one vendor after another selling fresh fruits, vegetables, spices and herbs, fabrics and beads and glassware and artwork.

"Your eyes are as wide as soup bowls," Edlin teases. "You all right?"

"I've never seen a food market before," Page says. "Not like this, anyway. Only in holos."

There are no twinges of familiar memory when she looks at these stalls, no whisper of some forgotten marketplace full of unfathomably fresh wares. If there was such a marketplace wherever she came from, she hasn't been to it.

Edlin weaves confidently between the stalls, making a circuit that's clearly familiar to him while Maelle and Page walk along with him. He pauses to haggle with some of the vendors, bartering with loose chits. He knows exactly what he's doing and where everything is; this is just a regular day for him.

At one stall, he holds up a large fruit, probing at the rind with his thumb before confirming his selection. Later he stops at a covered spice-cart, where he has an animated exchange with the seller inside. He emerges with five or six tiny paper packets, each hand-lettered with their contents.

It feels like hours that they wander between the stalls, looking at everything and talking about nothing in particular. The sun feels strange and welcoming against Page's skin—as chilly as it was last night, today is bright and warm.

For the briefest moment, Page allows herself to imagine living here. That *this* could be her life, wandering in the sunshine with a bag full of fresh vegetables and a family at her side. With *Maelle* at her side.

But that's impossible. Wherever her life ends up going, her path probably won't bring her back here. Like Maelle said last night: This is a business partnership, and it's best they keep it that way.

Maybe Page should still be on the lookout for escape routes. There are certainly a lot of people here, more than she's seen anywhere else on Laithe. It wouldn't be so difficult to slip away into the crowd, if *escape* were something she were still considering. But she just follows along after her hosts, and tries not to think of anything at all.

Maelle stops at a communal spigot to refill all their water bottles with cool, clean water, and then Edlin goes on ahead of them for a while. Page and Maelle stay near the water supply, watching a group of tiny birds flitting around, picking up crumbs next to a bakery stall. Page wonders if she's ever *seen* a real bird before now, and she thinks of the little bird that fell exhausted to the Greenworld.

"Reece still isn't budging on the scamships," Maelle says in a low voice. "I counted on her giving me a *bit* of trouble, but we need to be back at Felwae by tomorrow to meet back up with Zhak. We're running out of time." She sighs. "Reece probably thinks if she stalls me long enough, I won't leave."

We could stay here, Page wants to say. It's a wild, unrealistic thought. *We could just stay here, until the monk-ship is gone. Zhak will never come down to Laithe, and this will all be over—*

"What will we do if Reece doesn't change her mind?" she asks instead.

"She'll change her mind," Maelle says. "I'll talk to her again tonight."

Page is looking down at the ground, and she can't bring an answering smile to her face. "I've been thinking," she says hesitantly. "If this all fucks up... like the way it went with Rodin..."

"It won't," Maelle insists. "It *won't* go the way it did with Rodin, because that monk-ship isn't gonna shoot anyone down! It won't have external weapons. They don't even have their engines lit, which is why we can't track them by engine signature. That ship's *drifting*. It's on a slingshot course, completely silent through the cosmic void." She hums a little laugh at the turn of phrase. "They only fire their thrusters to change course. This is why these ships are so damn hard to track, and why there's such a small window of time for the monks to get back from a supply run. You've got to go back with them on their shuttle, it's the only way."

Page contemplates it in silence for a while. "You know an awful lot about this ship," she says at last. "If it's just... floating around out there undefended, and it's been out there for so long... I'm surprised no pirates have intercepted it before."

Maelle shrugs. "Most of our info came through the Nightblade's intel network. He's obsessed with Source artifacts, so he has contacts—and he's been tracking down details about this particular monk-ship for a while now. Apparently it's kind of a legend among treasure hunters. Couple months ago, he even bought an old schematic that shows the exact type of

Teyrian vessel it is. Honestly... I was a little shocked that this ship turned out to be real."

If something seems too good to be real, you've got to get out of there. Page's old mantra echoes hollowly in her head, but she doesn't say anything. She just scuffs the toe of her boot against the dirt, watching the little birds congregating on a fresh scattering of crumbs.

Then Maelle leads her over to the other side of the marketplace to rejoin Edlin, where there's another row of food vendors tucked in next to a section that sells mostly arts and crafts. A cloth bag slung over Maelle's back contains all the purchases they've procured so far, and Edlin shoves the small bundles he's been carrying through the open top.

"Targets acquired," Edlin says. "I found those treats Garin wanted for the jibbles, and the ink for Carleen; what are we still missing?"

"I think that's all," says Maelle. "Hmm. Did they say one other thing? What was it...?"

"Oh, wait, yeah! We still need to get the wine!" Edlin grins. "I think we cleared through a bit more than expected last night. C'mon, it'll be over this way, on the river side."

"Really?" Maelle shields her eyes against the sun. "They've changed things around, then. I thought the wine stalls used to be over by the other exit."

"Well, maybe you should come home more often, huh?" He gives her a playful shove. "They've been on the river side for ages."

"You mean, like... out back, where those rope swings used to be?"

"Yeah! Exactly! There's a whole other market section there now." He laughs. "Hey, remember that time Sal's shoe got stuck in the mud down there? And Rodin was trying to get him, but he wiped out and fell on his ass? Gods, that was fucking hilarious, I still think of it every single time I'm down there—"

Edlin and Maelle turn to the right, heading down the next row of market stalls. They keep talking, and they keep walking.

And Page... Page stops moving.

They're no more than a dozen paces away from her; she can still see them, right there ahead of her. There's Maelle's dark jacket, the bag full of market wares on her back, her blue-black ponytail swaying. There's Edlin's taller form, leaning down to talk to her, a floppy green sunhat on his head. She can still see Edlin's hat for a while after Maelle disappears from her view.

And then she can't see either of them anymore.

Page hesitates for a moment, imagining that she could simply turn around and walk in the other direction. It wouldn't take long for her to blend into the crowd the same way they have.

She could leave this marketplace, slip away into that town she can see over there, just down the next hill. She has a few unspent chits in her pocket that Maelle gave her for snacks. How far could she realistically get with that? How far could she run on a planet she doesn't know?

Does she even *want* to run anymore?

I'm in, she'd said. *You have your monk.* And she'd meant it. She can't run. What about the artifact, and the millions of credits, and Maelle's plan—

No. She has to go catch up to them, they can't have gone very far. And any minute now they'll circle back for her. She'd never make it to the town anyway.

Page is still standing there, looking around and considering all this, when something across the way catches her eye. A little further on, in the opposite direction from where Maelle and Edlin went, there are several woodworking booths. *Natural wood is Laithe's major export*, she remembers from that vid. And one of the booths has a selection of beautiful musical instruments.

Page's eyes land directly on one of the stringed vessels, with its rounded base and long, elegant neck. It's made of dark wood, carved with some intricate design along the open gap in its middle.

What *is* that? Something about it calls to her, as if it reaches right into her ribcage and tugs her sharply forward. And Page walks directly over to the stall before she can think about it.

"Excuse me?" she calls out to the stall-keeper.

The man turns around with the sort of wide, friendly smile you seldom see from a marketplace seller on Kuuj. Who on the outpost would be so trusting as to turn their back on their unguarded wares?

"I… I was just wondering… what's that called?" Page points to the polished, rounded instrument.

"Ah! That would be a *lyren!* My sister carves them. They're based on a traditional design from one of the Primes," the stall-keeper says. "Don't see many of these out this way, do you?"

"No… I guess not." Page steps closer again. "May I… come and see it closer up?"

The stall-keeper gives her a brief, searching look before he reaches to take the instrument off its stand. Page wonders if he's weighing up the likelihood that she could pay for it—or that she might snatch it and run. But he just sets the thing directly into her hands. "Of course! Here, go ahead. You can hold it."

Page cradles the instrument as one might a small child. It's a lot heavier than she had imagined, its wooden base smooth and cool against her palms. When she first looked at it on the stand, she didn't know which way around to hold it. But now that it's here in her grasp, a strange familiarity takes over, a muscle memory that guides her hands. And she knows that she's holding it *upside down.*

She turns it around so the correct section rests against her hip, then holds it aloft with her right hand, and her fingers find the correct positions along the strings.

"Know how to play?" the stall-keeper asks.

"I'm not sure," Page answers honestly. "I… think I used to play something like it. But I'm not sure I remember how anymore."

"Try it," he says. "It's just been tuned. Go on!"

Page's mouth goes dry with nerves. Does she even know any songs? Does she *really* know how this instrument works? But when she shifts it in her hands, somehow it feels as natural as breathing.

She doesn't need to think. She closes her eyes, finds the strings with her fingers and plucks, and a delicate chord whirls from somewhere within the instrument. She plucks again, and it is not the toneless cacophony of an amateur player. No, this sounds beautiful already. One, two, three simple chords blend into one another, growing into the shape of a song.

There's no clumsiness to it, no tentative notes, no missed strings. It comes to her right away, and her movements become a fluid cascade of gentle tones that build into something rich and wonderful. A few people passing by pause to listen, gathering around the stall in a semi-circle.

She plays only a single verse, but it feels like an eternity is suspended in each note. When she lowers the instrument again, Page is hardly breathing.

"Well! That was incredible!" the stall-keeper says with a look of astonishment. "Wow! How long's it been since you played, then?"

"I've... actually got no idea," Page says. "Until a few minutes ago, I would've said I'd never seen one of these before. But when I picked it up, my fingers just... started to play it." She looks down at the lyren. "I feel like that tune should have had words."

The man shrugs. "Sounded familiar, like something old. Most arrangements for the lyren are real old ones, you know... like, adaptations of Source stuff."

"Thank you," Page says. "*I give you thanks*." She hands the lyren back to him, reluctantly. Her vision blurs, and she realizes to her surprise that she's crying. (It's only much later, thinking back on the man and his instruments, that she suddenly realizes that she thanked him in Graya.)

Page turns from the stall and looks around. Maelle and Edlin are still nowhere in sight, and for a moment she can't quite remember which direction they went. The market seems impossibly vast, and too many of the rows of booths look the same.

"It's 'A Boy Found a Bird,'" a voice calls from nearby.

Page turns, unsure if she's being spoken to. "I'm sorry, what did you say?"

"'A Boy Found a Bird.' That's what you just played. An old traditional tune. It's one of my favourites."

A round-faced woman with sparse grey hair and a piercing stare stands in front of the neighbouring stall, looking directly at Page. A hairclip in the shape of a bird clings to her hair, just above one ear, but she is otherwise unadorned—she wears a beige, utilitarian jumpsuit that wouldn't look out of place in the cargo docks on Kuuj. Still, there is an air of wisdom about her, something serene and ancient that transcends her plain appearance.

She studies Page carefully, squinting at her as though she's scrutinizing her. "Come closer, child," she says, and her voice is equal parts comforting and commanding. "You look lost."

Page steps toward her. The woman's stall is a small, enclosed tent that Page can't see inside, its door covered by a thick curtain. A hand-lettered sign hangs from the side of the tent: *The Threads of Fate*.

"What do you sell here?" Page asks.

The woman only smiles enigmatically. "That is the wrong question," she says. "I would first ask you what you seek to *find* here."

"I'm... not sure," Page says, answering honestly. "I don't know what I seek to find."

"Then I have exactly what you need." The woman's strange smile widens, and she lifts up the edge of the curtain. "You might call me a prophet of sorts. Come inside, beloved child of the gods, and I shall read your fate for you. The mysteries of the past and future will be revealed."

She ducks into the tent, and Page follows, stepping hesitantly into the dimly-lit space. A strong, heady smoke spills from within, and Page coughs in surprise. She didn't expect to find a *fire* inside.

In truth, Page doesn't have the slightest clue what she expected of a place where the mysteries of the past and future might be revealed. But it certainly wasn't this. There's almost nothing in the way of ornamentation or décor. The sides of the tent are sheets of burlap, and the roof is a faded blue tarpaulin with several holes in it. There are two flickering lanterns hanging from the poles that hold up the tarp, and beside the prophet's table there's a dented metal bucket full of burning sticks—the source of that thick, fragrant smoke.

"Sit," says the prophet, gesturing at the cloth-covered stool across from her.

Then she reaches down toward the bucket, letting her hand linger around it for a moment, swirling her fingers through the smoke with careful consideration before she plucks out one of the burning sticks. She holds it out gingerly by the unburnt end, passing it to Page as she takes a seat.

"Here. Take this, hold it in your hand. That's it. Breathe deeply, be still... clear your thoughts... that's right. You have to open your mind before we begin."

Page takes a deep breath, and her lungs fill with smoke. She struggles not to choke as her eyes begin to water.

"Good, very good," the prophet says with a smile. "And now... hold that up for me and write your name in the air."

Page lifts the burning stick. Her hand shakes.

"Ah. Something is stopping you." The prophet studies her again, narrowing her eyes. "There is much uncertainty in you."

"I just..." Page takes another deep breath, wiping at her eyes with her free hand. "I... I've lost most of my memories. Post-suspension syndrome. I don't actually remember my real name."

"Real name? Ha!" The woman lets out an abrupt bray of laughter. "Names are not what is real, child! Names are something we give ourselves. They can be temporary, transient things... and the truth itself sometimes changes. Write the name you carry right now, or the one that seems most true to you at this moment."

Page lifts her hand, hesitates. And then she traces out the Graya words for *little darling*. She's slightly startled to discover that she knows the shapes of these letters.

"Good. Very good," the prophet says, tutting to herself. She wasn't even looking at the letters Page wrote out. Instead, it seems she was fixating on the movement of Page's arm. She reaches out and takes hold of it, her warm fingers pinching just over Page's right wrist.

Page must have jumped back in surprise, because the prophet tuts with exasperation.

"Your pulse," she sighs. "I'm simply getting the measure of you. Souls have shapes, you see, and they prefer certain kinds of vessels, one lifetime after another. If you have certain traits in one life, you're more likely to find them in another. And I'm not talking about your physical appearance, no, not the shape of your flesh. I mean the invisible traits you carry. Nervous tics. Grinding your teeth, or tapping your feet. The tempo of your heartbeat. The unique way you breathe. The things that catch your attention when all else is silent and still." She taps at Page's wrist. "Very few memories carry over from one lifetime to the next, but fear does. *Love* does, too. The things you experience, the things you feel… That all remains in your soul, if you know how to look for it."

The prophet reaches under the table and takes out what looks like a tiny broom. She brings it down toward Page's face, and trails the bristles gently from the top of her head down her nose, then across her cheekbones, then down over her neck to her collarbone and finally to the centre of her chest. The whole time, she hums to herself like some cosmic tailor making a measurement.

"Hmm…" she says. "Hmm, hmm… I see."

Finally, she puts away the brush and retrieves a handful of smooth, colourful stones. She takes the burning stick away from Page and pops it back into the bucket before she presses the stones into Page's open palms.

"These are god-runes," she says. "The right ones will show themselves when you tune in. There you go, hold them tightly for a moment... Focus! Infuse them with all of your hopes and fears. Steady, now... Breathe deeply. Concentrate, and I'll tell you more about your future."

Page holds the stones silently and breathes, trying not to choke on the smoke. She blinks back her frustration—it's her past she wants answers about, not the future. What lies ahead has always felt insignificant without a past to tie it to.

"What do you know of trajectories, child?" The prophet continues to speak, waving one hand around Page's head as if in a trance. "In space, things travel in the direction of momentum. So, by looking at where something is going, you can infer where it has already been. And so it is, too, with souls. Your soul has a momentum that sends it speeding across the cosmos. Predicting the future is infinitely easier than sussing out the past."

Page thinks of the blank space where the past should live in her head. Has she ever stood on Teyr?

The stones are growing surprisingly warm against her palms. One gets so hot it nearly burns her. But she holds fast, clutching them between her clasped hands, waiting for the prophet's instructions.

"Mmm-hmm, that should do," the prophet finally says, tapping the top of Page's hand with one knuckle. "Go ahead, then. Release them."

Page drops the stones on the table in front of her. They scatter, rolling further than she thought they would. But they all stop at the edge of the table, as though held there by some unseen force.

The prophet leans closer. She removes a slender pair of spectacles from a pocket in her jumpsuit, squinting dramatically at the glowing lines on the stones as though they hold some monumental message.

"Well?" Page's voice is shaking. "Do you... see something?"

"Indeed," the prophet says. "Oh, my! You are a rare one, little darling! You are a child of Teyr! Do you know what that means? In your future, I see... that you will be Teyrian, again and again, many lifetimes over. Which tells me... Yes, that's probably where you've already been. Teyr has a particularly mystical line, as far as the threads of the universe are concerned."

Page's arms prickle with goosebumps. "Teyrian," she whispers. "Are you sure?"

"Oh, yes, very sure. Now... hmm. I see here that you will be a rebel in the next life, as you have been in this one, as you always will be," the prophet continues. "Your lives have never been easy. You are a scavenger of things, of dreams, of stories—always at the edges, always watchful. But that also means you're perceptive. You learn things. You listen, and you grow with each lifetime you live. You know more than you think already. And you lead from the sidelines, in subtle ways. Your smallest actions can have a great influence on the destiny of the Worlds, perhaps even on the fate of humanity itself."

She looks back at the god-runes again, and taps a long, pointed fingernail against an orange stone that has rolled the furthest from the others. "And see this one here? This is the fire that burns everything down. But it is also the fire that restores. *Renewal*."

A heavy feeling settles in Page's stomach. She doesn't like the thought of it, of everything burning. Of fire. Of everything *disappearing*.

"The universe will burn down again and again," the prophet continues. "But you will rise from your own ashes, and you will emerge in the image of the Great Goddess. Fallen down as a little bird, raised up in love and light. Remember this, and your fortunes will rise, little darling."

Page stands up slowly, her knees shaking. She feels dizzy, like she's been spinning in circles. She has to get out of here. She has already started to turn toward the exit when the prophet jumps to her feet, and her surprisingly tight grip closes on Page's wrist.

"Ah-ah!" she says, the serene, trance-like quality leaving her voice. With her other hand, she shakes the small wooden bowl full of loose credit chits that perches on a pedestal next to her table. "Don't you think a little *donation* is in order, to thank the channel of this wisdom?"

Embarrassed, Page fumbles in her pocket. She pulls out the credit chits Maelle gave her and drops them all into the bowl, mumbling her thanks. She's nauseatingly dizzy now, stars clouding her vision and blurring the air in front of her.

And she can feel a blackout coming on. She has to go.

She stumbles back outside, punching her way frantically through the tent's thick curtain. At last, she falls on her knees on the strip of trampled grass outside. She heaves in a breath with difficulty, gasping for air. The fragrant smoke still hangs heavy in her lungs.

And then she's losing consciousness.

The bells—four, five, six chimes. Six chimes again.

A sky full of stars, a plume of fire descending among them, a ship coming down.

The lyren is playing sweetly, and a voice is singing along in Graya, the very same tune Page just played: 'One day a boy found a bird, found a little fallen bird—'

Now she's hiding, her breath quick and frightened. Crouched down behind a vast bookcase full of dozens and dozens of ancient-looking books, fragile and cloth-bound.

And someone shouts out a name—

The next instant, Maelle is at her side, shaking Page by the shoulders, shouting a different name. "Page? Page. *Page!*"

Her voice sounds shaken and anxious.

"Page, talk to me! Where'd you go, we've been looking everywhere for you!" She flings her arms around Page and clutches her tight to her chest. "Are you all right?"

"Dizzy," Page gasps. "I'm... Wow. I feel sick... There was... a lot of smoke in there..." She points back toward the prophet's tent.

Maelle looks over her shoulder, and then she rolls her eyes with a slow grin. "Ohhh. Damn it. God-smoke, of course. They told you to breathe it in, to 'open your mind'?"

"Wh—what?"

"God-smoke! You haven't had it before? Wild. It makes you talk out loud, so when they give you the stones to hold, and the burning stick to write with, and all of that, you're talkin' to them. Everything you're thinking, all that private stuff you think you're just imagining to yourself, you're actually saying it all out loud. That's how the 'reading' works."

Page rolls onto her back, struggling to understand the words Maelle is saying. She looks up at Maelle through half-lidded eyes, stars still dancing at the edges of her vision. Maelle looks angelic just then—she's so perfect and so beautiful. She looks as gorgeous as the rising Goddess when she's painted in her human form.

Maelle laughs. "Thanks. I'm flattered."

Page claps a hand over her mouth. "What—?"

"Yep, you're still talking." Maelle's eyes are sparkling with amusement. "Let me guess. You just got some foretelling that was remarkably applicable to the secret questions you were thinking of?"

"Shit. Yeah." Nausea roils in Page's throat again. Damn it.

"Hey, it's okay. You just fell for a little magic trick, that's all. Happens to the best of us." Maelle reaches out and tucks a strand of Page's hair behind her ear—an oddly affectionate gesture. "C'mon. Let's get out of here and get you a cold drink, huh? We'll have to look for Edlin after that—he went hunting for you round the other side."

"Ugh." Page staggers to her feet as Maelle supports her shoulder. "I really *wanted* to believe it, you know? She told me I was Teyrian in my past and future lives! She said... she said I was a rebel, and that I would do something important... but then..." Page stops, and sighs sadly. "Yeah... Wow. I guess she knew I wanted all that stuff to be true because... well, because I told her all about it."

Maelle laughs. "No offense, Page, but anyone can see that you're dying to have someone tell you something about your life. You were the perfect target. Someone totally lost."

Page's steps are still unsteady, and she leans heavily on Maelle. They walk slowly back toward the water spigot where they'd stood and talked earlier. The little birds near the bakery stall have flown off.

Maelle turns on the tap and Page tilts her dizzy head, letting the cold water run directly into her mouth as it soaks her face and hair, washing away the haze of the god-smoke.

Then they sit down together on the grass nearby for another moment. She lets her head loll to one side, her wet hair dripping over Maelle's shoulder.

"You know... Maybe I'm not *totally* lost. Because... if none of this had ever happened... if I'd stayed on Kuuj... then... I wouldn't have met you. And... I'm glad it happened, because I'm glad to have met you, and to have come here... even if you *don't* want me to trust you." She locks eyes with Maelle. "I know I'm talking, by the way. I'm saying this part on purpose."

Maelle smiles again. "Yeah," she says, her voice whisper-soft. "I'm glad to have met you, too."

DALYA
OF HOUSE EDAMAUN, IN HER EIGHTEENTH YEAR
First-City, Teyr

THE TWO TUTORS from Saymu Prime, Ker Minah and Ker Baulin, had come to Dalya just as Uncle had promised. They'd arrived at night, in a long transport with no lights on it—which Dalya found terribly odd—and thereafter they stayed in the library wing of the Edamaun residence. From there, they'd given Dalya many detailed lessons about the ways of the United Worlds.

When they first arrived, Dalya had feared the tutors greatly, and she did not quite know what to think of them. Their clothing and their hair ornaments were mostly like the dress of the Teyrians—though perhaps, Dalya thought, they dressed this way to fit in better here. But in their manner and their speech, they were always very different, and they seemed very strange to her.

Every day, Ker Minah schooled Dalya in the grammar, pronunciation and basics of the common language of the Union, a task at which Dalya luckily excelled. Meanwhile, Ker Baulin taught her what was called *interpersonal diplomacy*, the subtle art of conversation and gesture and social cues in the Saymu tradition, many of which differed from the Teyrian norms. The tutors would give her imagined scenarios and then ask Dalya to respond—with a letter, with a video message, with an in-person conversation.

Dalya never received any marking rubrics from these lessons, nor any feedback at all as to how she was doing. But in time, the lessons did become more and more difficult. The questions the tutors posed when they examined her became more complex, the answers less clear-cut with each passing month. So she knew she *must* be progressing, must be getting closer to some final validation that the endeavour had been successful.

Two years into their lessons, Minah and Baulin's peculiarities had become comfortable and familiar, and Dalya no longer shrank back from their brash voices or the blunt directness of their questions. She enjoyed her studies with the Saymu a great deal, and secretly, she was glad to have something to do that did not involve ceremonial duties or the mantle of the Edamaun family. Her tutors were eccentric and fascinating, and she grew to like them quite a lot.

Dalya did not know what the Saymu did to entertain themselves when they weren't teaching her, but they never seemed to leave the library wing. They were always down there, and she'd gradually grown accustomed to their constant presence. Uncle, too, spent much time with them inside the library when he was not at work. Perhaps they were researching something together among the old books.

Uncle never asked Dalya anything about her special lessons with the Saymu. They never spoke of it aloud—at breakfast, Uncle asked only about her regular lessons, the ones she was meant to be receiving from her Teyrian tutors. And she would answer dutifully that they were going well, thank you— even when she had not seen her regular tutors in weeks. She understood that she was never to mention her *extra* lessons to her other teachers, nor anywhere else in polite company. *Speak of it to no one save Heral,* Uncle had said, and so it remained.

She would very much have liked to speak to Anda Agote about it. But it had been years, now, since she had seen her old friend, and it pained her to think of it. Dalya did not see many friends now, only her tutors, and the hours of her lessons grew longer and longer until she was studying well into the night.

Dalya thought that the foreign tutors grew to care about her in their own way, although they always seemed to keep a careful distance from her. That, she supposed, was only proper; she was a god-child, after all, and they were simple mortals, doomed to live only one life.

Sometimes she didn't really know why they even bothered with helping her—her uncle, she supposed, must have paid them well, or offered them some other reward. She dared not ask him. But she wondered if Minah and Baulin minded it—the fact that when the whole universe was annihilated, they were told that their people would vanish into the ethereal void, while the Teyrians would be glorified and reincarnated at the beginning and end of all things.

In the most secret corners of her mind, sometimes Dalya did consider whether it mightn't be nice to vanish into the void, too, when her own life was over. To be unbound from the endless yoke of responsibility for the entire human species. There was a certain freedom in the thought. She never spoke it aloud, not to strict and serious Minah, not even to kind, sympathetic Baulin. And she certainly never mentioned anything of the sort to Uncle. But the thought was there, and it lodged in her mind like a splinter that she worried at in quiet moments.

What would it mean to have control of your own destiny?

Was it really so good to be *chosen*, if it meant you had no choice at all?

It was just the sort of thing Anda would have known a story about. She would have pulled out some scrap of the god-texts that answered the question perfectly, and the two of them would have laughed with relief. Remembering Anda always brought tears to Dalya's eyes.

Anda was still somewhere on Teyr, she thought, but they had not spoken, nor even exchanged a letter, since Uncle's sudden decree. She had overheard Heral and Uncle talking once about how 'the Agote girl' had gone up north, where most of the moonfolk were settled—but there was never any mention of Anda's uncle.

Dalya wondered if Ker Agote knew why Uncle no longer wanted his friendship. And she still desperately wished there were some way she might tell Anda she was sorry. But even Heral would not heed her, on the rare occasions when Dalya broke down and begged her to find some way to send Anda a message. Heral only shook her head and pressed a finger to her lips in silent apology.

And then a day finally came when Dalya saw Anda in the First-City again, for the briefest flash of a moment. They came across each other quite by chance, in the grand city square. Dalya was with her handlers, as she always was—on the way to visit a renowned tailor in the First-City to be fitted for a new ceremonial robe. And Anda, remarkably, was just coming out of the tailor's shop when Dalya's transport arrived.

Dalya almost didn't recognize her at first. Anda had grown taller and more slender since Dalya saw her last, and she wore an opaque blue mourning veil over her hair. But it was her *eyes* that Dalya saw first when they nearly collided on the stairs—those familiar, deeply sad eyes—and her heart leapt into her throat with disbelief.

Anda reached out for a moment and ever so slightly squeezed Dalya's arm, as though she were just trying to move past her. And then she lowered her gaze and rushed away into the crowded square before Dalya could react.

Anda! Dalya wanted to shout out. *Anda Agote! Wait!* But the words froze in her mouth, and in a blink of an eye, Anda was already gone.

Of course, Anda must have recognized her, too. Even if they hadn't nearly collided, she would have known the High Speaker's insignia on the big transport, the unmistakable uniforms of Dalya's handlers. And still, Anda hadn't stopped walking, hadn't said a single word.

She was right to be hurt, Dalya thought. And Anda *must* be hurt. Perhaps she didn't understand what had happened, or why she had been so suddenly banished from the Edamaun house. Dalya still didn't understand it herself.

When she returned home that evening, Dalya made up her mind to ask Uncle about it again. She'd kept her silence for more than two years now; surely she could plead for *some* answer as to what had happened with the Agote family.

Uncle's door was ajar when Dalya came to his study, but something stayed her hand just before she knocked. There was an urgent newscast playing quietly on Uncle's overhead monitor, the sound turned down too low for her to hear.

Dalya stopped there, her hand held in midair, waiting. Uncle never liked being interrupted if he was watching a 'cast. And if he was already cross with her, there'd be no chance to sway him.

The newscast played on, focused on a reporter's grim, serious face—it seemed that the 'cast brought dire news. Her heart raced to see a grainy image of the Union Flame—the logo of the United Worlds—in the background on the screen. From where she stood by the crack of the door, Dalya could just make out the subtitles running under the 'cast.

Alleged secret talks with offworlders. Treason in Moon-City. Saymu conspirator found dead on Meneyr.

In the foreground, an image appeared of the traitorous suspect, the one they were talking about. The dead spy from a Union world. A man smiling with incongruous friendliness—white-haired and sharp-featured.

Derin Agote.

THE STORYTELLER

Recording start 06:53:09

The Teyrian Job went real badly, in the end. It was bad for *all* of us, but some came out of it worse than others. And that part of my life ended the same way it began: with Vonnie at the helm of it all, setting the whole thing ablaze.

The job was almost over, and I can't say I wasn't glad of it. After Agote disappeared, the whole thing was always a mess – the comms were slipping, things got sloppy, and I never quite felt like I knew what was going on. But at last we were done with the whole thing, or close to it.

We'd delivered the last shipment of components for the death-hoop, and we were due to take our last batch of their payment back to Saymu Prime. It was all the usual stuff, all those crates of whatever old-world artifacts they were shipping. We were supposed to do a handover just inside Union space, and give these crates over to our Saymu contacts. And then they'd sign the job off as done, and give us our final payment.

At this point, we've done this shit dozens and dozens of times. As disorganized as things were on the Protectorate's side, on our side it was all running smooth as butter. But Vonnie... well, Vonnie suddenly decided that he was gonna go to Meneyr for this last run, that he'd be on the last ship himself to close things off.

It seemed a little weird to me, and unnecessary to go all that way there and back with them, but... you know. Vonnie did whatever Vonnie wanted. I didn't really question it. I just shrugged and said, all right, I'll see you when you get back. And so I parked up in the Saymu outer system at our base, same as always, and I was waiting for him there.

Now, I can tell you a million ways I should've seen it all coming. Truth is, when we care about somebody, it's easy to believe they'd go down swinging for us. That no matter what, they're gonna have our backs. But Vonnie was never really like that. From the very beginning, he only ever looked after one person: himself.

For as long as I live, I don't think I'll ever understand what he was thinking when he came up with this shit. The thing is, he was as overconfident as he was arrogant. I reckon he didn't tell me about what he was doing because he thought I'd try to talk him out of it... or that I'd quite rightly tell him he was out of his mind.

He was playing with fire, beyond anything we'd ever done. Because he got it in his head to double cross the Saymu, on this very last run. And through one of his other contacts, he hired a scamship crew... to fake an attack on our own ship.

Angel's Eye, that ship was called – it was one of our flagship cargo haulers. The deal Vonnie made was simple: as soon as the hauler crossed over into Union space, it would get attacked by these fake alien ships. They'd do it near enough to get witnessed by our Saymu contacts who were there waiting for the handover.

Of course, the Saymu ships would take off right quick – nobody wants to mess with aliens – and then Vonnie and his crew would make away with the whole haul of artifacts, and pretend the aliens blew his ship to bits.

Whatever was in those crates, the artifacts were worth way more than the payment we were due. And Vonnie'd always been interested in rarities, see. The Teyrian stuff in particular. He had a whole network of dealers trading in that stuff. It was always another scheme on the side, with him.

So, back to the handover. Vonnie was on the *Angel's Eye*, on the way to the rendezvous point... and that's where it all went to shit. I guess one of our Saymu contacts had been rumbled by the Union authorities, and the whole thing was compromised. So when Vonnie and his crew showed up at the handover coordinates, the area was already crawling with Union patrol ships. And of course, Vonnie had this scamship crew on the way in, and no way to call it off...

From what I heard, Vonnie panicked, and I guess he ordered the *Angel's Eye* to send out a distress signal. He thought he could still pretend he was just an independent hauler captain with no idea what he was carrying and no clue what was going on. He shot down one of the scamship pilots, too – his own damn hire!

But I never learned about any of this until years after it happened. Nine years later, to be precise – nine years that I spent on ice in stasis prison.

Because the Union authorities still seized the *Angel's Eye*, and they apprehended Vonnie anyway. He was travelling under an alias, of course – they didn't have a clue that he was actually the big boss.

But it turns out that the big boss was all those Union officials were interested in, really. They wanted Vonnie to give up the name of the person in charge of our whole operation, and the location of our base... and in exchange, they'd let him walk away.

And so, Vonnie told them where our base was.

And he did give up a name.

Mine.

CASE FILE #91116C

▮▮▮▮▮▮▮▮▮▮ HIGH SECURITY FACILITY
NAME: GUILLEM, AZERAN ("VOID SNAKE")

CHARGES:
- Misrepresentation of Transported Cargo
- Trade or Commerce in Illegal Weapons
- Trade or Commerce with Non-Union Entities
- Transport of Unregistered Antiquities
- Evasion of Union Trade Laws
- Possession of Illegal Communication Devices
- Unauthorized Contact with Non-Union Settlements
- Falsification of Transit Permits
- Conspiracy Against Union Interests
- Communication with Teyrian Protectorate
- Trade with Teyrian Protectorate
- 58 related minor infractions [see appended materials]
- 32 previously pending infractions [see appended materials]

SENTENCE:
- Suspended Animation, 9 years served at ▮▮▮▮▮▮▮▮▮▮

STATUS: RELEASED

PAGE FOUND
Felwae Deep Space Outpost

FELWAE OUTPOST IS exactly and precisely the same as the last time they were here, as unchanging as Teyr. It's only been a couple of days, Page supposes, but it's uncanny how similar everything is. Page sits on the same bench in the same peeling booth, eating the same sour candy as the last time. There's even a guy in a guild jacket standing in the same place at the bar.

But this time, Maelle is anything but relaxed. While they wait for Zhak's speedship to come and collect them, she fidgets anxiously, constantly checking the screen of her comm. Page watches as she locks and unlocks the screen, scrolls through old messages, then checks the home screen again before setting it down on the table. But there are no new pings. No messages from any of the Bereda family.

Page doesn't ask about how things have soured further between Maelle and her mother—she knows there was one more heated conversation after they came back from the marketplace—but Reece Bereda was conspicuously missing from the communal dinner table last night. The matriarch wasn't at breakfast either. And she didn't walk to the black gate with Garin and Edlin to see Maelle off.

Maelle has spoken little to Page in the hours since they left the planet; what camaraderie there was between them the day before seems suddenly to have cooled again. Page tries not to think about how much that stings. It's not as if Maelle didn't warn her. It's not like they were ever *actually* friends, much less anything else.

To pass the time and avoid the awkward silence, Page opens a note file on her 'pad. It's the biographical notes she's been creating about her false monk. Because everyone has some kind of a story, don't they? And most people even remember it.

Page's part in this whole scheme is almost painfully straightforward. All she'll have to do is convince those monks that she's one of them, for long enough to board their ship. Only one or two monks will come from the ship in a shuttlecraft, Zhak says. They'll be picking up supplies at an ancillary. And there, the 'lost monk' will intercept them.

It will seem like a happy accident, of course, when Page happens upon them—*the hand of the Goddess at work!* She'll give the monks a vague tale about having been revived from another monk-ship that ran into trouble... and then, perhaps after some verification of her tale and her stasis scars, the monks should take her back to their vessel. There, Page will activate the Q-link tracker and broadcast the ship's exact position to Zhak. And once they're back out in deep space... then Zhak will be able to find the otherwise silent ship.

This ship is on the way back to Teyr, but it hasn't been to the Protectorate for years, Page reminds herself. It's not as if anyone on board should recognize Page, not like they can dispute her claim that she belongs to the monastic order. But she still needs some kind of back story, just in case the monks need more convincing.

"If it comes to it, and they ask you something you don't know, you can always say you don't remember," Maelle had told her. "Everyone in their whole monastic order has been in stasis before, at least for a little while. So I'm sure they've seen their share of post-suspension syndrome, including memory loss."

"No," Page insisted. "*This* monk remembers everything. I'll make something up."

She's had enough of not remembering in her real life. Damn it, this character she's playing is going to remember every single detail of her past.

Page has been working on a loose outline of the story on her 'pad in spare moments, assembling a past from a combination of encyclopedia articles and image captures, and the bits and pieces of her own fragmented memories—if that's what they are.

> [File: Monk_biography]
> Grew up in First-City, Teyr. A very tall house, up high on a hill. White brick, large windows, with a huge balcony. I used to love looking at the stars from there. I miss the sound of bells tolling over the green hills.
>
> I had one sibling on Teyr. A sister. (Older or younger? Maybe a twin.) We used to run barefoot in the garden. We played music together – the lyren. In fact, that's our family name. Lyren.
>
> Parents deceased, but they were good believers. They loved me and they would have been proud of me.

Page still hasn't come up with a given name for the monk. She's scanned through a few lists of traditional names for Teyrian highborns, but none of them feel quite right. She tries to recall what name she heard in her dream the other day, but it won't come back to her.

When Maelle glances at the document Page has open on her screen, a pained look crosses her face.

"Page... listen. I was thinking," Maelle whispers. "If you do get on that monk-ship... you don't *have* to activate the Q-link to signal Zhak. You could just... not do it. You know that, right?"

"What?" Page's head snaps up. What in the hells would be the point of going through with all this if she wasn't planning to do it?

"That monk-ship is heading back to Teyr, eventually," Maelle says. "If you hunker down and just stay with the monks, it could take you to the Protectorate. If... you know. If that's something you want."

To the Protectorate. Page hadn't even truly considered that possibility. Her breath catches in her throat. To see Teyr for herself? To see if the things in her visions match up to anything real—surely that's impossible—

"What, you mean just... actually *go* with the monks?" she whispers back. "But what about the raid? And the artifact?"

"Reece wouldn't give me the scamships, Page. My plan is sunk," Maelle says, her face grim. "The minute you press that Q-link button on the monk-ship... Zhak's going to attack it with his raider crew, exactly the way he originally planned to. They'll probably take the engines out first, so the ship can't run even if it wants to... and then they'll take it over by force. Zhak will loot it for whatever artifacts are in there, and whether he finds the Bird's Heart or not, you bet he'll leave that ship adrift."

"Oh." Page's heart sinks.

"It's not a Union ship. It shouldn't even *be* here in Union space. There won't be any way for those monks to get help. Or to get home, if any of them survive."

"I... I don't think I'd want that to happen," Page says quietly. "Not at all."

"It's not what I intended, either," Maelle says. "With the scamships, it should've been easy. No raider boarding party, no firing the plasma guns. Just me and Zhak going in, and a bunch of monks who won't even look at us! With our own people there instead of Zhak's raiders, we'd have had a way to escape with that orb and leave Zhak behind. But now—"

Page looks down at her drink. There's a bleak disappointment in her, something that far outweighs the despair she felt when Zhak's ship first took her away from Kuuj. It's a chill in her whole body, as if the entire world has suddenly gone grey. What did she imagine would happen? Suddenly, everything feels every bit as pointless and futile as it did when she was pickpocketing for Tully.

"Look. You can still do this job for Zhak, I'm not gonna stop you from going through with it," Maelle says. "But... I think I'm out." She sighs, a long and defeated breath. "This was my best shot at setting things right, at getting some kind of justice for Rodin. And I couldn't fucking pull it off. But... yeah. I think it's over."

Page frowns, not entirely sure she's comprehending. "Wait, what? You're... leaving?"

"I'll play along and stay on the mission long enough to see you to the monks, if that's what you want," Maelle says. "But after that, I'm gone. I'll find my own way off the ancillary, and hitch a ride somewhere. I'm not having anything to do with Zhak's raid... and I'm never getting back on that asshole's ship again."

Page looks at the table numbly. *What if I went with you, instead?* she wants to say.

Don't leave me.

But just for a moment, she lets herself imagine that she could run away on the monk-ship. That she could let it bear her away, all the way to the Protectorate. And she pictures herself with her imaginary sister, running barefoot in the grass, high in the rolling green hills of Teyr.

ON HOW DIVINE OLANDRA TAMED THE HELL-HOUNDS

Adapted from the Sacred Texts; this version translated from 'Folktales of the Eternal: A Volume of Traditional Stories.' Original author unknown.

So we take up the divine tale of Olandra the Unafraid, who we call She Who Faced the Darkness and Tamer of Beasts and The Hand of Healing; she who tirelessly guards the realm of the gods against all that would do it harm.

After the quest of the Small Spirit revealed the intentions of the Oblivion, there was much caution among the gods, much fear that the Oblivion's beasts would rise from the shadows to attack once more. And it was Olandra the Unafraid who kept safe the Celestial Realm, perpetually guarding it with her wards and her all-seeing spells.

But Olandra's spells, bright as they were, could not penetrate the realm of shadows, nor could her messengers see through the perpetual darkness of the cosmic void. One day, Olandra ventured too far in pursuit of one of the Demon Queen's beasts, patrolling beyond the reach of the wards she had laid. And there, she was attacked by a numberless horde of the Oblivion's cursed creatures.

Chief among them were the hell-hounds, the fierce and never-sleeping, and they set upon her with relentless claws and sharp teeth. For five days Olandra fought them, her own magic just as relentless, smothering them with her goodness and her truth and her resilience. But still they fought on, and they bit and tore at her until she was near exhaustion. And brave Olandra did not cry out for help, for she did not want any of the other spirits to come to harm, in flying to her aid.

Five hounds there were, who persisted longer than the others. And with every passing hour, the beasts neared victory – but they, too, were on the last dregs of their strength. They did not wish to perish in the fight, for even shadow-beasts, it seems, have within them a will to live.

Still, these hounds dared not return to the Oblivion without some token of their victory. They would surely have been slaughtered by their mistress in failure, if they had allowed Olandra to escape after such a fight. An impasse there remained, for a further five days, but still the goddess would not relinquish the last of her strength.

And thus came an uneasy accord, a strange friendship as had never been seen: Olandra did offer the hounds her blessing in exchange for mercy. The beasts must join her, Olandra said, and must willingly offer their aid to the Celestial Realm. And in return, they would be rewarded with the favour of the Pantheon.

The Demon Queen's beasts could see in the dark for distances untold, and they could run in the shadows where even the gods dared not to tread. And thus the hell-hounds could provide the Celestial Realm with a new protection from the forces of darkness.

Four of the hell-hounds did accept Olandra's hand in friendship; they bowed their heads and offered her their aid. The fifth made a show of bowing to her, but when Olandra reached out her hand to grant her blessing, the hound did snap its jaws down and severed her glittering hand from her wrist, that it might run away to the Oblivion with the trophy of its pretended victory.

And so it was that Divine Olandra, Guardian of the Gates, lost one of her hands... but gained four loyal hounds who served her well ever after.

DALYA
OF HOUSE EDAMAUN, IN HER EIGHTEENTH YEAR
First-City, Teyr

THE MORNING AFTER the newscast naming Derin Agote as a traitor to Teyr, Uncle was not at breakfast. It was to be the start of another festival day in the city this morning—a new ship had come down from Meneyr—so perhaps he had gone ahead to the city centre a bit early, Dalya thought. They did not always travel together these days.

But there was an unease in her, a terrible dread that had not left her since she fled from the doorway of Uncle's study last night without making her presence known. Dalya had hardly slept, scarcely knew what to think, what to do.

Derin Agote, a traitor and conspirator? Surely, those terrible words must be wrong. The newscast contained many names and places Dalya didn't quite understand, but one had been repeated again and again. *Saymu Prime*, the Union world that Ker Agote allegedly had *secret dealings* with.

The very same world her tutors Minah and Baulin were from. The tutors she'd always been told to mention to no one, save Heral—

She must speak to Heral, she told herself, repeating the words to herself like a calming refrain: *Heral will know what to do*. Heral could make sense of anything.

But Heral did not seem to be at home this morning, either.

Her rooms were locked tight, and her house-shoes were not sitting on the little mat beside her door. Heral usually left a note about any unexpected engagements that took her away from the house. But there was no note, either. Heral, too, was away somewhere.

Biting down her disappointment, Dalya hurried to the library wing, already late for her first morning lesson. Her sessions with Minah and Baulin would typically be cut short on a festival day, since she was to appear at the ceremony later. But that early morning lesson was always on her calendar, and today was no exception. She wondered if her tutors would have anything to say about Derin Agote.

Of course they wouldn't, she chided herself. The tutors did not comment upon the news. They never spoke directly about anything that was going on beyond these walls; she could not think of a single occasion when they ever had. They would just greet her politely and take up today's lesson with a new, imaginary diplomatic scenario, as if nothing at all ever happened in the outside world. Surely, today's lesson would not feature a *traitor and conspirator*.

And yet, she wondered still why Minah and Baulin had never said much about their families, or their lives back on their homeworld, or anything about themselves. She wondered still why they had come here to teach her in the first place, or why they never left the grounds of the Edamaun house—

Dalya felt dizzy, as if too many thoughts were coming into her head all at once. Too many thoughts she did not want to consider too deeply. She must focus on the lesson for now, and get through this morning. She would look for Heral again afterwards. Heral would *have* to be there later to help her get ready for the festivities of welcome; Dalya couldn't put on her headpiece on her own, nor put on all the pieces of her heavy ceremonial gown.

But when Dalya arrived in the library wing for her lesson, her heart sank. Both of her tutors were absent. Minah and Baulin were not here at all. The lights in the library were off, and there was no scent of the herbal tea Baulin always brewed before lessons.

Perhaps they were both running late, Dalya told herself hopefully, though this had never occurred before. Minah and Baulin had always been perfectly punctual; they were always sitting ready in their places by the time she got there. And all their materials were gone, too—all their viewscreens and notebooks and the devices that displayed Union Basic. And those things were *never* moved.

No, something was terribly, terribly wrong here. Dalya's stomach turned anxiously.

Not knowing entirely what to do, Dalya set down the sweet cakes she'd brought for her tutors, placing them neatly on the table, and then she went to start Baulin's tea brewing for him. It seemed like the right thing to do. She had to pretend, had to convince herself they were coming, that any minute now, any minute—

Dalya picked up the water jug with shaking hands and turned to take it upstairs to fill it. And just then, she heard the door at the top of the stairs sliding open.

"Ker Minah?" she called out. "Ker Baulin?"

It was not either of her tutors, but Uncle coming down the stairs. He stood there in his ceremonial dress, the freshly applied gold paint for the welcome ceremony glimmering wet on his face. Dalya became suddenly, oddly aware of how *old* Uncle looked. A weariness seemed to have overtaken him these last months, as if the very life force were being drained from his bones.

Perhaps it was the stress of whatever was going on in the Gepcot lately, or the long hours he had been working. But it was the next thing she noticed that struck cold fear deep into her heart. His now greyed braid was covered by a sheer veil of dark blue cloth pinned at his temples. A mourning veil.

"Uncle! What's happened? Where are Ker Minah and Ker Baulin—"

"Shhh, Dalya," he said, raising a hand to silence her. "Your lessons with them are completed now. You have learned all you need, and you have no more need for tutors. Very soon, you will be called to... another task." He paused, and his face looked more serious than she had ever seen it. "You, my child, will be called to do something that Nathin could not accomplish. That is what you have wanted, isn't it?"

She nodded, her throat suddenly too tight to make a sound. At once she felt cold, as if she were surrounded by rushing water, as if she were about to be swept away. She had never been more terrified.

"Uncle, I don't understand—"

"Dalya... I must speak to you of an important matter," he said. It was the High Speaker's voice he used, the same strong, steady voice as when he addressed the people from a podium or in one of his speeches from the Council Rooms. "I had hoped it would be a while before it came to this. But sometimes, fate decides for us. The hand of the Goddess guides it all, and we are but carried along."

At some point between now and those long-ago days in the temple when Dalya used to earn a sharp look for clacking her polished shoes, Uncle had begun speaking to her as an adult. As she had always imagined he would have spoken to Nathin. She was almost the same age right now as Nathin had been when he died; perhaps Uncle had finally come to accept her in his son's stead, however much she had failed to live up to Nathin's ghost.

But there was not as much triumph in the realization as she had hoped there would be. It had been a very long time since Dalya had cried over her perpetual inability to fill Nathin's shoes, and the soft places in her heart where that wound used to live felt hardened now.

"I am listening with an open heart, Uncle," Dalya said, inclining her head forward. "My duty will be done, for the glory of all the gods, by the will of the Fair-Feathered Goddess." She spoke the invocation with all the reverence it was due.

"That it will," Uncle said, and there was something almost like sadness in his voice. "You will be sent away soon, Dalya. You will go first to the monks of the Golden-Feather, on Meneyr. And then, you will journey to another world."

"What? To the monks?" Dalya's breath caught, her stomach churning with disbelief. "A *new world?*—What are you talking about? Do you mean... that I shall have to leave Teyr?"

"Your passage outside our world will do a great honour to Teyr," Uncle said. "But it is through your sacrifice that the Greenworld will endure. You will go to Saymu Prime, to act as my emissary there."

Dalya's heart beat like a startled animal as she tried to swallow. Sent away! Away from green, everlasting Teyr? Perhaps this was a punishment, Dalya thought, for wishing that she had not been blessed. For wishing she could have seen Meneyr and other places. She had entertained those disrespectful fantasies about seeing the worlds outside Teyr since before she could remember... but she never thought it would actually *happen*.

Dalya had never truly wanted to be sent away, for surely that would be a failure. What greater calling could there ever be than to stand on the true Greenworld, the first of its kind, the very earth where the Great Goddess's footsteps once fell?

"We will be reunited one day, Dalya, do not fear," Uncle said. "You can never truly be torn asunder from your people. We will meet again as the prophecies foretell; you will be reborn on the Greenworld before the end of everything. Even if you do not return to us in this lifetime. Do you understand?"

The prophecies. Something about Uncle's words tugged at Dalya's memory like a stuck, stubborn claw, like a key struggling to turn—

And suddenly it came back to her. That terrible day when she and Anda had run from the library, when Uncle had been talking on his commpiece. The whole of what she had overheard, the words she'd pushed away to the depths of her mind—

Anda had kept running, too far ahead to overhear. But Dalya, too-curious Dalya, she had turned back. She had pressed herself against the wall, listening, trying to make any sense of it.

The prophecies, it's always the gods-damned prophecies, isn't it! Right, yes. Get the elders in line, and do it quickly. I want a new edict, unambiguous, and I want it out this week. The Moon-City's not for salvation, do I make myself clear? It's all a matter of... interpretation, isn't it?

"Do not look so frightened. The Goddess wills this, Dalya," Uncle said. "So long as we uphold our end of the bargain, so long as we remain steadfast and righteous, we will always be brought safely home. But you have learned the ways of the Saymu for a reason. Now you must go to them, to speak for us."

The moonfolk are not to be bargained with. Look, we told them to return, I shall not be held to ransom by those who defied the order! We need to head this off. Now!

"Do not cry for this burden. Rejoice in it, Dalya! You have been chosen to carry it gladly, as we all have. Now, listen carefully. As far as the people of Teyr are concerned, we will announce that you are being sent to the monks of the Golden-Feather. We will tell them you shall be launched away with one of their ships, to gain wisdom and grace as you sleep in the cosmic void—"

We can burn the Moon-City to the ground if they won't bend. Let them know that I will not hesitate to do what needs to be done. Do not defy me. And warn Agote that he is not to interfere with this again.

"I... I don't... I don't know if I can do it..." Dalya choked, her voice faltering.

"You can, and you will," Uncle said. "The time for doubt has passed. We do what we must, for Teyr. Are you ready and willing?"

"Yes, Uncle," she said. "I will do as I must."

"Long have I tried to love you as my child," Uncle said. "But there is no love in me that is stronger than my love for Teyr. And now come, there is something I must show you."

Dalya followed him wordlessly to the far side of the library, to the same bookcase where she'd once crept with Anda. Her pulse quickened with the memory, and though Uncle himself escorted her now, she still felt like that insolent child again, as if the very walls were about to give up her secrets, as if they would somehow reveal the press of the small hands that touched these books so long ago.

This part of the room was still the same as ever, rows upon rows of ancient books lining the wall. On the left, the Human. On the right, the Divine. *Biographies, Histories, Technologies. Traditional Practice, Philosophy, Theology.*

"Look around you," Uncle said, sweeping his arm in a dramatic circle. "What do you see, Dalya? We share space equally here—the Human and the Divine. Because we are one with the gods, and we will become even closer to them at the end of all things. We are two halves of a whole."

He beckoned her forward, into the Histories section. Then he walked around the pillar, around to the side that faced away from the door, and he removed a fabric-bound book with no title on its worn spine from a shelf near the very top.

To Dalya's surprise, when he opened the cover, there were no pages inside. It was a box, within which nestled a small, square device that looked like some kind of comm.

"What is that?" she asked him breathlessly.

"It is a Q-link device," Uncle said. "A connection to the outside world."

"But—" Dalya began. "But that is forbidden—"

"No, Dalya. It is a privilege, forbidden only to those who would not understand it. Your duty, now that you are coming of age, will be the same as mine. To protect Teyr and its secrets, to guard our old ways from the forces that would seek to tear us down." He paused, as though assessing her reaction. "To protect the good believers."

"But... the Saymu are not good believers," Dalya said slowly. "Why must I go to them, then?"

"Do you remember the story of Olandra's hounds?" Uncle asked.

Dalya nodded slowly. "Yes," she whispered, turning the story around in her head, trying to understand what he was alluding to. "Her hounds could run in the shadows... where the gods dared not to tread."

"Indeed," Uncle said, sounding almost proud. "And that is what you must understand. Sometimes, dangerous alliances are an act of bravery. An act of strength and conviction and sacrifice. Just as Olandra endured the bites and scratches of the beasts."

Dalya stared at her folded hands for a long time. "Derin Agote," she said quietly. "Anda's uncle... Was he... Was he one of the hounds?"

"Yes," Uncle said. "You understand now."

"Did you know that Ker Agote would be killed?"

"Dalya." He did not immediately answer in the affirmative, but he didn't meet her eyes. "I wish it were different, but we all make our choices. Ker Agote was a friend to us, and a friend to Teyr... until he was not. Sometimes the beast who refuses to be tamed must be put down."

A shiver squirmed down Dalya's back. She recalled the illustration of Olandra taming the hounds in a book she'd read many times as a child. She remembered how the image of those beasts had terrified her, how much she'd hated to see Olandra pinned to the ground with five great shadowy shapes swarming over her. The Oblivion's hell-hounds, tearing their prey to pieces, with their orange-eyed stares and their sharp, slavering teeth. Olandra's regal robes were in tatters, and her left hand had been torn away from her body—one of the hounds held it between its bloodied teeth.

Dalya had always turned that page over quickly so as not to see the hell-hounds and Olandra's severed hand for too long. On the next page was a peaceful image of several gods walking on the path toward the gates of the Celestial Kingdom. And beautiful, one-handed Olandra was there beside the gates, tall and slender and serene. Wearing the head and pelt of the traitorous hound as a cloak.

Around Olandra were the four other hounds from the previous page, now tamed and obedient to her. Their mouths were closed now, their eyes bright and golden, and they helped her guard the gate. One pair sat to either side of the path. And they wore pretty golden chains about them, with Olandra's sigil looped around their necks.

INVOCATION TO YHANNIS

Excerpted from Prayers to the Divine Pantheon:
Source Traditions in the Latter Worlds (Various Authors)

> The beginning is not the beginning.
> The end is not the end.
> The journey is the journey.
> Ever onward, in perpetuity.
> Watch over my steps, make steady my hand –
> Over land and water, through sky and stars.
> No matter how far I wander or where I pause to rest,
> Bring me back to the path, wise Yhannis who guides.
> Help me find the way home.

Many variations of this invocation exist throughout the Worlds. In particular, 'The Blessing for the Guidance Home' has been favoured by spacefaring travellers in hopes of a safe return, ever since the exploratory voyages launched by the First Primes.

Of the Primes, Anvaelia notably has the most planetside temples dedicated to Yhannis. This is likely because of the ancestral connection many of the Latter Worlds share with Anvaelia, as well as the planet's intense spacefaring activities during the Third and Fourth Expansion.

MAELLE KRESS
Zhaklam Evelor's Ship

MAELLE SITS IN the Dressing Room back on Zhak's ship, feeling the familiar engine hum beneath her feet as she stitches a new hem into a Teyrian cloak. She works with short, even stitches, breathing in time with the motions of her fingers.

In, out, stitch in, stitch out. In, out, stitch in, stitch out.

This isn't the cloak that Page is going to wear to meet the monks—she'll wear the feathered one, of course—but working with her hands still goes some small way to soothing Maelle's frayed nerves. So, as always, she's found herself something to fix.

Maelle and Page have spoken little of what transpired since they left Laithe, and they certainly haven't mentioned any of it to Zhak. Maelle didn't meet his eyes when she told him how she'd failed to find Reece Bereda, how her contact had left the system, a litany of excuses that she barely registered as they left her mouth.

Maybe it's for the better that the Beredas aren't involved in this. As furious as Maelle is at Reece, her mother's words are still echoing in her head. *What use is millions of credits if I have two dead children instead of one?*

She thinks of her family back on Laithe, and a shiver of dread hits her. She's always known that this plan was reckless, and that she was putting herself in the path of peril by working with Zhak. But if her scheme had come back on the Bereda family somehow—

She pushes that thought away. No matter, it didn't work anyway. It's over. And she's bailing out.

But Maelle never truly considered everything that might happen if the raid actually goes ahead without the scamships. If something goes wrong in the boarding, if the monk-ship does have armed guards—*if Page gets hurt*—

Any nervous energy she's soothed out of herself with the stitching needle comes back with a vengeance. She throws down the cloak and stands up, stretching the cramp out of her arm.

And she jumps back with a start when she sees Page standing there in the doorway, somber-faced and red-eyed. She's dressed in the Teyrian style, buttoned up to the neck in a light blue ruffled blouse, layered over loose trousers in the same colour. A shiny set of prayer beads is looped around her wrist.

"Zhak says, uh… He says we're nearly there," the junk thief tells her quietly. "He said… you should help me finish getting ready."

Maelle nods. "Yeah, all right," she manages. "Sure. Come over here."

Page steps inside, looking down at the avian mask and the long, feathered cloak that still sit on top of a pile of crates in their plastic wrappings. She doesn't reach out to touch anything; it's as though she's waiting for Maelle to place this mantle on her shoulders.

"Maelle," she says. "I'm not sure if I should—"

"I can't make this decision for you, Page," Maelle interjects before she can get any further. "This is something you've got to decide for yourself."

Page nods gravely as she lowers herself onto one of the crates. She slowly works those blue pointed boots off her feet, then peels off her socks, studying the red blisters on the backs of her heels.

"Apparently, monks of the Golden-Feather are supposed to go barefoot," Maelle smiles. "Don't know how appetizing that sounds in some grimy ancillary... but at least you can ditch those boots, huh?"

Page doesn't smile, and she doesn't answer.

"Right, come on, then. Let's do something with your hair," Maelle says. "One of those coiled-braid updos, maybe? Teyrians love those." She finds a comb and sets to work on Page's tangled hair, gradually separating and smoothing the dark strands as she works them into two thick braids and pins them into round coils.

Page keeps her eyes closed and sits perfectly still. For a brief moment as Maelle looks at their reflections in the mirror, she imagines what Page looked like in a stasis pod. Much like this, most likely, serene-faced and still, for all the long years of whatever journey she took. Like some ethereal fairy-tale character. Like the human-form goddess, floating in the void, waiting for Yhannis's hand.

Maelle realizes suddenly that she has never asked Page for Rodin's talisman back. But she doesn't say anything now. Her heart aches, and yet Page surely needs the Interlocutor's protection more than she does.

"I'm sorry," Page says quietly. "I'm real sorry that... it didn't work out with—"

"Shhh, shhh. No apologies. Let's not make this awkward, all right?" Maelle says. "Let's just get you ready." She reaches for the feathered cloak, removing it from its wrappings before carefully arranging it over Page's shoulders. "It's gonna be fine, Page. *You're* gonna be fine. Whatever you decide to do."

"Yeah? And... what about you?" Page asks. "Where will you go when you leave the ancillary? Back to Laithe?"

Maelle shrugs. "Doubt it. I think I've burned my bridges there for the forseeable future. I'll probably have to go somewhere else for a while. Haven't really thought that far."

Just then, Zhak appears in the doorway, those fake jewels

jangling obnoxiously from his sleeves.

"Knock knock!" he shouts, a breathless excitement in his voice. "We're almost there!" He grins toothily, making no attempt to contain his glee. "We're bang on time, we should be right in the window to intercept them. Get over to the speedship when you're ready. We'll shove off in a quarter hour."

He's addressing Page, pointedly avoiding Maelle's gaze. Still pissed off, then.

"I hope we can find the monks quickly," Page says, sounding nervous. "What if we don't run into them?"

"Oh, we'll find 'em. No trouble at all," Zhak says. "By the looks of it, there's barely anything on that ancillary except a bunch of warehouses and a little refueling hub. I doubt there's much traffic there besides a few cargo haulers and the monks' shuttle. There's only so many places they could be!" He laughs, almost maniacally. "This could not be a more fortuitous meeting! *Divine intervention*, here we come!"

"Great," Page says, and it's more of a sigh than a word. She looks back at Maelle, then picks up the bird mask. "Right... I... guess I'll see you at the speedship," she says.

Maelle turns her back, blinking away the tears she doesn't want Page to see.

This might well be the last time they get to speak alone. Maelle should really say something, she should turn around, she should call Page back, she should—

But by the time she turns, Page is gone, already out the door. All that remains are her blue boots standing side by side, her socks laid neatly over the top. It's an oddly endearing image.

And there, on the lid of the crate where she was sitting, Page has left Rodin's talisman.

DALYA
OF HOUSE EDAMAUN, IN HER EIGHTEENTH YEAR
Moon-City, Meneyr

THE NOVICE MONKS of the Golden-Feather—those who had not yet entered the Blessed Sleep—dwelled in a high tower on Meneyr, in the centre-most part of the domed city. They climbed as high as they could in order to reach closer to the cosmos, Dalya learned, to prepare themselves for their journeys into the cosmic void.

It struck her how surreal this all was—that the journey these novices awaited was the opposite of the Returning. They waited to *leave* the Greenworld, to leave the orbit of its moon, to journey further than most Teyrians had ever been in order to seek the Goddess's blessing. It was odd that this was even allowed.

But that wasn't even the strangest of it. Because here among them, Dalya awaited her own fate. Not the void-sleep of stasis, not the journey of the Golden-Feather monks, but a ship that would secretly take her away to serve as an ambassador for her uncle on Saymu Prime.

A single news camera had snapped a capture of Dalya boarding the voyager to the Moon-City. She could imagine the sort of thing that had been written about her in Teyr's daily missives. *Edamaun heir pledged to noble monastic journey. Dalya Edamaun answers call to the Everlasting. The Great, Glorious Choice of the High Speaker's Heir.*

What a great sacrifice Dalya was making, joining the monks! She would be gone for two years, the newscasts would claim, in which time she'd draw closer to the Goddess's grace, and she would surely bring the divine embrace closer to Teyr as the End of Time approached.

But Dalya had never felt further from the comforting embrace of the Goddess. Here, she was entirely and completely alone. She sat down in the window-seat of her room and looked out into the night, peering through the thick glass at the city that Anda had once called home. Beyond the glass, the Moon-City's lights scattered away into the distance, bright dots like starlight as far as her eyes could see. She had never been inside such a tall building.

Dalya pressed her forehead against the glass and tilted her head up, looking for the sheer, iridescent curvature of the dome even higher above the city. It seemed inconceivable that there was no clear line to the sky. That no rain ever fell here, that even those stars up there were only a distorted projection.

She had sometimes imagined what it might have been like, being here in the Moon-City... but she would never get to explore it. She'd be gone before she'd even *seen* any of it. Everything felt far away; the people below were faceless and distant, a crowd to which Dalya did not belong.

And Anda was not here.

In the monks' tower, no one spoke to Dalya. The attendants who brought her simple meals and water only gave a low, respectful bow before they flitted off out of sight again. She had nothing to do but sit and wait. They had left her with a single silver-framed datapad, unconnected to any network. There was nothing on it save for endless pages of the sacred texts, and a few vids of singing monks emerging glorious from their caskets with the words of the Goddess on their lips.

The datapad's gilded case bore an engraved image of a travelling Yhannis, walking among the stars with his tall staff. *The Interlocutor—He Who Guides*, said the curling text along the bottom. Dalya's heart ached. Anda used to love the stories about Yhannis and how he helped the little bird in her hour of need—those early tales from the sacred texts that the sages on Teyr rarely told.

Dalya thought of Anda, again and again. She thought of that long-ago day when Anda had told her that music was *the most human of humanity's creations*, a special thing, something to be proud of. Something they had that even the gods in all their glory and power and wisdom had not devised. The gift that humanity gave to the gods in return. The bird began to sing when she awoke because she had heard the music of the humans, and it lifted her small heart. And thereafter, the gods sent birds to all the green worlds, and all those birds, too, knew how to sing.

Was all of what was written in the sacred texts even true? How should one know which stories to believe? Dalya felt so lost, now, so uncertain of it all. She looked down at the Moon-City again, its buildings spilling in bright waves of light beneath her, and a new foreboding clenched in her chest.

Soon, she would don the pale feathered cape and beaked mask, and put on the guise of the little bird. She would walk down the spiral stairs to the grand monastic chamber, barefoot and silent, and she would be blessed a final time before she accepted the mantle of the Goddess and lay down in her gilded casket... or so it would seem.

Many would see her do it. It was imperative that Dalya be seen putting on the mask, and entering the stairwell, by as many people as possible. Except that Dalya would never get to the bottom of those steps. On a landing halfway down, she would exit through a small, narrow corridor, where another monk—a real novice in a matching bird mask—would be waiting to take her place in the casket.

And then she, Dalya, would be spirited off to meet her ship to Saymu Prime, to become Uncle's ambassador to a world far away. She would be like Divine Olandra, setting off to befriend the shadowy hell-hounds. Dalya tried not to think of the part where they ripped Olandra half to shreds.

Instead, Dalya carefully laid out the ceremonial dress she was to wear tonight—the last time she would be seen in public in the Protectorate before her flight. An attendant would surely come soon to help her put everything on. Oh, how she wished Heral were here. Heral had always done this for her before.

Would she ever see Heral again? Of course she would, she told herself. *Of course.* No matter what transpired, they would find each other at the beginning and the end of everything. On the Greenworld, they would be together again, and before, and forever.

Perhaps if Dalya just thought about it hard enough, somehow she could make herself believe it again, the way she did as a child. Perhaps she could forget the things she would rather not understand.

She looked down at all the pieces of her lush, ornamented ceremonial dress, spread out side by side on her bed. There was the beautiful new robe that she'd had fitted at the tailor's shop... where she'd last seen Anda on the tailor's front steps. Her heart seized with grief, recalling it.

The new robe was an impeccably made garment, its thick golden fabric richly embroidered with bright white thread. At the neck, there was a wide wreath of orange Goddess-blossom that encircled the whole collar. Each bloom was vibrant and silky, looking every bit as real as if the flowers had just been plucked from the garden.

Except—

Dalya frowned. There was an imperfection in that wreath of flowers, something she hadn't noticed before. It shocked her to see it, and for a moment she wondered if her eyes were deceiving her.

No, one of the blossoms really was a slightly different colour than the others. It looked larger and rougher-edged, as though the delicate fabric had not been properly cut out. When she reached out to touch it, it felt... *synthetic*, not soft and silky like the rest of the adornments.

Another painful memory lingered at the edge of Dalya's consciousness, dredging up the vivid image she hadn't thought of in so long. *Rain, so much rain falling in great, gusting sheets. A gilded pavilion ripping loose from its moorings, the fabric snapping perilously in the wind. Her cold and damp hair plastered to her cheeks. The sensation of the syrupy gold rune-paint running down her face, dripping inelegantly into her eyes.*

And a synthetic orange flower in Anda's outstretched hand.

Dalya took hold of the irregular flower and pulled. The bloom came away from the garment easily, as though it had only been hastily applied. Below it, there was a gap in the fine stitching along the robe's collar, an error in the otherwise flawless craft.

But under the partially unstitched edge, there was something—

Dalya removed what felt like a slim piece of card, working it loose with her nail. It was a pale grey rectangle only the width of her fingertip, with a computer chip embedded on one side.

A tiny data stick.

Dalya's heart pounded as she inserted the grey chip into the slot on the datapad, and for a moment it seemed as though time stood still. It took a few seconds for the contents of the chip to load, as though the device itself was uncertain whether or not to proceed.

Then the folder within finally opened, and there were only two files there.

The first was in an unfamiliar format, its icon marked with the word ENCRYPTED. The other was a regular vid-file, what looked to be a short recording.

With a shaking finger, Dalya selected the file.

And at once, it felt as though her heart had stopped entirely along with her mind, both of them unable to believe the sight before her. There was no mistaking it; here before her on the vid-screen was Anda Agote in her eighteenth year. The very girl she'd seen exiting the tailor's shop.

The girl who'd slipped this data stick into the seam of Dalya's new robe.

In the vid, Anda looked older and wiser and *angrier*. She was *so much more* than she had been, and yet she was still the same dear, lovely Anda.

"Dalya," her shimmering image said. "Oh, I so dearly hope it is you there watching this, Dalya. There is much that I need to tell you, and I need you to listen carefully."

Anda took a hurried, gasping breath, as if she couldn't get the words out fast enough. She spoke not in the Perfect Cadence, but in *Union Basic*—the tongue that had once seemed so coarse and strange to Dalya's ears. The language far less likely to be understood by any Teyrian who came across this.

"The Gepcot has built a great weapon above Teyr—a dark and awful thing. They call it a 'death-hoop,'" she continued. "The United Worlds long ago banned such weapons, due to the destruction they caused back in the Imperial Ages... but here, around our green world, they've constructed this horror anew. Your Uncle, the High Speaker, ordered the weapon built for Teyr's protection—to shield the planet from attacks from space. To protect us from the aliens! That is what *my* uncle believed he was doing, when he served the Protectorate all those years, and he helped to have it done. And perhaps that is all the Gepcot had first intended, too."

Anda cut herself off suddenly and glanced at the closed door behind her, as if she'd heard some unexpected noise. Panic flitted briefly across her pale face before she schooled it back into a fierce, undaunted determination.

"Dalya... we've learned now of a most terrible truth. The Gepcot intends to use the death-hoop to target Meneyr. Your uncle seeks to use it to silence the rebels in the Moon-City, once and for all. A strike like deadly lightning will soon pierce one of the domes... and it will cause a catastrophic failure that will spread to the others. The entire dome-shield will fall, and anyone on the surface will perish. If this comes to pass,

An Unbreakable World

then all but the underground levels of the Moon-City will be completely lost."

Dalya's breath left her chest, as though some great weight had just collided with the middle of her ribcage. Her uncle had made many veiled threats these last few years, had given many dire warnings of what could befall Meneyr's rebels if they did not turn back to the proper path. But surely he would never—

"This is a horror in which we have all played a part, whether we knew it or not," Anda said, lowering her head. "My uncle sought a different end to this tale. It broke his heart, knowing how much of this was his own doing. But he had only sought to secure the safety of the Protectorate—for me, for all of us. To keep us safe from the aliens. When he learned what the Gepcot intended, when he saw that your uncle would not change his mind... he tried to expose everything. And..." She drew in a half-choked sob. "The Gepcot named him a conspirator and a Union spy... and they killed him for it."

A small part of Dalya wondered if she was dreaming all of this, grasping at the tenuous hope that it wasn't true. This couldn't possibly be happening. Surely, at any moment, she would awaken back in her familiar bed in Uncle's house on the green hill, on everlasting Teyr, and none of this would be real—

"We are almost out of time, Dalya. The order has already been given," Anda's flickering figure went on. "The order is annihilation. They are only awaiting the all-clear. The Gepcot will be waiting for the ship carrying their *new ambassador* to leave orbit. That is to be the signal. As soon as your ship has left Meneyr's orbit... they will activate the weapon."

No. *No, no, no, no*—

"It does not matter now, Dalya, that you didn't believe me about my parents when we were younger. I forgive you. I know why you could not listen. It matters only that you believe me *now*. Please." There were tears in her eyes. "My uncle died trying to change the Gepcot's course, and he probably thought he'd failed. But he didn't, Dalya. He hasn't! Not yet. Because he sent a copy of the proof to *me*."

Anda's jaw tensed, and she turned and looked behind her again. "They will come for me, I'm sure of it. I don't know if I'll make it back to Meneyr in time, or at all. But you—you're going there soon. *You* can still stop this. You have to."

How, Anda? Dalya mouthed, tears welling in her eyes. *What can I do?*

"You need to find the rebels in the underground shelters on Meneyr, and get this data to their leader."

The rebels? Underground? Anda, I am here locked in a monastery tower, how can I possibly find—

"Above all, you must not get on that ship, Dalya. You mustn't leave Meneyr. So long as you remain in the Moon-City, your uncle won't give the signal."

Still, something in Dalya's chest writhed and screamed silently against it, her heart beating, *no, no, no*. How could Uncle—how could Luwan Edamaun, the High Speaker of the Great, Everlasting Planetary Council of Teyr—

But Anda had never lied to her.

"I'm so sorry, Dalya," Anda whispered. "But you must fly like the little bird did, now. And warn them what's coming."

MAELLE KRESS
Zhaklam Evelor's Ship

THE ANCILLARY AHEAD of them is arranged in a hexagonal shape: six tall blocks of enormous warehouses anchored around a small refuelling hub. The whole thing is barely lit from the outside, except for a few exterior running lights to help ships line up on the docking clamps.

As Zhak predicted, there are very few ships currently in dock. In fact, Maelle can't see any ships there at all as they approach, at least not on the side they're descending from. There's nothing clamped in any of the bays, not even a shuttle. The refuelling hub in the centre is dark. The place seems utterly deserted.

"This doesn't look good," Maelle says. "No ships at all? Where in the hells are the staff?" She turns to Page. "Ancillaries should have a perpetual skeleton crew, and live guards. Also, it doesn't look like your monks are here yet."

"They'll be here," Zhak says confidently. "Look, that monkship's drifting on a slingshot course, they can't just change plans. If our intel is good, they only have a window of a few hours to shuttle out, grab some supplies and rejoin their ship. Even if there's not a damn soul out here, they'll show up. And we'll be here to let them in if they need help." He grins. "This could turn out even better for us than we thought."

"I don't know," Maelle says. "It makes me nervous, that's all. Why's it dark?"

Zhak is on the speedship's comm, checking in with his raider crew. "Raider ships are taking position," he says, sliding away the display. "We're good. Now we just gotta get on that ancillary and wait for these monks."

He takes out and examines his plasma pistol, then tucks it back into his belt.

"Uh... should we really be going in armed, if we plan to meet pacifist monks?" Page asks. "Is that good manners?"

"Manners?" Zhak laughs. "You'd be out of your mind not to be armed, busting into a dark ancillary. And besides, you're the only monk among us. We're just giving you a ride. Don't you think we ought to protect our little birdie?"

He goes off into one of the small supply compartments and returns with a beam torch, which he throws to Maelle. "Take that. Doesn't look like there's anyone working the docks, so we might need to rip through some doors if there's nobody home."

Maelle seethes inwardly at the way he throws orders at her, but she takes the beam torch and slings it over her shoulder without comment. She has half a mind to just slice through him with the beam torch and be done with it. An ancillary full of dark warehouses seems as good a place as any to do it, if she was ever going to. Her hands tighten into fists.

But no. Page needs this chance to make up her mind. To meet the monks—to go with them, if she wants to. Maelle owes her that much.

As the speedship descends, rotating slowly into position toward one of the empty docking bays at the refuelling hub, she looks up at the towering structures above. Many of the storage spaces are unmarked, but here and there, a company logo or name is emblazoned on one of the gateways, illuminated by a single floodlight.

And there, Maelle's gaze lands directly on the one about four levels up.

The familiar shape of a semicircular saw, stencilled on the side of one of the gigantic warehouses.
BEREDA FINE WOOD FURNISHINGS.
This is Ancillary Nineteen.

ZHAK'S RAIDER CREW
Private Channel

RAID LEADER: Raider Zero Eight, position check?
RAIDER 08: Fanning out, we're in position. I'm in local comms range of the ancillary.
RAID LEADER: All confirmed. Zhak, we're set. On your mark.
ZHAK: Right, hold position. I'm just docking the speedship, we're going inside.
RAID LEADER: Hey... Hey, Zhak, you getting this alert they're sending out? Apparently an orange zone's heating up not far from here.

[ANCILLARY NINETEEN – PUBLIC BULLETIN – ALL CARGO TRANSFERS AND WAREHOUSE ACCESS SUSPENDED DUE TO NEARBY ALIEN ACTIVITY – EMERGENCY DOCKINGS ONLY – ALL CARGO TRANSFERS AND WAREHOUSE ACCESS SUSPENDED DUE TO NEARBY ALIEN ACTIVITY]

RAIDER 06: Oh, wow, yeah. Is this a mission pull? Looks like it.
ZHAK: [static]
RAIDER 08: You seeing this report, Zhak? Worst I've seen in a long while. Apparently there's activity all around here.
RAIDER 04: Tons of Felen traffic, about a four-hour radius. Some closer.
RAIDER 02: Fuck, this has to be a mission pull. We've gotta get out of here.
ZHAK: Absolutely not, you're not going anywhere. Hold position, wait for my signal.
RAID LEADER: There's nobody else out here, Zhak. Emergency dockings only. I don't even see any ships on that ancillary. You sure this is where –

ZHAK: Target will be incoming shortly. We hold position, don't move till I say so.

RAIDER 08: No way we're getting paid enough for this.

ZHAK: I'm docking with the ancillary. You'll hold position till you hear from me. The mission proceeds as planned.

RAID LEADER: Zhak, hey! Hey! We getting a danger bonus here, or what?

ZHAK: [*static*]

PAGE FOUND
Ancillary Nineteen, Deep Space

As they make their way through the airlock into the main thoroughfare of the deserted refuelling station, Page can't suppress a shiver. Not for the first time, she wonders if maybe she really should have bolted back in the marketplace on Laithe.

Maybe she could have delayed Maelle long enough to miss Zhak's pickup window at Felwae. Maybe this never would have happened, and she wouldn't be standing here in a deserted ancillary, barefoot and feather-cloaked, with her heart threatening to burst out of her chest, wondering if she truly has made the biggest mistake of this life.

Zhak's tracker, with its dense, very real Q-brick inside, is heavy in her bag, resting against her hip. Waiting for her to carry it onto the monks' shuttle. Waiting for her to make up her mind.

If you do get on that monk-ship... you don't have *to activate the Q-link*, Maelle had said. *You could just... not do it. You know that, right?*

She could refuse to push the button, and just let the monk-ship bear her away with it into the fathomless deeps. Or she could signal Zhak's raiders, complete the job... and probably condemn all the monks on board to death.

She knows what she's *not* willing to do.

But none of that will matter if they don't get through the first part. Maybe the monks aren't even here. And so far, there's no sign of them. There's no sign of anybody at all.

Zhak takes the lead, walking ahead of them into the darkened thoroughfare with a flashlight in his hand. There's no sound except for Zhak's booted footsteps, echoing loudly over the corrugated metal floor, and the accursed jangling of the jewelled chains on his sleeves. Page's bare feet are soundless on the floor, and Maelle steps quietly behind them, clutching that beam torch like her life depends on it.

"Hello?" Zhak calls out. "Anybody home 'round here?"

His voice reverberates through the cavernous, empty space. His light illuminates large cargo lifts to either side of them, and several exits that look like service passageways. Nowhere that a visiting monk is likely to be. They would surely be down here in the main thoroughfare of the refuelling station, looking for crates of basic supplies or replacement parts for their water purification system.

Page wonders vaguely how a monk-ship from the Protectorate pays for resupply. Do Teyrians even have Union currency anymore? Perhaps they have to barter.

But there's no one here to barter *with*, all the supply vendors seem to be closed.

"Hello?" Zhak shouts again, flashing his light up into the higher catwalks.

The sound of his voice echoes back again, but this time it's... *strange*. It's not only his own voice that returns, but several voices, merging into a long, low hum, like the beginnings of a chant.

"What's that?" Page whispers to Maelle.

But before Maelle can say anything in reply, a narrow door that Page didn't notice before slides open on the far wall, and a single figure slips through it. Page quickly pulls down her beaked mask and settles it properly over her face, assuming her straight-backed, monastic posture.

Unfortunately, it's no monk of the Golden-Feather who emerges from the door, but a young man in a guild jacket, walking toward them with the hurried steps of an administrator.

"Ah! So sorry, we weren't expecting anyone to be docking! As you've probably noticed, the warehouse facility is temporarily closed, what with all the alien activity that's been reported," Guild Jacket says. He gives them a wide, congenial smile. "What's your emergency? Anything I can do to help?"

Page and Maelle turn to glance at each other at the same time, a look of silent astonishment passing between them. *What in the name of the stars is Dex the supply-aider from the Felwae bar doing here?*

Dex's gaze betrays no immediate recognition, as his eyes pass over first Zhak and Maelle, then settle on Page in her bare feet and her odd, bird-like garb.

"Oh! Well, damn!" Dex says, bringing both hands to his mouth. "*Another* one of you bird-monks?"

"Another?" Zhak presses forward, alarm in his voice. "What! Do you mean to say that you've seen others of her order, here? Have they gone already?"

"Nah, I reckon they're still around somewhere," Dex says, shaking his head with a nonchalant shrug. "It sounded like they were... waiting for something? I didn't quite understand what they were saying. They don't speak Union Basic."

"Where are they now? Where is their shuttlecraft?" Zhak demands, gesturing at Page. "Listen, their god-sibling here is searching for them, we've got to get to where they—"

As if on cue, that low, chanting hum suddenly grows louder, and at the same time, all the overhead lights in the refuelling thoroughfare come on. Maelle and Zhak are both looking around in bafflement, first at each other and then back at Page. *What in the hells?*

Three more figures are shuffling into the thoroughfare from around a still-darkened corner, awkwardly steering a wide pallet of supply crates between them. A couple of them wear ornate shirts and trousers in that Teyrian style, and the third one is outfitted in the avian cloak and mask, just like Page.

"*Blessed Everlasting Lady,*" one of them exclaims in Graya. They stop, all of them staring at Page. "*What's this? Are you... one of us? How is this possible?*"

They abandon the pallet of crates and all hurry over, arranging themselves in a row with the bird in the middle. The bird-feathered monk steps forward, reaching an open hand toward Page.

"*Tell us you are one of ours,*" the monk says reverently.

"*God-siblings! Yes, I am of your own kin. The hand of the Goddess guides me,*" Page says, her heartbeat pounding in her temples. "*Long have I been lost from the Sanctum of the Golden-Feather... but today we are reunited at last.*"

The Graya words dance from her mouth almost before she can think them through. She holds her breath, waiting for their reaction. And for a few seconds that feel like an eternity, they all just stand there staring at her.

There's that same sense of recognition in the back of Page's mind—the absolute certainty that she has seen such monks somewhere before—but she feels no *kinship* when she looks at them. No sense of being one of them.

In fact, in this moment, she has never been more certain that she doesn't actually want to get on that monk-ship at all. This is wrong, something about this is wrong.

Page dares a small glance back at Maelle, wondering if she shares Page's apprehension. But Maelle seems preoccupied. She's looking somewhere else—watching Dex sauntering back toward that narrow door he came from. Walking away from them calmly, as if this business is quite simply nothing to do with him anymore.

There's a deep frown on Maelle's face as she watches him go. No doubt she also feels that there's something strange going on.

"*I cannot believe it, our blessings are innumerable,*" Zhak says to the monks, pulling out his theatrical, formal Graya. "*We made an emergency docking here on account of some engine troubles... and to think, the threads of fate have led us here! Long has my dear friend sought her kin with no way back home."*

"*And* your *ship has brought her to us!*" The feathery one's attention pivots to Zhak, all three monks moving to surround him. "*This is your doing, honoured friend?*"

"*Indeed! Truly, the hand of the divine must have guided us today,*" Zhak says with a self-satisfied smile. This is surely going better than he'd imagined. At this rate, they're going to invite him onto the ship and ask him if he wants to hold the Bird's Heart in his hands, Page thinks wryly.

"*I suppose you are aware that there is a reward for anyone assisting in the safe return of a monk of the Golden-Feather to their companions?*" the monk on the right says.

"*Oh?*" Zhak clearly did not expect that; his chin straightens and his eyes widen suddenly. Page is sure he isn't feigning his surprise. "*I hadn't thought—no, of course not! I wish no reward but to see my friend here safely returned among good believers. You will take her to your ship with you, I presume?*"

"*Most certainly, we will!*" the feathered monk says. "*We will bear her toward the Greenworld with us, with great joy.*"

Page takes a long, steadying breath and says, "*Don't you wish to hear the story of how I came to be stranded here? To learn if I am who I claim to be?*"

Do they not wish to question her, to ask where on Teyr she was born, to see the scars of the void-sleep? To hear of her twin sister and the orange flowers on the altar and the six-chime of the bells?

Next to Page, Zhak's shoulders stiffen visibly at her words. What is she *doing?*

Page is not entirely sure of it herself. Does she *want* the monks to catch her out as a fraud? Or does she just want so badly to make her imagined story real, as if by telling it to them and seeing them believe it, she might weave it into a lost truth? Who's to say she's *not* a monk of the Golden-Feather?

"There will be much time for sharing tales later," the monk on the left says. *"We shall hear it gladly, and rejoice in your company. But our time runs short, now—we must rejoin our ship before it passes us by. We should leave here as soon as we can."*

Page turns again to look at Maelle. She's still staring at the closed door, but Dex is gone now, the passage he came from sealed shut once more.

Zhak looks inordinately pleased with himself as the feathered monk gives a long, deep bow before him. *"Now... in reward for such selfless friendship,"* the monk is saying, *"I should like to grant you a portent. Perhaps a little divination? Would that please you?"*

From somewhere under his cape, the feathered monk produces a deck of worn paper cards. On the back of each card is an image of the Great Goddess in humanoid form, faceless and golden, resplendent in a long, billowing dress and shining like a sun. Around her is a whirl of white birds, some of which are sitting on her arms.

"Perhaps you could help me with this?" the monk says to Page, and her breath catches in her throat.

Have the monks seen through her? Maybe this is some kind of test, because Page has absolutely no idea how to do this—nothing like this was covered in any of the dozens of articles she'd read.

"By that I mean... could you hold the cards, please, to amplify their divine energy?" the monk clarifies, clearing his throat. And Page breathes again.

The monk shuffles the cards before he passes them over to Page, setting the whole deck into her outstretched hands. The cards are well-used, the corners soft with wear, and they feel warm against her palms. Each iridescent image of the goddess is covered in a web of cracks and creases.

"Now we are ready," the bird-monk says, waving his hands around slowly in midair. *"We just need to let divine inspiration speak. Let your friend select a card."*

Page holds the deck out toward Zhak with shaking hands. Zhak makes a perfunctory skim of the card edges with his fingertips, just enough not to seem uninterested. He closes in on one card that protrudes slightly from the deck, and pulls it loose.

"*Wonderful,*" says the monk, plucking it quickly from his hand. "*Shall we take a look?*"

At the same time, Page turns over the remainder of the deck in her hands, curiously spreading the cards between her fingers. To her surprise, the painting on the other side is identical on *every single card*.

A shining serpent, with a large lozenge-shaped head and two piercing yellow eyes, stares back at her dozens of times over, its coil of gilded black scales wrapped around the hilt of a dagger.

"*Ah!*" the monk exclaims with almost childlike delight, flipping Zhak's chosen card toward him. "*The Void Snake!*"

Then all the lights in the thoroughfare go out again.

Page screams.

INTERPRETING THE TRADITIONAL GODDESS-DECK: A PRIMER

Card meanings and their mythological contexts
Card #55: The Void Snake

The traditional illustration for this card shows a coiled snake pierced through with a dagger lodged just behind its head – a mortal wound. But the snake's head is raised, its eyes and mouth open, its fangs proudly bared, as though it intends to strike with its dying act.

Snake imagery is prevalent in the mythological art of the Primes, and is typically associated with positive change, renewal, reinvention and revival – probably because many species of land snake regularly shed their skin. The snake is also strongly linked with the goddess Moehrga, the bringer of change, who is sometimes shown carrying a snake-shaped staff.

Thus the Void Snake card, with its wounded and dying snake, is sometimes read as symbolizing the opposite within the context of a reading: that is, there are barriers to one's reinvention, or serious obstacles standing in one's way, or a strong resistance to change.

This card's meaning is sometimes associated with revenge or retribution, or the dealing of some deserved misfortune. The appearance of the Void Snake in a reading can also signify the act of overcoming something, or of reaching for a goal at any cost, even when that cost is steep.

There is a notable sense of triumph and perseverance with the appearance of this card – the pictured snake, despite its mortal wound, is not cowed and will nonetheless strike its intended blow.

DALYA
OF HOUSE EDAMAUN, IN HER EIGHTEENTH YEAR
Moon-City, Meneyr

DALYA STEPPED DOWN the spiral staircase of the tower. The marbled stone was cool and smooth against her bare feet. One step, then another, then another. The heavy, feathered cape pooled on the steps behind her; the bird mask was tight against her face.

There were little alcoves or doorways at almost every landing she passed. Some led to winding corridors, some to other unlit stairways that coiled away into the dark. This tower was a labyrinth, intended to represent the Goddess's confusion when she lost her way in the cosmic void. But all Dalya needed to do was walk straight ahead.

Her path was clear; there was a bright golden stripe painted on the centre of each stair to guide her way. She must get halfway down the tower—*one foot in front of the other, almost there, almost there*—and there she would come upon her bird-cloaked replacement, waiting in one of the alcoves.

The two birds would slip silently past one another, and Dalya's replacement would descend to the gilded casket in her place. And then, Dalya supposed, someone would come to escort her away. By tomorrow, she would be on the way to Saymu Prime. *And the Moon-City will be no more.*

For one wild moment, Dalya imagined that the replacement

bird wouldn't be there in the alcove. That instead *she*, Dalya, would step the rest of the way down these stairs, and she'd simply lie down in the casket, and allow the Blessed Sleep to overtake her. Maybe then, she need never think about the little data stick clutched in her hand. She need never think of Uncle's terrible decree, and the death-hoop suspended above Teyr, and Anda's message—

But no. She could not lose her courage now. *Fly like the little bird*, Anda had said. Like the Small Spirit, voiceless and alone, she must soar into the dark.

Sometimes, disobedient footsteps do take you to the right place. And sometimes, when you feel it... when you feel a path calling you to go somewhere unexpected... that's the divine inspiration in you.

Those were Uncle's own words, and they rang strangely now in Dalya's memory. And yet—

She had no idea how she could possibly find the rebels, or even how she could leave this building. But she had to try.

She stepped down, and down, and down, following that shining golden line. She was completely alone here in the silence, passing between one landing and the next. No one behind her, no one ahead. She turned from side to side, and the alcoves were both empty.

But just ahead and to the right, another vacant stairwell curved away into the dark.

The distant six-chime of the bells reverberated through the tower, echoing down into the stone. It was funny, Dalya thought, that a tower that stood on this moon that had seen no rain, where no green fields grew, where the Goddess had never stepped, could feel so *ancient*.

Dalya took a long breath, holding the little chip of Anda's data tight in her palm.

She turned to the right, into the darkened stairwell.

And she ran—

No. She *flew*.

ZHAK'S RAIDER CREW
Private Channel

RAIDER 03: Whoa! Leader, I'm getting a lot of pings here all of a sudden –
RAIDER 08: Oh, damn! Yeah, same, it's lighting *up!*

[*PROXIMITY ALERT*] [*PROXIMITY ALERT*] [*PROXIMITY ALERT*]
[*PROXIMITY ALERT*] [*PROXIMITY ALERT*] [*PROXIMITY ALERT*]
[*PROXIMITY ALERT*]

RAID LEADER: Zhak! Listen, I'm seeing a lot of action right now. We've got alien activity out here from two different directions. Confirm that we're pulling the raid?
ZHAK: [*static*]

[*PROXIMITY ALERT*] [*PROXIMITY ALERT*] [*PROXIMITY ALERT*]
[*PROXIMITY ALERT*] [*PROXIMITY ALERT*] [*PROXIMITY ALERT*]
[*PROXIMITY ALERT*] [*PROXIMITY ALERT*] [*PROXIMITY ALERT*]

RAIDER 07: Leader, what's your call?
RAID LEADER: Zhak! We calling this? We've got to pull, I've got Felen traffic on all the scanners here –
ZHAK: [*static*]
RAIDER 08: Right, that's it, I'm going dark. Powering down.

[*RAIDER 08 OFFLINE*]

RAIDER 04: Oh, hells, no. I'm not getting caught drifting. We gotta get out of here!
RAID LEADER: Zhak!
ZHAK: [*static*]

[PROXIMITY ALERT] [PROXIMITY ALERT] [PROXIMITY ALERT] [PROXIMITY ALERT] [PROXIMITY ALERT] [PROXIMITY ALERT] [PROXIMITY ALERT] [PROXIMITY ALERT] [PROXIMITY ALERT] [PROXIMITY ALERT] [PROXIMITY ALERT] [PROXIMITY ALERT] [PROXIMITY ALERT] [PROXIMITY ALERT]

RAIDER 07: Good luck, everybody. I'm out.
RAID LEADER: Right, I'm calling it. Power down if you're playing dead – everyone else, on my mark. Fall back and follow me.

[RAIDER 02 OFFLINE]
[RAIDER 01 OFFLINE]
[RAIDER 07 OUT OF RANGE]

ZHAK: [static]

MAELLE KRESS
Ancillary Nineteen, Deep Space

THE LIGHTS IN the thoroughfare are all out. Maelle can't see anything at all in front of her; the whole space has been plunged into pitch darkness.

A few paces in front of her, Page is still screaming. Maelle lunges for her in the dark, seizing her by the edge of the feathered cloak.

"Too dark! It's too dark."

"I've got you," Maelle gasps. "It's me. Shhh, Page, shhh—" She pulls Page away from where she *thinks* Zhak is, turning her around, dragging her toward one of the outer walls.

"They're—not—monks—" Page pants. Maelle is tripping over the feathered cape where it tangles around Page's bare feet. She steers Page by the shoulders, now pushing her forward. "They weren't monks, Maelle, I think it's some kind of a trap—"

"Oh, you *think*?" rages Zhak. He flicks his flashlight back on, pointing it around the thoroughfare, and Maelle pulls Page against her and freezes. Zhak is spinning in small, frantic circles. But there's nobody there, nobody in range of his light. "Maelle! Show yourself!"

Nothing except Zhak is moving. It's silent as a tomb again.

The monks—or whoever they were—seem to have gone, as if they've just vaporized into the shadows. Back to their shuttlecraft, if they ever had one, or further into the ancillary. *Did they go up into the warehouses? And where in the hells is Dex?*

"What did you do?" Zhak demands, shouting into the dark. "Maelle! What did you do? What kind of setup is this? You conniving, traitorous little—"

Maelle drops to a crouch and continues to move toward the outer wall, little by little. She feels Page drop to the floor alongside her, hears the soft sounds of her panicked breathing.

"Maelle!" Zhak screams again. "Maelle, gods damn it, I know you're here! Where are you?"

Maelle's elbow makes sudden contact with a hard surface, and she bites back a yelp, dropping to one knee. It's not the wall—it's the pallet that the monks left behind, piled with crates. She tugs on Page's wrist, moving around the pallet to put it between them and Zhak. Luckily, she thinks, Page is well practised in the art of sneaking.

Somehow, Maelle manages to quietly shoulder off the heavy beam torch and shrug free of it, setting it down. But not a moment later, a flash of bright pink sends a new panic into her chest. That's a plasma charge gauge. Zhak has armed his weapon. Maelle flattens herself almost to the floor, and she and Page crawl together behind the pallet.

Then Zhak fires twice in random directions, and Maelle flinches. Her hand presses into Page's. Both shots hit the distant walls with a crackle of burning wires, briefly illuminating the thoroughfare.

Zhak goes silent again, his flashlight turning in a slower circle as Maelle peers around the edge of the pallet. She ducks back again when he starts moving toward them, blocky boot heels reverberating on the metal floor. There is still no sign of Dex or the monks coming back.

Page and Maelle lie flat to the floor as Zhak comes closer, his flashlight sweeping over the top of the crates. He's close to them now; all he has to do is take a few steps and turn his light to the left, and he'll be looking right at them.

But he's stopped. The light flicks off again and he stands in silence, as though listening for movement. A moment later, Maelle hears the soft beep of him activating a comm channel.

"Raid Leader! Change of plans, I need armed backup at the ancillary," Zhak says sharply. "Bring it in, come to me and dock up here. Weapons ready."

There's nothing but silence and faint static on his line.

"Raid Leader, hello? I need everyone down here on the ancillary, do you read me?"

At last, a tinny voice comes through, a terrible connection as though the sender is reaching the very edge of communication range. "We're on the way out of here, boss. Raid's been pulled! There's loads of Felen traffic out here, congregating on the ancillary. You'd better get out, too!"

"What?" He swears, a long chain of curses—half in Union Basic and half in Graya, but Maelle doesn't need to understand them to guess at their meaning.

Her heart soars. It's *Reece*, it must be. The Bereda warehouse is right here, only four stories above them, full of the best hybrid builds around. But how—

Maelle holds perfectly still, clutching Page with one arm, and they wait breathlessly. Zhak walks past them again, to the farthest end of the pallet, his light sweeping over the crates.

His foot clatters against something on the floor, and he curses again as he sweeps his light downward.

Damn it, she thinks, *the beam torch, she left the beam torch—*

Zhak leans down and picks it up, his light bobbing briefly as he hefts the heavy tool onto his shoulder.

And just then, Maelle's comm ringer goes off.

She hadn't thought to silence it, because it's set to local calls only. Fuck, who's calling her? Her hand flies to her belt to switch off the sound, but it's too late. Zhak turns, and in seconds he's on them, his flashlight on their faces.

"Found you," he growls.

Maelle's comm is still flashing and buzzing with an incoming transmission, clutched in her hand. Instead of going for his weapon again, Zhak lunges forward and grabs Maelle's wrist, wrenching her hand up.

And when he turns her wrist over, there's an unhinged grin on his face in the glow of her comm's screen.

"Oh, look at that! A friend of yours calling?" He laughs, and he turns the screen toward her.

[*Incoming local-range comm-call*]
CONTACT: REECE

"You think you're so smart, Maelle, the smartest around! You did all of this. You think I don't know what you're up to? That's Bereda's scamships out there!" He laughs again, a high and deranged sound. "What in the fuck have you done?"

Page is shrinking back, pressing herself against the crates as though she could disappear into them. "Run," Maelle hisses to her through clenched teeth. But Page doesn't move.

The comm is still buzzing.

Then Zhak abruptly lets go of Maelle's wrist. He draws the plasma pistol again, and he points the weapon at Page.

"Go on, Maelle. Answer it," he sneers.

Maelle swallows hard, staring at the incoming call.

"Say hello, Maelle. Do it, or say goodbye to the birdie," he whispers, pressing the gun against Page's neck.

Maelle activates the call. "H-hello?" she manages.

"Maelle? Can you hear me?" comes Reece's urgent voice over the comm. The connection is tenuous, the sound dropping in and out with a crackle. "Hello? Listen… Baby, I was trying to come get you… on the way to the ancillary… had to fall back… can't get to you… Felen traffic everywhere around the warehouse!"

"What?" Maelle whispers. "Where are you?"

There's another loud hiss in the line. "Are you there?" says Reece. "Maesie, say something. We've got to fall back—"

"Reece! Where are you, how far from the ancillary?"

It seems an eternity until Reece's garbled voice returns.

"Shit. Shit. This is real bad, baby," she's saying. "We've got eyes on the ancillary now... they're closing in on you... thorn ships coming your way... got to be two dozen of them—" Reece's voice disappears again, lost in the noise.

Static hisses. And then... there's nothing at all.

"Reece?"

Nothing.

"Reece!" Maelle's voice cracks as the light on the comm line blinks out, replaced by an orange error bar. "*Mama!* No, *no*—"

[*Connection lost*]

At once, a row of emergency lights flashes on along the perimeter beams, intermittently illuminating the thoroughfare. The look on Zhak's face in the flickering light has shifted from anger to horror.

But he's not reacting to Maelle's emotional slip. He's looking at the orange warning pulsing between the emergency lights.

[ALERT – LOCAL ALIEN ACTIVITY REPORTED]

"Fuck. That's *not* Bereda's scamships? This shit's *real*."

Maelle suddenly feels dizzy, a wave of cold fear overtaking her as she grabs tight hold of Page's hand. She looks back at the silent comm. "No, no, no," she whispers. "No, Reece, come on—"

[*Connection lost*]
Reconnecting...
[*Connection lost*]
Reconnecting...
[CONTACT OFFLINE]

Zhak has already turned his back on them, his fury forgotten in the wake of his terror. He's taken off running, his bootsteps echoing into the dark as he hurtles back toward where the speedship is docked.

"Maelle! What should we do?" Page whispers breathlessly as they both clamber to their feet.

"I don't know, I don't know... I think... Gods, I think we've got to get off this ancillary before the Felen open fire on it..."

Their best hope is that the aliens are planning to ransack the warehouses first, and that they won't fire on the ancillary right away. But those are thorn ships out there—the Felen's smallest, deadliest destroyers, the same ones whose hulls the Beredas refit into hybrids. Two dozen of them could annihilate this whole place in minutes if they've set their sights on torching everything—which they all too often do.

Maelle spins around, squinting into the shadows. The thoroughfare is still partially lit by the flashing emergency lights. Over where the monks had been before, she can see the feathered cape and mask lying on the floor amidst the scattered divination cards. But there's no one else here.

"There must be other ships around here, somewhere," Maelle says, fighting to keep her voice calm. "Maybe they're docked around the other side. But I don't know how to get over there. For all we know, the others already took off."

"Zhak's gonna leave us," Page gasps. She's pulled her own bird mask off now, and it hangs around her neck. One of the strips of gilded feathers is hanging loose and torn. "He's gonna leave without us and strand us here!"

Maelle reaches for Rodin's talisman in her pocket, running her thumb over it in silent invocation.

"I really am glad I met you," Page says tearfully. "And... Maelle, if we don't—"

"No. Don't you do that. No saying goodbye. We're getting out of here!"

The end is not the end. The beginning is not the beginning. Help me find the way home.

"Come on," Maelle says. "We've got to go after him."

* * *

MAELLE AND PAGE run back through the darkened thoroughfare, back toward where Zhak's speedship was docked. It takes time to power that ship up, Maelle tells herself, it takes *time*. He can't possibly have taken off yet, it's impossible, he'll be there, he'll be there—

But they don't get as far as the ship. Zhak's stopped right at the exit. They can see him there, silhouetted in the bright light of the beam torch, which he's using to cut through a metal grate covering the gate control panel.

A piece of melted grate clatters to the floor, and then Zhak turns around with a feral scream. "Get back!"

He hurls the still-lit beam torch toward them, but it's too heavy to get any distance. It spins away across the tiled floor, and the smell of burning synthetics wafts thick through the air as the beam sizzles through the tile. Then the tool's failsafe kicks in, and it switches itself off harmlessly, spinning to a stop.

"What are you doing, Zhak?" Maelle demands. "Can we get back to the ship?"

"It's saying 'all unclamping processes are suspended due to emergency,'" he growls. "But I'm getting this ship loose… and *you* aren't coming."

"There's no other way out of here!" Page pleads.

"Believe me, you're not going anywhere, little birdie." He reaches to his belt and re-arms the plasma pistol. "Understand me?"

Page shrinks back, pulling her feathered cloak around herself. But before Zhak can move, Dex is there, barreling toward them—whether he came from the thoroughfare or from another door somewhere, Maelle didn't see.

"Hey! Are you out of your mind?" Dex screams. "Weapons off! The aliens track plasma signatures, we need to hide! We're about to get boarded here!"

"Correction, *you're* about to get boarded," snarls Zhak. He turns to slam the release button behind the grate, to let himself into the airlock. "*I'm* leaving—"

He trails off mid-sentence, his hand halfway to the button. His head tilts back.

And he looks *up*, toward the high, hexagonal skylight where the warehouses tower above them. Their blocky outlines are just visible by the floodlights, the dim stars beyond providing scant illumination.

But it's not the stars Zhak is looking at—there are other lights there, many of them. Brighter and closer, closing in fast.

A sea of triangular running lights is descending on the refuelling hub, like a flock of migrating birds. *Thorn ships*. The aliens are coming, angling their sleek craft toward the empty docking bays, like so many falling leaves.

Maelle's blood turns to ice in her veins. There's nowhere to go.

Zhak's face is contorted in wild-eyed terror now. He switches off the plasma pistol and tosses it away, backing toward the thoroughfare. "Where's the safe room?" he shouts at Dex. "Come on, come on, now! We've got to go—"

He whirls on his heels and Dex gives chase, and now the two of them are running back in the direction of the thoroughfare.

Neither Maelle nor Page have moved. Page is frozen in place, still staring at the descending ships, her mouth open in unmitigated awe. The iridescent black thorns with their bright running lights are setting down, and yet more are still hovering above, between the warehouses.

This is far, far more than two dozen ships. It's more alien craft than Maelle has ever heard of in a single sighting.

Page reaches for Maelle's hand, clasping her fingers around Maelle's. They hold Rodin's talisman between them, Yhannis's smooth synthstone pressed between their joined palms.

"Can… can we say goodbye now?" Page whispers.

A part of Maelle's mind is screaming out in terror. She should be looking at the alien ships, she should be following Dex, searching for cover. She should be picking up Zhak's plasma pistol, for all the good it will do against the Felen's impenetrable shielding. But she can't look away from Page's face.

"Yeah," Maelle whispers back. "I reckon so." She pulls Page against her, her other hand clasping a handful of the feathered cape. "I'm glad I met you, too. I'm sorry that we took you off Kuuj like that. I'm sorry for—for whatever *this* was. That you never got the chance to find out—"

"I don't care anymore, Maelle, I don't care what happened in my past," Page cries out. "All that time I was searching, and I wasn't seeing. I wasn't *seeing!* I lost my life twice, once when I went into stasis, and once when I wouldn't let it go." Her voice is shaking. "I just wanted a chance to *live*. And if I could do it over again—"

Her words are drowned out by the loud clank of several airlocks activating with eerie synchronicity. One, two, three, four—all of the circular doors are engaging, the clasps uncoupling, gates raising, soon to unleash whatever beasts are in the bays beyond.

Page and Maelle turn to face them, still clasping Rodin's stone between their palms.

YOU'LL KNOW IT WHEN IT'S OVER [VARIOUS ARTISTS]

Excerpted from THE COMPENDIUM OF CLASSIC HITS

There is some debate over which is the earliest recording [1] of "You'll Know It When It's Over," but the song first rose to prominence on unlicensed interlink channels before being reinterpreted by several contemporaneous artists [2].

See also: <u>List of prominent covers</u>

On several worlds, it came to be considered a wartime anthem of sorts, with its mixing of metaphors about a cosmic mythological conflict and lyrics about the breakup of a relationship between two people. The track was a runaway hit for years across various Union territories.

The song contains references to myths and legends including the flight of the Small Spirit in bird form, the evil and destructive gaze of the Oblivion, and the Unbreakable World. Many of the most popular arrangements include an eerie melodic sampling of monastic chants, and the bridge of the song often contains the sounds of a lyren, a traditional instrument of the Prime Worlds.

The story told in the song begins with the narrator in the role of the fallen bird, crushed by their broken heart, and ends with a triumphant reversal in which the destroyed has become the destroyer, with the narrator effectively taking over the role of the Oblivion.

MAELLE KRESS
Ancillary Nineteen, Deep Space

MAELLE WANTS TO close her eyes, but she can't, this isn't right, this isn't how it was meant to go. *I don't like hiding. It's not the way I was raised. I was always raised to confront things, to fight things face to face.*

She jerks her hand away from Page's, and the talisman falls between their fingers. It clinks on the tile, rolling away across the floor, but Maelle is already diving for Zhak's plasma pistol, picking it up, brandishing it in front of her with shaking hands.

"Go!" she shouts to Page. "You run! Go find Dex, I'll try to hold them off for long enough—"

Page turns and starts to run, and for a moment, Maelle thinks she's obeyed. But she doesn't head back to the thoroughfare. She picks up the discarded beam torch, fumbling to ignite it.

"I'm not leaving you, Maelle. I'm not, I won't, I won't."

And then, the first group of alien figures emerges at one of the airlocks: dark, crouched shapes spilling through the gate. Maelle has seen enough vids to know what the Felen look like, those tall, four-eyed creatures whose limbs aren't in quite the right configuration to be humanoid—

"Just like Olandra," Page is mumbling under her breath. "Like Olandra and the shadow beasts, we'll be overwhelmed, but we must not falter—" She lapses into Graya, into some murmured invocation.

"Weapons down," a voice commands in Union Basic, the warbling reverb of a voice modulator.

The black-suited, helmeted creature that leads the charge is definitely humanoid, and *tiny*. At its full height, it would scarcely reach Maelle's shoulder.

"Maesie, put it down. Listen to your mother."

"What?" Page breathes.

The black helmet snaps up. "Guess I do remember how to fly, huh?" Reece says.

Maelle's mouth drops open as she lowers her weapon, staring at Reece Bereda—Little Fearless—in her ink-black flight suit.

"Mama! But—how—all the Felen ships, they—they—"

"Ours. They're all ours, baby. I'm so sorry, but we had to make it seem real," Reece says. She's already rushing forward to embrace Maelle. And then Maelle's clutching her mother and Page at once, clinging to them both with tearful disbelief.

Other helmeted pilots—all very much human—are pouring in. There's a wash of pink lights as they arm their weapons and line up behind Reece.

"Where is he?" someone shouts. "Did they get him? Where's *Zhak?*"

Maelle looks back toward the thoroughfare.

"There," Page gasps, pointing. "They went that way."

THEY ALL RUN to the hub together, both Maelle and Page ignoring Reece's commands that they stay behind.

The emergency lights are still pulsing along the perimeter beams, but there's a single spotlight illuminating the hub now, framing three green-clad figures clustered near the middle of the space. To her shock, Maelle recognizes two of the monks who'd been speaking to Page and Zhak—the third must be the one who'd been wearing the bird mask before.

They're no longer dressed in their Teyrian garb; now they all bear green guild jackets like Dex's. And Maelle notices for the first time that the two yellow lozenges on the jacket's lapels are two bright golden eyes.

"Bring forth the Nightblade," one of the false monks commands.

It's Dex who pulls Zhak forward, bringing him into the illuminated circle.

"What is this?" Zhak is shouting. "This is a mistake. I don't know what you—I have no idea who you mean—"

There's blood streaming from his mouth and nose, staining his ruffled collar. His hands are tied behind him with the jangling chains from his sleeves.

"The Bird's Orb. A legendary relic," Dex says. "Some say it's an archive of the Source civilization, or else some lost star chart or a map to a long-forgotten cache of Source weapons."

Zhak spits on the floor. "I don't know what you're talking about—"

"It was a convenient little set of clues you bought, wasn't it?" Dex goes on. "First the monk-ship itself; its history, its trajectory; its previous sightings, some going back years. Even a schematic! Quite the research you did—on something that doesn't exist."

"How—? What did you—?"

"And fancy that, next you got intel that led you to a Graya speaker, just in the nick of time—intel brought to you by a sister of the pilot you shot down with the *Angel's Eye*." He looks toward Maelle and Page and Reece. "And then you tried to hire his *mother* to fly your scamships."

The narrow, half-concealed door that Dex came through earlier slides open.

"But it's like you said, isn't it?" Dex says. "Sometimes, illusions are the only thing that counts."

An eerie melody has started playing from somewhere beyond the open door—it sounds like old traditional music overlaid with soft chanting, before it suddenly bursts into a chorus of modern instruments and drums. Zhak's head snaps up, his eyes widening with something like horror.

Maelle recognizes the song, vaguely. It's one of those classic tracks from Reece's generation that still gets played all the time. The kind of song that's embedded itself somewhere deep in the collective consciousness. A refrain she's heard turned up in a bar at closing time on at least a half-dozen different outposts, one of those songs that Garin's always had rattling from the speakers in the hauler as he sings along—

You'll know it when it's over... You'll know it when your world lies broken there at your feet... You'll taste your defeat...

Zhak is thrashing around now, attempting to jerk away from his captors. He's scrambling backwards, trying to get up, but the guild-jacketed 'monks' hold him in place.

And then a solitary figure steps out through the door.

The woman is encased from waist to feet in a shimmering walk-suit. A network of metal plates connects to the bionic exoskeleton, and a glowing power system webs up over the cuirass that covers her torso. Several handheld weapons are attached to brackets framing her hips.

"What song is this?" she says, pausing to tilt her head dramatically.

The shadows swirl over her face as she walks slowly forward again. And then she steps into the light and lifts Zhak's chin with the point of his own jewelled knife.

"Hello, Vonnie."

DALYA
OF HOUSE EDAMAUN, IN HER EIGHTEENTH YEAR
Moon-City, Meneyr

She should not have come here! Oh, woe, what now has befallen her! She is lost, and she is small, and she despairs of ever finding anything but shadow ever again.

Everywhere she turns, there is only darkness, and more darkness. The cosmic void is as inescapable as it is vast. There is no more 'up' or 'down,' no light by which the little bird can see. No hope for a foolish little spirit with more courage than sense.

The Curious One is frightened. Here, so far in the depths, no god nor spirit will come to her aid. Here, there are only the Oblivion's creatures, hunting her through the void.

She grows tired, so very tired. She is certain that she has been flying in circles. She can no longer take a breath, the very shadows are choking her—

Something was wrong with the air.

There was a strange, acrid taste in the passageways down here, and Dalya's breaths had grown laboured. Had she truly become the little bird now, the very shadows choking her?

Was she still in the monks' tower somewhere, or had she exited the building? It was impossible to tell. All of the lights seemed to have gone out. What had she been thinking?

In the dark, in the distance, someone screamed.

"This way!" a voice was shouting in Union Basic. "I think she went this way. Get your breathing masks on, they're flooding the passageways with this stuff!"

Somewhere up ahead of her, Dalya heard a crackle of static, like a bad comm connection. The high, clear ping of a message coming in, then more worried voices whispering in the dark.

"What is it?" one of them hissed. "What's happening?"

"Massive energy fluctuations in orbit. I think they're turning on the death-hoop."

"*What?* But she's not even on the ship yet, nothing's taken off—"

"We need to get as many people as possible to the bunkers! There's no time to find her! We have to go back up!"

Dalya's pulse pounded a terrified rhythm in her chest. Uncle wouldn't give the order to destroy the Moon-City, surely he wouldn't! Not if she was still on the moon's surface.

But if he knew she had run away? If he thought she'd *betrayed* him, the way Nathin never would have done—?

There is no love in me that is stronger than my love for Teyr, Uncle had said.

No, *no, no, no, no*—

The data stick burned like a small sun against her palm. She felt very unsteady now, and the air felt as thick as the Oblivion's shadows in her lungs. It was burning her throat.

Was she dying? What was happening?

"Help," Dalya gasped. Her voice was nothing but a dry creak, scarcely a hoarse whisper passing between her lips. She pitched forward, slumping to her knees.

She could see a bright beam ahead of her, like a doorway opening. A group of figures in pale robes were moving at the edge of her straining vision. *Monks!* Surely the monks couldn't hurt her. They wouldn't.

Dalya desperately needed to *breathe*.

She had dropped her beaked mask long ago, somewhere behind her in the dark, but the feathered cloak felt like a suffocating weight around her neck. She tried and tried, but could not unclasp it.

It was too late now to find the rebels. It was too late for everything.

"Please..." she croaked, pulling herself along the stone floor. "Help me... I need help—"

And then one tall, slender figure was moving toward her, wreathed in a dazzling halo of brilliance.

A *light!* There was a portable lantern shining in his hand.

"Over here!" the monk shouted. "Quickly!"

As the light grew closer, Dalya made out the man holding it. The monk wore a thick brown travelling robe and a pale cloak overtop of it. There was a rounded breathing mask, like something a medic would wear, tightly covering his mouth and nose. And above it... a shining rune inscribed in paint on his forehead.

The rune of *Yhannis*. This monk wore the guise of the Interlocutor! Dalya's heart leapt with sudden hope. He grabbed hold of her with both hands, leaning in to take a closer look at her.

"Dalya?" the monk whispered, almost reverently. "Graces be! It *is* you. Come, hurry. We must get you to safety."

His voice was deep and soothing, slightly muffled through the mask. He spoke the Perfect Cadence like a First-City Teyrian, she thought, the way he embraced the full, rich tones of their ancient tongue with that mellifluence that the moonfolk never quite achieved.

The Interlocutor handed his lantern to another monk beside him, then lifted Dalya into his arms. When he looked into her eyes, for one strange, heart-stopping second she imagined that she saw Uncle before her.

Uncle, if he were younger, that is—his hair still ink-black, his sharp eyes so much kinder and gentler than she had ever known them to be, the web of lines at the corners less pronounced.

Uncle? she mumbled, and it was perhaps more a thought than a word. Her mouth wasn't working anymore, her head felt oddly heavy.

"She's inhaled a lot of the gas," the Interlocutor said. "We have to get her some oxygen! Now!"

Dalya felt another set of hands taking hold of her. She was being lifted higher, hoisted over the Interlocutor's shoulder. Another person supported her legs, and they jostled together into a narrow hallway. A door closed behind them, and she heard the tone of an engaging seal, like an airlock.

They lay her down on something flat—a gurney, she thought, but maybe it was just a table—and she felt a mask being pulled over her mouth. She took a long, gasping breath, and sweet, blessed clean air poured into her lungs.

"Air quality's stabilizing," said the Interlocutor, looking at a panel on the wall. "We should be fine in here—for now. Seal off the upper level, get everyone moving toward the bunkers!" He leaned in close to Dalya again. "It's all right," he said gently. "Be still. We're taking you down to the underground shelters."

"Are you… are you… with the rebels, then?" Dalya gasped out.

The Interlocutor laid a hand on the top of her head with a surprising tenderness. "I am with the truth-tellers, Dalya," he said. "That is what I have always been."

The truth-tellers. *Anda's data stick*, she suddenly remembered. It was still in her hand, her fingers clutched so tightly around it that they'd grown numb.

"I have—something—for you—" she whispered. "I have—*the truth*—"

Her head lolled to the side, her voice failing her again. But she stuck her arm out, and she could feel the monk opening her fist, prying the little rectangle from her clutching fingers.

"What's this—?"

There was a blur of movement in Dalya's peripheral vision, a flurry of noise, a flash like a bright light coming on. She bobbed in and out of consciousness—how long had passed? a minute? half an hour?—and then she jerked to alertness again.

Where was the Interlocutor?

Dalya struggled to sit up, looking around for her rescuer.

"Fire up the broadcast system!" someone was calling out. There were so many voices here, all bleeding into one another, a chaos of urgent shouts.

"They're going to shut us down!"

"Hurry! Now, now!"

"Open the link, we've got to pour this data into the network!"

"I've got it, here it comes—"

Dalya looked around frantically. There! There he was, right across the room.

The Interlocutor was shrugging off his layers of monastic robes, letting the guise of Yhannis drop to the floor. Beneath it, he wore a plain black tunic and trousers; ordinary, unornamented clothing. He had removed his breathing mask, revealing the rest of his face. And that startling familiarity struck Dalya once more.

He had Uncle's sharp chin and high cheekbones, the same arch to his nose. Even his hair fell exactly the same way, more curled on the left side than the right—

A broadcast camera, like the ones that surrounded Uncle when he made speeches to the public, was being hastily positioned in front of him.

And the erstwhile monk of Yhannis, this Interlocutor with the eerily familiar face, arranged himself in front of the camera. His skin shone with sweat under the bright light, and he dabbed at the dripping rune on his forehead.

When he pulled his hand away, there was paint smeared over his knuckles. He wiped his hand on the edge of his tunic just as someone started the recording.

"My name is Nathin Edamaun, and I speak for Meneyr," he said. "I speak on behalf of us all."

PAGE FOUND
Bereda Spaceport, Laithe

IT'S AN UNSEASONABLY warm evening on Laithe when the lander shuttle descends to the Bereda spaceport. And just before nightfall, Page and Maelle walk together to meet it.

They speak little as they walk beneath the lengthening shadows, and Maelle's headlamp casts a circle of brightness onto the uneven road ahead of them. The jibbles run back and forth around them, daring to venture about three paces from the road before they come bounding back.

There's nothing dangerous out there, no animals that could eat them, no real way they could get lost with their electronic chips. Perhaps the small creatures don't understand how safe they actually are; perhaps something in them fears the encroaching dark, just like Page always has.

Or perhaps… perhaps they aren't afraid, but they just want to stick close to those they trust. They're practically under Maelle and Page's feet as they wait at the edge of the landing pad, their round eyes glittering in the dim light.

The descending vehicle is compact and streamlined, a sleek grey shuttlecraft with angled lights on the front that remind Page of snake eyes. The shuttle sits for a while before the door slides open. And their guest appears in the open doorway, a lone figure framed by the artificial light spilling from inside.

Page hadn't expected the woman herself to come to the surface. She'd thought it would be a messenger—Dex, maybe, or one of her other crew. But no, it's *her*, in person, holding a bulky black carryall slung over one shoulder.

Azeran Guillem. The Void Snake.

Close up, she's grim-faced and serious, with dark eyes so sharp and steady that it's difficult not to flinch under her gaze. Her brows are close-knit, meeting over a nose that's set slightly off-centre, as if it's once been broken. She probably looks older than her years, accounting for the effects of post-suspension syndrome, although her skin has retained its rich brown colour.

When she turns to close the metal door of her craft, Page sees the line of thick scarring that gnarls over the side of her neck, so much less refined than her own neat triangle of stasis port markings. In stasis prison, there's little regard for the cosmetic effects of the procedure.

Although, Page thinks, the Void Snake is surely the type who uses her scars as a mark of intimidation. If anything, the cut of the metallic cuirass she wears above her walk-suit seems designed specifically to display them, dipping low in the back where her dark hair is gathered up on her nape to expose the top of her spine. Her exoskeleton may be necessary as a mobility aid, bracing the limbs permanently numbed by her time in suspension, but she has made it a show of strength.

"Well, well," the Void Snake says, her voice surprisingly warm. "Please, don't be shy. Come closer."

She motions them forward, fixing that piercing gaze first on Maelle and then on Page. There's an amusement in her sharp eyes when she notices the incongruity of Page's fancy Teyrian blouse with her plain grey linen trousers and sturdy work boots—boots that *fit*.

Maelle and Page look at each other for a moment and then move forward in unison, standing before her like soldiers before a commander. The jibbles still hover at their feet, yipping excitedly. Maelle picks them up to quiet them, and the Void

Snake reaches over to scratch their heads, smiling widely.

"Jibbles!" she says with obvious delight. "I love them! Damn, I haven't seen a jibble in years. Used to have a little grey one as a child. I was so small, I could hardly pick it up, but I carried it around everywhere like a toy."

Page finds it difficult to imagine that the Void Snake has ever been a small child. It's a startling thought, like her own disconnected past.

"I, uh. I suppose we owe you our thanks," Maelle says after a moment. One of the jibbles gives a squeaky little *yip,* as though in agreement.

"I don't know about that," the Void Snake says. "Feels more like *I* should be thanking *you*. But for the sake of avoiding unnecessary argument... let's just say that we did each other a favour." She shucks the black carryall off her shoulder, letting it drop onto the landing pad in front of her with a loud *clunk*. "Nonetheless, I'm not one to let a favour go unappreciated. And so... this is for you."

Maelle slowly crouches and sets down the jibbles, keeping her eyes on the Void Snake as though she might still decide to snatch the bag back up. But she's just standing there smiling, her arms folded over her dark breastplate.

Maelle unfastens the bag and lifts the outer flap, and Page sees at once what's inside: rows upon rows of shiny credit chits, stacked into thick blocks. Page's mouth goes dry as she does some quick mental arithmetic. She glances down at Maelle, and sees the shock dawning on her face as she does the same sums.

If the bag is full of the same, it's got to be close to two million credits.

"I thought Reece had already received your payment?" Maelle says quietly. "I understand it was quite generous."

"Yes. Full payment has been sent for the... furniture delivery." A smile quirks at the Void Snake's lips. "This is for you two. For your trouble. Consider it an apology of sorts, that I was not straightforward with you." She looks from Maelle to Page and back again. "That's one-point-nine million credits—it's what *he* gave me many years ago, when we started our business." She nods down at the carryall, which one of the jibbles is currently trying to climb into. "Split it between you, or use it together. I trust you'll make better choices than I did, in every respect."

"Gods. Thank you so much," whispers Maelle, at the same time Page says, "*I give you great and most honoured thanks.*"

Page's words come out in Graya, and at that, the Void Snake's smile turns wistful. She stares off into the middle distance for a moment, up into the tree-lined hills, as though her thoughts are far away.

"Right," she finally says, her eyes snapping back to Page and Maelle. "As far as I'm concerned... you two never worked for Zhaklam Evelor. You've never heard of the Nightblade. We have never met... and this will be the end of it all. But if anyone in the Bereda family needs anything"—she turns in the direction of the Compound—"I trust Reece knows how to find me."

Maelle nods. "Reece says she's getting out of the scamship biz. We'll see about that... but our Edlin's going to be taking over the day-to-day on the business, so it'll stay in the family regardless," she says with a smile. "And Garin reckons he might try his hand at our good old ancestral trade of woodworking. So, you know, if you ever want any *actual* wooden furniture..."

"I might just take you up on that." The Void Snake chuckles. "I'm building myself a new house, planetside on Gedringa. Wouldn't mind a nice new dining table," she grins. "And if you're ever out travelling that way—Gedringa's weather is just about perfect, year-round. Might even give Teyr a run for its money."

Page lowers her eyes. She's far less concerned about escape routes these days, but she's not likely to go planetside on many Union worlds without a proper ident. Page Found has always done better skulking at the sidelines.

"Ah! Speaking of travel. Before I forget..." The Void Snake reaches to her belt, and for a brief, heart-stopping moment

Page thinks she's reaching for a weapon. But she only removes a thin, silvery round disc, of the kind that usually houses a Union ident.

"I believe I have something of yours here, Page," she says with a sly look. "One more little gift. Organized on behalf of your friends here on Laithe."

"Something of *mine*?" Page stares at her. "What do you mean?"

"Have a look."

Page reaches out and takes hold of the shining disc, turning it over on her palm. Immediately, a Union cit-file unfolds from the surface. There's an image of her own face in the middle of the circle, a row of what looks like biometric data spiralling down one side. Page hasn't seen Union idents all that often, but it definitely *looks* legit.

"Whoa," she gasps. "An ident? I—I don't even know what to—"

"It's a good fake—solid as they come—but you'll still have to be a little careful," the Void Snake says. "Just don't apply for any high-ranking government jobs or try to move to a First Prime." She winks.

"Wasn't planning on it," Page says. She turns to Maelle, who's grinning almost as widely as she is.

"And as for the particulars there—well, someone insisted."

Page lets her eyes skim downward over the shimmering data.

The birthday is the same as the estimated birth date they'd put on her Kuuj residency.

And as for the rest—

BIRTHPLACE: **FELWAE OUTPOST**
NAME: **PAGE FOUND BEREDA**

YOUR SUBMISSION TO HUMANITY'S PRESERVATION PROJECT: A WARTIME ARCHIVE OF HOPE, HISTORY AND SURVIVAL

Thank you for choosing to submit to *Humanity's Preservation Project*! We are one of many collectives working on the preservation and archival of the human experience and our civilization during this time of peril, conflict and uncertainty.

It is our hope that future generations of the United Worlds of Humanity will survive to unlock this time capsule, not as a tragic reminder of what has been lost, but as a testament to the resilience and renewal of humanity. And as an act of kinship, a gift from the present to the future – our stories, passing from our hands to theirs, across the reaches of time.

This is your chance to record your personal missive, and to add your voice to the many accounts we have already collected. *Humanity's Preservation Project* is your opportunity to preserve stories or experiences that might be of interest to future historians – and also to our descendants, the children of humanity yet to come. Join us in creating a collective diary of how we lived and loved and survived in wartime, and how we persevered.

You are the Storyteller, so tell us your story today!

- Honesty, sincerity and emotion are encouraged. We ask that you be as truthful as possible, and that you recount primarily your own lived experiences.
- Speak naturally; it may help to imagine that you're telling your story to a friend.
- All subjects are welcome. It could be a funny childhood story, the memory of a heartbreak you endured, a lesson you learned, or an experience you feel represents you as a person. It might be something you want to get off your chest,

or something you haven't told anyone during your lifetime. Don't be afraid to get vulnerable and share from the heart.
- You can use the question prompts to get started, or simply speak in free form.
- There is no time limit, so long as your recording fits in the required file size. Please upload completed audio files to the portal in the listed formats only.
- Tag your submission with the categories and keywords from the list. After choosing up to three categories that best describe your submission, you may select as many additional keywords as you feel apply to your story.
- Submissions in any language or in multiple languages are welcome; please be sure to tag your language(s) to help us archive your story.
- If you fill in your name and key details on the form, these will be used in the search index to help archive and retrieve your submission. However, anonymous submissions are welcome, and you do not need to append any identifying biographical data.
- Anonymous submissions will be attributed to **THE STORYTELLER**.

THE STORYTELLER

Recording start 07:31:23

I think that's enough about all that, isn't it? This feels like the part where a good story would pretend to wrap things up all nice. Where I tell you that it turned out okay, and that it's all going to be fine.

Sometimes, we don't find out what happened to everybody at the end of the journey. Sometimes we never know why our hearts broke, or what in the hells it was all supposed to be for.

Maybe you want to know if humanity turned the tide of the war with the Felen, or whether some of us managed to live happily ever after. Well, the war's still going on, so I suppose that part might be *your* story to tell, whoever you are.

But amidst it all – yes, even in the darkest of times – sometimes we were happy. And if you're listening to this recording... then I guess somebody made it after all.

Sometimes, with a little ingenuity and a lot of perseverance, it does just work out. That's what we've got to hope for, right? That's what we have to believe.

Comes to a point, you've got to believe *something*.

// SUCCESSFUL Q-LINK TRANSMISSION //

FROM: [Code] [REDACTED] SECTOR 6FR >>
TO: [Code] INDEPENDENT MOON-CITY, MENEYR

Dalya, my dearest, my most steadfast of friends –

Communications to the Protectorate are still being blocked, but I am told there is a brief window now to send this transmission, and that it might be captured by Meneyr's new satellite. I do hope that this missive will find you safe and well.

So little news has reached me of what is happening on Meneyr, but my heart rejoices to hear any news at all from the Protectorate. I give thanks every day that the city has survived, that the death-hoop has been destroyed, that Nathin Edamaun now leads the Independent Moon-City. That you are there with him.

I hope you know that I have never blamed you for your uncle's deeds, nor for my uncle's death. My uncle knew what he risked; he knew what he stood for and what he fought for, despite the mistakes that he made. He died trying to correct his course, and I have done what he intended to. I finished what he started.

Now, I must carry out my final journey. Renewal is my hope now – that I might be raised again into light and goodness and glorious peace.

I am reminded of the line you chose from the sacred texts, when at last you picked a favourite: "Courage is not always a bright flower in full bloom; sometimes it is a bud awaiting the moment to open." I have clung much to it in these last days, held it close to me. It belongs to the sacred texts, but in my mind, it also belongs to you.

Soon, I am to reach for the embrace of the Goddess and enter the void-sleep. But it is no monk-ship that will bear me away into the cosmos, but a vessel departing from the edge of mainspace, carrying out an experimental study in faster stasis revival methods. They tell me that the contract will gain me safe passage into the Union, and that

I will receive a Union citizenship in compensation when I wake –
although I do not know if I believe them.

In truth, a part of me hopes that I will be granted freedom from this
life. Perhaps I will not wake. I wish only for a new start, whether in the
United Worlds or in my next incarnation. No longer Anda Agote, but
a little nameless bird, dropping to a green world, carrying only the
hope in her heart.

By the time you get this letter, I will be gone to the cosmic void.
Wish me safe travels; may Yhannis reach for my hand. I hope that
you, too, will find peace.

I told you once that my family would not be waiting for me at the
end and the beginning, and that I did not expect to see them again
in the bright hills of the Greenworld. I do not know what I believe
anymore. But if we do go somewhere after we die... then I should like
to think we will all go to the same place.

Perhaps we will be reunited one day on the Unbreakable World,
wherever it is.

Always and forever your friend,
Anda

ACKNOWLEDGMENTS

FIRST OF ALL, my everlasting gratitude goes out to the readers who expressed so much affection and excitement for my debut novel, *Under Fortunate Stars*. You are the reason why *An Unbreakable World* exists, and why there will be more stories in this universe. I'm forever honoured to travel the stars with you through your bookshelves and e-readers!

To my agent Ernie Chiara: your incredible passion and indefatigable support have propelled this book from its inception, and I appreciate you more than words can say. Thanks so much for all that you do!

A massive thank you to my editor, David Thomas Moore, who first took a chance on this universe and has returned to it with such enthusiasm. Thanks also to my copy-editor and proofreader, Donna Bond and Sophie Clark, and to Jess Gofton and Natalie Charlesworth, Chiara Mestieri, Dagna Dlubak, Owen Johnson and Simon Read, and everyone at Rebellion whose hard work has helped bring this book into being.

To Dominic Forbes, for another brilliant cover design, and to Mathias Kom, the bard of the Union Quadrant, for another unforgettable song.

To Monica and Rebecca, for their invaluable insights and encouragement as I drafted this manuscript, and for their unbreakable belief that it would become a book.

To all my beloved friends, writer crews, and creative communities that sustain my heart, with special thanks to Harry, Bethany, Chance, Kate, Claire, and Kerbie, who have loved bits and pieces of this story since it was only a handful of ideas and a dream.

To my wonderful family, born and chosen, who have been there through every twist and turn of this unpredictable journey.

To Michael, my best friend and perpetual first reader, whose love has carried me through the chaos.

And to E, who first showed me the question.

Ren Hutchings

Ren Hutchings is a speculative fiction writer, writing mentor, editor, and lifelong SFF fan. She loves pop science, unexplained mysteries, 90s music, collecting outdated electronics, and pondering about alternate universes. Ren is the author of twisty sci-fi books including *Under Fortunate Stars* and *An Unbreakable World* (Solaris Books) and *The Legend Liminal* (Stars and Sabers), as well as short fiction.

🦋 @voidcricket.bsky.social
📷 @voidcricket
🌐 renhutchings.com

FIND US ONLINE!

www.rebellionpublishing.com

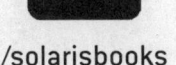

/solarisbooks /solarisbks

/solarisbooks /solarisbooks.bsky.social

SIGN UP TO OUR NEWSLETTER!

rebellionpublishing.com/newsletter

YOUR REVIEWS MATTER!

Enjoy this book? Got something to say?

Leave a review on Amazon, GoodReads or with your favourite bookseller and let the world know!

"LEAVES THE AUDIENCE GASPING" – *The Times*

MICKEY 7

STARRING ROBERT PATTINSON
NOW MAJOR MOTION PICTURE MICKEY 17
DIRECTED BY BONG JOON HO

EDWARD ASHTON

www.rebellionpublishing.com